CALL ME ZELDA

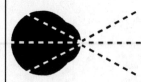

This Large Print Book carries the
Seal of Approval of N.A.V.H.

CALL ME ZELDA

ERIKA ROBUCK

WHEELER PUBLISHING
A part of Gale, Cengage Learning

GALE
CENGAGE Learning·

Detroit • New York • San Francisco • New Haven, Conn • Waterville, Maine • London

GALE
CENGAGE Learning®

LIBRARY OF CONGRESS CATALOGING-IN-PUBLICATION DATA

Robuck, Erika.
    Call me Zelda / by Erika Robuck. — Large print edition.
        pages ; cm.
    ISBN 978-1-4104-6211-4 (hardcover) — ISBN 1-4104-6211-0 (hardcover)
    1. Fitzgerald, Zelda, 1900–1948—Fiction. 2. Fitzgerald, F. Scott (Francis Scott), 1896–1940—Fiction. 3. Authors, American—Fiction. 4. Psychiatric hospital patients—Fiction. 5. Psychiatric nurses—Fiction. 6. Female friendship—Fiction. 7. Baltimore (Md.)—Fiction. 8. Psychological fiction. 9. Large type books. I. Title.
    PS3618.O338C35 2013b
    813'.6—dc23   2013019819

Published in 2013 by arrangement with NAL Signet, a member of Penguin Group (USA) Inc.

Printed in Mexico
1 2 3 4 5 6 7 17 16 15 14 13

For *my* Scott

■ ■ ■ ■

FIRST ACT

■ ■ ■ ■

"Ah! How rapidly descending,
Falls the avalanche of fate!"
— Tobia Gorrio, *La Gioconda*

ONE

February 1932, Phipps Psychiatric Clinic
Johns Hopkins University Hospital, Baltimore,
Maryland

The ward was never the same after that February afternoon when Zelda Fitzgerald stumbled into the psychiatric clinic with a stack of papers clutched to her chest, eyes darting this way and that, at once pushing from and pulling toward her husband like a spinning magnet.

I opened my arms to her. She would not look at me, her nurse, or allow me to touch her, but walked next to me down the hallway to her room. We left Mr. Fitzgerald at the desk preparing to meet with the resident in charge of his wife's case, when Mrs. Fitzgerald suddenly stopped and ran back to him, nearly knocking him over with her force. Her husband wrapped his arms around her and kissed her hair with an intensity that filled me with longing and squeezed my heart. They both began to cry like two lost, scared children. They were not what I expected in any way.

As quickly as she'd run to him, she pulled herself out of his arms and came back to me. It was then that I met his gaze — ice-green eyes underlined by dark circles, his hair and clothing a rumpled mess. I was overtaken by a sense of pity for the two of them and thought that he too might benefit from a stay with us.

"On my left, my left," said Mrs. Fitzgerald.

"Pardon me?" I asked her.

"You must walk on my left. I can't see out of the right eye."

I knew the doctor's notes said she claimed to have blindness in her right eye, so I obeyed her wishes as we walked down the hall. I noticed a red rash creeping up her neck that she scratched with her jagged nails. By the time we reached the room, she'd succeeded in making her neck bleed.

As soon as we arrived, she collapsed onto the bed, still clutching her papers as if they were a precious infant. She cried in a low moan. An orderly carried in her bags and placed them on the shiny floor next to the door.

"Mrs. Fitzgerald, I'll need to look you over for admission," I said. "Is it okay with you if

I take your blood pressure and listen to your heart?"

"My heart," she whispered. "My poor broken heart."

I walked to her and gently pulled her to a sitting position.

"May I place your papers on the bedside table?" I asked.

She looked at me with fear in her eyes, and then out the door.

"Don't show him. He can't see it," she said.

I wondered who she was afraid would see the papers. Was she referring to her husband? If so, why was she simultaneously distressed at being separated from him, but emphatic that he not see what she clutched in her hands?

"If you'd like to keep the papers with you," I said, "I can work around them."

She nodded with some reluctance and put the papers on her lap. I glanced down and saw pages of what must have been her handwriting, surprisingly straight but with the loops and embellishments of a young girl. I was curious about their contents but didn't want to press her, especially since she began to wheeze.

"I have asthma," she said while she gasped.

There was a note in the file about asthma, but here, watching her, I thought it more likely that she had panic-induced breathlessness. Her heart rate was elevated and her blood pressure high.

"There, there," I said. "You are in a state. Let's try to get you calm."

The place on her neck that she'd scratched needed attention, so once she seemed more settled, I stepped away to fetch some antiseptic and a bandage. When I returned, she still sat on the bed, clutching her papers, crying out every now and then in anguish. I cleaned her wound, but she soon began to recoil from my touch and questions as if they were flames licking at her face.

I watched her eyes glass over and she entered into the catatonic state sometimes present with schizophrenic patients. She looked through me with her large gray eyes in the most unsettling way, and I had the distinct feeling of having encountered such eyes before, but could not place them. Her limbs were stiff, but I helped her to lie on the bed and moved the papers close to her heart. I covered her with a blanket, drew the curtains, and locked her in the room.

As I left her, dread pushed down through my shoulders and into my chest. It was as if someone closed a fist around my lungs, and sweat beaded along my brow. I stopped and leaned against the door to catch my breath, wondering whether I was suddenly becoming ill, when it hit me: Mrs. Fitzgerald's eyes were like my own, reflected in the mirror across from my bed years ago, after the war and my great losses.

Memories of my husband and daughter roared up like waves in my ears, along with the crippling sensation that accompanied the remembrance of their absence. I could not think of them here in this place, so I wished them away and they retreated.

Later. Later.

Mrs. Fitzgerald's eyes, however, would not leave my mind. I had no idea what those haunting eyes would lead me to do. If I'd known then, I don't think I would have become as involved as I did.

No, I still would have.

Mr. Fitzgerald's strain was palpable in the room.

We sat near Dr. Meyer's desk in his warm study — young resident Dr. Mildred Squires, Scott Fitzgerald, and I. We let Mr. Fitzgerald talk while we took notes, each of us judging him in spite of ourselves, and trying to understand his broken wife.

It was clear that Mr. Fitzgerald was near a

breaking point himself. His hands shook and he chain-smoked. He often stood to pace the room while he gathered his thoughts. Then he would sit abruptly, cough, and continue. I listened to him with great interest, for he spoke like a storyteller.

"She was born and raised a free and indulged child in Montgomery, Alabama," he began. "Her mother allowed her at the breast until she was four years old and never told her no. Her father was a stoic and admired judge."

"Was her relationship with her father difficult?" asked Dr. Meyer, a stern, spectacled German in charge of the Phipps Clinic.

"Yes, I'd say so," said Mr. Fitzgerald. "Judge Sayre was a practical sort of old Southern gentleman. He didn't understand his daughter."

"But Mrs. Sayre did?" asked Dr. Squires.

"I don't think she understood Zelda, either," said Scott. "She encouraged her, especially as a wild debutante."

He stood again, walked to the window, and lit a new cigarette. His nervous energy disturbed all of us. Out of the corner of my eye, I caught the usually steady and solid Dr. Meyer squirming in his chair.

"Zelda is strong willed and stubborn.

Hates taking instruction," continued Fitzgerald.

"I know she was previously at Malmaison and Valmont clinics in Switzerland and diagnosed as schizophrenic," said Dr. Meyer. "What precipitated her first collapse?"

"There was a" — he faltered a moment — "relationship of mine with a young actress when we were in Hollywood in 'twenty-six or 'twenty-seven that affected her. Entirely chaste, mind you, but Zelda wouldn't hear otherwise. This was following a relationship Zelda had with a Frenchman. Then there was her suicidal practice of ballet. She'd dance six, even eight hours a day until her feet bled and there were pools of sweat on the floor. That's the pattern, you know. She gets manic about some form of art, becomes closed off from me, aggravates her asthma and eczema, then breaks down."

I was fascinated by his justification of his affair and her behavior patterns. Was either of them unfaithful? Was Zelda punishing herself through art or trying to find herself? My thoughts again returned to the stack of papers she'd guarded so closely.

"What are the papers she brought?" I asked.

His laugh was bitter. "Her latest obsession: a novel. She thinks she will outdo me."

His pretension could not hide that he felt threatened by her. Did he wish to be the only one in their marriage with any accomplishment? Did he undermine her attempts at expression? Or perhaps she antagonized him.

"Once she gets an idea in her head she won't change it for a stack of Lincolns," he said. "Do you know she thinks I dallied with Ernest Hemingway?"

We all looked up from our notepads.

"I did not, of course, but she's convinced."

His weary tone caused me to believe him, though I wondered what made her make such an assumption. I began to pity him again.

He returned to his chair and asked for a glass of water. His skin was pale, and sweat formed along his upper lip. I poured him some water from a pitcher on Meyer's side table, and Fitzgerald met my eyes directly when he thanked me.

"That is enough for today," said Dr. Meyer. "It's clear that you both need rest. Will you be staying in Baltimore long?"

"No, I'll return to Montgomery tomorrow. My daughter, Scottie, needs me. I don't want to uproot her again. Not yet, anyway."

I knew in some vague way that they had a ten-year-old child. The fact was in a file somewhere in black and white, and at the time I'd read it, I did not internalize that information. Now, however, seeing the emotional state of the two of them, my heart went out to the young girl. How did she manage with parents like these? Inevitably, I thought of my own daughter, Katie, and that she would have been thirteen this year. Just a bit older than Scottie.

Suddenly the room seemed very small and full of people. Mr. Fitzgerald's wool coat on the chair next to me scratched my arm, and the pungent aroma of his cigarettes made me nauseous. The clock on the wall behind Meyer's desk showed two o'clock. I still had three hours in my shift.

I had to get out of the room.

I stood and placed my notebook on the desk. The others stood around me. The meeting was over. There was a shaking of hands, discussion of a call, and an exchange of addresses. Mr. Fitzgerald picked up his coat and again looked into my eyes.

"You'll take good care of her," he said. It was not a question, but a reassurance to himself.

"Yes, sir," I said. "The very best care."

His face relaxed and he even smiled. I saw

a hint of what he must have been in his younger days. He kept his gaze on mine and reached for my hands.

"Thank you," he said.

With that, he was gone.

I walked out after him and watched him move down the hall and out the doors. The afternoon slipped in for a moment, then was shut out. Everything in the ward seemed different now, and I no longer felt its calming presence. The Fitzgeralds stirred something in me that had been dormant for a long time, and I was not prepared to face it.

An hour later, I returned to Mrs. Fitzgerald to reassess her vitals and begin a relationship with her. It was Dr. Meyer's philosophy that people with mental illness needed a comforting place of physical and emotional calm to work out their disturbances. He was revolutionary in the practice at a time when sanitariums often involved starched areas of decay and neglect, overcrowded dormitories polluted with the noise of people with not only mental illness, but all forms of physical handicaps, sexually transmitted diseases, or simple homelessness.

But this was not a public institution. It was an expensive private clinic connected to a research hospital, for those with the means to afford it. The wall hangings and tapestries were warmly colored and calming. There were moldings, chandeliers, and various rooms of amusement for billiards or bridge. It had the look of a posh hotel, and I'd felt an enormous sense of relief since I'd begun working here, years ago. The schedule and routine framed my existence in small, manageable blocks the way Walter Reed General Hospital had done at the start of the war, and the clean, muted environment soothed me.

Until today.

With Mr. Fitzgerald gone, at least the air seemed lighter. Mrs. Fitzgerald was standing at the window when I knocked and opened the door. Her bags were open and she looked as if she'd brushed her hair and washed her face. She continued to hold the papers.

"White February, with the crispness of a paper envelope," she said in her graceful Southern drawl, nodding to the snow-sprinkled garden outside her window. "Sugarplum fairies were playing in the bushes there, but your knock scared them off."

She gave me the smile one would give a child. I returned it, relieved to see her lightness and feel my own.

"It's the white uniform," I said. "Intimidating."

Mrs. Fitzgerald's smile touched her eyes, and she regarded me warmly, seemingly happy that I played along. This was a very good sign and one I'd not expected.

"He's gone," she said. "My husband?"

"Yes, Mrs. Fitzgerald, he left to tend to your daughter."

"But he can't really leave if we don't drop his name, can we?" she said. "Call me Zelda."

Her gentle voice, which had been so light just moments before, grew as sharp as an icicle. I'd meant to address her formally and as a lady of some position, but she clearly resented the shadow his name cast.

"I'd be glad to call you Zelda," I said. "I'm glad we can cut the pretense. I'm Anna, and I'll be your nurse while you stay with us."

" 'Had I on earth but wishes three, the first should be my Anna,' " said Zelda. "Robert Burns. The poetry of ballet is something to consider but seems so far from this cold, weary desert."

Her thoughts flitted through her mind and out of her lips in a tumble I had trouble following, though her words suggested her brilliance.

I needed to reassess her vital signs, and

she allowed me to lead her back to the bed, but the shift from personal to professional conversation once more set the emotional barrier between us. She wouldn't look me in the eye, but kept her gaze fixed at the window.

I slid her blouse open to listen to her heart and noted her prominent collarbones and the eczema that continued to splotch her skin. She suddenly grimaced, then broke into an enormous smile. I couldn't help but look over my shoulder at what she saw, but was greeted with only the window. Her face must have been reacting to a film of memories I could not yet access.

"Your blood pressure is much improved, as is your pulse," I said.

She blinked and directed her large eyes at me, again unnerving me. She slid her gaze over my face and down my arms to my hands, where it lingered there a bit.

"Long, graceful fingers with short blunt nails," she said. "The hands of a piano player. Chopin, Debussy, Beethoven."

Patients rarely noticed me so closely, and commented on me even less, so her scrutiny felt strange, though not unpleasant.

"I do play a bit. I used to a lot," I said, allowing my thoughts of Ben to hover at the edges of my consciousness, teasing me. I had a sudden memory of him behind me as I played, his fingers along my collarbone, his arms lifting me off the bench, my hands in his hair —

I snapped the memory shut, but a faint heat remained in my neck. She saw the flush, stood abruptly, and walked back to the window, again recoiling from me.

I was astonished by the height of her perception. It was clear that she read others well — maybe too well. Dr. Meyer would not be pleased. He often spoke to us about the emotional sensitivity of his patients to the feelings of others. I had never seen anything to this degree, though.

"Dinner will be served in the dining room at five thirty," I said. "Your evening nurse will arrive at five o'clock to introduce herself and escort you there. Tonight you may rest and read if you'd like. Tomorrow we'll begin counseling with Dr. Meyer and Dr. Squires. Do you have any questions for me before I leave?"

She looked at me and shook her head in the negative.

"Then good evening, Zelda," I said. "I'm glad to meet you, and I look forward to working with you."

She continued to stare at me and it was difficult to remove myself from her gaze, but I managed a nod and turned to leave the room.

"Play again," she said.

I turned back to her. "Pardon me?"

"The piano. You should play again."

I forced a smile.

"Good advice," I said. "Thank you."

She turned back to the window, and I locked her in on my way out.

It was waiting for me when I pushed open the door to my apartment. The piano, that is. Stiff, upright, accusing.

A neglected wife, I thought.

Where have you been? it said with its posture.

My fingers longed to touch its keys, but sound is memory, so I resisted the urge. I was of no mind to raise old ghosts.

I closed the door behind me and placed my bag on the table next to the door. I could hear pats and thumps from the girls above me, two ballerinas from the Peabody Institute. The muffled melancholy of an opera singer conjured by the point of a needle on a gramophone competed with the scrape of strings on a violin in the apartment below me, where an intense Romanian musician lived.

I had fallen in love with the building in

Baltimore's Mount Vernon neighborhood on a walk after my shift at the hospital years ago, when my mother had encouraged me to find a place of my own. Its rounded, swirled, and layered woodwork, chimneys, and impressive leaded windows gave it the appearance of a Victorian dollhouse. The little colony of artists felt safe, though I did feel a bit out of place. When I had asked the landlord whether he was sure a psychiatric nurse fit in with dancers and musicians, he laughed and said I couldn't be a more welcome addition.

When he'd shown me the room, the piano was the only thing in it. It was covered with a sheet, but its presence was heavy. I flinched when I saw it. He must have seen, because he said, "We can have it moved if you'd like. It's been in the house forever, though. The last one who lived here was a painter, so it never got used beyond being a prop for canvases."

"I do play," I'd said.

"See, you're a good fit," he had said. "These rooms were waiting for you."

I thought of this as I stood by the window and stared outside. Winter's dark muted the city and left me feeling tired to my bones. Hoping to ward off any illness that might be trying to nestle into my body, I had a bowl of chicken soup for dinner and retired early.

Sleep had long been an antagonist that thrilled as well as tormented me, so I fell into it easily, the way one would opium. The dreams were getting further apart until entire months went by without Ben or Katie in any of them, but I knew from my experiences with the Fitzgeralds that day and the emotions they'd stirred in me that someone from my past would be waiting in my dreams.

It was Ben.

It was the day at the train station when he had to return to the front. Emotion had rendered me speechless all morning. Ben's eyes were dark and heavily lashed, and his newly shorn brown hair made him look so young. He brushed a tear away gruffly with the back of his hand.

"I'm not doing this to you," he said. "I have to do it for them."

This stirred me enough to shake loose the hold on my throat.

"For whom?" I said. "To them you're just a speck on a map. A number. To me . . ." I wouldn't continue. I couldn't say it any more.

"If I didn't go back, I couldn't live with myself — not with all of them fighting. I have to go back."

I looked down the platform at the women and men kissing and embracing one another. I saw a man nearby chuck his little son under his chin. He saluted the boy, who saluted back. A brave little soldier for his mother, who struggled with an infant on her hip.

Ben's eyes followed mine down the platform and rested on the family. We looked back at each other and at once, I understood. I finally allowed myself to hug him.

He felt so warm in his uniform. I buried myself in his neck, clean and shaved. It would soon be covered in grime and stubble. I wanted to press myself into him so I could go with him, but the departure whistle blew, and I pulled away.

"I'll be back," he said.

"I'll be waiting."

He stepped up into the train and slid into the seat nearest the window. Our lips formed *I love you* at the same moment. This made us smile. He put his hand on the glass.

Then the bomb slid through the air with a scream, destroying the train and everyone before me in a ball of fire and smoke.

I woke up, sweating, with my heart hammering in my chest.

I hadn't had the dream in so long, and it

took me some time to recover, to tell myself that he didn't get blown up at the train station, to allow the little bird of hope, which had weakened through the years, to continue to flutter in my heart that he might still come back to me the way my daughter never could.

TWO

"I can't continue with Mrs. Fitzgerald," I said. Zelda had been in my care for only two weeks and already I could see that I needed to be shaken free from her.

Dr. Meyer regarded me with a sharp eye. When he looked at me I could feel him assessing all the time. I closed my mind and emotions to him as much as possible, willing a sturdy wall of confidence. He mustn't see my unease. He allowed only those with the strongest, steadiest mental health to work in his ward, and I couldn't bear to lose my place there.

"Might I ask why that is your opinion?" he said.

I faltered a little. I couldn't let on how upset I was. My nausea, elevated heart rate, flashbacks, and now nightmares caused me serious alarm. If I continued with Zelda, how much worse would it get?

"I just feel that someone better versed in

dementia praecox might help her more," I lied. "She is extremely fragile, by my assessment, and would benefit from Nurse Thompson or even Nurse Lombard — women more maternal by age. Women with whom Zelda might feel safe and nurtured."

"You do yourself a disservice," he said. "Age makes no difference. You exude as much maternal warmth at thirty-five years of age as Nurses Thompson and Lombard in their fifties, and you don't even have children."

I flinched and hoped he didn't perceive it.

"I'm sorry, but I need you to stay with her," he continued. "If for no other reason than she calls for you often in the night."

I was startled by this. "Pardon me?"

"Yes, the night nurse recorded that Mrs. Fitzgerald wouldn't allow her to touch her, take her vitals, or interact with her in any way. She wants you."

I was at a loss. I never expected that Zelda would have thought twice about me once my shift was over, because she often paid me no attention. In the weeks that she'd been here, she had not even been able to complete a full therapy session. She was too volatile and unsettled. Hearing that she called for me softened me, and I nodded.

"Good," said Dr. Meyer.

I prepared to leave the room when he stopped me.

"Are you all right, Nurse Howard?" he asked. "Is anything bothering *you*?"

I looked at my hands, mindful of keeping them still and folded over each other. My heart hammered so hard in my chest it threatened to betray me. Meyer knew nothing of my past. He was entirely professional and made no attempt to get to know his staff outside of the hospital. It was why I liked working for him.

"No, Dr. Meyer."

"Very well. I'll see you and Mrs. Fitzgerald at eleven o'clock for counseling."

There is nothing that underlines an uncomfortable silence as much as a ticking clock.

We sat in Dr. Meyer's study in the same formation as the day of Zelda's admittance, with one Fitzgerald traded for another. Zelda did not tremble or shake as Mr. Fitzgerald had done. She did not look pale or sweaty. Her features were relaxed. Only her fingers picking at her nails and occasionally reaching up to scratch a patch of red skin betrayed her facade.

"Mrs. Fitzgerald," said Dr. Meyer.

"Zelda," I interrupted. "She prefers to be called Zelda."

Zelda flicked a smile at me, then turned her attention to the window just over Dr. Squires's shoulder.

"Zelda," Meyer said, looking slightly aggravated at the reminder, "Dr. Squires is a resident here and will be handling your case along with me and Nurse Howard."

"I hope they'll have tomato sandwiches at lunch," said Zelda. "I adore tomato sandwiches and lemonade. It's all I ate in Alabama."

Dr. Meyer furrowed his brow, but Dr. Squires, a young, fresh-faced resident with a kindly countenance, picked up Zelda's thread.

"And could you tell us a bit about your childhood in Alabama?" asked Dr. Squires, pencil poised, a look of alert interest on her face.

Too soon, I thought.

Zelda ignored Dr. Squires's question.

"I'm also keen on cucumbers," Zelda said. "Cucumber sandwiches are a good, clean meal. I like clean foods. Clean people."

"And did your mother keep a clean house?" asked Dr. Squires.

What a ridiculous question. I looked from her to Dr. Meyer and saw he thought the same.

"Zelda," said Dr. Meyer, "if you'd prefer

not to speak about your childhood, perhaps you can tell us about your thoughts on your diagnosis from Valmont."

"You know very well what my diagnosis is."

Dr. Meyer studied her for a moment. "Am I correct in assuming that you do not wish to speak of your illness at this time?"

Again, the ticking clock.

Dr. Squires sat up straighter in her chair and started to write something on her notepad, but reconsidered and placed her pencil on the desk. Dr. Meyer did not fidget. He stared directly at Zelda, waiting her out. It seemed that an eternity passed before she finally spoke.

"It's been a pleasure sitting with you all this morning," said Zelda, "but I'll require a bit of rest before lunch. Do you think they'll serve tomato sandwiches?"

Dr. Meyer's face was unreadable, but the air felt as if Zelda had won some unspoken confrontation.

"I'm sure that can be arranged," he said. "We want you to feel rested and comfortable while you are here."

Zelda stood and walked out of the room, victorious.

When my shift ended, I went to Zelda's

room to wish her a good night. She sat in the dark, staring at the door with her papers on her lap.

"Zelda," I said. "I have to go. I hope you have a nice evening."

The light from the hallway cast a ghostly pallor across her face. Her eyes appeared as black as marbles. She could have been an actor in a haunted house, and I felt goose bumps rise on my arms.

"May I turn on the light for you?" I asked.

She did not respond at first, but blinked her eyes rapidly. When she finally made eye contact with me, her gaze looked somehow more normal. Perhaps it was just the light from the hallway contracting her pupils.

"My eyes hurt," she said.

"Here," I said, going to the small lamp on the table by the window. "I'll turn on a low light. Then you can read or write a little before dinner."

I returned to the door. "Well, good night, Zelda."

I moved to leave, but she called me back.

"Anna." Her voice shook. "Will you stay with me tonight, at least until I go to bed?"

I was touched by her request. I had spent many nights with patients during my old days at Walter Reed General Hospital, long after my shift had ended. Grieving families had often kept me tethered to bedsides while their loved ones passed on. It had been a long time, however, since I had felt compelled or anyone had asked. I was sure Zelda's night nurse wouldn't mind the help.

"Yes, I think that would be fine," I said. "Just until you go to bed."

Her face relaxed and she smiled at me with gratitude.

I led her to dinner, helped her bathe, and read to her a bit before lights-out. Dr. Meyer was pleased that she trusted me so much, and Nurse Wilson was glad to have a lighter caseload. And I felt good to be needed by someone.

By eight o'clock, however, my back ached and my skin longed to be free of the starched uniform. Mercifully, Zelda's eyes grew heavy, and within minutes of starting her book, *Modern French Painters,* she was sound asleep. Her eyelashes rested on her cheeks like a girl's, and I was overcome with pity for this child-woman who had broken down so far that she needed to live apart from her husband and daughter in a sanitarium. I hoped with all of my heart that we'd be able to restore her to some version of her better self so she could live normally.

I knew the pain of living without. I often thought grief was like madness — the lack of control, the overwhelming waves of emotion with unexpected triggers, breathlessness, night sweats, nightmares, and the feeling of utter aloneness, like that of standing on a ledge in a violent wind.

I shivered.

An orderly walked by, breaking the spell, and I set the book on the bedside table. When I stood, I placed my hand on Zelda's hair and silently wished her good dreams.

Mercifully, when I got home and slept that night, there were no nightmares to plague me.

THREE

Zelda looped her arm through mine and pointed at the moldings and chandeliers as we walked to morning therapy. I was pleased about the suggestion of intimacy and trust she exhibited by initiating physical contact with me. She had also regained the light in her eyes, which helped me forget how like my own they were.

"This place is like the Biltmore Hotel, Anna, and we will go there together so I can show you."

"I've never taken time to sightsee in New York City."

She stopped and grabbed me on the shoulders. "Never?"

"Not once," I said.

"Then I'd better hurry up and get well so I can show you around."

She relooped her arm through mine as if we were two friends on a social outing. We stepped through the door to Dr. Meyer's office, where he sat scribbling notes and Dr. Squires waited like an eager student. Dr. Meyer looked up, his face unreadable.

"You are utterly reliable, Dr. Meyer," said Zelda. "A wise owl in a tree. A trusty bookend."

I'd hoped to see a flicker of a smile cross Meyer's face, but his expression remained inaccessible. That was disappointing. I thought he'd get further with a woman like Zelda by responding positively to her at least a bit.

As the meeting progressed, Zelda passed from topic to topic, dodging questions as a politician would, but with less concern for keeping up appearances. Her hands fluttered like skittish birds while she talked in her low Southern voice. She crossed and uncrossed her shapely, taut legs, allowing them to peek out of her skirt where she had missed several buttonholes. She leaned conspiratorially toward whomever she addressed in conversation.

"Don't be afraid to smile, Dr. Meyer," said Zelda. She rested her elbows on his desk and leaned into him as much as the furniture allowed. He looked at her with a mixture of superiority and tolerance, as one would a precocious child.

"It's a pity you don't have dances here,"

she said. "The way the men love me, my card would be double-full for every song. I might even save a whole dance for you." She winked at Meyer. As I looked away to suppress a smile, I saw Dr. Squires's mouth pop open like a fish's. She quickly clamped it shut.

I enjoyed watching the exchange and found myself silently rooting for Zelda, though I didn't understand why. Dr. Meyer was a superb physician, widely respected by patients and colleagues alike. Perhaps the underlying sense of unease I felt now in the ward showed that Meyer's facade was, in fact, penetrable and that a steady temper in any person at all times was impossible. This both comforted me and unsettled me, and watching their exchange play out was morbidly fascinating.

"Zelda," said Dr. Meyer. "What are your personal goals?"

She slouched in her chair and wrapped the fingers of her right hand around her left, slowly bending her hand back along the wrist until it looked as if it would snap. She looked out the window. The ticking clock reminded us it was there.

"Not longevity," she said. "Not peace. Not some chloroformed happiness. Not tranquillity. They are all such *common* goals, aren't they, Dr. Meyer?"

"Convention does not suit you," he said.

"No. I want audacity. High color. Total independence."

"No one can exist in a totally independent state, Zelda," said Dr. Meyer. "Nor would I suspect that they would ever really wish to."

Zelda cleared her throat and sat up in her chair. "Do you know that I once called the fire department as a child and told them I saw a girl stranded on a roof, just before I climbed onto that roof and waited for them to come and get me?"

We all sat in various states of unrest waiting for her to continue.

"I could have climbed down from the roof at any time," she said. "I enjoyed having them at my disposal."

The skin rose on my arms, and for the first time since she'd arrived I felt suspicious of Zelda, and my allegiance slipped back to its proper alignment.

Zelda stood, scraping her chair against the floor and knocking her knee against the heavy wood of Meyer's desk.

"I must get back to work," she said.

"What work is that?" asked Dr. Meyer.

"My novel."

"A writer," said Dr. Squires. "Like your husband."

"No. He's more like me than I'm like him."

I smiled at her confidence.

"It's wonderful to have two talents in the family," said Dr. Squires.

"Yes," said Zelda. "But I don't know how Scott will write with me locked up."

"Why is that?" asked Dr. Meyer.

She spun toward him, piercing him with her glare, at once fierce, vulnerable, proud, and angry. Her emotions were like a jewel whose facets caught the light in succession.

"I am his words."

As if to punctuate her declaration, the clock struck the hour and she stormed out of the room.

Her pen did not leave the page for two hours after her therapy session. Every time I checked in on her she was scribbling, the stack of papers accumulating like winter snow on top of her bedside table. After my morning rounds I was able to sit with her while she wrote, trying to pick up some of her mumblings, but none of it made any sense to me. She told me, however, that I was a comfort to her, so I was glad to sit with her and catch the intermittent smiles and offhand comments she'd throw me. In truth, her attention felt like the sun coming out from behind the clouds, for it revealed in brief flashes the woman she was before all of the hurt and pain and illness blotted her out.

Lunchtime was approaching, and I wanted to warn her to give her some time to transition from the state she was in. I cleared my throat and reminded her of the schedule, anticipating that she would ignore me as she had during the last hour whenever I asked whether she needed anything. I was surprised when she dropped her pen and stretched her hands.

"A good stopping place," she said.

Her cheeks were flushed and her eyes glassy, as if her writing had induced a creative fever.

"You look well," I said. "Your memories become you."

Her smile was luminous.

"That night at the Champs-Élysées theater," she said, "Josephine Baker arrived onstage wearing nothing but a skirt, breasts bare like ripe, caramel-covered apples, and we all were mesmerized by the beautiful grotesquerie of it."

"I'm afraid it would've caused me to blush," I said, feeling heat in my cheeks at the mere thought of it.

"We were too tight from the champagne

cocktails to feel the burn of the blush," she said. "That time in Paris in the twenties was the edge of when it all turned."

I felt suddenly alert. She was beginning her remembrances. I didn't want to lead her at all, so I remained quiet and attempted to mute my expression. Perhaps if I could just blend into the walls she'd speak as if she were alone.

"Those were the days we ran with the Murphys, the Hemingways, Dos Passos, Duff Twysden. That damnable Stein, who always banished the wives to tea with her *wife* while the artists and writers got high on each other's bold ideas." Her voice became brittle.

"There were too many parties, too many salons, too many nights watching half-naked Negroes, half-sober painters, half-mad homosexuals. . . ." Her voice trailed off for a moment. "Waking up mornings was the worst part. It was like the sickly, bitter flavor on the tongue after drinking coffee. It was so good going down, but the aftertaste made you damn near hate it."

My eyes moved over the pages and it occurred to me that her writing allowed her to open up. I considered this for a moment, then made my thoughts known.

"How would you feel about writing to Dr.

Meyer instead of talking to him?" I asked.

Her gaze met mine straight on and I understood that being direct was the only way to get through to her. She was no fool. Tricks would not get her to reveal anything.

"About what?" she said.

"Your illness. Your past. What you think precipitated your collapses," I said. "It's all he wants, you know. It's all any of us want: to help you reach in and determine the source of the problem to help you avoid it in the future. To heal. To prepare you for living outside of a clinic."

She did not recoil from my words as I anticipated she would. After a few moments, she nodded her head.

"I'll do it," she said. "What shall I write?"

"Start at the beginning, wherever that is to you."

"Can it be like a story?" she asked.

"It can be anything you want. Whatever feels natural."

"Could I only write for you?"

This presented a problem. Anything my patient shared I was obligated to tell the entire team caring for her. I didn't want to lie to her, but I also didn't want to betray her. I decided to put her at ease for now, and later decide what to do if she wrote anything.

"Yes, you may write just for me," I said.

"And you promise not to show Scott."

"Of course I won't show him," I said.

"He thinks expression ruins me," she said. "Why?"

"Because he thinks he should be enough for me. He needs me to orbit him. He wishes to pluck me from orbit when he needs me and then send me back once he's used me up."

Herein lies the problem, I thought. But it was a common enough problem in marriages. Didn't we all want devotion? Undivided attention? Why did it break the Fitzgeralds so badly?

"You clearly crave creative expression," I said. "I know about your dancing. Do you play an instrument? Paint? I feel that more outlets would nurture your physical and mental health."

"I do love to paint. I studied with the best in France. I love to make things with my hands, too. You should have seen the dollhouse I made for Scottie at our home in Delaware."

Her words fell flat and her face contorted. A sob rose in her throat and she collapsed on the bed. It had been too much. I needed to back off, but I wanted to calm her. I approached her carefully and reached to touch her back. She flinched but did not push me off. I sat next to her and rubbed her back in wide, slow circles. She turned her body and wrapped her arms around me, crying until she fell asleep.

Four

The taxi stopped at the entrance to the pebbled drive, and Lincoln, the driver, opened my door and helped me out like he did once a month. He treated me as if I were the most important and elegant woman who'd ever ridden in his backseat.

"You sure you don't want me to take you all the way up to the door?" he asked, as he always did.

"No, sir," I said. "I like the walk through the trees. But you are the finest gentleman I know for asking."

He smiled his wide, half-toothless smile and ran a hand over his black, stubbled hair.

"Aw, honey, you make an old man feel young."

I reached into my pocketbook to pay him and he hurried back to the passenger seat.

"No charge today," he said, rolling up his window. "I won at cards last night, and I said to myself, 'If I win, I'm not chargin'

Anna.' "

I laughed, and opened the door to shove the money down the back of his shirt.

"Don't get fresh with me, young missy," he called. "I'll tell the wife."

Lincoln talked only about baseball and his wife, the former being his greatest love. Time for him was marked by the passage from preseason, to season, to postseason. He was fond of telling me he bled black and orange for his beloved Baltimore Black Sox, and that his favorite player, Jud "Boojum" Wilson, would have been good enough to play against any of those major leaguers, if only colored men were allowed.

Lincoln and I had a standing date once a month. On every third Saturday morning he delivered me to my parents' place in the rural part of Towson just outside the Baltimore suburbs, argued with me about paying before he drove away, and returned Sunday evening to take me back to the city.

I closed his laugh into the car and started up the drive.

Though it was the end of February, the day was a lazy sort of cold. The sun slipped through the clouds in bursts, reminding the landscape that it was still there, prodding snow piles to relax into puddles and stirring sleeping seeds under the ground.

My breath always caught when I looked at my parents' house. It was a brown ranch style nestled among poplars and pines, with shiny green holly lining its front porch lattice in the winter and deep blue hydrangeas in the summer. It was equal parts comfort and affliction for me. It held so many happy memories and my parents, whom I adored, but it also reminded me of the daughter I'd lost, and the time we lived here after the war.

I saw my mother in the window smiling out at me, and the tension left my shoulders. When I opened the unlocked door, the aroma of coffee and banana bread greeted me first, followed by my mother, limping around the corner, clutching her cane.

"Please stay seated," I said. "I saw you there."

"Let me get up to greet you while I still can," she said.

At fifty-nine, my mother still held the beauty of her youth, with only a peppering of gray hair at her temples and the faintest lines around her eyes. She wore her brown hair in a loose bun at the base of her neck. Her warm brown eyes had a glint of mischief, and she still dressed every day for visitors, though she and my dad didn't often have them. Her body, however, had betrayed her, as she often said. She was diagnosed with multiple sclerosis around the time I began working at the Phipps Clinic, five years ago. I embraced her and she allowed me to walk her back over and lower her into her chair. I took the seat across from her.

"Are you losing weight?" I asked, worried by the prominence of her bones I could feel through her sweater.

"Now, don't start fussing over me as soon as you've walked in the door," she said. "Tell me about your month."

I'd been waiting for this query with great anticipation for weeks. I usually had nothing of any importance to report. I'd say so and watch my mother's face fall from a mixture of boredom that I had no news and worry that I was not embracing life — points that, I reflected, she had a right to worry about.

But not this month.

Dr. Meyer did not want us to speak about our patients outside of the clinic, but I rationalized my guilt away by telling myself my mother needed stimulation and I needed advice. My eyes flickered over her bookshelf, bursting with well-worn spines, and immediately found the object of my glance. *This Side of Paradise* and *The Beautiful and Damned* winked at me from their positions, causing me to smile.

"You have news," she said with genuine pleasure. "Tell me!"

"Maybe I'll make you guess," I said, raising an eyebrow and enjoying her anticipation.

"You've found a man!" she said.

What she blurted out so completely surprised and shook me that it took me a moment to remember what my news actually was. I thought of Ben and felt a cold sweat form on my forehead. She could see she had said the wrong thing and reached for my arm.

"I'm so sorry, honey," she said. "You just looked so animated, I thought . . ."

"No, it's okay," I said. "I shouldn't have made you play a guessing game."

An awkward silence settled over the room. I watched a male cardinal fly past the window and land on a nearby branch, shaking off the light coating of snow that clung to it. I looked back at my mom and smiled at her.

"Let's try again," I said. "You'll never guess who's been admitted to the clinic."

"Who?" My mother leaned forward in her chair.

"Mrs. F. Scott Fitzgerald!"

"No!"

"Yes!"

The awkwardness dissolved and I told my mother all about Zelda and how she came to Phipps. My mother wanted to know what she looked like, what she ate, and what she did all day.

"Wait," she said. "Did you see *him?*"

"I did. And he looked as broken as his wife."

My mom sucked in her breath and shook her head. "A terrible shame."

"What's a shame, Janie?" asked my father as he walked into the room wearing his red flannel jacket and wiping his hands on a brown towel. His fair gray hair was wispy from the breeze.

"Anna was just telling me that Zelda Fitzgerald, the famous writer's wife, is at the Phipps Clinic!"

"Which writer?" he asked. "The one who wrote that *Sun Rises* book?"

"No, Paddy, the man with the flapper wife."

"Oh," he said, clearly unimpressed and uninformed as to whom exactly we were talking about. He gave me a kiss on the cheek.

"Your nose is cold," I said. "How long have you been out in that shed?"

"He wants the chimes ready for Spring

51

Fest," said my mother. My father had been a boilermaker for many years, and in his retirement he now devoted his time to making copper wind chimes. It was a hobby he'd picked up from his father but couldn't devote his full attention to until now. I always associated the sober, beautiful sounds of wind chimes with my family home. Their music sat behind many days of beauty and heartbreak in my life. I couldn't help but think of Katie, and rubbed my temples.

"Are you okay?" asked my dad.

"Is it a headache?" asked my mother.

"No, I'm fine," I said. "I guess I just need some coffee."

They met each other's concerned gazes and then looked back at me. My mother seemed to want to probe the matter further, but my father clapped his hands and announced that it was snack time. She was clearly uneasy, but resigned herself to dropping the subject.

"Perfect," she said. "And then I'll let Anna read Peter's letter from Rome so she can hear the good news."

With my mother resting for the afternoon and my father at the market picking up ingredients for dinner, I pulled on my boots and opened the door to the backyard. I wanted some time in the wind shed, as we called it, before the bustle of evening dinner preparations. The ground was muddy from the melting snow, and the air smelled fresh. I stuffed my hands in my pockets, feeling the sharp edges of Peter's letter.

I enjoyed the way my boots stuck in the icy mud. They made a pleasant squelching sound over the patter of the thaw dribbling from the trees and running into the little streams that threaded through the woods. The sounds reminded me of my childhood — a happy childhood — spent amidst the tulip poplars and maples with Peter trailing me on our adventures. They also reminded me of how Katie had hopped along the paths, chattering like a finch. I could almost see her small form leading me to the wind shed.

Just shouting distance from the house, the wind shed was an old barn my father had converted to a workroom. As one walked nearer to it, the worn dirt path from a thousand trips my father made back and forth turned to oyster shells we'd collected from our summer visits to Maryland's Eastern Shore.

The barn itself was dark brown and had two large doors directly across from each other that my father left open most of the time to create a wind tunnel. It was along the beams running from one doorway of the barn to the other that he hung his wind chimes, which played perpetual scales in response to the breezes blowing through the doors.

I felt my shoulders relax as I drew nearer and walked under them, and thought that Zelda and our patients would benefit from the healing sounds of the chimes. Perhaps I'd bring some back to the clinic.

My father had left the woodstove burning for me. I sat on the old upholstered chair next to it and fished Peter's letter from my pocket.

February 5, 1932

Dear Mom & Dad,
Buona sera!

The bells of St. Peter's are announcing the evening with so much drama and romance I could almost trade in my collar for a girl to kiss. But not for now. I have wonderful news about my future assignment that I've known about for some time but could not share until the official announcement.

The Archdiocese of Baltimore has approved my installation at the Baltimore Cathedral! I'm overwhelmed with happiness to be so close to you and to Anna, because I love you all and because I love your cooking, and hope to be fat as Friar Tuck by the fall on soda bread, corned beef, and cabbage.

In all seriousness, before I return I'll be on a pilgrimage to San Giovanni Rotondo, where I hope to meet the holy man, Padre Pio. The Vatican issued an official decree not to revere him as many around him have done due to his non-conformity, but you know authority telling me not to do something only hastens the time in which I do it. I've written to my dear friend Aldo, who lives there, and he has assured me the man is no grifter. At the very least I'd like the good padre to hear my confession and hope some of his reverence wears off on me, since, as you well know, irreverence is my one and only deficit of character.

I can hardly wait to see you all, and I pray for your well-being daily. I don't want to alarm you, but I've had some recent bad dreams about Anna, and I sincerely hope she is in a good emotional state. Please kiss her for me and tell her that her pesky younger brother will be home soon to remind her what a trouble-maker she used to be and how I'd like to see a bit of that again.

Con affetto,
Pietro

I was more than a little troubled by his words. I tried to mute my worry by concentrating on my happiness over his return to Baltimore. I hadn't seen him since Christmas of 1930, and felt his absence acutely. To have him so near would be a great gift to us all.

The barn was suddenly filled with darkness from a cloud passing over the sun, and the chimes began to clang in a frenzy from a passing wind. The woodstove could not compete with the sudden return of winter elements, and I was no longer comfortable in the shed. I stood and walked to the doorway facing the woods and saw that it was not a single cloud, but a bank of clouds that threatened winter rain. I shoved Peter's letter into my pocket and hurried back to the house.

After dinner, I sat by the fire with my

parents talking of Peter's good news. We all avoided the closing of his letter and what it implied, and instead focused on how happy we were that he was coming home.

"I see that even the influence of the Holy See has not tamed your brother," my mother said with a mixture of exasperation and pride. "I hoped his study in Rome would . . . sober him a little."

"God likes him crazy," my dad said, much to my amusement. "Otherwise he woulda made him serious."

"They must think highly of him to install him in such an important parish," I said. "Peter will probably end up pope one day."

The room was quiet for a moment, but then we all had a good laugh. Peter dated girls every summer he was home from the seminary to "get it out of his system." He smoked. He drank. He loved to dance. He seemed far more youthful than his thirty-two years, though he could be profoundly spiritual and insightful.

"We should introduce him to Zelda," said my mother. "I bet he could help her."

"He'd probably encourage the behaviors that led to her downfall," I said. "I would be interested to hear what he has to think."

"His theory would be outlandish, for sure," said Mother, "but probably accurate."

"Amen to that," said my father.

We all sat watching the fire burn out, and I noticed my mother starting to nod off. My father saw her too. He looked at her with such tenderness that I felt a wave of emotion I had difficulty containing.

"Dad, would you like me to help you get her to bed?"

"No, honey," he said. "I'll just sit here with her for a bit longer. She'll wake in a little while and then I'll take her."

He spoke from experience.

"Well, good night, then," I said.

I walked down the hall, running my hand along the faded Sears, Roebuck flowered wallpaper, to the room that had been mine as a girl. I fell asleep as soon as my head hit the pillow, but I did not sleep the peaceful sleep of my youth. Instead I dreamed that Zelda called for me over and over in the night from her room at the clinic, and Peter called for me from a dormitory in Rome, and my mother called for me from down the hallway, and Katie called me from the wind shed, and Ben called to me but I didn't know where he was.

The flickering light of a dying bulb inside the apartment of the Romanian violinist tapped its Morse code on the sidewalk outside of my building. I started up the front stairs as Lincoln drove off, but felt too anxious to go inside and shut myself in my apartment for the night. I thought a quick walk around the block before the darkness really set in would calm my nerves.

I'd always been one with a vivid and morbid imagination, which I attributed to the profusion of Poe tales my mother had read to me and Peter as children. I enjoyed visiting Poe's grave several blocks away and fancied myself connected to the dead writer the way Peter probably felt connected to his dead saints. I did not worship Poe, only imagined I saw him around street corners, cemetery gates, and in and out of the stacks at the Enoch Pratt Free Library.

The street had a heavy Poe sensibility about it that night in the winter dark, and more than once I considered turning back. My eyes scanned the sidewalks and avenues, seeking students or symphonygoers, Fords or trolley cars, but except for the smell of smoke from fires burning in row house chimneys, the city seemed vacant.

I pulled my coat close around me and noticed the weight from my overnight bag and pocketbook heavy on my shoulder. I shifted them to the other shoulder and turned down Madison Street. I hesitated a bit and stepped slowly over the uneven cobblestones. Mr. Poe would have made note of the fog that seeped into the alleyways and doorways in the yellow glow of the street lamps. I suddenly felt the hairs on the back of my neck stand.

It made no sense to turn back, because I was equally as far from my apartment on the other side of the block. I continued walking, but at a quicker pace. The wind blew with great intensity through the streets between the buildings, and I cursed myself for my poor judgment.

The sound of footsteps behind me interrupted my thoughts. I stopped and turned my head, but all I saw was the pattern of low light and deep shadows between the lampposts. Did I see movement in the pool of darkness at the corner? It was most likely a rat. They seemed to be getting fatter as the depressed city grew thinner.

Whether it was a rat or not, I wanted to get home. A distant siren wailed from another neighborhood, sending chills up my arms. Out of instinct, I made the sign of the cross over myself as my mother taught us, to pray for those in danger. As the siren died, I heard footsteps again. This time I was sure.

My heart began pounding in my chest. I

hesitated a moment, but I did not want to turn around again. Fortunately, I was nearing the corner to the last section of block before my street. I increased my pace but didn't run. Hopefully it was just someone out for an evening stroll.

In the winter.

At night.

The footsteps also quickened.

I abandoned all pretense and broke into a run.

The bag felt like a sack of bricks on my shoulder. My face stung from the cold, and fear chilled my heart. I couldn't help but turn my head to the side. Out of the corner of my eye I saw a man in a long dark coat pursuing me. My worst fears confirmed, I sprang forward, running as fast as I could. That fear held me by the throat and I could not make any sound besides the gasping from my lungs, tight from exertion in near-freezing temperatures.

As I neared the corner, I realized that I didn't want him to know where I lived, but I didn't have anywhere else to go. I didn't have much time to contemplate an alternate route, however, because I felt his hands pulling my hair. I finally managed a scream, but only for a moment before his filthy fingers clamped over my mouth.

I threw my bags at him, hoping he was just looking to rob me. He made no move toward them, and I knew from the evil in his small blue eyes that there was something else he wanted. Panic sent a surge of energy through my body, and I bit his fingers and screamed for help. As my voice echoed off the pavement, he tackled me and slammed me to the ground. The back of my head hit the sidewalk and I saw sparks in my field of vision. The sting of blood filled my mouth where I'd bitten my tongue. I spit in his face and tried to bring up my fingers to scratch his eyes, but he had my hands pinned too tightly at my sides.

My leg pulled itself from under his, and I managed to knee him in the groin, but he was tall and I could bring my knee up only so much, so he didn't get the full force of the impact. He grunted a little, raised his fist, and struck me across the face, this time causing my vision to go black for a moment.

It was suddenly clear to me that I was going to die in the worst way I could imagine. All I could think of was that I didn't want my parents to find out, because it would hurt them too much.

My God, I had to get him off me!

But he pressed onward. I could feel him fumbling with my skirt, poking at me. I heard a snarl and felt as if I would vomit when suddenly he was jerked from me and thrown into the slushy mess in the street. My eyes still weren't focused, but I saw the blurred outline of a dark figure punching my attacker repeatedly until the man lay still in the gutter. Then my helper was at my side. His face and hair were dark in the light. For a moment I thought it was . . .

"Ben?"

"Shhh," he said. "Do you think I can lift you?"

That accent. It was not Ben. Where had I heard it before? I squeezed my eyes shut and opened them again to see the face of the Romanian from my building.

"I'm all right," I said, attempting to pull myself into a sitting position. Overtaken by a dizzy spell, I fell back to the pavement. He moved his arm under my neck just before my head hit the street.

"I will carry you," he said.

I looked over at my attacker and my heart raced.

"No, please," I said. "Please call the police. We can't give him a chance to get away."

"I will not leave you in the street next to him while I call for help."

He stood and walked back to the criminal

and ripped off his filthy cap that was covering a mostly bald head with only wisps of greasy gray hair along the fringe. He had a mouth of rotten brown teeth, and those slits of blue eyes were swollen from the Romanian's punches, which my rescuer again administered for good measure. I flinched in spite of myself, and was surprised that a figure so seemingly meek and quiet was capable of such violence.

"We have had a good look," he said. "If he crawls somewhere before I return, we will be able to describe him to the police."

With that, he lifted me and carried me into the apartment building and into his rooms on the first floor, where he'd left the door ajar. He placed me on a threadbare couch and ran his fingers through his hair.

"Stay here," he said unnecessarily. I couldn't have gone anywhere if I wanted to.

As he left the room, I fell back on the worn couch, grateful that I was here instead of on the street. My vision stopped its shifting, but I could feel the beginnings of a headache. I began to shake, certain I was in some kind of shock and thankful that the Romanian had seen me when he did. My God, if he hadn't been there —

My teeth chattered and my hands shook, but I was able to slowly sit myself up and look around the apartment. Music sheets littered the floor in a bank of crumpled balls. A plain wooden chair sat by a music stand in front of a great arched window that lent an air of grace to the room. Candles flickered on a table next to a plate of bread crumbs and an empty glass of wine, and logs glowed in a fireplace behind the dining table. The only adornments on the peeling plaster walls were a pencil drawing of an intense, robust man with dark eyes and a dark crop of hair, and an ornate cross that seemed to be at odds with the poverty of the room.

I felt unaccountably safe in this simple place with the faucet leaking from the kitchen. I reached my hand to touch the back of my head and felt a lump, but no blood, so I lay back on the couch. I thought I dreamed the sound of the police siren.

The Romanian's name was Sorin Funar.

After the police officers had taken a statement from each of us and hauled my attacker off to jail, I told Sorin I wanted to go home. He carried my bags, which he'd retrieved for me, in one arm, and let me lean against him with the other. He was my height and thin, and I again wondered how he had overcome the criminal. When we got to the second floor, I thought I was going to be sick, so I allowed him to escort me into my apartment.

I could see that the piano commanded his attention in the turn of his head as he led me past it and into my bedroom. He placed my bags on the floor and helped me sit on the bed. I was so overcome with relief and gratitude to be safe in my apartment that I began to cry. His face turned red and I could see his discomfort.

"I'm sorry," I said. "I'm just so thankful you were there. If you hadn't been there . . ."

"It is all right," he said.

"How did you know?"

He looked down at his feet and shuffled his worn shoes against the wood floor.

"I saw you arrive," he said. "I was at the window, practicing. Then I saw that you did not want to come in."

"I was stupid," I said.

"No," he said. "I did not think anything of it until I saw him."

"Follow me?"

"Yes, after you started your walk I saw him cross the street and turn the corner you had just turned."

"If you weren't at that window," I said as my tears slowed. "If you hadn't come out on the street."

He nodded. I saw him flex his fingers open and closed, and I felt my stomach drop. He needed those hands. They were everything to him and he'd used them to punch my attacker.

"Are your fingers all right?" I asked.

"A little stiff," he said, finally smiling. "But not broken."

"Where did you learn to punch like that?"

"I lived in a tough town," he said. "A skinny boy with a violin needs to learn how to use his fists at a young age."

I smiled at him.

"Well, I'll be forever grateful," I said. "I can't thank you enough."

He started looking around the room and shifting from foot to foot. I could see he wanted to leave. I stood to show him the door but he stopped me.

"I will let myself out," he said. "Good night."

"Good night."

He left the room and I heard the door close a few moments later. I stared after him, unable to sleep for the remainder of the night.

FIVE

I was in agony from the headaches, and because I was sure Zelda felt abandoned by me. In the three days I'd been out of work, I sensed her turmoil in my body the way an arthritic senses a coming storm.

I was sick of hiding in my apartment, scared to walk outside, anxious about sleep and the terrible dreams I'd been having. At least the piano didn't taunt me the way I thought it would. It looked somehow softer, pliable, more inviting; though without any music on its stand it did have a barren feel. I regarded it and was suddenly overcome by an urge to make it an offering of sorts while bringing a piece of Ben to these rooms.

I went to my bedroom and jostled through shoes and old nursing uniforms in the back of the closet. The box I was looking for was in front of a box of my daughter's things that I deliberately did not look at. I slid it out and sat with it on the floor, watching the dust motes rising from it, dancing in the afternoon light. With a deep breath, I lifted the lid and was overcome by the smell of one of Ben's uniforms after all these years. I slammed the lid shut and shoved the box back in the closet with my heart racing. I walked over to the window and put my hands on the sill, breathing deeply until my heart steadied.

During the war, I had used this technique to cope. I would walk away for just a moment, breathe, steel myself, and return. I used to pride myself on keeping grace under pressure. Other nurses envied me for it. Doctors depended on me because of it. I stood up straight and turned to face the room with more determination.

When I pulled out the box and lifted the lid this time, I was prepared for the scent of Ben's uniforms under years of dust and neglect. The smell was there, but I did not recoil. I inhaled it and allowed him to fill me with each breath.

I reached into the box and pulled out the framed photograph of the two of us at my parents' house on our wedding day. We were standing against the side of the barn, but my brother had taken the picture without our knowledge. In it, Ben had his hand on my lower back, I had my arms wrapped around his neck, and our foreheads were touching. It was beautiful.

Forcing myself to stand, I carried the photograph out to the living room, and as I placed the picture on the piano, the lonely, aching sound of Sorin's violin drifted up the stairwell and into my apartment. I hadn't seen him since the night of the attack, and I wanted to thank him somehow, to show him my gratitude.

I decided to take him some of the loaf of my mother's banana bread I'd just baked, but when I took the bread down the stairs and knocked on his door he didn't answer. I listened at the door, but he didn't make any noise. I didn't want to leave the bread in case of rodents, so I knocked again, much harder.

A muffled sound came through the door, like a rustling of paper. A distant cough. I knocked a final time and called, "It's Anna. I've baked some bread for you. It's here."

I placed the bread on the floor outside of his door, made sure the paper was closed tightly around it, and went back up to my room. The tea I'd put on the stove was whistling, so I poured myself a cup, added half a teaspoon of sugar, and set it on the piano to cool. I went back to the hallway and looked down the stairwell to see that the bread was gone.

Soon afterward, I knew I'd overdone it. My head felt split in two, and I was overcome with fatigue. I slept the rest of the afternoon.

For the next two days I continued my strange routine. I moved pictures from Ben's box in the closet to various places around the apartment. I sat at the piano without playing, but let my tingling fingers rest on the keys, finding the scales without pressing them. I continued to leave offerings of gratitude at Sorin's apartment. Wednesday, I left him half of a roast I'd cooked. Thursday, several mason jars of mulled cider. I also gave some of the cider to the ballerinas, and they accepted it with hearty thanks and invited me in. I declined as they regarded my bruised face with curiosity, and I left them before they could ask any questions.

By Friday, echoes of pain continued to shoot through my head, but I was ready to return to work. I'd spoken to Dr. Meyer by phone and he was glad to hear I was well enough to return, even if it was only for one day before the weekend. I decided to keep my attack a secret, and told the clinic that I'd had a bad cold. It was a traumatic experience, and I didn't want Dr. Meyer to know about it and scrutinize me for it.

When I got to work, I hung my coat in the nurses' room and quickly started down the hall to Zelda. Anxiety and anticipation had my heart racing and my palms clammy. I gave her door a knock, counted to ten to allow her to ready herself for a visitor, and opened it. At first, I did not see her.

"I'm in here, bathing, Mildred," she called.

My voice felt stuck in my throat. Mildred? When had Zelda and Dr. Squires gotten on such good terms? I felt a sudden pang of something I did not understand.

"It's me, Anna. Do you need assistance?"

Silence was all that greeted me. I glanced around the room and saw several piles of papers. It looked as if she had many writing projects under way. I wondered whether she had written anything about her illness or her past for me to read. There were some sketches on an easel in the corner of the room closest to me, and an assortment of tubes of gouache paint. I stepped closer to the sketches and flipped through them.

In the front rested several landscapes that appeared to be views from her window, though they were rather distorted. There was one strange drawing of a ballet dancer with such unusual lines and prominent feet that it looked as if the dancer were swollen with terrible pain. The last sketch was of Dr. Squires.

My spirits sank. Zelda had transferred her trust to Dr. Squires while I was away.

"Zelda, may I come in?"

When I heard no answer in the affirmative or negative I began to worry. What if she couldn't make a decision and needed my assistance? What if she'd hurt herself somehow?

"Zelda, I'm coming in."

Still no response.

When I stepped into the doorway of the bathroom, she was sitting in the bathtub with her arms around her knees, staring at the water.

"Are you all right?" I asked.

Her face was blank. She acted as if she hadn't heard me. I felt like an apparition undetected by a human person. It was terribly unsettling.

"May I help you out of the bath?"

She sat still for another moment, and then she laughed as if I'd just said something funny. As quickly as she made the sound, it was over, and she looked troubled that she'd laughed at all. She finally looked at me and her gaze stopped me in my tracks. I had never been on the receiving end of such an accusatory, venomous glare.

"If it's not too much trouble," she said, with heavy sarcasm.

My fears were well-founded. She'd felt abandoned by me.

"Zelda," I said, "I'm so sorry I wasn't here this week. I've been . . . ill."

She cocked her head to the side and regarded me suspiciously before looking away. I had prepared a lie for her, but I felt I owed her more than that. She was far too perceptive anyway.

"I was attacked," I said. "By a man at night."

That got her attention.

"Anna," she said. "Are you all right? Did he . . ."

"No, no. Thank God," I said. "My neighbor saw us out the window and came to help. Everything's all right; I just hit my head and needed to rest for a few days."

This seemed to soften her.

"And here I was thinking you were like all the rest," she said. "What did Meyer say?"

"I'm not going to tell him," I said. "I have a feeling that he'd force me to take off more time and possibly suggest some kind of therapy, but I want to be here. With you."

She looked up at me with large, adoring eyes before her face darkened. She looked as if she wanted to cry.

"My friend. My dear friend," she said. "Poor Anna."

She stood up from the water and stepped onto the tile. I moved to wrap a towel around her and pressed it into her skin to absorb the water. She allowed me to help her dry off, but put on her underclothes and dressed herself. Then she sat at the mirror and handed me the brush. I began brushing her tawny blond hair away from her face, and she closed her eyes and put her head back.

While Zelda wrote that morning, I sat in a staff meeting with Dr. Meyer and Dr. Squires, and they briefed me on what had gone on in my absence.

"Zelda's making incredible progress on her novel," said Dr. Squires. "She's allowed me to read it and it's quite good. She's calling it *Save Me the Waltz.*"

I felt the pang again, and forced a smile. "Really? How nice."

"Yes, it's quite unique and unlike anything I've ever read," she continued. "It has a rambling, conversational tone to it, but is also highly literary. I'm afraid I can't explain it."

"Perhaps she'll let Nurse Howard read it

sometime," said Dr. Meyer. "I know she won't let me. She seems to have a deep distrust of men."

"And yet a dependence on them," said Dr. Squires. "It's as if she both craves and resents the men in her life."

I was interested to hear Dr. Squires expand on this.

"Has she spoken to you of the past yet?" I asked.

"No, not actually," said Dr. Squires. "Her novel, though, is autobiographical. I'm learning a lot about her past through it."

So Zelda did feel comfortable expressing herself on the page. I longed to read the book and at once recognized the pang I'd felt. It was jealousy gnawing at my belly. I could not loathe Dr. Squires, however. She was kind and open, and her support of Zelda was a good thing. I just hoped there was room for both of us in Zelda's attention.

The meeting came to a conclusion and we all stood.

"I'm so glad you're back," said Dr. Squires just before she left Meyer's office.

"Thank you," I said. "It's good to be back."

Dr. Squires squeezed my hand and walked out the door, heading to her next patient meeting. I started to leave when Dr. Meyer called to me.

"Nurse Howard," he said. "Please close the door."

I did so, hoping he'd reveal something new to me about Zelda. Instead, I was the subject of his observation.

"Your headaches and cold," he said with concern. "Are they better?"

I willed myself to keep eye contact with him. "Yes, Dr. Meyer. I hated being away for so long."

"I see," he said. "And how did you get that bruise on your cheek?"

I reached up and touched the fist-size, yellowing bruise. I'd prepared a story, but as I faced Dr. Meyer, it seemed preposterous. Still, I could not speak of the attack. In my years of psychiatric nurse training, my instructors focused so strongly on maintaining boundaries in clinical relationships. Without limits, relationships could become ambiguous or even corrosive to all parties involved. I told myself that these boundaries needed to extend to my relationship with Dr. Meyer to keep his confidence. I wouldn't want him to think I was suffering emotionally. What I wouldn't allow myself to recognize, however, was that I couldn't stand the thought of being separated from Zelda.

"It happened at my parents' place," I said. "I ran right into a barn beam."

"Really," he said. "I wouldn't have taken you for a clumsy one."

"It was muddy."

He smiled a little, as if I'd reassured him. "Well, I'm glad you're back."

I felt a pang of guilt over the lie and was able to manage only a nod. He turned from me and began shuffling papers on his desk.

Suddenly, an animal-like howl rent the quiet. We ran out of the office and started down the hall to Zelda's room, where the sound originated. We reached the room just as Zelda was being restrained by an orderly while she shredded a piece of paper in her hands.

"Bastard. Goddamn him to hell!" she shouted.

Dr. Meyer ordered the attendant off Zelda and she slipped into the corner of the room and continued shredding the paper.

"I just gave her the mail and she started this," said the man.

I stepped forward. "What is it, Zelda?"

She stopped shouting and started mumbling to herself. "No books, no fiction. 'Stop your writing. You'll put yourself over the edge.' I'd rather hear that I'm his locked-tower princess than take all of his damned instructions and diagnosis." She spit at the papers and flung them to the floor around her bare feet. Then she placed her head on her knees and exhaled. When she looked up again, her face was unlined and peaceful, as if nothing had just happened.

"What's for supper this evening?" she asked. "I'd love a cucumber salad or some tomato sandwiches with a spray of parsley on the side to remind me of his eyelashes when I loved his eyes and they were like the Mediterranean Sea to me instead of the icy glare throwers they've become. I can see him looking out of the paper at me and I can't stand it."

At that moment, I had the eeriest feeling that Mr. Fitzgerald could see us. Zelda watched the goose bumps rise on my arms.

"You feel it, too," she said. "I'm not alone."

We returned to her room after lunch, and she walked to her papers and ran her hands over them as if she were stroking a cat. I stood at the window and watched her until she looked up at me.

"I'm glad these are under lock and key with me in this big safe so he can't steal them," she said.

"Do you really think he would steal your work?" I asked.

"Wouldn't be the first time," she said.

"What other times has he stolen your work?"

"*This Side of Paradise, The Beautiful and Damned, Gatsby . . .*"

"What are you saying?" I asked. "Did you write those?"

She stood to her full posture and suddenly became indignant.

"No," she said. "No, you mustn't think he's not a great writer. He's the finest writer of our generation."

"I think he is a fine writer," I replied, carefully choosing my words. "It's just that I interpreted your words as an insinuation that he used your writing and passed it off as his own. I apologize if I misread you."

"No, you didn't. I flit like a butterfly. Can you keep up?"

"I can try," I said.

She sat heavily on the bed and stared out the window. "But he is a plagiarist."

That was a strong accusation. I didn't want to further upset her, however, so I remained silent, waiting for her to continue.

"Sometimes I think if I could just find the diaries he stole . . ."

"He stole your diaries?" I couldn't help myself.

"Yes," she said. "I used to keep diaries, and when we first got married he took them and wouldn't tell me where he'd put them. Said that I was done with all that now."

"And have you seen them since?"

"No."

"Do you think he still has them?"

"I hope so," she said. "Otherwise there is no hope for me."

"Why?"

"Because the roots of my soul are in those books. If they're gone, so is my soul seed. I might as well die."

My mind started racing. I felt something coming at me on a wave. Inevitability. A task. To restore her identity and present it to her.

"I have not forgotten what you asked of me," she said. "Writing my past. My remembrances."

"Aren't you doing that in your novel?" I asked.

"I am, but it's just a piddly small account of a portion of our timeline. I want to take you back, and I will. I just have to get this novel out of me."

"I look forward to it," I said. "But please know that there's no pressure. Perhaps the novel will be enough."

"It won't be enough, because it's for everyone. When I write for you, I will write *only* for you. My confessions."

I decided, right there on the spot, that I would not share her confessions with anyone. She needed someone in her life not to betray or use her in any way. I would be that person. I could share my insights with Dr. Meyer, but not Zelda's words.

"Of course," I said.

"And then we'll burn them," she said. "Like the salamander."

"I'm not familiar with the salamander," I said.

"A mythic lizard, purified by fire," she said. "A woman who burns through men to find her one true love."

She struck a match and lit a cigarette, inhaling deeply and filling the space around her with her exhalations.

Six

The next day, Zelda pressed papers into my hands and told me I was not to share her remembrances with anyone.

"Not even Dr. Squires?"

"Not even Dr. Squires."

It pleased me to be in her confidence. I realized this was not healthy, but I had no way to stop my feelings. I wished I could write to Peter that I was someone's confessor. Perhaps we could discuss it when he came home. I was sure he would have much insight for me.

I waited for the bus outside the hospital. Since my attack I'd been unable to walk home alone. Even though the dark of winter was crowded out a bit each day by the impending equinox, and in spite of my knowledge that my attacker was in jail, I still couldn't enjoy my city walks — not yet. After the war I didn't think I could ever be frightened of anything again.

I was wrong.

The bus dropped me very near my apartment, and I walked briskly through the fading light to my building, pausing just a moment to glance at Sorin's window and see whether he was there. He was and nodded at me. I waved and hurried in the door to show him how responsible I was. No more nighttime walks for me.

I heard the faraway pounding of the ballerinas on the third floor to a brisk mazurka. I loved how it competed with Sorin's violin, and privately imagined my piano nudging into the atmospheric score. This thought made me smile. In fact, after I opened the door and locked it behind me, I walked over to the piano and played a quick scale. I could swear that all musical life outside my apartment stopped with my playing, but it soon resumed, making me wonder whether my imagination was running away with me.

Anxious to get to Zelda's papers but wishing to savor them without distraction, I hurried through a scrambled egg, a slice of toast, and a small can of peaches. I washed my face, brushed my teeth, and slipped into my flannel nightgown. I tucked myself into bed and started reading.

Dear Anna, I'm writing my confessions for

you alone. I am no victim. I am no saint. Yet he has paid me back more than he owed and does not know how to stop.

Montgomery, Alabama, 1918
Can you hear the faraway music coming from the faded country club? It is old and the daylight isn't kind, but the night and the lights along the lip of the roof and the winks of the fireflies and the delicious pines framing it give it an air of romance and mystery. The scent of honeysuckle hangs in the darkness like the thick glop of sugar at the bottom of a glass of lemonade.

Do you see her as she dances the "Dance of the Hours" for the admiring soldiers and the scowling, envious women? She moves with grace and suppleness, and she should have stayed with the dance, but that's for later.

There was one soldier who looked out of place. It was his large, sad eyes she noticed first, the heavy fringe of lashes. He was pretty enough to be a woman. She could see that she had him already, which was a shame, because she did like a challenge, but he'd do. At the time he was just another stub in her scrapbook, a pressed flower, a name on a dance card: "Scott Fitzgerald."

"And how do you do, Mr. Fitzgerald?" she asked. "Have you ever seen so fine and beautiful a dancer?"

He was taken aback but pleased. A slow smile spread across his face. Ooh, she could love that face.

"I don't think I ever want to see someone dance again after such a swell performance," he said. "Do you think she'd dance with me if I asked her?"

Do you hear how he played with me? I always loved when people played with me.

"I don't know," I said. "She is awfully fast. You'd best stay away from her."

And I pirouetted away, counting in my head to see how long it would take for him to follow.

One. Two. Three. Four. Five.

"Excuse me," he said, touching my arm

with his slender fingers like a sweet little breeze. "Tell her I'm not afraid, would you? And tell her I can keep up."

And then he walked away and I was shocked. How dared he walk away? I certainly couldn't go after him, but the challenge was placed. I was on unsure footing and it excited me. I did not want to lose the advantage, however, so I quickly made eyes at the nearest male and had a partner in no time at all.

One. Two. Three. Four. Five.

Scott interrupted the dance, much to the dismay of the soldier.

"May I?"

"You most certainly may not," said the soldier.

I turned and took Scott Fitzgerald without hesitation, leaving the soldier sad and wounded on the dance floor. I imagined him a seared pile of ash behind me, and it dawned on me that my imaginings were in poor taste, since he was soon shipping out to become a pile of ash. But that was no matter. I was the salamander.

"What is your name?" said Scott.

"Formally, Miss Sayre, but you may call me Zelda."

"Zelda," he whispered.

"You're a fiver," I said, slipping comfortably into the cradle of his arms.

"Pardon me?" said Scott.

"A fiver. One, two, three, four, five. That's how long you took to come after me."

"How does that compare to your sad beau you left over there?" He nodded in the direction of the sulking soldier. I smiled my sweetest sugar-baby smile and waved, enjoying the cruelty of the gesture.

"He's a two-er, so you don't have to worry a bit," I said.

I enjoyed the vibration of his laugh through my body, though it made me clench my teeth. My, how I felt him as if he and I were the same being. That scared me, because sometimes I could barely keep up with myself. My breath caught as he stroked my neck under my hair. He started singing along with the music in my ear as he led me all around the dance floor. I let him, intoxicated, vaguely aware of the stir we created. Sulking men, green women. His voice in my ear.

"They're all looking at us," he said. "That's good."

Good, good, I thought.

They kept looking at us.

I placed the pages on my lap, imagining the humid Southern night, the beautiful young woman and man. The foreshadowing of trouble. The onlookers. I wished she'd written more.

When I read back over the material I was struck by her change of tense from *her* to *I,* as if she'd become more fully herself once he arrived. But that didn't make sense, given that she now needed to be away from him to calm herself. I needed to ask Zelda about this.

Patience, I reminded myself. This was just the beginning of the story. I reread the anecdote, placed the papers on my bedside table, and turned out the light.

Patience.

"Patients!"

I was confused. Where was that voice coming from?

"Nurse Howard! Patients!"

The doors of the hospital train scraped open and we were suddenly engulfed in a wave of bleeding, crying, screaming men. Nurses rushed about clearing areas, making space where the sterile white would soon be red and brown and all shades of pain and suffering. I quickly snapped out of my daydreams and started on triage as voices rose and fell all around me.

"Name?" I asked the medic.

"Unknown."

"Injury?"

"Skull."

I paused and looked at the patient. His lower mandible was gone and his eyes were wide. He'd die before the hour was up. His eyes were blue. It wasn't Ben.

I'm ashamed to admit that was what I always checked first. We all did, though none of us would have admitted it out loud. It was clear by the gasps when names matched or hair color worried us, or something in the look of the eyes reminded us of our men. How badly we all wanted them to show up in the base hospital with a survivable sprinkling of bullets across the surface. Pin on a medal. Send him home. God, how we wanted that, but it was not to be.

Ben hadn't written to me in over three weeks. He'd never gone this long without some kind of contact. I knew he was in a terrible area, and I heard from medics and wounded soldiers that it was hell. I was somewhat reassured by the fact that none of the other girls with men in Ben's unit heard anything. They couldn't all be dead, was what we told ourselves. Also, I had peace because I knew that if Ben had died I'd feel some kind of wrenching in my gut, and that wrenching hadn't yet occurred.

My patient gave a gurgling, guttural cry, and I sent him to surgery with a look of reassurance I did not feel and a prayer, and wondered whether prayers were triaged.

Ridiculous, Peter would have said. *God has no limits.*

Then where the hell was —

"Next!"

The medics brought in what could only have been a boy, underage but in uniform, and in possession of tremendous dignity in spite of his years, with the lower half of his legs missing. He did not cry but he was a ghastly shade of green.

"Name," I said.

The patient answered for the medic. "Private John Bates Junior, ma'am."

"Injury."

"Loss of limbs," said the medic. Private Bates's face contorted into a sob. I felt my heart ache for him. He should have been home at some northeastern college, talking sports and wooing pretty debutantes. I reached out, squeezed his hand, and ran my fingers over his strong shoulder.

"We will heal you, Private John Bates Junior," I said. "Surgery."

I nodded at the nurses and they wheeled him away. I turned my attention to the door. The next soldier came through.

"DOA," I said. The medics seemed surprised as they looked down at their patient, blue as an icicle and already showing signs of rigor mortis. They wordlessly carried his stretcher to the morgue.

"Next. Name?"

"Gavin Murray."

I looked at him and saw his face hanging open like a flap where metal had slashed through it. He, too, was just a boy.

"Injury."

"Is my buddy okay?" he asked. "Is John

gonna be okay?"

I thought of the boy who'd just come in with missing limbs and the massive quantities of blood staining his sheet.

"We'll do our best," I said. "He looks like a fighter."

"He is," said Gavin. "We both are."

"You just worry about yourself and we'll take care of your friend," I said, squeezing his hand for reassurance, before he was wheeled away to be cleaned and stitched.

"Next. Name?"

"All we got was Ben."

I felt my head go dizzy and slowly turned to look at the patient. Red hair, green eyes. Not my Ben. I had never felt so disheartened and relieved at once.

"In . . . injury?"

"Shrapnel."

I gestured over to the bed nearest the door for surgery, where a nurse would be able to handle the picking and cleaning. I suddenly saw stars in the corners of my field of vision and thought I'd faint. I grabbed the stretcher and squeezed my eyes shut.

"Nurse, are you okay?" I felt a hand on my arm. I breathed in and out, and opened my eyes when the world steadied. I nodded and released the stretcher.

After the last of the men was admitted, I

walked out into the cold, away from the base hospital, crunching over the frozen grass with my arms wrapped around myself. I ended up at the edge of the forest, bare of leaves, vacant of animals, and held up by sopping cold earth. I searched the growth with my eyes, yearning for a small sign of life, something that belonged in a forest and remained untouched by war, something to buoy me up in this barren wasteland. But there was nothing.

SEVEN

I knocked before I had time to lose my nerve.

Thin, pale, their hair plaited and limbs entwined, the dancers answered the door together and looked at each other in surprise to see me there.

"Pardon me for coming so early, but I heard you were awake," I said.

I blushed as I realized it must sound like I was spying on them.

"It's okay," said the taller of the two. "May we help you?"

"I have a question about a dance."

They smiled. A pair of Cheshire cats.

"Come in."

Their rooms had the ethereal quality of a dream. The scents of talc, sweat, and camphor hung in the pale pink mesh curtains that adorned the windows and doorways. Dried flowers rested in glasses and old cans covered in fabric, the relics of gifts from past performances. The gramophone sat near a wall, at rest, out of the faint morning sunlight that nudged its way into the cool room.

"I'm Anna," I said as I settled on the sofa where they'd directed me — springs poking my back through the floral covering.

"Julia."

"Rose."

"Pleased to meet you," I began. "I have a . . . friend who recently wrote to me. She told me she danced the 'Dance of the Hours' for someone, and I couldn't imagine the scene, though it was one I wished heartily to imagine." My voice trailed off. It seemed silly asking them instead of Zelda, but I wanted to ask Zelda only questions of deep importance so she did not get sidetracked. In case this was an incidental detail, I wanted to know before I saw her.

The smaller of the two, Julia, stood and walked to the large box next to the gramophone.

"Ponchielli, *La Gioconda,*" called Rose from across the room.

Julia leveled a gaze at Rose as if to say, *I know.* She fingered through the records until she found what she was looking for. Her eyes lit and she pulled the object of her search. She slid the record from its worn paper covering and set it upon the machine. She wound the crank, released the break with her ballet-slippered foot, and placed the needle about a third of the way onto the record. The scratch of the needle preceded a loud, vigorous chorus and she lifted it. She moved it slightly closer to the center and placed it down again. A chorus faded, there was a moment of silence, and then a gentle, lilting, almost playful melody began.

Julia did some halfhearted steps along with it, as if she were posing for stills, but when the music became swinging and somber she began to dance more seriously. Rose joined her and they danced with all of the poise of an onstage performance. The harp and violins quieted the mood for a few minutes, but the finish was sweeping and dramatic — almost frenzied. Then came the sound of a bell.

"A funeral bell," said Rose. "Signifying the pretend death of a woman administered a sedative to take her away from her terrible husband to her lover."

"Assisted by a woman who also loved the lover but whose purity and goodness longed more for his happiness than her own."

"A beautiful tragedy," finished Rose.

I was touched by the music and the story. The progression from light to somber to frantic seemed to carry some greater connection to the Fitzgeralds' life that had been almost prophetic. What if they'd listened to the message of the song that first night at the country club? Would their story end well or with the frenzied dawn and the tolling of the bell?

Suddenly overcome by emotion and realizing I would be late, I excused myself to the confused and troubled faces of the ballerinas and hurried to catch the bus to the hospital.

Zelda sat with her back to me as I entered the room.

"Anna," she said.

"How did you know it was me?" I asked.

"Because you make almost no noise at all when you walk, and yet I could feel someone enter."

"My mother used to reprimand me for that," I said. "Said I used to scare her to death."

"You couldn't scare a mouse," she said. "Sometimes I pretend I made you up. My imaginary friend. A ghost."

I didn't know how that was supposed to make me feel. She said it kindly, but it was strange to be told I was a quiet enough personality to almost not exist. I wanted to defend myself.

"I took up more space before the war," I said.

She turned and faced me and patted the bed as an invitation to sit down.

My psychiatric nurses' training came back to me, cautioning me to keep boundaries with my patient, but it felt so good to talk to her. As so-called mental nurses, we were encouraged to share a little of ourselves to inspire trust, but not to ever give our problems to our patients. I was sure I wouldn't give her my past pain, since I couldn't even face it directly myself. I would just tell her the good parts that wanted remembering.

"Who was Anna before the war?" she asked.

"I was musical, adventurous, passionate." I leaned into her and widened my eyes. She whistled long and low.

"Tell me about your boys," she said. "Did you have dozens of suitors or one smooth, handsome man who stole all of your interests?"

"One dark, handsome soldier. He had very expressive brown eyes and a full mouth. He was tall."

"Is that how he kept your interest? Those eyes? That mouth?"

"Those hands, that kiss," I said.

She "oohed" and leaned back with a deep, throaty laugh.

"My God, I wish he'd come to Montgomery," she said. "The officers there were a dime a dozen. They stood in a neat line waiting for my attention. I kissed them all, and right in front of the others."

"Until that one," I said.

The smile left her face, and I regretted the reference to Scott. She became unreadable, but her eyes and mouth began working in response to a memory, an emotion she could not pin down. I saw a flash of anger, a softening, then exhaustion that made her eyes heavy and moist.

Since there was no going back, I pressed on. "I read your paper." I held it out to her and she snatched it away, reading over it as if she'd never seen it before. Her features softened again and she pressed it to her chest when she finished.

"If I could just put that night and a couple others on a record and play them over and over again," she said, "everything would be okay."

"You started well," I said. "The beautiful young debutante. The handsome soldier. You understood each other immediately."

"Immediately," she echoed. "It's almost as

if we share a mind or a soul, except there's not room for both of us. We're forever nudging each other out of the space allotted to us and it wears us out."

"And when did you show him your diaries?"

"He saw them early on, I think," she said. "Listen, I was a narcissistic girl. If he wanted to read my diary it was fine, because it was about me. And he seemed enthralled by my words. Imagine, a writer being enthralled with the words in my diaries."

"Did you give them to him?"

"Yes, no, I don't know." She was quiet for a moment. "I think I first showed him the diaries to make him jealous. If he saw all the dance cards and soldiers' photos, letters, and mementos, he'd see how desired I was, and it would make him want me more."

"Did you quarrel often?"

"Oh, yes," she said. "Big, messy, bawling quarrels in the parlor, with my father asking him to leave and my mother sighing on the stairs. We were always making a scene. Still are, I guess."

"Were there ever quiet moments?" I asked. "Sipping lemonade on a porch, taking a walk on a lane, sitting together in silence?"

"Yes," she said. "The night was a great friend of ours. In bed. Not in the way you think, but in the quiet dark where we could curl around each other in a drowsy embrace and let our words and thoughts and breath mingle. I'd put the night on that repeating record of mine."

She laid the papers in her lap for a moment as we allowed her words to sit in our thoughts. I wanted Scott to hear her say this. These were words that could restore a marriage: sweet balm and remembrance to help them reclaim what they had lost. I thought that he should come to Baltimore.

That is, until Dr. Squires showed me the letter he had sent to her.

EIGHT

March 1932

Mr. Fitzgerald had a tantrum that started in Alabama on paper, continued as he crashed through the doors of the Phipps Psychiatric Clinic, and exploded as he thundered, gin-soaked, into Dr. Meyer's office.

"This is my material, *my material,*" he insisted, as he smoked and paced around the office. "How could she go behind my back with *your* doctor and submit to *my* editor before I had a chance to read it? I've been working on my novel for years, stopping over and over to shit out these short stories to pay the bills and keep her in comfort, and not only does she steal my material, but you help her to do it!"

He shoved a chair, rocking it dangerously until it settled back on its four legs.

"Mr. Fitzgerald," said Dr. Meyer, "I would be glad to have a discourse with you on the subject, but if you continue to act out in a violent manner, I will have you escorted from my hospital."

Fitzgerald's breathing began to slow. His gaze shifted from the chair to me and then to Dr. Squires at the door. I could barely make eye contact with him, because I was afraid I'd betray my loathing of him at that moment.

And my guilt.

Zelda and I had talked long past my shift one night. She told me that Scott wouldn't approve of her novel, but that she was desperate to send her voice into the world. She told me that she wanted Scott's editor, Max Perkins, to see it without Scott's edits, to tell her what he thought. I knew that Dr. Squires said *Save Me the Waltz* needed editing, but the meat of the story and Zelda's knack for sensory detail and figurative language were unlike anything she'd seen.

I had encouraged Zelda to go through Scott first, but she insisted that I send it directly to the editor. She said if Scott touched it, it would be stained, and she would never know whether her writing was worthwhile on its own. She told me that Perkins wouldn't mind, and if Scott found out he would be only a little mad. I caved in to her pleadings, which was a horrible mistake. I should have anticipated Scott's response, but I didn't know him well then, and thought it would be a harmless way to gain Zelda some validation outside of her husband.

I had helped Zelda package the novel with a short note to the editor and told Dr. Squires I'd post it for Zelda. I did not mention that I was sending it to Perkins and not Scott, but Dr. Squires did not ask, so I told myself it would be all right.

But it wasn't.

To think of the terrible things Scott wrote to Dr. Squires and to Zelda about his outrage at them for not sending him Zelda's novel first. To think that he demanded his wife ask permission from him before submitting her work to the editor.

I stood in the doorway of Meyer's office, feeling layers of unsettling emotions and shaking in my white shoes, wishing I could sneak away, but fascinated to watch Mr. Fitzgerald in enough of a state of disarray to qualify him for admittance to the clinic.

"Look," Scott said, turning back to Dr. Meyer, "I am not an unreasonable man. You know how devoted I am to her — you *know* it. You have to understand the betrayal I feel. To have my greatest novel yet begging for my attention while I'm forced to slave over these little vignettes for the *Post* or *Collier's* or whoever will take the goddamned things for Zelda's care. To try to keep my daughter three states away in some sort of stable environment while her mother is here sinking deeper and deeper into madness. Then to have Zelda take my novel and turn it into hers. Can't you understand why I'm frantic? Am I so unreasonable?"

His eyes darted from Dr. Meyer to Dr. Squires and then to me. When he met my gaze, I recognized his anguish. The stress he was under was enormous, and he did an enviable job of keeping his wife in comfort. Yet he referred to the events that inspired her novel as *his* material. It was her life — her story. The material he thought he owned was Zelda's life. But perhaps I'd made a mistake in interfering.

Dr. Squires spoke. "Mr. Fitzgerald, I must apologize for angering you so. I do understand your frustration, and I regret that we didn't speak about this before the manuscript was sent to her editor. I had assumed the manuscript was being sent to you. But even if I had known its true destination I can't help but think I would have argued on Zelda's behalf. She's worked on her novel tirelessly for the past month and a half, and it is her life story. Surely she has the right to

106

tell her own story."

I felt a wave of gratitude for Dr. Squires. She could have easily placed the blame on me. It was my interference that had escalated their troubles. I looked at the floor in shame.

"But she knows that I pay the bills," he said, "so it is my right to use our lives and our stories. She knows that my novel centers on her breakdown. By writing it she stole the freshness from my work. I don't know if Scribner's will even take my novel now."

"With all due respect to your wife," said Dr. Meyer, "you are the great novelist. She is just looking for a mode of expression."

Dr. Squires and I both turned to look at Dr. Meyer. I thought she must be thinking what I was thinking: How dared these two men belittle Zelda's rather magnificent achievement of creating an entire novel in six weeks by making it sound like a hobby or amusement? Dr. Squires looked at me and widened her eyes, confirming that she and I were of one mind.

Fitzgerald seemed appeased by Meyer's words, as I was quite sure Meyer intended, and he sat in the chair he'd recently tried to overturn. Two red blotches formed on Dr. Squires's cheeks. She was quivering, but unable to challenge the men. Her frustration seemed to fuel some sort of courage within me, and a desire to fix what I had broken.

"Might I suggest a collaboration?" I said.

They all turned their eyes toward me. I hesitated a moment, but again found my voice. "Mr. Fitzgerald, why not work with your editor to promote Zelda's novel?"

"Don't you understand why I don't think it should be published?" said Scott.

"I do, but I have a different view," I said. "It's possible that readers will want to hear both sides of the story."

"Nurse Howard," said Dr. Meyer, "we aren't here to debate Mrs. Fitzgerald's literary career, but rather the best treatment for her that will enable her to live in the real world without incident."

"With all due respect, Dr. Meyer," I continued, "I feel that recognition of her creative impulses might satisfy a craving that will enable her to function more normally."

I looked at Scott, and his eyes bored into me with an intensity that made it hard to concentrate. It would have been easier to speak if he looked indignant instead of gazing at me with what seemed like adoration.

"She might be right," he said quietly.

Now I really didn't know what to say. Dr. Squires rescued me from my sudden muteness.

"Yes, I agree with Nurse Howard. Have you ever finished one book on a subject and suddenly longed to read more about it?"

"All the time," said Mr. Fitzgerald.

"So why not give readers more? Start with Zelda's novel; then release yours. They will still be very different novels, so even if the subject or themes overlap, you each have a unique way of presenting them."

He nodded his head in the affirmative.

I looked at Dr. Meyer and saw that he was more stoic than ever and refused to meet my gaze.

"Can I see her?" asked Mr. Fitzgerald.

"I'm afraid that would not be advisable today," said Dr. Meyer. "If you'll pardon my interference, you appear somewhat inebriated. I cannot allow you to visit Zelda unless you're sober."

Anger flared across Fitzgerald's face.

"Let's get this straight, Meyer," he said. "I'm paying you the king's share to make my *wife* better. You leave me out of it."

"And you need to understand that your health — mental and otherwise — is tied to that of your wife. I would suggest that you stop drinking altogether if her recovery is truly what you wish for."

"A man is entitled to a drink if he chooses. My drinking has nothing to do with her condition."

"Perhaps it does not," said Meyer, "but her condition requires stability and peace. In your current state you will not be able to provide that. If you wish to see her, you will not drink before you visit."

Fitzgerald stood and started out of the room. Before he left, he met my gaze and gave me a slight nod. He passed me like a storm, leaving an alcoholic wind in his wake. I couldn't imagine that he'd ever see his wife again.

Before I left that evening, I went to Zelda's room to wish her a good night. She sat with the curtains drawn, with the smoke from her cigarette encircling her head. Only the light in her bathroom was on, and it cast an eerie glow in the room.

I did not tell her that Scott had been there earlier that day. I didn't want to upset her more than his letter had already done. I did feel as if I owed her an apology for assisting in her submission to Scott's editor without fully thinking through the consequences.

"Zelda, I'm sorry how all of this turned out. If I'd had any idea how he'd react, I would never have allowed it. I hate that I've added in any way to your marital discord or stress."

She gave no indication that she heard, only inhaled and exhaled the smoke from her cigarette.

"Dr. Squires is hopeful that Scott might consider relenting on his opposition to your novel," I said.

She stubbed out her cigarette in the ashtray on the bedside table. Her hands began to crawl and twist over each other.

"I don't want to excite you," I continued, "but you should know that the idea has been introduced that publication of your novel might feed readership of his."

She turned her attention to the curtained window and then looked from the floor to the dresser and to the bed, as if she'd lost something. She looked terribly confused.

Her vagueness saddened me. It was painful to watch her slide suddenly from coherence to near catatonia. It was like losing an old friend each day and never knowing when she'd return. I thought of Scott and felt shame for judging him. If I, her nurse, felt this way, how much more painful must it feel to be her husband or her daughter?

"Well, good evening," I said. "I'll see you in the morning."

I started to leave when I heard the padding of her feet on the floor. I turned and saw her pull a pile of papers out from under her pillow. She rushed over to me and thrust them into my hands before scurrying to sit on the bed. I looked down and read the title: "Manhattan Baptism."

My heartbeat quickened.

"I was hoping you'd written more today," I said. "May I take this home?"

She nodded, allowing her nod to turn into a rocking motion that overtook her body. I looked down at the papers and then back to her as she rocked herself, soothing some old hurt that needed comfort.

As much as I longed to read the papers on the bus, Zelda's confessions deserved my total concentration in the quiet of my apartment. I looked out the window, willing my attention away from the girlish handwriting, and noted with pleasure that the light hung in the evening just a bit longer than usual. Daffodils and hyacinths bloomed in tiny town house gardens, and buds swelled on trees that had looked like mere sticks just yesterday.

There was a new energy on the streets around my building. Art students painted in the park across the way. Musicians played on street corners. Small gangs of children ran along the avenues and alleys wearing unzipped coats. Cars slowed or stopped at corners so friends could wave and punch the bag about nothing at all. The city was reawakening after the long, cold winter.

When I arrived at my building, I hurried up the front steps and ran straight into Sorin, nearly knocking his violin case to the ground. I was embarrassed at being caught bounding up the stairs like a girl with spring fever, and apologized profusely. He smiled and I noticed how very young he was. He had to be at least ten years my junior. I must have been so shaken the night of the attack that I hadn't realized.

"It is all right," he said. "I am glad to see you are feeling much better."

"I am, thank you."

"And thank you for the bread and everything," he said. "I am sorry I did not answer the door when you knocked. I was mid-composition and I was afraid to stop and interrupt the flow, you understand?"

"I understand," I said.

"Maybe I could play it for you sometime."

"Yes, that would be nice."

He nodded and continued around me. I watched him walk down the street. As he turned the corner, he looked back and grinned. I smiled in return and walked into the building feeling light and pleased.

MANHATTAN BAPTISM

The nuptials were an early blur of sweet sunlight, midnight blue suits, and Easter lilies we left in a pot, wilted, while we ordered spinach-and-tomato sandwiches the hour before midnight before our revolving-door, taxi-riding, jazz-club revelries began.

He'd taken my diaries by then, so I couldn't record it all, though I wish I had.

I would have told of how they all desired me. You should have seen me walk across a lobby. I'd see women grabbing the faces of their men, turning them away from me, and I'd laugh to myself, with good reason, enjoying the halo of the cigarette smoke about my finger curls, my painted lips, the stockings with the line from heel to thigh, my squirrel coat — my God, that coat.

Scott watched me always.

He'd watch me while I bathed, asking me questions through the steam about the boys I'd kissed, my favorite boys, whether I plotted to make them love me or if they all just loved me. He'd watch me in the mirror while I fastened my garters and brushed my hair and picked through the piles of clothes on the floor for a clean slip, asking me why I didn't keep up with the laundry, why I didn't pick up the clothes, whether I ever intended to keep the rooms. His breath would be on my neck — a foul, alcoholic mist that encircled us both — while he'd beg me to behave, to make love only to him, to stay away from theater critics and lawyers and former college mates. We'd slide into the cab and he'd ask me what I thought of the night, and the driver, and the popular songs, and the Biltmore. He'd bring my drinks — one after another — and then scribble on slips of napkins while I hopped on tables, and danced with men, and smoked and smoked.

And when I'd drag him home to wring him out, he'd beg me to tell him that he satisfied me above all men, only I wouldn't. I was vague in my cruelty: "Yes, yes, Goofo, you're fine, just come up a little short," I'd say. Then he'd cry and I'd say, "No, you misunderstand; you are my incomparable love," and he'd kiss me feverishly, wishing to prove to me that he was the best man, but the knocking would begin, and a pile of men would be at the door with booze and noise.

He would sulk, but the lure of the drinks was too strong for him to ignore, so he'd have just one more until he couldn't speak and I got so fed up with it all and frantic from the energy bouncing from the men into me that I'd have to leave. They'd follow me in confusion, misunderstanding me. I wished to flee, but they thought I wished them to follow and to watch.

And with their eyes watching me I charged into the fountain in my white clothes, looking for a baptism in the penny-stained water, opening my hands to God for release and to the water for purity, when the only thing that answered me was the siren on Fifth Avenue stealing the holy order of it all.

NINE

May 1932
Play for me, Anna.

Even though Ben's face blurred in my mind, his voice seemed ever at my ear these days. Calm. Low. The remembrance of its vibration made the hair on my skin rise.

I sat on the bench and spread out the music.

Mendelssohn's *Songs Without Words*.

The first chord cut the air in the room and made me jump. I felt sweat form on my forehead and the back of my neck, and stopped.

I heard the bells of the cathedral announce the hour as I looked up at our wedding picture. My dress, which had been my mother's, drew my gaze. The dress was soft and elegant like a spring breeze, with none of the Victorian, high-necked fussiness that had been popular at the time. The white silk embroidered with tiny white leaves and

117

flowers and the vertical ruffles that sat gently against the sheer neckpiece invited the groom to lean in a little closer.

My mother had had the dress boxed up and put back in her closet after the wedding for her future granddaughters. I imagined it still gathered dust, since her only grand-daughter would never be able to wear it. But here in the photo it was in its prime and perfection, immortalized in black and white. Here we both were. I remembered how he smelled fresh and starched in his uniform. I remember his body heat reaching through his jacket to my skin in a prelude of what was to come that night, when he slid the dress off me one button at a time until I couldn't stand it.

Heat rose on my neck and I started the piece over.

The opening of the introduction was like the music of a slow, mournful carousel. Then the melody arrived, a moody ballerina jewel box at once wistful, passionate, and melancholy, especially on a piano in need of tuning. I continued through to the end and was surprised how much playing the piece had lightened my mood. I'd anticipated a rise of sorrow in resurrecting the song he had loved so much, but instead I felt peace. Calm. Wholeness.

With renewed vigor I started to play again when I heard a knock at the door. Whoever it was had to have heard me playing, but who would visit me? My heart started pounding. Then the knock resumed, but this time it turned into a beat.

Boom, boom, boom, ba, doom, boom, boom, boom.

It sounded like a jazz drum solo.

I jumped up from the seat, ran across the room, and swung open the door with a grin on my face.

"Peter!"

When my brother told us he had decided to become a priest, we all had a good laugh, but for once he was the one who had remained serious. Once the giggles evaporated and the silence became nearly unbearable, my mother spoke.

"Good for you, Peter," she had said. "We are proud of you."

"We are," echoed my dad.

Peter's emotion had been evident but contained in his shiny eyes. I remember thinking how kind and generous my parents were. I knew that, in spite of their great pride, it must have been a blow that their only son would never have children. I thought of all the hearts that would break upon hearing the news, and I had felt guilty. Somehow, I knew that my losses had something to do with his decision.

And here Peter stood, handsome as ever, but with a lingering sadness in his eyes that gave him a mysterious look. I lunged at him for a hug.

"What are you doing here?"

"Nice to see you, too," he said. "My train just arrived and I'm not due for duty until next week. I thought I'd escort you to Mom and Dad's after work tomorrow. After all, you look like an old lady with that streak of gray I see forming in your hair. Are you sure you're only thirty-five?"

I slapped his hand away.

"At least my butt hasn't disappeared completely," I said. "What do you weigh now, eighty, ninety pounds?"

"Hardly," he said. "Ninety-five."

We sat up talking late into the night, brewing pot after pot of tea, and catching up on each other's lives. He confessed that his Lenten fasting had gotten a bit out of hand and he was trying to regain the weight he'd lost. He was overjoyed at his placement in Baltimore and looked forward to human interaction, since he'd just completed a year of intense study at the Vatican.

"But enough about me," he said, stubbing

out his third cigarette. "Tell me how you're getting along."

I looked at him for a moment, our eyes locked in silent remembrance of the time I'd been through hell and back all those years ago with him at my side.

"I'm . . . well," I said, meaning it. "I have a new patient who has touched me and given me renewed purpose."

He smiled at me, chasing away the sad lines around his eyes. "That's swell," he said. "Tell me about your patient."

"Pretend we're in the confessional, Father," I said.

"It's between you, me, and God."

"Good. Zelda Fitzgerald is my patient."

"The flapper?"

"Yes!"

"What's her diagnosis?"

"Schizophrenia."

"How has she touched you so?"

"Because her eyes look like mine when I lost Ben and then Katie."

"Empty."

"Yes, empty."

He lit another cigarette. "Do you think she's just dissatisfied? Depressed over her wild youth fading into the humdrum of adulthood?"

"No, it's much more than that. She is

121

mentally ill."

"Beyond help?"

"Maybe," I said. "But I think I may have a way to help her restore some of her sanity, or at least give her some sense of peace."

"What can you do?"

"Help her find the diaries her husband stole from her and used in his work."

Peter became quiet, and worry creased his forehead. "Did she instruct you to do this?"

"We worked it out together."

He seemed to want to speak but was trying to hold back.

"What?" I asked. "You look upset."

"Just be careful," he said.

I suddenly felt defensive. Since my dark time, I had sensed an unseen shifting in our roles, in which Peter acted as if he were older and wiser than me. It annoyed me that on our first night reunited he had to insert advice.

"I'm going to look for a diary," I said, "not disarm a bomb."

"But you're taking a side in a marriage, and that's a dangerous business."

"She needs an ally."

"She's mentally ill. Do you know his side?"

"Not entirely, but it's pretty clearly a violation the way he used her diaries."

"Is it?" he said. "Maybe she gave him her diaries. Maybe she enjoyed being his subject."

"I'm sure she did for a time, but it went on too long."

"And now you think that finding her diaries and giving them to her will accomplish what?"

"It will give her control of herself again," I said.

"I thought you said she was mentally ill."

"She is."

"Then pardon me for saying it, but you're taking a simplistic view of a much bigger problem, and one that might cause trouble for you."

"Let's just drop this," I said. "Pardon *me* for saying it, but you are a *man;* you've never been married and you can't understand."

"You're right about that," he said. "But I'm approaching this from a clerical perspective in defense of the sacrament of marriage, which is bigger than both of the parties involved and should be treated as sacred."

"But what if they are destroying each other?"

"Then that's between them and God, but it's not between them, God, and Anna."

I stood in a huff and walked into the kitchen so I wouldn't strangle Peter. I picked up a towel and wrung it out the way I'd like to do with his neck. He followed after me shortly, wearing a sheepish grin and holding his hands in the air in surrender.

"I'm sorry," he said. "I've been debating theology for three years. I'll just nod and say *okay* next time."

"Good."

"And I'm proud of you for your renewed vitality."

"Thank you."

"And clearly something has awakened inside of you, because I see you've got the wedding picture on display, and when I approached your door you were playing the piano."

I placed the towel back on the stove handle and folded my arms in front of my chest. I tried to maintain my stern expression, but he looked so disheveled and contrite that I couldn't help but smile.

"Let's go to bed," I said. "We can argue on the way to Mom and Dad's tomorrow."

I left Peter to go to work the next morning, eager to get back to Zelda and discuss her Manhattan narrative. When I arrived, I was surprised to hear that Mr. Fitzgerald was in her room, visiting with her.

"He showed up very early and very sober," said Dr. Squires. "I suppose he has to come first thing in the morning to make that possible."

"How did she react when he appeared?"

"It's hard to say. I can say with certainty that she was elated, aggravated, serene, and angry about it, and that was just as he walked in."

I smiled at her and checked the clock. I supposed I could see to my other patients before Zelda. I felt a guilty stab at my emotional neglect of the other women in my care. One was an elderly woman prone to alternating bouts of hysteria and catatonia, much like Zelda but without any lucid moments to bridge the swings. Another was a young woman who had suffered a breakdown after the birth of her third child. Her husband was devoted and efficient and kept asking when she'd be "right" to come home. He didn't yet know that in her most recent therapy session she'd confessed to wanting to kill her baby or herself. My final patient slept all day and wandered the halls at night. She scared Zelda, who forever thought she was being haunted.

Zelda's room was the first I passed, and

her door was ajar. As I glanced in, Mr. Fitzgerald saw me and called me into the room. I hesitated, unsure whether Zelda would appreciate the intrusion, but I was pleased to see that her face was open and peaceful. A large and lush bouquet of white calla lilies and bloodred roses sat fragrant and bright on the windowsill. It was an extravagant gesture, and I was sure Zelda loved it.

"Nurse," he said.

"Anna," said Zelda, not unkindly.

"Anna," he echoed. "Please come in. We have an idea we'd like to run by you."

I felt wary and ill at ease, and thought that if a schizophrenic and an alcoholic had an idea, there was a definite chance it would not be a good one.

"I found a house," he said. "Nearby. Do you think Meyer would approve of partial residence there for Zelda?"

I knew it was silly and even wrong, but I felt a strange tug at my heart at the thought of her not being here. From a practical standpoint, however, I did not see how Dr. Meyer would support Zelda's release at this time. Her behavior was still erratic in spite of overall improvement. I decided to be honest.

"While I can't speak for Dr. Meyer, I think

we'd need a bit more consistency of behavior before the approval of outings."

It hung in the air that Zelda was not bound to the clinic. She was a voluntary patient, and could, therefore, check out at any time.

"How do you feel about that, Zelda?" I asked. "Would you like to leave the hospital for part of the day if Dr. Meyer supported the request?"

She thought in earnest, looking from me to her husband.

"Only if you come with me," she said.

Mr. Fitzgerald stared at her like . . . well, like she was mad.

"Why didn't you say that before?" he asked.

"I just thought of it," she said. "I forget how much I like Anna when she's gone. But now she's here in her dark, slender, tragic beauty, and I want to place her in my pocket and carry her everywhere with me."

I couldn't help but laugh at the absurdity of her description. Then the Fitzgeralds looked at each other and joined me in my laughter.

I worked my fingers through Zelda's hair, creating a rich, fragrant lather with the French shampoo Scott had bought for her.

The aroma was like a lavender field, and I inhaled deeply. Zelda fingered a rose she'd plucked from the bouquet, twisting it in her fingers.

"The Manhattan piece you wrote was magnificent," I said.

"You are very kind, Anna," she said. "All of us were so young and alive, fragrant and intoxicating like thousands of red poppies. I should say intoxicated. Intoxicated."

"You said Scott had taken your diaries by then. What did he do with them?"

"He kept them in his writing desk in whatever hotel we'd set up lodgings. One in particular he'd pull out late at night at parties and read passages from it. He'd say, 'Isn't she a genius? A beauty and a genius.' "

"Then he was proud of your work," I said.

"Oh, yes. Too proud. He wanted to claim it. When Scott loves someone or something, he wants it to *be* him or part of him. If he could have eaten me, I think he would have."

"You would have tasted like lemonade and tomato sandwiches," I said.

We laughed at this. I loved the deep, raspy sound.

"And squirrel," she said.

We laughed again, and I rinsed the shampoo from her hair with the warm, sudsy water. She handed me a cloth, and I started on her neck and shoulders.

"I remember that he loaned my diary to a friend of his to read," she said. "I was so angry at him. I told him that I might as well sleep with the man if he was going to pass me around like that."

"How did he respond?"

"Weeping: vast drunken weeping, like the spray off a champagne fountain."

"Did you see the diary after that?"

"Yes, miraculously the friend returned it. Scott was so sanctimonious. 'See,' he said. 'See, I told you he'd return it.' 'Yes, but the rape is finished, so it does not matter now,' I said."

Her flatness of voice chilled me. I dipped my arms in the warm water to smooth the goose bumps.

"Where were you living at the time?" I asked. "Could he have left the diaries there?"

She thought for a moment, then shook her head. "No. We were at the Biltmore, then the Commodore. No, he had the diaries when we moved to Westport."

"Connecticut?"

"Yes. We moved there the summer after we married. He needed quiet from the city so he could work."

"And did you achieve that quiet?"

"Ha!" she said. "All the New York bastards just followed us there."

"Will you write it for me? A piece about Westport?"

She did not answer, but started humming some nameless tune, and continued to play with the red rose in her hands. I didn't want to push her, so I simply washed her arms and hands, then her legs and feet. The steam and my awkward angle as I leaned over the bath were beginning to get to me, so I hurried to finish. When I looked up she was staring at me.

"What is your hair color?" said Zelda, reaching out and running her hand through it. Her hands were wet from the bath, so they stuck a little, pulling at the strands, stinging my scalp as a few strands snapped away on her fingers.

"It's changed as I've aged," I said.

"Yes, but it's no color, like your eyes. Not black, not brown, just dark."

Yes, just dark. Like a shadow. Perhaps my lack of color was why Zelda could open up to me. She felt no threat.

I watched her break the thorns off the stem of the rose and drop them into the water. When she reached up and slid the rose behind my ear I could see that her fingers bled a little.

"There," she said.

I looked at her for a moment before I turned to face the mirror.

There, indeed.

TEN

When I opened the door the next morning, I thought it would be Lincoln letting me know he'd arrived early to take us to my parents' house. I couldn't have been more surprised to find Sorin standing there, his hair wild from the rake of hands through it, dark circles under his eyes. It looked like he'd been on an all-night bender.

"Are you well?" I asked, opening the door to him and motioning him inside.

"Yes," he said. "Very well, thank you."

On closer inspection I could see a gleam in his eyes and a certain excitement quivering from him, making the papers in his hands shake. He reminded me of Zelda's feverish state when she completed a piece of art.

"For you," he said, thrusting a pile of music into my hands.

I looked down and flipped through the handwritten papers. It was an instrumental piece for piano. My eyes flicked back to the top.

"Anii."

"Anii?" I said, confusion in my voice.

"Uh, your word *succor, help,*" he said. "Helper. And it is a play on your name."

His face burned red, and it suddenly became clear that he had written the piece for me. It wasn't long before my face matched his in color.

"I . . . I'm honored," I said.

"You have been playing," he said.

"Yes."

"Late at night," he said.

"Does it disturb you?"

"No. No. It is good."

"Well, I look forward to learning this," I said. "I hope I can do it justice."

"You will."

Peter came around the corner in a T-shirt, fastening his belt. Sorin's eyes grew wide, then dark. He muttered something and turned quickly away, starting down the stairs before I could grab his arm.

"No, wait," I said.

My God, he must think . . .

"Sorin!" I called.

"It is okay, Anna," he said. "I have to go."

He hurried down the stairs and out the front door.

133

I turned to Peter and smacked his arm. "What?"

"He thinks that you're . . . that we . . ."

"Oh, no! Ew! I'm sorry!"

"You should be," I said. "Do you know how shy he is? He probably worried all night before working up the courage to come to the door."

"I'm sorry," he said, raising his hands in surrender. His eyes flicked to the papers. "What's that?"

I felt embarrassed and protective of Sorin's gift, and clutched the pages to my chest.

"Just some music," I said.

Peter broke into a grin.

"An-na," he sang. "Do we have a potential love match here?"

"Ugh, please," I said, turning toward the piano so he couldn't see my face. "It's nothing."

I shoved the papers into the music book on the stand and walked toward my bedroom to get my overnight bag and to avoid my brother.

"He's kinda young," yelled Peter with mischief in his voice.

"I didn't notice," I called.

I heard Peter laugh from the other room and again wanted to punch him. He knew exactly how to get under my skin. I was worried what Sorin thought, so I quickly scribbled a note to him that I intended to slip under his door before we left: *Dear Sorin, I can't thank you enough for the music. I'm sorry you couldn't stay and meet <u>my brother.</u> Maybe we can all have dinner together sometime. Sincerely, Anna.*

I thought it was a bit excessive to underline *my brother,* but I wanted to be sure that Sorin understood.

"He's good-looking in a moody musician kind of way," said Peter as I returned to the living room.

"Peter, stop. I am married, after all."

He stared hard at me until I had to look away.

Lincoln narrowed his eyes, wearing as much suspicion of Peter as Sorin had.

"Lincoln, meet Peter, *my brother,*" I said.

"Brother, ay?" said Lincoln.

"Yes, sir," said Peter. "It's a pleasure to meet you. Anna's told me all about you."

"Good thing you're not a suitor, or we'da had to settle this like men." He slapped Peter on the shoulder and loaded our bags, laughing to himself.

I slipped into the cab and closed my eyes, massaging my temples. I felt a headache playing at the edges of my skull and hoped a nap on the way to my parents' house would take care of it. I opened my eyes as we drove away from the apartment building and caught Peter watching me.

"You okay?" he asked.

I nodded and closed my eyes. I felt his hand cover mine.

"So, Lincoln," said Peter, "how are the Sox gonna do this season?"

I opened one eye and smiled at Peter. He gave me a wink. I slipped in and out of sleep on the drive to the steady hum of Lincoln's voice.

We agreed that Peter would surprise our parents. He waited on the path five minutes after I approached. I was able to corral Mom and Dad on the front porch by then, when Peter came jogging around the bend, like an Olympic runner at the tape.

Mom actually screamed and managed a small jump in the air. Dad hurried off the porch to meet him. They wrapped each other in a huge hug. Then Peter let go of Dad and ran to give Mom a hug. He lifted her off the ground and spun her around. I flinched, but even when he put her back on the porch she beamed. Dad grabbed my hand and we all went into the house in a whirlwind of greetings, questions, and admonitions about our weight.

It was the first time I'd returned home in years without the burden of history.

"I'm sinking into a coma," said Peter.

"A food coma," said Dad.

We sat on the back porch listening to the sounds of the wind chimes and watching the quarter moon glow stronger as the night darkened the woods behind the house. Our stomachs were full from my dad's crab cakes and corn on the cob, and we punted lazy, half-finished conversations to one another, content in one another's company, finishing one another's thoughts in our heads.

"It's heaven to have you both here with us," said Mom. "This is a good, good night."

"I wish I could bring Zelda here some-time," I said.

I felt embarrassed for voicing that aloud.

"You've grown attached to her," said Mom. There was no judgment in her voice, so it calmed me. "Have you had to stay many nights with her, like that first week?"

"On and off," I said. "She has extreme highs and lows. I stay with her during the lows."

"I always said you should have just set up a room wherever you worked to be on call at all times."

"Separation does Anna good," said Peter. "Then she can't forget to take care of herself."

-"I am sitting right here," I said, nudging Peter on the arm.

The wind picked up, increasing the symphony of the wind chimes.

"I think Zelda needs to spend more time outdoors," I said. "She seems to thrive on exercise. And she'd enjoy the chimes."

"Bring her by on a day trip if you can get permission," said Dad. "I'd love to meet her."

"Me, too," said Mom. "Could she bring her husband? I'd love to meet him."

"That probably wouldn't work so well," I said. "He's a bit of a stressor for her."

"How sad," said Mom.

"It is sad," I said.

"All I can think of is a flapper with a cigarette and a feathered headdress doing the Charleston up the drive," said Mom.

We sat with this idea for a moment, each of us imagining the Fitzgeralds sauntering through our woods. It seemed out of place even in a fantasy. Then Dad laughed and changed tack.

"All I can think of is Peter running around that turn like he used to when he was a boy home from school or camp or seminary."

"I like to make an entrance," he said.

"It's a shame you can't greet the congregation at mass like that on Sunday mornings," I said.

A ripple of laughter went through us.

"How did someone with your personality size fit into the monastery in Italy?" asked Mom.

He gave a nervous laugh. "Not well at first, I must confess, but I was at my most penitent, since it started during Lent, so they didn't get my full wattage."

"You saved that for me," I said.

"And your neighbor," he replied.

"What neighbor?" asked Mom.

I shot Peter a look and he let the question die.

"I actually almost stayed at the monastery," he said.

"I don't believe you," said Mom.

"I did," said Peter. "The friar I spoke of, Padre Pio — he had a profound effect on me. He's being held prisoner of sorts at the Rotonda by the Church because they want to prove him a fraud."

"Why?" I asked.

Peter hesitated. "He has the stigmata."

Dad whistled low through his teeth.

"Did you see it?" asked my mother.

"He wears gloves, but I did see the blood seeping through on several occasions," said Peter.

"And you believe it's real?" I asked, unable to hide the skepticism in my voice.

"Yes, Anna," he said.

"You don't believe the wounds are self-inflicted?"

"No," he said. "It's not something I can explain. There's more to it than that. Anyway, he suffers greatly."

"How else?"

"I don't want to go into it and have you rolling your eyes at me," said Peter. "Not everything can be explained by science."

"I won't roll my eyes," I said. "I promise."

"He's been in two places at once. He has an aura of flowers about him that seems most potent when the wounds actively bleed. He is tormented by demons at night."

"What?" said my mother.

I felt the goose bumps rise on my arms.

"You know, I don't really want to go on," said Peter. "Just know that he taught me two things. The first is that confession is the clearest way to unburden ourselves and grow in our spiritual and overall health."

"And the second?" I asked.

"We can take on the suffering of others,

not only for their redemption, but also for our own."

ELEVEN

June 1932

The way Dr. Meyer looked at Dr. Squires, Scott, and me made me feel like a naughty schoolgirl in the principal's office. Our conspiracy, as he referred to it, angered and shocked him.

"It's only for half days," said Dr. Squires. "She'll return after lunch and spend nights with us."

"And she'll get to be with her daughter. And Anna will be with her at the house and at the clinic," said Scott. "Zelda will always have Anna to lean on."

My turmoil over the plan left me unable to say a word. Part of me felt strongly that this change would benefit Zelda. The other part believed it would destroy the fragile web of stability she'd woven around herself. It was cowardly of me, but I allowed the others to make the case while I stood stoic, awaiting my fate. I had to pray that I'd end up in the place meant for me.

"We'll have Nurse Howard keep Zelda to a strict schedule, just as she does at Phipps," said Dr. Squires.

"You yourself said Zelda has had barely any outbursts in weeks," said Scott.

"What will happen to Nurse Howard's other patients?" asked Dr. Meyer.

"With recent discharges I will be able to rearrange the schedule while she's with Zelda evenly among the other nurses," said Dr. Squires. "She'll be able to do her rounds during the other half of the day. Besides, Nurse Howard and I discussed that her connection to Mrs. Fitzgerald has much more potential than the clinical relationships Anna has with her other patients."

"And if it doesn't work out," said Scott, "we can always go back to the way it is."

I glanced at Fitzgerald and he looked at me with a half smile. I noticed that his hands had a slight tremor and he looked pale, but he was sober. His sobriety probably had something to do with his trembling. Nonetheless, I was proud of him for coming to the hospital this way. It allowed me to feel some hope for the couple.

Meyer looked at me.

"What do you think, Nurse Howard?" said Dr. Meyer. He would not let me go without expressing my opinion. "You are closest to her."

All eyes turned to me. The room felt close, and that annoying clock underlined every moment I did not speak.

Well?

Well?

Well?

I wanted Zelda to have a chance at a normal life. Her husband wanted it. Her daughter deserved it. But this little feeling, a fluttering low in my stomach, warned me that Zelda probably would not get better and the experiment would fail. And yet Peter always told me of faith and miracles. Ask and I shall receive. My answer would be the start of my prayer for Zelda and her family.

"She deserves a chance at freedom," I said. "She hungers for it. Sterility does not . . . become her."

I saw an emotion flicker over Meyer's eyes that I could not read. Defeat? Yearning? Sadness? No, I could not discern it.

"Very well," he said. "Let her try. Bring her in."

Scott beamed and Dr. Squires smiled. I excused myself to fetch Zelda and relate the good news. When I arrived at her room she was hunched in a ball in the corner, biting

144

her lip, covering her ears with balled-up fists. My heart sank. I raced to her side and placed my hand on her back.

"Zelda," I said, though she would not look at me. "Zelda."

I sat next to her on the floor and put my face in my hands, knowing how crushed Scott would be that I could not recommend that she be discharged like this. It pained me to think of how upset her daughter would be to find out that her mother would not be coming home for visits after all.

I suddenly felt Zelda's hands pull my own away from my eyes. Her lip bled a bit where she'd bitten it, but otherwise her countenance had completely changed. Her relaxed face did not reassure me.

"Can I go?" she asked.

I didn't know what to say. How could I allow her to go after what I'd just witnessed? My gaze flicked out to the doorway, where I half hoped I'd see Dr. Squires so she could back me up. Zelda gently turned my face toward hers.

"I know you're worried," she said. "But it will be okay. Do you see how I fixed myself? It was only a minute, and I was able to fix myself."

I stood slowly, and she rose with me and brushed the wrinkles from her dress. She reached up to smooth her hair and caught my gaze. She cocked her head to the side and smiled her warmest debutante smile.

"You won't keep me from my life now, will you, Anna?" she said.

It was raining the day I arrived at La Paix, the house Scott had found for them several miles north of the city. It was a persistent, chilly pouring that soaked me through the soles, so that when I knocked I must have looked like something the Jones Falls had kicked up. I was supposed to have left with Scott when he'd picked up Zelda from Phipps that morning, but Dr. Meyer had a mountain of paperwork he insisted I complete before going. The bus stop was a half mile or so down the road from the house. At least Scott's secretary would drive me back to Phipps with Zelda at one thirty, after lunch, so I wouldn't have to get soaked again.

The house was a rambling old Victorian with a wraparound porch framed in maple trees that looked like a dollhouse Zelda might make for Scottie. It was located on the lush estate of a wealthy Baltimore family in the Rodgers Forge area, just miles from the city but with a rural feel. The grounds outshone the house, which looked as if it needed remodeling, but in spite of its aged appearance La Paix was nicer than any home I'd ever lived in.

Scott opened the door in a rush and glanced over me from head to toe.

"Anna!" he said with the drama of a Hollywood actor overplaying his part. "So good of you to agree to this."

Scott did not invite me in but turned and started walking down the hallway, his gray flannel robe flapping behind him, a trail of smoke and the smell of something prescriptive in his wake. I did not think he meant for me to remain outside the door, so I crept over the threshold and waited in the foyer as he disappeared around a turn.

The interior of the house had dark-paneled walls and an imposing grandfather clock in the hallway that chimed the hour while I stood there. Fitzgerald poked his head out of the room at the end of the hall and without removing the cigarette from his mouth said, "Come, come."

I walked down the hallway and entered the sitting room. A storm of yellow note-pads, broken pencils, papers, and books littered the tables and floor of the room, along with a collection of empty beer cans. It looked as if a party of wild librarians had just cleared out.

"Anna," he said.

"Yes, sir," I replied.

"Scott. Please call me Scott." He said this with a great amount of joviality, almost as if he were a liberal politician intent on dispelling the class system for an audience.

"Are you cold? Would you like some tea?" he asked.

"No, sir — Scott, please, I don't need any tea," I said.

He looked at me for a moment, then motioned for me to sit. He chose to stand.

He gave me a speech that sounded rehearsed about what he would need from me as a nurse at the house, as if I'd never cared for Zelda, as if we'd never spoken of these things. As he talked, he dribbled ashes all over the carpet, stepping on them with his slippered foot. I had a tremendous urge to stub the cigarette out, but contained it by folding my hands tightly in my lap.

"Here, finally, I will complete my novel," he said. "It's been on hold for years, and now I can feel the momentum pushing forward, urging me to finish the book. I will finish and I can't have distraction."

I wondered why he wanted Zelda here if he couldn't have distraction. Did he truly depend on her for inspiration? Would his muse behave for him?

It was clear that although it was only ten o'clock in the morning, Scott was drunk. I was furious. The hope that had started in Meyer's office was now completely slashed; the first puncture had come when I found Zelda on the floor of her room at Phipps, and now here, with him, was the final cut.

"There are things you should know," he said, his voice losing the full, warm quality it had had moments ago and assuming a tone of grave seriousness.

"The house is sometimes . . ." He searched the air as if looking for the word. "Unsettled."

To my horror, thunder punctuated his sentence by rumbling low over the house at that moment. He paused, half smiled, and redirected his attention to me. The hair on the back of my neck stood.

"And not due to my daughter, Scottie, who's here, by the way, running my secretary ragged."

I glanced at the framed photograph nearest me and saw the apple-cheeked child to whom he referred, and felt a sudden lift in my heart at the thought of finally meeting this little girl I'd so often thought about.

A movement by the heavy drapes in the corner caught my attention, and I was shocked to see Zelda emerge. Actually, she didn't emerge; she'd just been standing next to the drapes like a specter all this time and I hadn't noticed her. Scott's eyes darted from Zelda back to me. He'd known she was there.

My skin crawled. How could I not have seen her in the corner? It was as if she haunted the house, though she was alive. It was also as if she were seeing me for the first time.

Zelda chewed at her lips for a moment, then broke into a smile, suddenly an entirely different being from the pale, darkened figure in the drapes. Yet the smile unnerved me more than her previous countenance. My heart began to pound. I thought of her huddled on the floor in her room at Phipps. I thought of her emerging like a ghost from the curtains. It was suddenly clear to me that I'd made an error of terrible proportions.

She should not be here.

TWELVE

It was nearly the end of June, and Peter's last night with me before taking up residence at the cathedral. He said he wanted to go somewhere trendy and illegal, so I led him over to the Owl Bar, the best speakeasy in town, located in the Belvedere Hotel.

The Belvedere looked like it belonged in Hollywood — elegantly lit letters, ornate columns, a gilded facade, and a red carpet that led from the street into the lobby. The Owl Bar inside had exposed brick walls, a shiny tiled floor, and long light fixtures that reflected off the arched window. To Peter's excitement, the eye of the wise old owl over the bar was blinking the "all clear" wink when we arrived, so we found a table, ordered up two gin rickeys, and kept our eyes on the door and on the owl's eye in case of coppers.

"Why do you want booze at a bar where you can get arrested when you can drink the church wine any old time?" I asked.

"It tastes better when it's forbidden, Doll Face," he replied with a wink.

I laughed and squeezed his hand. "Peter, you are my favorite priest."

"Damn right," he said.

It was Friday night, so we passed on the meat and ordered oysters on the half shell and two fish and chips. I hadn't eaten three bites of my dinner when I suddenly wasn't hungry. Scott Fitzgerald had walked into the bar.

It was strange seeing him there, out of context. He wore a sharp gray suit. His hair was heavily gelled and parted in the middle. The warm light of the bar softened his features and gave his skin color. His eyes glowed bright green, and I realized with some discomfort how handsome, or rather pretty, he was.

Peter followed my gaze, then snapped his eyes back to me.

"Is that him? Fitzgerald?"

"Yes." I looked down at the oysters, trying to think of a way I could crawl under the table without being noticed. I did not want to have to engage in uncomfortable small talk with my patient's husband, especially when that husband was a famous writer.

"Anna!"

Damn.

I looked up and feigned surprise. "Scott! Hi! Swell to see you here."

"Yes, quite!"

He seemed genuinely pleased to see me. He stood and stared at me as if he were waiting for something.

"Hi, I'm her brother, Peter."

An introduction, yes.

"I'm sorry," I said. "I've forgotten my manners."

"No, no," said Scott. "It's a bit wacky for us to be together without Zelda, right?"

Somehow the mention of her name made me feel even more awkward than before.

"Yes. No. I mean . . ."

"Why don't you join us?" asked Peter.

I kicked Peter under the table. He was not my favorite priest anymore.

"I'd love to," said Scott.

The waiter came over and Scott ordered what we were having.

"Darn, Pete, I thought Anna was on a date," he said. "And you, just her brother."

"He's a priest," I said. "Though he's incognito tonight."

"She should be on a date," said Peter, swinging the conversation back to me.

"Pretty girl," said Scott.

I drained my gin and motioned the bartender for another. This was going to be a long night.

I watched the hands on the clock turn slowly around while Peter and Scott rambled on endlessly about the Jazz Age, Catholicism, Europe, Princeton. It was as if they'd been friends for life.

"The French Riviera," said Scott. "Heaven on earth."

"I've never ssset sandal there," said Peter. I noticed his speech was becoming more slurred by the minute. My own view had blurred at the edges, but at least the embarrassment had gone. The rickeys left me feeling faintly drowsy and as if I were in a dream.

Scott slapped the table and laughed loudly. "Sandal, Jesus, I love it. Did I say heaven on earth? No, it was hell, too. Feckin' French aviator."

"What, are you turning more Irish the drunker you get?" said Peter, while I tried to hang on to that detail. Scott laughed harder and his face turned flaming red. What French aviator? But the detail slipped through the well-oiled cogs in my mind for the time being.

"Anna," said Scott. "Have you been? To the Riviera?"

"She honeymooned there," said Peter.

That sobered the table.

"Huh?" said Scott.

"Excuse me; I have to find the ladies' room," I said.

I leveled Peter with my gaze and he quickly changed the subject.

"I just got back from Italy and a visit with a future saint," he said.

"Italy, God, awful," said Scott. "Zelda and I were never so sick and tired as our time there. The Italians didn't get us."

The crowd swallowed their conversation as I made my way to the bathroom at the back of the bar. I placed my hand on the cool brick for support and pulled the door handle of the lavatory.

"In a minute," called a muffled voice from the other side.

I leaned back against the wall and closed my eyes, trying to stop the room from slipping about as it did. Trying to find that thought again that had piqued my interest. A pilot?

The door opened and out spilled an amply bosomed woman in mile-high heels.

"Your turn, hon," she said. "Snazzy dress!"

I slipped into the bathroom and closed the door behind me. There was a mirror straight ahead and a dim light on the ceiling above it. My cheeks had a pleasant flush from the alcohol, and my hair still had a nice wave from when I'd set it earlier. And it was a snazzy dress. I'd bought it last season for myself as a birthday present, and this was the first time I'd worn it. It was the most enchanting shade of aquamarine — a bit like Scott's eyes when they turned that way, in fact. Before I left the bathroom, I reapplied my red lipstick. I felt a surge of confidence and gave myself permission to enjoy tonight and stop worrying about Zelda or Ben or any other thing in the world.

When I returned to the table, Peter had gone to the restroom. Scott stood and pulled out my chair.

"You are a vision tonight, Nurse Anna," he said.

"Why, thank you, Writer Scott."

"You remind me of the good old days in that dress with that lipstick."

"You are very kind." I took another long drink of my gin and rested my chin in the palm of my hand.

He leaned a little closer to me; then his eyes widened. "You are Brancusi's *Margit.*"

"Pardon me?"

He pulled two cigarettes out of the pack

in his pocket, lit them both, and offered me one. I declined with a shake of my head. He placed his elbows on the table and held up a cigarette in each hand. He took a long drag from one.

"A brass sculpture," he said. "We met in Europe. The artist Brancusi made it of an art student, Margit. You are the image of the girl in that sculpture." He exhaled to the side.

My face colored. I did not enjoy the scrutiny as much as I had resigned myself to it in the lavatory.

"I'll have to see it sometime," I said.

"Perhaps Zelda should try sculpture," he said. "She needs a medium where I don't dabble."

"You didn't dabble in ballet," I said.

"No, you're right about that."

"You don't dabble in paints. She enjoys her painting."

"True."

"Besides," I said, "I don't know that Zelda dabbles."

"She dabbled in men when we were young." He inhaled the other cigarette and blew to the other side.

"But dabbling is a thing of youth," I said. "Habit, discipline are what you have now."

"Mania is what we have now, love," he

said. "I'd give anything to go back to Princeton. I was so young, with every single day before me, and every single thing in the world ripe for my plucking. I should have reached higher."

"You did pretty damned well for yourself," I said. "A novel published when you'd barely started shaving. The most beautiful girl in the South."

"It's true," said Scott. "But you only really get one bite at the apple, I think. I took it when I'd just stepped out from under the shadows of those ivy-covered Princeton arches, when I should have waited for them to mature a bit more. Maybe then I could have handled it all better."

Peter sat down heavily. Scott passed him one of the lit cigarettes.

"Friends. Sisters. I'm tight," said Peter.

"Then surely you won't mind if I ask, are you a fairy?"

Peter wrinkled his forehead. " 'Scuse me?"

"A fairy, you know?" said Scott.

His voice was too loud, and the people sitting nearest us gave Scott a look of distaste.

"Otherwise, why'd a guy with your looks become a priest?"

"Keep it down, would you?" said Peter. "I'm not . . . what you said, but there could

158

be future parishioners of mine around here, and I don't want them thinking their pastor's a drunk of . . . alternative tastes."

Scott finished his cigarette and drained what was left of his fifth glass. He began to laugh, quiet and resigned at first, but then it grew in volume and intensity until he was sobbing.

Oh, no. Zelda often told me that once he hit the weepy stage of intoxication, trouble started.

"You know that bitch accused me of that," said Scott. "She's just calling the kettle black, is what she's doing. She was in love with her ballet teacher and her nurses in Switzerland and the other patients on her floor. Probably with you, Anna."

This went through me like a jolt. I didn't have time to dwell on it, though, because I saw the bartender motion toward a bouncer at the door. The large man approached the table.

"Around here we keep it down, sir," said the bouncer in a firm but respectful voice. "We don't like to draw attention to ourselves. One warning, sir, and you're out."

Scott nodded and waved him off. Tears ran down his face. He looked ridiculous here, crying his eyes out in the middle of a bar.

"Scott," said Peter. "Use Zelda's Christian name. No need to cut her down with foul words."

Scott began to shake his head. "I'm sorry, Father. I need confession; can you do a confession? Right here and now? Can you absolve me?"

I touched Peter's arm and nodded toward the door. When I looked for the waiter he had the bill for us in a moment. Scott insisted on paying.

"Indulgences," he said, dropping money on the table. "Can this get me indulgences, Father?"

His crying turned back into a laugh, and we walked him outside into the warm air. He laid his head on my shoulder while we waited for a taxi.

"Margit, you are lovely," he said.

His gin-soaked breath was on my neck. I felt a strange turmoil of emotions in response. It had been a long time since a man had shown me any interest, so while my emotional and intellectual selves were repelled and a little horrified, my physical self was intrigued. I didn't have to worry too long, however, because a taxi soon pulled up. I gave the driver his address while Peter loaded him into the car.

"You're my best friend, Peter," said Scott.

"My very best pally."

"You too," said Peter. "Drink some water when you get home. Tell your wife you love her tomorrow."

"I love her," he said.

"You do," said Peter. "Tell her."

"I love her." The weeping resumed, but we shut him in the taxi and sent him home.

We didn't say much on the way back to the apartment.

Sorin's lights were dark, and I wondered whether he was asleep or if he had friends to meet in city bars. The ballerinas' rooms were also dark. We trudged up the stairs and into the apartment. Peter sat on the sofa and took off his shoes while I filled two glasses to the brim with water. I brought him a glass and sat across from him on the piano bench.

He clinked my glass.

"Cheers."

We were both bottoms up in less than a minute. He took the glasses into the kitchen for a refill and we drank more water. When I finished I looked at my wedding picture on the piano and prepared myself to tell him my big news. I took a deep breath.

"I resigned from Phipps," I said.

Peter was silent for a moment. "What's

that?" he finally said.

"I resigned. From the clinic. To be Zelda's private nurse."

"When did this happen?"

"I put in my notice last Friday. We are in a period of transition."

He placed his empty water glass on the table and shook his head.

"You need to ask for your job back," he said.

"It's too late. They've already replaced me. It happened a week ago."

"Is this for her?" he asked. "For them?" He said *them* as if it were made of poison.

"It's for me. And for her."

"You can't allow yourself to be absorbed by them."

"I'm not worried about that."

A lie.

"Is it because they're famous? You have to guard against that. Those who are famous have a way of making people serve them."

"That's not fair, Peter," I said. "I do want to serve them, especially her, but it's not the celebrity."

"Then what is it?"

"I'm needed. Me. Personally. Not because I'm a nurse, but because I have a special connection to someone who needs *me,* Anna." I stood and walked over to the piano

162

with my back to Peter. "I haven't been needed in a long time. I forgot how good it feels."

Peter was quiet for a moment. When I turned to face him, he spoke kindly but with conviction. "Anna, you can certainly make your own decisions, but I can't help but think this is a mistake."

"He's paying me fifty a week," I said.

"Oh."

"I'm making more money than I did at Phipps, but it's not just that. I feel that I'm called to be there."

"After meeting him tonight, I think you'll earn every penny."

"You seemed to get on well enough," I said, not hiding my sarcasm. "You didn't say no to any drinks, either."

He started to protest but then fell silent. "I feel bad. I shouldn't have drunk like that," he said. Peter put his face in his hands and rubbed his eyes. "I just think you'll regret your decision."

I knew that he was probably right, but like an addict I felt no power to restrict myself. Zelda had made little progress in the weeks she'd been at La Paix, but quite honestly, she had made little progress at Phipps. Was she supposed to be institutionalized for the rest of her life?

I couldn't believe that. I had to hope that she could improve and her family would find a way to live as one, her little family of a man and a wife and a daughter. Two pieces of my family were gone, and I knew that if they were here I would do everything — I would risk everything — to keep us together. I had to try to help the Fitzgeralds so they could fit together and run the way they should.

But maybe it was my selfish desire to be needed. Maybe it was their celebrity. Deep down I knew I longed for the blissful anonymity of becoming part of something beautiful and tragic and even historic — like a single stroke of paint on a large and detailed landscape.

THIRTEEN

Against the recommendation of Dr. Meyer, and in spite of the fact that there was no measurable improvement in her condition, Zelda was formally discharged from Phipps Clinic on June 26, 1932. Scott was tired of dealing with Meyer, whom he did not respect and who insisted regularly that Scott stop drinking, and felt that my full-time attention would benefit his wife. I tried to assert that Zelda should still spend half of her time at the clinic, but Scott would agree only to weekly therapy.

I was determined to keep Zelda on Meyer's schedule and to help her find healthy ways to satisfy her creative impulses, while maintaining the peace with her husband. Meyer regimented her eating, reading, dancing, painting, tennis, horseback riding, and outpatient therapy schedule. I tried to push her from one activity to the next like a child in primary school.

It was a task beyond my qualifications.

One stiflingly humid July afternoon, I placed a watercolor of the dancers Zelda had just finished on the side table to dry, and rinsed out her brushes in the sink. Her small room at the top of the house felt especially close with the hot air rising, the open window only bringing in more heat, and Zelda's sudden need to move through ballet positions.

When I turned back to her, I noticed her picking at a patch of eczema beginning on her neck and chin, flaring like a red flag. The skin irritations and obsession with work had historically produced major break-downs, so I decided to steer her toward more restful activity. I thought perhaps I could interest her in a walk under the shade trees when a sudden noise in the hallway was followed by Scott bursting into the room. His eyes were wild and he looked as if he wanted to catch us at something. I didn't know exactly what he was looking for, but he seemed almost disappointed not to have found it.

Since our night at the Owl Bar, Scott and I had made a silent agreement that we would not speak of it. Zelda would make more of it than necessary, and Scott at least had the good sense to understand that

Zelda must think me entirely hers if there was to be any trust between us.

"I'm not writing a word, you terrible bastard, so get the hell out of here," she said.

Her vehemence surprised me.

"Don't act like I don't have cause to be suspicious," he said. "Anna, is she? Was she just working on her new novel?"

"She was not," I said. "She just finished painting."

"Show me," he said.

I gestured to the drying paper and he walked over to see it. He ran his hands over the picture, smearing some of the color.

"Just go on," said Zelda. "Destroy it. Like you destroy every part of me. I am nothing but a cadaver to you. Perform your autopsy, dear. Tell me what's inside."

"You've already started for me by clawing away at your face."

"Once I wanted to live inside your head. Now I'd just like to tear it off."

"Then please do. And put me out of my misery."

I stepped between them.

"Please, both of you," I said. "Scott, everything was okay here. Please leave us."

The two of them stared each other down with the ferocity of boxers in the ring. Scott finally pivoted and left the room.

"I want to go back to Phipps," she said. "Or I want to die. Pick one, but do not leave me here with this man tonight. One of us won't make it through."

"Zelda, you don't mean that."

"I mean it with every breath it takes to speak the words."

She stormed over to the door and slammed it as hard as she could. I cringed, waiting for his footsteps to return. Instead I heard the front door slam downstairs. I went to the window and watched him charge down the path to the car, get in, and speed away, kicking up a cloud of dust in his wake.

"Good," she said, shaking her head. "Good."

"Did you quarrel last night?"

She laughed with a sneer. "Did we quarrel? When do we not quarrel?"

She walked over to her closet and pulled out a pile of papers that I knew to be the very thing that Scott had asked her not to write. She sat down in the chair at the table facing the window, dropped the papers on the watercolor painting, and started writing. The wet color bled through onto her words, but she did not seem to notice or care.

I watched her for a moment in her silent rebellion, trying to decide whether I should take her threats of murder or suicide seriously, when I heard the sound of a child's voice through the window. Zelda stopped writing and looked out front to see Scottie skipping up the drive with her friend Andrew. They were having a race, and Scottie was winning. Through the open window drifted her laughter and narration.

"Up ahead is the brilliant, beautiful, worldly, and dashing Scottie Fitzgerald, first-place skipper and three-time Olympic champ."

She was breathing so fast it was hard for her to get it out, but she did all the same, and collapsed into a fit of giggles with Andrew as soon as they reached the oak in the front yard.

I saw Zelda watching her daughter. Her shoulders began to rise and fall heavily and I could see that she was crying. I stepped behind her and placed my hands on her back.

"We've done one thing, just one thing right," she said.

"It's the most important thing," I said.

Scottie and Andrew scampered off into the woods, leaving their happy echoes behind them.

"But she's not a bit mine," said Zelda. "Her face, her name, her manners. He won't let her be mine, and she knows it, so she treats me with the polite distance of a lunatic aunt."

"Why don't you try to do something with her? Just the two of you. Take her on a horseback ride. Help her with tennis. Swim in the reservoir. Whatever. She'd be happy to do it with you."

"No. I'd do something wrong. Something bad would happen. It's better if I don't poison her with my atmosphere."

"Zelda, that's not true. You must stop."

She raised her hand to me.

"No more," she said. "I don't want to speak of it anymore."

Zelda stood up and wiped her eyes. She picked up the papers, walked them over to the closet, and placed them back on the high shelf. Then she took down a folder and walked over to the fireplace. She motioned for me to join her.

She pulled all the essays she'd written for me out of the box, along with a photograph of a handsome man on a beach. She placed them in the bottom of the fireplace, opened the book of matches on the mantel, and struck one. She watched the flame until it burned almost to her fingertips and then threw it into the fireplace. The papers ignited and curled into little piles of ash. The quick flare of orange reflected off her face and wide eyes, giving her a demonic look.

The smoke didn't drift up the fireplace, but slipped out into the room, surrounding us with its odor and adding to the oppressive heat. I worried that the chimney was clogged, and retrieved the water from Zelda's painting. I poured it over the papers, adding another layer of scorched air to the room.

Zelda inhaled deeply.

"Do you feel it filling you up, purifying you?" she asked.

"I feel it, but I do not feel cleaner."

"I do," she said. "I only wish I could add my diaries to the pile. Someday I will, but for now, good-bye, 'Dance of the Hours'; good-bye, New York fountain; good-bye, aviator."

I felt a flicker of recognition, then remembered Scott's words at the bar.

"Aviator?"

"Shhh," she said, walking back to the window and looking for Scott.

"Who is this aviator?" I asked.

"He is nothing anymore, but once he could have been everything. If Scott hadn't locked me up all those weeks."

"Where did he lock you up?"

She laughed suddenly, that terrible out-of-context laugh that seemed to disturb her as much as it did me. Her neck was redder than ever and I knew it was time to stop.

"I'll write it," she said. "Something more intimate than what I wrote for my novel. Something just for you. And then we'll burn that, too. Like salamanders."

It seemed that speaking of this aviator set her more on edge, and I was growing increasingly uncomfortable with her need to burn papers. It was hard enough to leave her each night; I didn't want to add worry about her setting fires. I tried to steer her in another direction.

"Why don't you start with Westport and we'll work up to the aviator?" I said.

"There's nothing to tell of Westport," she said. "Westport: the great Manhattan martini glass spilling over, tipsy-turvy with all of our terrible friends and lovers drowning us, distracting Scott, terrifying my parents, alienating my sister. Westport was a drunken mess. France is what you need to know next."

"Did the diaries make it to France?"

"I don't know. I'll have to think about it. But France is where it cracked and couldn't be repaired."

"Your relationship?"

"Our relationship, my head, all of it. The

great chasm started in France and has never stopped starting since."

THE RIVIERA, ST.-RAPHAEL: SUMMER 1924

We watched the houses push out of the blue sea and shake off the sand to wait for us and our little party of four: an underused mother, a lush father, a bubbly baby, and a dictatorial nanny. The villa that was meant for us — the house of the nightingales — bloomed, a quick garden fragranced with boredom and a quiver of unease. Even the flowers trembled with it.

With barriers of language all around and the buzzing of planes like silver bees over the house at all hours of the day and night, we made for the little oasis of a beach. It had a new, just-raked quality about it. A well-polished man rose from the water and told us it was his, and we were welcome, and wouldn't we just dress up his parties like shiny Christmas ornaments.

So we did. Party after party. A stew of wealthy, useless people of vast opinion with a peppering of artists to season the pot. A cubist here, a dramatist there, more writers.

I longed for those parties all the bored long days while the cook swatted me from the kitchen, the nanny swatted me from my girl, the husband swatted me from his work. I felt like a fly they all wished to splat against the window glass. Or one of the planes buzzing overhead.

Have you ever heard the terrible drone of bees? It's a sound that carries a warning of sting and death with no winners. Death to the stung. Death to the stinger.

The death began the day I locked eyes with the aviator.

It was like those terrible fairy tales where the princess meets the prince and every-thing starts to conspire against them to keep them apart. I don't know if the drunken husband saw the first eye lock or even the second. I'm quite sure he didn't notice the dancing or the kisses by moon-light. It took a plane buzzing our house with my aviator's wave and the dropping of a package for the husband to finally notice another man might be a threat.

But still he worked. Still he drank. Still he ignored, fussed, instructed, placated, and swatted me away.

The nights on the French Riviera make the shadows for the secret whispers the people wait all day to make. But I chose to stand in the middle of the dance floor under the light of the moon, to show my husband that it was okay and it was not okay. I thought if he saw me dancing he'd cut in. He did not. Why did he not cut in anymore?

The music of the three-piece jazz ensemble chased away my longing for my husband and forced me to attend to what was in front of me. This golden god of sun, vibrantly alive, pressing into me with his body and his sad eyes, hypnotizing me with his French words I could only partly understand. I didn't have to understand the words, though. I felt their meaning searing the insides of my heart, cleaning out what had occupied it for so long, replacing it with a reminder of what used to be there.

Suddenly the Riviera was pulled away like a sandcastle by the tide. One wave, two, three — it was gone, and around me the old country club in Montgomery erected itself. Paper soldiers lined the walls with wilting female flowers on their arms, and it was just me and some faceless uniformed man whispering unintelligible things in my ear. My eyes locked with Scott's in the corner, his once soft green eyes now hardened like jagged shards of arctic ice. I pleaded with my eyes, *Come to me, come to me, interrupt us.*

But still, he did not.

Later that evening, I sat on the front porch with Zelda, reading her confessions by the pink glow of the setting sun, while I waited for Lincoln to arrive and take me to my parents' house. She chewed her lips and picked her face beside me. I reached over while I read and gently pulled her hands down to settle in her lap. The moment I finished, I heard the crunch of tires on the road and looked up.

It was Scott.

My heart started to pound, and Zelda jumped visibly in her chair as I stuffed the paper in my handbag and zipped it shut. He slammed his car door and just stood, staring at her without saying a word. He came around the car slowly, like a panther watching his prey. She wrung her hands in her lap. He staggered a bit as he approached the front porch stairs, started up them, and paused at the top.

"Tonight I will work," he said. "I don't want any interruption. I don't want hysterics, theatrics, or pyrotechnics of any kind. Scottie is staying with the Turnbulls, my secretary will be leaving shortly, and you, Zelda, are to go to bed at eight thirty. Do you understand?"

"May I listen to my records?" she asked.

"No," he said. "I will not stand for any distraction."

"Then tonight I will kill myself. I have enough pills saved."

"As long as you do it quietly," he said.

Lincoln pulled up as Scott disappeared into the house. I slipped Lincoln the fare and told him to go home. I wouldn't need his services tonight.

The house was frightening enough during the daytime, but at night, with the vacancy left by Scottie, the sounds of Scott pacing the halls downstairs talking to himself, and Zelda's groans and cries while she slept, it was almost intolerable.

After bathing her and brushing out her

hair, I had sent Zelda to bed with a light sedative. As much as it frustrated me, I could not ask her about the result of her affair, if that was what it could be called. I had no notion whether she had actually made love to the aviator. That conversation would have to take place at another time. Whether or not she had, it was clear that the power shift in the relationship took place at that time.

I noted the dosing on her chart and made some notes for Dr. Meyer, then sat with Zelda until she slept. Once her breathing was deep and rhythmic, I left the room to read in her project room upstairs.

The watercolor she'd worked on that afternoon was nearly ruined from Scott's hands and Zelda's writing papers, but I did not discard it. Zelda might be able to fix it. I sat on the chair and ran my hands over the now dried lines of the grotesque ballerina. I could feel the pain of the dancer in her monstrous, bulbous legs and contorted frame. We'd been taught that art was a mirror to the emotional state of the patient. This painting was the work of a disturbed individual, and it hit me with a wave of sadness that this real-world experiment was failing. Zelda and Scott could not continue to destroy each other at this rate.

Unfortunately, I think money was part of what motivated Scott's decision to pull her out of Phipps. Money and a disdain for a clinic that advised him to stop drinking when he just wanted treatment for his wife. He could not see how his use of alcohol contributed to the turbulence in the house; or rather, he would not see it.

I pulled Zelda's proofs for her novel closer and picked up where I'd left off the day before, just at the point when Alabama and David arrived in Connecticut. I was helping Zelda prepare the manuscript of *Save Me the Waltz* for Scribner's and thought it had the ingredients of brilliance without an ounce of control. Scott had helped her with some of the editing, but either from fatigue or malice he'd stopped work on the project to resume his own.

I tried to read for several pages, but my thoughts slipped from my guilt after my mother's silence when I called her to tell her I wouldn't be coming for the weekend, to frustration that Peter would probably judge me poorly for it. I pushed these thoughts away but still felt unsettled. I moved from the chair to the couch and tried to read a bit more, but the words soon blurred and I fell asleep.

■ ■ ■ ■

I opened my eyes and couldn't remember where I was.

Sheer netting surrounded my bed. Morning light crept through the wood-framed window, giving the room a rosy glow. I felt the weight of an arm draped across my stomach. Ben slept next to me, his face young from sleep. I felt elation in my heart until my eyes slipped to the corner of the room, where Scott sat with a tumbler of alcohol in his hand, and I knew it was a dream.

"You are dreaming," said Scott.

"Go away," I said.

I realized that now it was only me and Ben in the room. It was the morning after the first night of our honeymoon. Wineglasses holding small, sticky red pools stood on the bedside table. A white flower Ben had picked for me from the garden path at night opened from an empty wine bottle he'd filled with water.

I ran my hand along his forearm and up to his shoulder. He stirred and smiled before he opened his eyes. I felt my body, still a bit sore from the previous night, begin to want him. I turned him to his back and rolled on top of him, nuzzling my face into his warm neck. He wrapped his arms around my waist.

"Anna," he said.

"Anna."

"Anna." My eyes snapped open and took a moment to adjust to the darkness. Zelda knelt on the floor in front of me.

"We must burn it now."

I pushed myself into a sitting position and she pressed herself into my knees and put her hands on my thighs.

"The aviator piece," she said. "He's asleep. We need to burn it right now."

"We can wait until morning," I said. "It's in my purse; he won't look there."

"Now!"

I shushed her and stood, still shaky from my sleep, and found my purse. She followed me. I felt around the handbag, pushing aside my wallet, my keys, a tube of lipstick. I found a paper and squinted to see whether it was Zelda's writing. It was my discharge letter from Hopkins. I felt around again and could find no other paper.

"Can you see it?" she asked. "Shall I turn on the light?"

My heart began to race. There was no other paper in my purse, but I worried that if I told Zelda she'd break down. I opened the purse a little wider, saw that her paper was gone, and made a decision.

"Here, let's burn it."

I stood and carried my letter to the fireplace. I crumpled it into a ball so she wouldn't see the typewritten words and threw it deep into the ashes of the previous writing she'd burned. She struck a match and watched it flare up, and mercifully did not notice as the paper curled that it was not her handwriting on the sheet.

She left the room when the letter was gone, mumbling to herself, "Now I can sleep."

But I could not.

I felt his eyes on me while I moved around the kitchen preparing tea for myself and a tray to take up to Zelda when she awoke. I placed the toast on the tray with a shaking hand, picked up a napkin from the counter, and slid it under the butter knife. All the time I could see his form in the doorway out of the corner of my eye but couldn't force myself to look at him.

" 'But still, he did not,' " he said.

I stiffened under the stony inflection with which he read, and looked up to see that he had Zelda's aviator paper in his hand.

"But still I did not," he said. He exhaled a

short laugh, shook his head, and ran his hand over his eyes. The dark circles were so heavy and his face so pale, I felt the nurse in me long to send him to bed and care for him, but his disgust was a barrier between the two of us that I dared not cross.

He laughed again in a few short bursts, and then continued until he worked himself up to hysterics. I prayed Zelda wouldn't come down the stairs.

"Scott," I said.

"Mr. Fitzgerald, actually," he said. "Nurse Howard, I'd feel better if we returned to formality, because we are not a team. No, we are in opposing camps and you have chosen your side, and for that, you may call me Mr. Fitzgerald and give me the respect I deserve."

"Please allow me to explain," I said.

"Explain what? Explain that you are encouraging my wife in the very hobby I've forbidden? Explain that you are a willing participant in making sure that my next novel never reaches completion because of the stresses you're feeding in this house? Explain that you yourself probably sent Zelda's book to Scribner's in the first place and started this whole war?"

His words slipped into me like arrows, but I took issue with his last statement. I was not responsible for his marriage problems.

"I understand that you do not wish Zelda to write, and I will admit that I asked her to write little essays for me to help me understand her background and where her breakdowns occurred so that I may assist her in preventing them in the future. These essays are therapeutic and we've been using them for some time, and we are, I believe, making great headway in allowing Zelda to discover exactly where it is that she lost herself and how we can help her restore at least a bit of it."

"Essays?" he said. "So there are more?"

"*Were* more. They are destroyed and we intended to destroy the one you've *stolen.* It gives Zelda pleasure to burn these things. It's become a purification ritual for her, and if she finds out you've found this piece and read it, you will cause a serious setback in her mental state."

"Ha! As if it could get any worse."

"Let me assure you, *Mr. Fitzgerald,* it can and will get much worse if you continue to use her as you would a marionette to position and hang before you like some sick stimulus."

"Sick? She's my wife. A wife should support her husband."

"Support, yes, but you don't want support. You want to consume her. You want to use her up. And you've used her up many times over, but she is not a phoenix and she cannot crawl out of the ashes reborn over and over again, because she is human."

"You're wrong," said Zelda. She appeared in the doorway wearing an obscene pink tutu and smoking a cigarette. She looked like a manifestation of the ballerina painting on canvas, larger than life, blotchy with eczema, and flicking her glassy gaze around the room. "I am no mortal. I am a salamander."

Mr. Fitzgerald looked disgusted. "Here is your subject, Nurse Howard. See her progress. Maybe we can take her to Scottie's school for show-and-tell?"

"That would be lovely," said Zelda. "I do love a show."

I quivered with frustration. I was well aware that Zelda took two steps back for every small gain, but I didn't know how to communicate to her husband that no matter what her mental state, she deserved to be treated with dignity and not used up and wrung out until there was nothing left.

Zelda played her record as loud as she could while thumping around above me in her room upstairs. I placed a cool rag to my

185

neck and wondered how she could stand to exert herself in such heat.

As I rinsed the lemonade pitcher at the kitchen sink, I stared out the window at Scottie and Andrew running around the yard in bathing clothes, soaked from their swim and, mercifully, oblivious to the strain in the Fitzgerald house. When I turned off the water, I heard a sob from somewhere downstairs. I could hear Zelda's continued dance on the ceiling above me, so I knew it wasn't her weeping. I crept into the hallway and to Fitzgerald's study where he wrote. He sat at the desk, crying, with his arms crossed over his yellow notepad. There were papers taped on the walls all around him, papers littering the floor, and empty beer cans everywhere. I was moved but immobilized by indecision. Would he want my comfort? Did I have a right to give it?

He sat up and jumped when he saw me standing in the doorway. He had such a look of hopelessness that I went to him.

"I'm sorry about earlier," I said. "I just want to help to restore her so that your lives can improve."

"It's me who should apologize," he said. "For bringing anyone into this madness. For my poor Scottie." His voice trailed off and he began sobbing again.

It disturbed me beyond words to see a grown man so broken. I crouched before him.

"You are a good father," I said. "I've seen how you care for your daughter. And you must know this: She's a happy child. You've sheltered her well; at least, as much as you possibly can."

"Maybe I should send her away," he said. "Do you think I should send her away to school so she doesn't have to be around this?"

"No," I said. "It's good for her to be around you, but you have to take care of yourself."

His skin was pasty pale, and he was covered in sweat. I was quite alarmed by his pallor and put my hand on his forehead. It burned with fever.

I reached for his arm. "May I?"

He extended his wrist and I took his pulse. It was extremely high.

"Mr. Fitzgerald," I said.

"Scott."

"Scott, I think you should consider checking into Hopkins for some rest."

He started to protest, but I raised my hands.

"You are not well," I said. "And you have to stay well. If not for yourself, then for

187

Scottie."

He shook his head and tried to stand, but collapsed into a coughing fit in the chair. I helped him up and guided him over to the couch.

"I'll pack some things for you, and call the doctor," I said.

"What will you tell Zelda?" he asked.

"I'll tell her the truth."

FOURTEEN

Scottie walked up to the bank of the reservoir where I sat watching Zelda slice through the water with strong, bold strokes for her morning exercise.

"She's a good swimmer," I said.

"Yes," said Scottie. "I think she feels best when she's exercising."

"I agree," I said.

Scottie sat next to me on the grass. It pleased me that she was comfortable enough to do so.

"Are you enjoying living here, in Baltimore?" I asked.

"Yes, very much. The neighbor's son, Andrew, is fun. And I look forward to going to school here. I visited last week and I thought it very pretty."

I was impressed by her fine speech and manners. Scottie had been taught well and seemed to possess an ease of temperament that neither of her parents was blessed with

— at least not in their current states.

"You seem very grown-up for a ten-year-old," I said. "Your parents are proud of you."

Her face lit with a smile.

Zelda continued her laps. She'd been swimming without rest for thirty minutes, and the ripples and splashes she'd made now filled the entire reservoir. It was easy to imagine her dancing herself into exhaustion.

"Would you like to join her?" I asked. "I could fetch your suit for you."

"Oh, no, thank you. Mommy's focused right now. Best not to disturb her."

Scottie's matter-of-fact tone saddened me. She spoke from experience and yet she did not seem to possess a shred of self-pity or sadness. To Scott's credit, he worked hard to protect his daughter and give her a sense of normalcy.

A boy appeared through the trees and motioned for Scottie to join him. She jumped up and brushed off her behind.

"Bye, now," she said. "It was nice talking to you."

"You, too, dear," I said.

I watched her disappear into the woods, warmed by our conversation but sad that such a sweet child had a father in the hospital drying out and a mother who was so unstable. These recent interactions with Scott and Scottie stirred me in a new way. Perhaps Zelda was beyond help, and I was called here for them. Perhaps they needed me more than she did.

Scott stayed in the hospital for two weeks. I visited him on the way home from La Paix every day, and encouraged him on his progress with his novel. At first, Zelda seemed more at ease when he wasn't there, but as time passed she started to grow anxious.

I'd made plans for a field trip to the ballet for Zelda, scheduled for the day before Scott's return. I knew Scott would never agree to her going out without him, so I wanted to get it in before he came back. My stomach was nervous at the thought, but my excitement overshadowed my reserve. We had never attempted such an outing, and I had high hopes that it would stitch one of her torn emotional places, as music had often done in my own life.

"When is he coming home?" she asked. "I'm ready for him to come home."

"He'll be home tomorrow," I said.

"Oh, Anna, help me set my hair and pick out a dress. It will be just like old times. I'll be my old self and we'll all be new and shiny again."

Her complexion was marred by the eczema she picked at, and her hair had grown wild. She wore a stained tutu and had chewed her nails to nubs. Scott would surely be repulsed to see her in her present condition.

I sent her up to the bath and searched her closet for her most becoming dress. I would tell her about my plan to take her out after she was dressed and primped, and her hairdo could carry over to the following day. Once Zelda was scrubbed clean, her hair set, and she had a little rouge on her cheeks, she looked fresh and young. Her pale blue dress showed off her tanned skin, and her eyes looked alert.

"Do you think he'll love me, Anna?" she asked.

"He always loves you, Zelda, more than he can bear."

She nodded. "Yes, I know he does."

"So," I said, "would you like to know why I had you dress up tonight?"

"To prepare for tomorrow?"

"Not exactly," I said. "I have a gift for you."

"Is it my diaries?" she asked.

I felt the nerves in my stomach start as I

shook my head. I tried to make light of her question. "No, silly. When would I have been able to go on a trip to find them?"

She rolled her eyes and shrugged her shoulders. "I don't know. Nights? Weekends?"

I heard a car pull up and the horn beep.

"I'm taking you on a field trip," I said.

Her eyes got a wonderful, mischievous glint. She hunched her shoulders up to her ears. "Oh, Anna, where are you taking me?"

"You'll just have to see," I said, giving her a coy wink. "I'll change my clothes and we'll be on our way."

I walked to the front window and waved down at Lincoln. He gave me the thumbs-up.

My dress hung in the hobby room closet. I had bought it with my pay last week — a chiffon frock that moved like zephyr and was the exact shade of pinky salmon that Zelda loved. I pulled off my work clothes and kicked off my clunky shoes. The dress was so light and pleasant, I knew it would be perfect in the heat, and so were the strappy heels I'd found at the consignment shop down the street. Zelda watched me dress and pin up the sides of my hair, ooh-ing and ahhing over my transformation.

"Nurse Anna, look at you! Togged to the

bricks. I think I want to marry you!"

"Get in line," I teased.

Zelda laughed her deep, warm laugh, but when I turned around to face her she looked very serious. She stared at me with an expression of sad confusion on her face.

"Why aren't you married?" she finally said.

Her question killed all of the happy energy in the room, but it was too direct to ignore, and how I wished I could have ignored it.

"I am married," I said.

She stared at me for another interminable amount of time before she spoke. "Where is he?"

Lincoln beeped the horn.

"Let's talk about this later, huh?" I said, painting a false smile on my face.

"I want to talk now," she said.

"No," I said, a little sharper than I intended. "No, I would love to, but this night is about you and a gift I'd like to give to you."

Her face hardened and she pursed her lips. This was not going as I'd planned.

"Now, don't pout," I said with a lightness I did not feel. "Here, I have one more surprise for you. An accessory you haven't used in far too long."

I turned back to the closet and opened

the box on the shelf inside of it, carefully removing its contents and spreading the gorgeous blue feathers of the fan before turning to her.

She gasped and covered her mouth. "My fan," she stammered. "Where did you find my fan?"

"Scott had it on the table when he was writing late one night when I stayed over. I asked him about it and he told me that it was the first present he bought for you when you were a young debutante and you adored expensive, decorative, unique gifts."

She took the fan from my hands while tears ran down her cheeks, cutting wet lines in her powder.

"Now, don't cry," I said. I picked up one of Scott's handkerchiefs from the table and walked over to blot her tears. She continued to stare at the fan, seemingly oblivious to my presence. I was glad and hoped she wouldn't ask me any more questions.

I held her face in my hands and directed her gaze back to mine.

"Let's go," I said. "We don't want to be late."

I felt a mixture of emotions raging inside of me. Zelda was very quiet on the cab ride, and nestled trembling into my side. I didn't know whether she was scared, excited, or both, so I put my arm around her and squeezed her shoulder for reassurance. She clutched the fan with white knuckles and didn't speak.

Her eyes grew wide when we arrived at the Maryland Theatre. It was a grand place in Hagerstown, Maryland, with an opulent facade, a thick velvet red curtain, ornate balconies, and seating for more than one thousand. Lincoln opened the car door for us and told me he'd be just around the side of the theater sleeping if I needed him. I would be sure to pay him extra for working late tonight.

When I led Zelda into the lobby, she seemed to shrink into herself even further. It was rather stuffy with the mobs of people, the heavy scents of women's perfume and cigarette smoke, and laughter and noise filling every space we turned. I was finally able to navigate through the loitering theater-goers to a side staircase, where we showed our tickets to an usher. He led us to the box nearest stage right and I felt like royalty as we stood above the glamorous crowd. The lights flickered almost as soon as we sat down, and within moments we were plunged into darkness.

Zelda's hand reached for mine and

clutched it. It was sweaty and she continued to tremble. The stage lights gradually turned on and highlighted Zelda's nose and forehead. Her eyes and the hollows of her cheeks remained in the shadows, giving her a cadaverous look, and I felt my spirits sink. Zelda was supposed to be gay and animated, not like a woman living in a nightmare. I began to sweat and pondered leaving with her. When the orchestra started and the warm, round voices began, Zelda's face suddenly turned to a smile, and I felt relief wash over me.

"*La Gioconda*," she whispered. "Oh, Anna."

Yes, *La Gioconda,* the tragic opera of a woman who sacrificed herself for her lover's happiness, the story of blindness and sight, misunderstandings, and the cruelty of fate. The opera included the "Dance of the Hours," the song playing when Zelda danced at the Montgomery country club the first night she'd met Scott. Zelda clutched her fan with one hand and my hand painfully with her other. I felt trapped by her, but didn't dare move. I was afraid to break the spell.

When the "Dance of the Hours" began, Zelda laughed out loud. Several of the people in the rows below us looked up and then back at the stage. My heart raced.

"Anna," she said with her voice at full volume. "Anna, it's my dance!"

I managed a stiff smile and put my finger to my lips to encourage her to speak in a whisper. She ignored me and turned back to the stage.

She began to move her feet in time to the music, and alternated between short bursts of laugher and terrible strangled sounds like sobs. To my horror, she released her grip on me, stood in the box, and began to dance. The usher was there within moments and pointed to the chair. Zelda put her thumb on her nose and wiggled her fingers at the man, but did sit down.

I felt as if I couldn't breathe, and began planning how I was going to get her out of the theater without making a scene. Luckily, the song ended and it was as if a curtain closed on her features. Her face took on the look of a statue, and she barely moved for the rest of the act.

As the final act began, I noticed tracks of tears on her face. She placed the fan on her lap and began to twist her hands and rock back and forth. I knew I needed to get her out of the theater.

"Zelda, let's go before the crowds," I whispered as I placed my hands around her shoulders.

"Not yet," she said, again at full volume. "Don't you see?"

Her face contorted and she began to shake her head and weep.

"Gioconda will sacrifice herself for him," she said. "For them. She will allow him to be free and will kill herself; watch."

The people just below us shushed her, but she continued to cry. The beautiful, melancholy sounds of the woman about to take her life filled the theater, interlaced with Zelda's sobs. I felt as if my heart were being torn open, and I could feel the tears on my own cheeks. I tried now to pull her from the box, and mercifully, the usher was back and helped me to carry her out and down the stairs. Zelda suddenly started screaming about her fan and I realized we'd dropped it. I left the poor man with my mad patient and took the stairs two at a time back to the box, where the fan lay in a tangle on the floor. I could barely see through my tears as I raced back down the stairs and out to the street. The usher held Zelda like an orderly at Phipps while she wailed and scratched at his face.

"There!" I shouted, pointing at the taxi waiting at the other end of the long alley.

I stumbled to the door and threw it open, startling Lincoln awake as I pushed Zelda into the backseat. I closed the two of us in and screamed for him to drive, and he complied.

Zelda sobbed during our entire trip back to La Paix, up the walk, through the front door, up the stairs, and into her room. Lincoln helped me every step of the way. I was so grateful that Scottie was sleeping at her girlfriend Peaches's house.

Lincoln stood next to the bed with his hat in his hands while I injected Zelda with a sedative and her cries turned to whimpers.

"I don't think I should leave you like this, Anna," he said.

"I'll be all right now. It's best if you go. I'm sorry."

He looked from Zelda to me with worry, then started for the door.

I realized I hadn't paid him, so I chased him down the stairs and gave him twenty dollars from my wallet. He looked at the bill and shoved it into his pocket. It was the first time he'd ever taken my money without a fight.

I closed the front door, locked it behind him, and slid down to the floor, placing my head in my hands.

My God, what had I done?

FIFTEEN

October 1932

Peter and I walked down the stairs just off the breezeway behind the church and into the crypts and caverns below the Baltimore Cathedral. He dragged a match against the brick to light his cigarette, and deposited it in a pile of rubble in a hole in the wall. I found it dark and creepy under the church, but Peter enjoyed watching the progress on the architectural reinforcements going on underground. The ceiling was so low, we practically needed to stoop.

"You were right," I said.

"Are you referring to your tenure with the Fitzgeralds?" he asked.

I laughed. "My tenure. Yes, if that's what you'd like to call it."

"I hate to say it, but you do look awful."

"Thanks, Pete."

"You know I say that out of concern," he said. "When I first caught sight of you in

201

the pews I didn't recognize you. Dark circles under your eyes. An overall worn look about you."

"Enough," I said. "I've got it."

We paused in the mausoleum full of dead bishops and cardinals, their caskets ordered in rows in the walls like safe-deposit boxes at the bank.

"You'll be buried here someday," I said.

"Ha," said Peter. "Their coffins would spring out if the likes of me were slid in there."

"I hate to admit it, but you look swell."

"Thanks," he said. "I feel swell."

"I'm very glad to hear it."

We walked deeper underground and Peter flipped on a crude light without a fixture, illuminating parts of some passages while leaving others in eerie shadows. It looked like an abandoned subway tunnel, and I half expected a train to come roaring toward us from the dark brick arches. I breathed in the musty underground air, and turned back to Peter. "Why did you bring me down here?" I asked.

"So I could smoke."

"Oh, I thought you were going to give me a lesson on the necessity of building a foundation as it relates to faith and mental health."

"That, too, but since you seem to understand the moral, there's no need to waste air."

"Then how about a lecture about putting people like the Fitzgeralds on pedestals and arranging one's entire life around their well-being when they are just as regular and broken, if not more so, than you and me."

"Couldn't have said it better myself," he said as he exhaled. "But truly, the more I think about it, the more I don't think that about you. You are a giver. It doesn't matter who is in your care."

I stopped and looked away from him at the dark arches of brick that held up the massive cathedral: simple pieces of rock piled one on top of the other to support an entire building. I caught the white stare of two stone angel statues facing us from the tunnel to our left, and shivered.

"So you don't want to tell me I should leave my work with the Fitzgeralds at once, and find a nice man who will marry and keep me so I don't have to work?"

"No, Anna. Not anymore."

I cocked my head to the side and gave him a look of suspicion.

"You need to stay on with them," he said.

"Do you think I should recommend that they take her back to Phipps, at least on a part-time basis?"

"Do you think it would benefit her?"

"It depends on the hour you ask me. When I see her chewing her nails, expending her manic energy on meaningless tasks, and arguing with her husband, then yes, I do. But when I see Zelda share a hug with her daughter, or walk in the garden, or sit next to Scott with her feet up talking about the old days while he writes, I can't imagine her anywhere else."

"Then she probably should not return to Phipps. And if she did, you'd be out of a job."

"I'm aware of this."

"Just keep at it, Anna. This is right."

"Where is this coming from?" I asked. "You just told me I look horrid."

"You do."

"Then why do you think I should stay on with them?"

"Because it recently occurred to me in prayer that you are exactly where you are supposed to be."

"Do you care to elaborate?" I asked.

He started walking again, and I fell into step with him.

"Not really," he said. "You'll just ignore me anyway."

"Probably, but I'm burning with curiosity.

At least help me satisfy that."

"No," he said. "If I bring up Padre Pio, confession, and atonement you will shut down."

"You're right," I said. "Let's not talk about it."

We reached the end of the passage, and climbed up the stairs and out of the front entrance of the cathedral. It was a relief to breathe the fresh autumnal air. A large banner showing Edgar Allan Poe hung from the windows of the Enoch Pratt Free Library across the street.

"I love reading Poe at this time of year," he said.

"Me, too. Though I feel as if I've been living in a Poe story in that creepy house with those unsettled people."

"Then you really must stay," he said, "if for no other reason than to see how the story ends."

"I just hope it doesn't end with the house collapsing in on itself and its haunted inhabitants."

"And their psychiatric nurse, ooooohhhhh." He held out his hands like a Frankenstein monster and squeezed my shoulders. I couldn't help but laugh at the old woman passing us, watching with disapproval at the priest behaving like a schoolboy.

He waved to her and then pulled me by my hand. "Come on."

"Where to?"

"Poe's grave."

The fall sky wore the marbled gray threat of precipitation, and a chilly wind slid between the city buildings. We pulled our coats up around our necks, remarking on the sudden change in the weather.

The Poe grave was located at the corner of Fayette and Greene streets. The large stone monument was supposed to mark his grave, but rumors persisted that his real burial site was in the back of the cemetery. The monument was a beautiful tribute to the troubled writer, with its impressive arched top, large engraved name, and black bas-relief bust of the man's face.

Peter and I stood before it for a moment, then walked around the cemetery noting the older, more crumbled slabs and remarking on the macabre beauty of our surroundings. Near the back, I came upon a headstone of a child. She was only five when she had died, and I felt connected to those who had lost her. My daughter, Katie, rested across town in the Green Mount Cemetery. It was one of the reasons I'd chosen to work at Hopkins and live in the city: to remain near her. It had been a long time, however, since I'd visited her grave. Too long. I was surprised to find that thinking of her did not depress me, but rather, reminded me of the time I'd had her, a human thread connecting me to Ben and to who I once was.

I felt Peter's hands on my shoulders and reached up to touch one of them.

"Are you okay?" he asked. "Would you like to leave?"

I turned to him. "No," I said. "No, it's good to be here. To remember things."

"I've always admired you, Anna," he said.

I was surprised by his words and couldn't think why he said them.

"Why?"

"Your courage," he said. "I don't have a tenth of your courage. It's why I am what I am."

The wind picked up around us, rattling the newly colored leaves of the tree hanging over us. One of the leaves let go and floated down to rest near a gravestone.

"How can you say that?" I said. "You have the hardest job of all. I can't imagine doing what you do, being alone like you, responsible for so many the way that you are."

"How is that different from you?" he said.

"I guess it's a little bit the same, but so, so

different," I said. "At least I have my freedom."

"Don't you see, though? I'm free. You, who've loved as you have, who have lost what you lost. Look at you and Ben. Katie. Look at Scott and Zelda, slowly killing each other by stray bullets meant for themselves. That's what happens with love. It ends. By death or separation."

"I never knew you to be such a pessimist," I said.

"I'm a realist. All human relationships will end. I've already lost my love, the Lord. Now I just have to live well to get back to him. I couldn't bear what you've lost. You're a far stronger person than I could ever hope to be."

I looked down at the red leaves that had fallen prematurely, and let his words sit heavy in my heart.

I'd invited Peter to dinner that night and told him I'd include Sorin. Sorin hadn't spoken much since the day he'd delivered the song. Though he knew Peter was my brother, I believed the strain of reaching out and giving me the song had irreparably taxed his nerves. He blushed whenever he saw me, stuttered responses to my greetings, and made a general mess of every small interaction we had in the hall.

I had been practicing "Anii" on the piano for weeks and knew he had to have heard through the walls of our building, as I often heard him. The music was exquisite. Two simple melodies drifting in and out of each other, with the sadness of Chopin and the depth of Beethoven. It made me cry the first time I played it correctly from start to finish.

It also worried me. There was so much feeling in the song, and while I couldn't deny that I was drawn to Sorin, I felt as if I didn't deserve his affection and couldn't possibly return it. It occurred to me that his creative fevers reminded me of Zelda's, and while this fascinated me, I did not need another project.

As I pulled the rosemary-scented chicken out of the oven, the phone rang. It was Peter, full of apologies. The bishop and a number of notable clergy were coming to dine at the rectory, and he hadn't found out about it until that afternoon.

"That can't be true, Peter," I said. "You set me up."

He laughed and I knew I was right in spite of his insistence that he didn't know.

"You just want me to have a date with Sorin, and I don't appreciate your meddling in my love life."

"Anna, if I could swear on the Bible, I would. I did not set you up. I have to confess that I'm glad it worked out this way, but I didn't orchestrate it."

I groaned and hung up on him, frantic at the thought of dining alone with Sorin in my apartment, but thankful for living in the city where I at least had a telephone and could be notified of such a late change in plans. Maybe I still had time to invite the ballerinas. I checked the clock and saw that I had ten minutes before Sorin was due to arrive. Taking the steps two at a time, I reached Rose and Julia's door out of breath. I knocked and waited, but no one answered. I knocked a little harder, but they weren't there.

Would it be rude to back out, fake sickness, and send Sorin a plate? As I started down the stairs contemplating how I could get out of this awkward situation, he walked up from his apartment. His hair looked freshly cut and he carried a bouquet of wildflowers. I couldn't help but smile.

I put on an Al Jolson record and poured two glasses of boot-legged wine. I hoped the music and the alcohol might help me relax.

"Those are beautiful," I said, pointing to the flowers. "Peter won't be able to join us. I made so much food I thought I'd ask Julia and Rose to come, but they weren't there."

"They would not have eaten much anyway," he said.

"You're probably right."

We stood and stared at each other for a moment before turning away and studying various items around us so we wouldn't have to look directly at each other. I was horrified to think that Sorin might suspect I had finagled a dinner with just the two of us. I felt terribly awkward until the buzzer on the stove let me know the rice was ready. I ducked past him into the kitchen.

"Can I help you with anything?" he called.

"No, thank you. I'm just about ready."

While I put the rice and vegetables into bowls and set the table, I saw Sorin walk over to the piano and touch the sheet music. I returned to the kitchen to slice the chicken, and when I came back to the table with the platter, Sorin had my wedding picture in his hands. It startled me and I nearly dropped the plate of chicken. It landed on the table, rattling the cups and plates. He looked up.

I wiped my hands on my apron. "I'm sorry. I'm a little clumsy."

He held up the picture. His brows were furrowed.

"This is a beautiful picture," he said.

I knew I had to tell him something so he didn't think the worst about me.

"Thank you," I said. "My husband, Ben, fought in the war."

I wanted to explain, but I just couldn't find the words.

"But he did not come home," said Sorin. So simple.

"Yes," I said.

"Do you want to talk about it?" he asked.

I shook my head in the negative. Sorin placed the picture on the piano and walked over to me. He reached for my hands and I placed them in his. His palms were calloused and warm, and his face was open and kind.

"Thank you for inviting me here," he said.

I exhaled and felt relief filling me. The awkwardness left the room and our connection from his simple physical gesture put me at ease.

"It's my pleasure," I said.

He looked at the food and then back at me. I clung to his hands.

"Anna," he said.

"Yes?"

"I am starving."

I laughed and released his hands.

It gave me such pleasure to see Sorin enjoying the meal so much. He ate his first helping quickly and looked bashful about asking for seconds.

"Please," I said. "Eat it all. And I'm sending you home with what you don't eat now."

"Thank you," he said. "You are a good baker."

I smiled at him. "Thank you. It's nice to cook for someone else."

"You are alone much, yes?"

"Yes," I said. "Well, no. I have my work, and my family is close by."

"You are a nurse."

"Yes," I said. "I'm a psychiatric nurse."

"What is this psychiatric?"

"I help people who suffer from mental illness," I said, pointing at my forehead. "Schizophrenia, melancholia, other such ailments."

"Ah, yes, melancholia," he said. "Do you like the work?"

"I do, mostly," I said. "It's hard, though. In a regular hospital I could help patients heal from physical wounds. Wounds of the mind aren't so easy to fix."

"I can believe that," he said. "Why do you do it? This kind of nursing."

That was a hard question to answer without dragging in too many of my past hurts, but I tried. "After the war," I said, "I realized that some wounds are worse than those of the flesh. I wanted to help those people."

"I understand," he said.

A dog barked from somewhere outside on the street, and the bells of the cathedral rang the hour. When they finished, Sorin asked, "Your brother . . . Peter, is it? You are close to him."

"Yes, Peter. My difficult little brother." I couldn't help but smile.

"Do you fight?"

"We do battle a bit, yes," I said. "He knows how to set off my temper, but I still adore him. How about you? Do you have any brothers or sisters?"

It was Sorin's turn to smile. "Yes, I have two sisters and two brothers. I am the youngest."

"How old are you?" I asked.

"Twenty-five," he said.

I rolled my eyes. "So young!"

"How old are you?" he asked.

"It's not good form to ask a lady her age," I said, pretending offense.

"Surely a young lady like you does not mind a question like that," he said with a

214

devilish smile. I was tickled to see him acting playful.

"Surely," I said. "But I can't tell you everything the first time I have dinner with you."

"So there will be more times you have dinner with me?"

He held me still with his dark eyes and I felt the pressure return. He did not flinch in his gaze, but I looked down at my hands. It took a moment for me to find my voice.

"You have a nice big family," I said. "Is it hard for you to be away from them?"

He looked at me for a moment before he spoke but finally he answered.

"Yes," he said. "But my mother is a great lover of music. She wanted me to come here and study and make something of my life."

There, I thought. *A return to safe subjects.*

"You couldn't do that in Romania?" I asked.

"In other parts of Europe, maybe, but it is not good in my village," he said. "And my mother thinks I could be a world-famous musician."

"I think you could, too, from what I hear."

"I make a mess of noise here," he said. "You should hear me in concert sometime."

"I'd love to," I said.

"Would you play 'Anii' for me?" he said.

I was taken aback and felt myself blush.

"It is okay if you do not want to," he said. "But I have heard you, and you play beautifully. You do not have to be scared of anything with me." He spoke the last words quietly.

I didn't know what to say. The only man I'd played for in a private setting was Ben, and it had always aroused us both to distraction. I felt the heat rising on my neck when I thought of the way Ben would pull me onto his lap on the piano bench, or the way he'd run his hands over my hair and my back while I played until the last note hung in the air, and we wrapped ourselves in each other's arms while we'd stumble to the bedroom, if we could even make it that far. The music had become such a part of my intimacy with Ben, I didn't think I could share it with anyone else.

The music was not only about intimacy for me, either. It was about conjuring the past to remember and to heal. I'd learned from experience that playing old songs seemed to mend old wounds, but only with concentration. It was like prayer.

"I will play with you," he said, a note of pleading in his voice. "I have a melody I can add with my violin that will complete the song."

I met his eyes again and saw that he wanted this. In truth, I felt as if I owed him something from when he'd saved me. All the baking in the world wasn't what he wanted. It was the music.

I nodded and he broke into a smile and stood from the chair. "I will get my violin."

He was out the door in a flash. I sat at the table for a moment trying to steady my nerves, reassuring myself that it was just a song. Sorin couldn't know what playing meant to me. It would be okay.

I stood and cleared the plates, hoping the physical act of cleaning up dinner would soothe me and help me distance myself from my emotions. By the time Sorin returned, I had everything put away and felt in control of myself again.

"I am sorry," he said. "A string broke and I had to rethread it. You did not change your mind, did you?"

"No," I said.

"Good."

We walked over to the piano together and I sat, willing myself not to look at my wedding picture, and acutely aware of a feeling of darkness around me. I stared out the window and noticed the streetlights hadn't yet turned on. I reached for the lamp near the piano and pulled the chain, hoping to

217

chase off any troubled spirits with its glow.

Sorin sat on the right side of the bench, and his back grazed my arm. I could feel the heat coming off him and flinched. I glanced out of the corner of my eye at him and he nodded.

"Whenever you are ready," he said.

I took a deep breath and looked at the music, letting my fingertips rest on the keys that I was about to press. The keys were cold, and I left my fingers on them until I couldn't feel the separation of my skin and the instrument. Once we connected, I began to play.

Sorin did not play right away. He allowed me to work through the introduction for eight measures before he eased into the song. Then he began a high, slow vibrato that met the highest notes on the piano until it slipped into the lower register, resting between the lines of music, adding the final piece of what I hadn't even realized was missing from the song. The music was rich and layered, and I found myself lost in it. When it ended I looked at Sorin and his eyes were closed. He opened them and turned his face toward mine.

I couldn't describe the tangled feelings I had at that moment. I was aware of Ben in the picture, just inches away. I was hypnotized from the music. I watched Sorin place his violin and bow on the floor and felt his heat as he returned to my side on the bench. I thought how young he was as his face moved slowly toward me. And I was shocked by the sensation of his lips on mine.

Sorin gave me a soft, slow kiss and my body seemed separate from my mind, responding to him in spite of my confusion. His kiss was so unexpected it fascinated me. These feelings hadn't been tapped in so long it was like waking up after a long, cold hibernation. I felt his hands on the sides of my neck sliding back into my hair, and our kiss became more intense. I dared to open my eyes, and Sorin's were closed.

Suddenly the streetlights turned on and blazed through my window, illuminating the piano and shining on my wedding picture.

Sorin moved his lips off mine and started down my neck.

"Anna," he whispered, and my eyes found Ben in the picture.

I slid out of Sorin's hands, stood, and leaned, breathless, on the windowsill. Sorin looked like a drowning man who'd just lost his life preserver.

"Anna," he said. "I am sorry."

I put up my hand and shook my head. "No. Don't apologize."

My eyes returned to the picture and then to Sorin. He saw where I was looking and understood. He reached down, picked up his violin and bow, and stood.

"I should go," he said.

I didn't glance at him, but nodded and crossed my arms across my chest.

Sorin walked over to the door.

"Thank you for dinner," he said. "Good night, Anna."

He closed the door and left me in my apartment, alone.

Sixteen

I saw very little of Sorin in the coming weeks, which left me confused and frustrated. When he left that night I felt as if I would explode. As ridiculous as it sounds, I even felt something like anger at Ben for interfering. Like the coward I was, I ended up writing Sorin a note expressing how glad I was that he had come over and how much I had enjoyed the music. I apologized for the abrupt end to our dinner and asked that he tell me when his next concert was so I could hear him play.

He did not write back.

In the meantime, Zelda's novel, *Save Me the Waltz,* was released by Scribner's, and met with a lukewarm response. Scott had assumed an I-told-you-so air but seemed satisfied that at least she could not be crowned queen of his domain. It gave him a surge of confidence and a dictatorial place in the house regarding both Zelda's care and Scottie's rearing.

Under Scott's strict observation, Zelda became more and more unglued. Dr. Squires had left, and Zelda would no longer open up to Meyer during their weekly therapy sessions at Phipps. She had become hostile and unresponsive, and Meyer was finally finished with her during the session in which Zelda kept repeating over and over that the word *therapist* was actually *the rapist* when you spread out the letters.

Dr. Meyer assigned Zelda to a new doctor, Dr. Thomas Rennie, though Meyer would still consult. Rennie was a handsome young bachelor with whom Zelda bonded immediately. She began to dress well for her sessions and flirted shamelessly with the young man. He blushed and seemed a bit in awe of her celebrity, but overall, he was a good fit for her. He had empathy for her situation that allowed her to trust him, and she took great delight in teasing Scott about her new beau Rennie, as she liked to refer to him.

"Do you think Rennie'd be a two-er or a fiver?" she asked one fall afternoon while she and I walked under the autumn trees.

"Excuse me?" I asked.

"You know, how long the boys took to come back to me once I left them."

"Ah, yes, I'll have to think about that."

"I think he'd be a three-er," she said. "He has a look of the Trinity about him."

I smiled a little, amused at her bizarre yet arresting use of language.

We circled back to the house and found Scott on the front lawn throwing a football with Andrew while Scottie stood on the front porch reciting lines of poetry. She had tears running down her face, and Andrew was noticeably uncomfortable. We could hear Scott's voice as we drew closer.

"Again," said Scott, with all the emphasis of an army sergeant.

"Daddy, please," begged Scottie. "I can't stand it anymore."

"You will recite it again until it's perfect. Next time, get a better grade in speech and this won't be necessary."

"I got an A!" she cried.

"But only a ninety-seven percent," he said. "You can do better than that."

Zelda sighed loudly as we approached, and he looked at her with daggers in his eyes.

Scottie continued her recitations.

"Funny," whispered Zelda in my ear. "He was an appalling student."

When we got closer, Zelda called to Scott, "Is this really necessary? Girls should care

223

about parties and dresses and dance cards. You'll turn her into a damned spinster."

I cringed inwardly at Zelda's assessment of what should concern girls, but kept my mouth shut.

"A lot of good that did you," he said. "You're nothing but a lapel decoration that's lost its bloom."

Zelda's face turned pale. I could not contain my anger.

"How could you say such a thing to your wife in the presence of your own daughter?" I said.

Andrew looked from me, to Zelda, to Scott and then took off running down the path to his house. Scottie stared at all of us with a dark, unreadable expression. Scott slammed the football to the ground.

"How am I wrong?" he asked. "Tell me."

"You are wrong to abuse her, especially when she's vulnerable," I said.

"But I am not wrong," he said. "It is you who encourages us to speak the truth, but I think you'll agree that it is not always best."

He turned back to his daughter. "Again!"

Scottie looked from her father to her mother and back to her father. She began to recite the poem with a full, clear voice, all trace of tears gone.

■ ■ ■ ■

A curious calm settled over Zelda at the start of winter. Preceding her argument with Scott about her "usefulness" as a woman, she'd become so unwound that she would no longer write about her past for me. She also wouldn't speak of her past, and had difficulty sustaining any conversation. But strangely, since the fight Zelda had stopped trying to interact with her husband and seemed to accept that they would never again see eye to eye.

As she gained strength from the distance she placed between herself and Scott, he deteriorated more and more. He relapsed shortly after drying out at Hopkins, and his drinking was worse than ever. They'd been through several maids and cooks because he'd corner them, recounting all sorts of inappropriate stories from his youth with Zelda, and ask the poor, shaken women questions too personal in nature. Like me, his secretary, Isabel, remained in their service. She, too, seemed attached to the family, and practically speaking, regular pay in such a burdened economy was not to be taken lightly. Isabel helped him meet dead-lines, typed and retyped his work, paid bills to creditors before they took action, and was kind and nurturing to Scottie.

In December, Scott had to again return to Hopkins for help with his drinking. He dried out for a few weeks, but was soon back home to poor habits, insomnia, and generally disruptive behavior. We avoided him as much as possible by staying in the little hobby room upstairs, where Zelda worked on a set of paper dolls for Scottie.

Zelda spent hours hunched over the dolls — the little Fitzgeralds — decorating them with rich detail and color and cutting them to perfect precision, as if she were trying to remake her own family. Rubbing her strained eyes, which hurt from the effort, but continuing on, Zelda poured herself into the dolls as an expression of her deep but often inexpressible love for the child. I hoped that one day Scottie would recognize these exquisite and unique works of art for what they were.

I was there the day Zelda presented the dolls to Scottie. Scottie's face lit with such pure and absolute delight that I had to struggle to hold back my tears. Scottie hugged Zelda and gave her the sweetest and most heartfelt thanks, making me ache for my own daughter, inspiring me later that night to dig out my photographs of Katie and place them around my apartment, hidden no more. My relief was profound.

When Zelda finished the dolls, she began another writing project.

"What's this one?" I asked.

"I'm calling it *Scandalabra*," she said. "It's a play. If he doesn't want me to write novels I will write a play."

If nothing else I admired her dogged stubbornness and determination to express herself.

"Do you feel up to writing for me?" I asked.

She continued to write, and nodded her head. "Yes, I think I'm ready again."

"Good," I said.

"But only if you tell me first."

"Tell you what?"

"About your husband."

Fair enough, I thought.

She put down her pencil and reached for my hands.

"I don't know you, Anna, and you know me inside and out."

I looked down at my hands.

"It's not that I want to keep things from you," I said. "It's just that psychiatric nurses are trained to separate our emotional lives from our patients' so they don't get confused. Dr. Meyer would agree. We should not burden the patient in any way. You don't need any of my baggage weighing you down."

"To hell with Dr. Meyer and all of them," said Zelda. "We aren't in a clinical setting anymore. You are a part of my life, whether you like it or not. You are more my friend than my nurse. You have to treat me like a friend."

And our lives are connected, I thought. *Inextricably.*

"Very well," I said.

"Let's go outside," she said. "It's so tight in here. It might help your words if they can breathe the fresh air."

I nodded. *Yes, that would help.*

The grounds of La Paix were covered in a light dusting of snow. The ground crunched under our boots, and we walked arm in arm under the naked deciduous trees by the frozen reservoir and empty tennis courts, our breath mingling in steamy clouds around our heads.

"It was cold like this at the base hospital in France the day I lost him," I began. But no, that wasn't the right place to start. I needed to start here, in Baltimore, in the fall of 1917, when all the young men went to war and I worked as a nurse at Walter

Reed General Hospital.

"No, let me start at the beginning," I said.

Zelda stayed quiet, seemingly allowing me space to gather my thoughts, build my story, figure out the parts I wanted to tell, the important parts, the ones I could speak.

"I always knew I wanted to be a nurse. I never flinched from patching hurt animals or wounded little brothers. While I trained, the world was at war, and America teetered on the brink, so after nurse training school, I worked at Walter Reed so I could serve my country.

"One of my favorite patients, Will, was a doughboy wounded in his first battle in France. He was recovering from several shots to his leg, but he'd be all right. Every day he told me about his fiancée, when they'd get married, and to stop loving him so much because he was taken. I'd tease him and tell him that with his baby blue eyes and blond crew cut, he was too young to get married and might be mistaken for the ring bearer.

"I was more outgoing then," I said, "having never experienced a single heartache aside from watching my mother grieve a couple of miscarriages. I flirted with him and all of my patients, and I was a general favorite."

"Still are," said Zelda.

"Thank you," I said. "Anyway, one day I pulled back the curtain and said, 'Is today the day you're willing to throw your girl over so we can get married?' as I did every day, and this man with a huge grin that gave me butterflies in my stomach stood at Will's side. 'I don't know about Will,' said the soldier, 'but I'd sure love to.' Well, I was just as red as a rose, but I gave him my best 'get in line' line and tended to Will, while trying to pretend that the soldier with the crinkled eyes and tanned skin and mischievous smile wasn't in the room laughing behind me and heating me up from two feet away.

"I soon found out that man's name was Benjamin Howard and he was two months away from shipping out. He and Will were best friends and had grown up in southern Maryland. They couldn't wait to get back to the farms and waterways after the war. He hung around Will and me like a fly, but it wasn't until an autumn dance that I fell in love."

"Oh, how romantic," said Zelda. "Keep going."

"Ben had been asking me out for weeks and I kept saying no. I didn't want to get all wrapped up with a man about to be sent to his death, though I didn't tell him that. But he continued to come every day. One morning in late November, Ben showed up with a bouquet of calla lilies and a smile that fully cracked through the wall I'd put up between us, and I surrendered.

" 'One date,' I'd told him, and he was over the moon. I tried not to let on that I was, too, but later, he told me that he knew I loved him long before I admitted it to myself.

"That night was magical. An early snow fell. Young men in uniforms, young women with shiny eyes and hearts swollen with love for them and their country, the wartime energy pulsing off all of us. After the dance, we walked along the Baltimore Harbor holding hands and watching the snowflakes dissolve into the glassy black water. We stared at each other for a long time with all the world spinning around us but barely there until he finally said, 'Anna, may I kiss you?' I smiled at him in encouragement and felt his mouth on mine, and knew without a doubt that it wouldn't be just one date. That these were the only lips I'd kiss forever."

"Oh, how wonderful," said Zelda. "To feel such certainty. I've never felt certainty about anything in my life, except Al Jolson's music and tomato sandwiches."

We had a good laugh over that one as we

231

crossed a snow-sprinkled field, leaving boot tracks behind us.

"So we began our happily ever after," I continued. "We fell head over heels in love, spent as much time together as possible, married at a little church north of Baltimore barely a month after we'd met, had a small reception at my parents' place in Towson, and spent our first night together at the Belvedere Hotel."

"Then he shipped out on a boat made of newspaper and sank," she said.

"No, we had more time together."

"Thank God. Tell me more."

"General Pershing was pushing hard for nurses for war field hospitals. I couldn't stand being away from Ben and thought that if we were at least on the same continent we'd get to see each other again. I had a hell of a time getting approval, because they wanted nurses who were at least twenty-five and I was only twenty-one. My supervisor was able to pull strings, though, because I'd already graduated nurse training school and because I worked at Walter Reed.

"In Ben's letters, he begged me not to come. Having seen the horrors of war, albeit briefly, Will pleaded with me not to go. My poor mother and father were a wreck because my brother had enlisted and had also shipped out to fight, but I told them all about love and duty, and they understood."

The pines and red cedars muted the day and surrounded Zelda and me in cold shadows as we walked through the forest that led to the Turnbull house on the grounds of La Paix. We moved closer together on the path for warmth and for comfort in the chilly air.

"After the long trip overseas, my team of nurses reached France and turned an old hotel into an evacuation hospital. I was unprepared for the horrors I would come to know, but I'd achieved my goal. Later that year, Ben and I were able to coordinate our leave to visit the French Riviera, which became our belated honeymoon."

Zelda stiffened a bit and I looked at her profile.

"Do you want to hear more," I asked, "or have you had enough?"

"More," she said. "But speak quietly, because I can feel his breath on my neck."

I felt shivers on my arms and stopped walking. Behind us, the path was shadowed and strange.

"Who?"

"Scott," she said. "Do you hear him? Coming from the knob in that tree? It's like

233

he's speaking on a microphone."

The voices. It was never a good sign when she heard voices, and though I knew what she said was impossible, her surety was unsettling.

"Let's turn back," I said.

"No," she said. "I can't stand to go to that house until supper. Finish."

I hesitated, worried that we'd get stuck outside in the dark and that Scott would grow angry. I could also feel the cold in my bones, and I was weary from sharing so much about Ben.

"Zelda, please can we head back?" I said. "I promise to keep speaking, but I'm so cold and tired."

She did not reply, but allowed me to turn toward La Paix. She hung behind a little, but I urged her forward, and soon we were walking in step on our way back to the house.

"The time away on the Riviera made me half-mad," I said, threading my arm through hers. "Rather than restore me for a return to the front, leave left me restless, skittish, and fearful. I indulged in runaway fantasies that I started speaking out loud to Ben. At first he humored me, but then he told me to stop. That he would never step away from his duty. We had terrible quarrels. He knew he had to stay and see the fighting through, especially when friends of his with children were doing so. I told him he'd given enough and what about his duty to me. He urged me to return home, but I told him we were a package deal. He didn't like it, but he went back. And we stayed on.

"The fall of 1918 was brutal. The miserable cold rain, the muddy trenches, gassed soldiers, influenza — it was hell on earth, but every day that I didn't receive a report that he'd died I counted as a good day. His letters were becoming increasingly erratic and troubling. He seemed to lose his hope and his good cheer, and in the last letter he sent to me, he apologized for keeping us in the war. He wrote that he had been horribly wrong and that he lived in hell for it, and that if it weren't for his men he'd flee and take me with him. Those were dangerous words to put in writing."

We stepped out of the woods and walked back over the field as the sun set. The temperature seemed to have dropped ten degrees since we'd started out. I felt my voice stuck in my throat and wished I could stop speaking. But I kept on because I wanted more from Zelda, and I owed this to her.

"His unit fought at Argonne, where thousands died. The armistice was signed at five in the morning on a train on November eleventh of 1918. I waited for him at the base hospital for weeks, but I never heard from him again. No one did. I received an MIA letter that December. They've never found him."

"No," said Zelda. She stopped walking. "To this day?"

"Never." I shook my head. "Ben and more than one hundred thousand others. Lost."

"My God." She placed her hand over her mouth. "How can that be?"

"Massive explosions. The nature of modern warfare."

Zelda trembled against me. I decided that I would not speak of my pregnancy at the time of his disappearance. That would remain my secret, at least for now. So would the five years of heaven on earth I had with that little angel, Katie, who tied me to Ben until pneumonia took her from me.

"And here I am," said Zelda, "complaining about my husband and egging him on and distracting him like a damned fly when you'd give anything to find yours, either alive and upright or in a grave, so you could finally get some rest."

I flinched.

"Wait," she said, "he could still be alive.

Did he flee? Is it possible?"

"I've always thought so," I said, suddenly unafraid to speak my deepest hopes to this woman who would not judge me, the only person who would not judge me for my foolish hope. "I never felt the air change the way it would have if he no longer occupied this earth. I interviewed every man left alive and found in his platoon. He was loved by all as the bravest soldier, and yet no one can remember seeing him after he crossed a little peasant bridge. It was as if he vanished into thin air."

"Have you been to the bridge?"

"Of course," I said. "My poor brother, Peter, went with me six times. Six times we combed the landscape there. We knocked on doors. Followed dead leads. Sifted through wards of mumbling, incoherent, shell-shocked soldiers. But we never found him.

"I wrote to Will while I searched in Europe, but he wouldn't accept that Ben was missing. I saw him once, after the war. He visited me at my parents' house, and cried in my arms for an hour. I never saw a man cry like that. That was the last time I ever saw him."

We arrived back at the house as the final light left the sky, and Zelda stopped me on the porch stairs.

"Thank you for telling me everything," she said.

I nodded, feeling a bit guilty about the large part of the story I'd left out, but sure Zelda should not know it. At least not now.

"I'll write for you this weekend," she said. "I'll write to you about the mansion in Delaware where we used to live, after Scott made love to that vapid young actress and put a stake through my heart."

Lincoln was in the driveway, right on schedule. I gathered my things and embraced Zelda, and as I pulled away from La Paix, I saw Zelda's dark form on the front porch, a specter in a troubled house, a wilted lapel flower.

I was startled by Lincoln's furrowed brow. He had nodded his head and pulled away from La Paix without speaking. He was rarely serious, but I reflected that since our night at the theater he hadn't said much at all. I tried to make small talk, but it wasn't getting me much more than grunts and mumbles. Finally, he spoke.

"I need to talk to you, Anna."

"Yes, sir, this sounds quite serious, sir," I said.

"It is," he said. "I'm worried about you at

that writer's place."

I smiled at him from the backseat.

"You are kind to think of me," I said, "but everything's okay. I know I made a mistake by taking her to the ballet that night, but I sure won't do that again."

"That's part of it," he said, "but not all."

"What do you mean?"

He rubbed his neck and turned his eyes back to the road.

"You just spend so much time there. You left your job at Hopkins. You've missed your parents' house a couple of times — not that I'm judging, mind you, I've just never seen you do that before."

I fixed my gaze out the window and felt my defenses rise. I didn't appreciate Lincoln's judgment. I needed a taxi driver, not a therapist.

"And you seem tired, Anna. Tired to your bones —"

"That's enough," I said.

I caught his eye in the mirror again, and his forehead was creased with worry. I turned away in my seat and didn't look at him or speak a word for the rest of the ride. My feelings alternated between anger at his interference, guilt that I'd snapped at him, and the little nagging thought I kept swatting away that he might be right.

The taxi ride seemed to take ten times longer than usual, and a cold rain started as soon as we pulled up to my parents' driveway. I dropped Lincoln's fare into the front seat, jumped out of the car before he had a chance to open my door, and started up the long driveway, cursing myself for forgetting my umbrella. Lincoln was shortly at my side with his umbrella over the two of us, and I felt awful for the way I'd behaved. When I tried to apologize he put up his hand.

"Anna, I love you like a daughter, and I have a daughter, so I know all about moods and things. You're not going to get rid of me with one tantrum."

I was embarrassed to feel tears in my eyes, and I tried to smile at him.

"Now go see your parents and take care of yourself this weekend," he said. "Just do me a favor: Try to leave that other life behind you to get a little rest while you're up here."

I nodded. "I think I can do that."

"Good girl."

He deposited me at the front door, kissed my head, and left.

Mom was tired and spent much of the weekend resting in bed. She said the cold weather and early dark made her feel worse

240

than usual. I worried, not for the first time, that my father might need more help here with her. He always swatted my queries away, but I could foresee that soon the tides would turn.

How would I split my time? I had to be here when they needed me, but my job with Zelda had taken over my life. I started to obsess about why I had let it consume me. Was it because I'd been so alone and needed to feel useful? Or was it because of a more sinister issue: their fame? I hated to admit that I could let such a thing influence my attention to a patient and her family, but the idea nagged at me. I reminded myself that I'd always had a hard time separating work and life, that I'd spent nights in the hospital with patients who had needed me at Walter Reed, at the field hospital, at Phipps, and I'd certainly never before taken care of anyone famous.

Recalling Lincoln's words about leaving my life in the city behind, however, gave me permission to stop thinking about Zelda and focus on my family and myself. The quiet of the woods was a balm, and the hours my mother spent resting gave me time to spend with my father in the barn.

Saturday afternoon he got a fire going in the stove and cut the copper tubes for his wind chimes while I wired them to cedar blocks. We wore fingerless gloves and sipped coffee while we worked, and didn't say much of anything. My dad wasn't one for long speeches; he let his presence and our actions do the talking. Even as a girl, I'd learned lessons at his side: how shapeless, ugly things like metal could be pounded and soldered to make beautiful music; how it took patience to find the right tubes for the tones that would harmonize best together; how concentrating on the act of creating something with my hands could heal troubles in my heart; how the pretty things we made would hang from others' back porches and trees and bring them some sort of release.

Zelda tried to wiggle into my thoughts, but I pushed her out. I gave my energy only to what was around me.

When I sat at the dinner table that night, I felt restored. The crisp air had cleared out my lungs, my fingertips had a pleasant soreness from the wire, and the wind from my walk by the woods had put a little color in my cheeks. My mother remarked on my improvement.

"You look so fresh and lovely," she said. "I think being here did you good."

"I think it did, too," I said. "I'm sorry I've

242

let some time go between visits. I'm a little caught up with the Fitzgeralds, I must confess."

"I can see how demanding they are of your attention," said Mom, "but you've always been that way. A caretaker. It's why you became a nurse in the first place."

"I suppose you're right," I said. I took a bite of the pumpkin pie my mother had made and it nearly melted on my tongue.

"Just make sure you come up for air every now and then," she said. "Don't be afraid to set boundaries."

Boundaries. Dividing lines. Therapy with Zelda didn't work that way. It was all or nothing. In or out. And I didn't want the boundaries, truth be told. I received satisfaction from small successes with her. I felt as if I was fulfilling my purpose when I was with her, and I didn't want to think of what would happen when I couldn't help her anymore: if she'd get sent away if the money ran out. I could only focus on the days in front of me and hope they stretched long into the future, where we could untangle her knots, strike the right chord, and wire her together so she'd work as intended.

Seventeen

Ellerslie: 1927

A one-act play illustrating the effects of cheap Hollywood romance, and how violence breaks more than just a nose.

PROLOGUE:

The location of this house is in Delaware, but it could be any haunted old estate where people live beyond their means trying to destroy one another with lovers and parties and alcohol, and where the day moves from morning to afternoon to twilight to night and back again faster than in other places in the world.

When we meet our friends there is a party with many drunks and fancy people. Of special notice are the following characters: ACTRESS, a hollow young Hollywood sort who tries to convey innocence through wide eyes and white dresses while she's dirty as a harlot in her panties. A washed-up WRITER who can't stop drinking long enough to produce anything but rapturous adoration from ACTRESS. CHILD whom everyone forgets about and who wanders the rooms talking to herself. And DANCER trying to make meaning of the music in large mirrors and pale pink dance clothes.

Bootlegged records of Negro music play, while a thunderstorm rages outside that has sent the guests indoors to disturb the calm of the house and the balance of DANCER.

ACTRESS: (*Placing her hand on the arm of washed-up WRITER*) I can see how you are unable to write with all of this distraction. If I had a secret tree house, I'd hide you up there with your typewriter and guard you so you could write and the world could read the words it wants from you.

WRITER: (*Draining his fifth glass of wine*) I wish I'd married you. You understand me and the importance of what I do. And you . . . what you do with your roles. America's a better place because of what you show them when you act.

DANCER: You forget, dear, that she was still pissing in her diapers when you married, so that wouldn't have worked.

WRITER: Yes, and she was already ambitious and thoughtful as a child and has filled her life with work and purpose before she's even reached the age of others when they were jumping in fountains and showing their knickers on New York tabletops to any dandy who'd buy her a champagne cocktail.

DANCER: I would still show my knickers for a champagne cocktail if the right dandy offered.

DANDY: What's this you say? Lift up your tutu, beautiful dancer, and show us what you've got.

DANCER lifts her skirt to the applause and enthusiasm of the assembly, while ACTRESS covers her eyes and runs from the room, offended by the boldness of

DANCER. CHILD looks on, trying to make sense of the scene, but before she can find it, NANNY drags her up the stairs to her room, where the ghosts of the house will scare her to hysterics all night with the storm and the party noise.

DANCER: But where has Writer gone?

DANDY: He's there, scribbling at the large living room table, writing down all you do so he can have it instead of you.

DANCER: Did you get it all, Writer? Do you have enough material or shall I perform more?

WRITER: If you could just do the part again where you lift your skirts, I could have the material I need.

DANCER: What kind of third rate are you to need repeats? If you can't keep up it's your loss.

WRITER becomes enraged and throws DANCER's favorite vase — colored like the sky at twilight's epilogue — right into the fireplace. DANCER says she wishes he would die. WRITER begins weeping like a child.

DANCER: Shall we call your mick cop of a father to mediate, or shall I ask Actress to bring us a burp cloth to dab at your baby tears?

WRITER jumps up from the table and strikes DANCER across the face. The party gasps and blows away into the night and the storm. DANCER feels the blood leaking out of her nose as it mingles with the perspiration from her practice. She wipes the blood away and watches it blur in the sweat on her arm, giving color to her skin from the outside in.

CURTAIN

June 1933
My mother's hair danced in the breeze that moved through the wind shed. Her eyes were closed and she wore a grimace of pain on her brow while a smile played at her lips. I watched her and made a mental portrait of her under the wind chimes.

"Please take Zelda a set," she said. "They have healing powers."

"I will," I said. "I'd thought of bringing

her here, but after that awful night at the opera I'll never do that again."

"Poor Anna. I'm so sorry to hear about that."

"And after last Sunday I don't know if the Fitzgeralds can ever be repaired."

"What happened?"

"Scott had Dr. Rennie to the house so Scott could 'document' his grievances and instruct Zelda to stop writing. No understanding, no empathy, no love. Only bitterness."

A crow flew by the barn door and rested in a nearby tree, making a noisy production of its presence.

"My God, if you had been there," I continued. "If you had heard the terrible things Scott said to Zelda, you would have struck him. I wanted to strike him."

"Was it that bad?"

"Worse than that bad," I said. "Hours of listening to him belittle her, boast about himself, indulge in a tantrum about her writing."

"What was the outcome?"

"They want to divorce each other. And Zelda no longer wants to live with him."

"Is there any hope at all?"

"I really don't know."

For the first time, I began to think that

Scott and Zelda should be separated. Not just because of how Scott put down Zelda for her faded beauty or failed attempts at ballet or writing, but because she was his cancer, too. She taunted him and tortured him every chance she got, was inconsistent in her relationship with her daughter, and sadly, was spending more and more time in her inner world than in the real world.

Days would pass without a coherent conversation between the two of us; then suddenly, it was as if she'd returned from a vacation. It was hard keeping up with her, and even in the best moments, I always felt as if we were at the threshold of disaster.

We heard a noise on the path and my father entered the wind shed. He walked over the dirt floor and kissed my mother on the cheek.

"You are beautiful," he said to her. My heart melted.

She smiled. "Clearly, your sight is failing. Any goodies in the mail?"

He waved off her comment and thumbed through the letters he'd just picked up from the post office.

"Mostly bills," he said. "But something for Anna."

"Me?"

"Yes. From a Will Brennan."

"Will," I said. My hospital Will. Ben's friend. My partner in grief. I took the letter.

"Who's Will?" asked Mom.

"He was Ben's best friend," I said.

"Oh, yes," she said. "Now I remember. The boy with the limp who wept for Ben."

"Yes, the boy with the limp who wept for Ben after I told him about the MIA letter."

I'm sorry to inform you that Sgt. Benjamin Howard went missing on or near the Argonne forest. All attempts have been made at rescue, but we are unable to locate any trace of him. We will keep you abreast of any discoveries made pertaining to his case.

When I had written to Will to tell him about the MIA letter, he'd written back the saddest note I'd ever received. He said it felt as if he had lost a brother. They'd grown up together. They wanted to marry girls and move home. Raise their kids. Then Will came to visit me here, saw Katie, who was still a baby, and broke down. His grief had deepened my own. A sharp pain went through my heart and I closed my eyes.

"I'm going to take a walk," I said.

I left the shed holding the letter, curious to see what it said. Will and I had corresponded for several months following the day he'd visited. He had married and was back in Solomons, Maryland. He managed

251

his father's farm and a general store but had said that the town had lost so much for him now that Ben wasn't there. After a while, I had stopped answering his letters. He always brought up Ben while I was trying to heal, and reminded me too much of what I'd lost.

But now, years later, things were different.

I opened the letter once I hit the path to the woods, eager to receive his news, and unafraid of any references to Ben.

June 1, 1933

Dear Anna,

I know it's been a long while since we've been in contact, but I found myself thinking of you when I read a piece in the paper about Walter Reed Hospital. I love remembering that time when Ben and I hung around playing cards, full of carelessness and confidence, and when you and Ben fell in love. It was a beautiful thing to watch and be a part of, and I will always cherish that time in my life.

I'm still in southern Maryland, running the farm and store for my dad and writing a column for the local paper. I hope you received my card when I heard about Katie all those years ago. I'm sorry as hell for your loss. I don't have any kids, myself, so I can't imagine what you went through. I lost my mom a little while after the war, but I know that doesn't compare.

Anyway, I pray that you're in good health and doing well. I'd love to hear from you if you get a chance.

Sincerely,
Will

I smiled at the thought of our card games on Will's hospital bed, with Ben teasing Will about his phantom fiancée and the two of them teasing me to death about everything. I wondered about Will's wife and about his life in the quiet town where he and Ben had been raised.

I decided I'd send him a letter when I got home from my parents' house, and update him on my life and my work. My letter would be sadly brief. I needed to actually live more to call it a life.

When I returned home after the weekend, Sorin saw me through the window. We'd been waving politely for months, but I couldn't stand how we'd left things that night, and wished to make amends with him. I knocked on his door before I could change my mind, and he invited me in.

The first thing I noticed about his apartment was how clean it was. There were no papers strewn about the floor. The walls were bare. No empty cups littered the table. Three boxes were stacked near the couch. He followed my gaze.

"I am leaving," he said.

Was he leaving because of me? How had I let so much time pass without coming to him to assure him it wasn't his fault?

"Why?" I asked.

"I graduated," he said.

Of course. The ballerinas had left late last week.

"Congratulations," I said. "Are you returning to Romania?"

"No," he said. "I am off to New York to audition for the New York Philharmonic."

"I'm so happy for you," I said. "And I'm sad I haven't heard you play with the orchestra."

"I did not think you would really want to," he said. "After that night."

I don't think I could have felt any worse than I did at that moment. He looked pained, too.

"Sorin," I said, "I need to apologize to you."

"No," he said. "I should not have done that to you. After your attack. With your husband's picture."

"Stop," I said. "You did everything right. That dinner with you. That kiss."

I blushed, but I continued, determined to assure him.

"You reawakened something in me," I said.

Now it was his turn to blush.

"I wish there could have been more. It was my fault, not yours. I realized how young you were and felt my husband looming over us."

"But, Anna, he has passed on," said Sorin.

"Probably," I said. "But all I have is a piece of paper that says he's missing and he was never found. And he is a part of me and I've never felt that part of me lose its grip the way I would if he was really dead. So I still feel married, and that isn't fair to you. He's always there."

Sorin looked at his feet. "I see."

"I know I'm foolish," I said. "I can't explain it, and I haven't been able to get over it after all these years. I'm held prisoner by the idea that he's just missing and not dead."

"I am very sorry for you," he said. "You deserve someone, Anna."

"And you deserve someone who can give you every part of herself."

I reached for his hands and he took mine. I pulled him closer to me.

"But you helped me, Sorin. You wrote that song in which my name means *helper,* but it is you who shook something loose in me. You gave me healing that night, and I'll never forget you."

He lifted one of my hands to his lips and kissed it. I had to will myself not to step toward him and kiss him, but I knew I had to let him go. Instead, I wrapped my arms around him and held him until he pulled away and kissed my forehead.

I played his song over and over that night. I hoped he heard and understood how very much I meant what I had said to him.

Eighteen

It was only eight o'clock in the morning and the heat was nearly unbearable. Maryland gave us only two weeks of spring that year and jumped mercilessly into a humid Southern summer. As I stepped off the bus and wiped my forehead, I thought Zelda would probably want to swim today and that I'd tell Scottie to join her mother. I was always looking for ways to bring them together.

I had packed a set of wind chimes for Zelda and was eager to give it to her. I knew she'd love the gift. I just hoped we'd get a little wind to stir their music. The air was so thick and still. A fly landed on my leg and bit me, as if to emphasize my musings. As I reached down to slap it, the sound of a fire truck siren called me from my thoughts. It got nearer and nearer until it slowed to turn down La Paix Lane. I jumped out of the road so I wouldn't get run over and soon saw another truck racing in behind the first.

As the smell of the smoke hit me, I felt a sudden panic in my heart. With only a few houses on the lane there was a very good chance that there was trouble at the Fitzgeralds' place.

Zelda.

I began to run up the side of the lane and was horrified to see my worst fears confirmed. The house was on fire. The upper floor that held Zelda's hobby room was throwing flames out its window like a roaring furnace.

"Zelda!"

When I got to the front lawn I saw Scott running in and out of the house in his bathrobe, throwing furniture and paintings onto the front yard, while neighbors helped remove as much as they could get their hands on. Scottie, Andrew, and several other children stood at a safe distance, staring at the house in shock. I could not see Zelda anywhere, and threw my belongings on the ground. The violent clang of the chimes in the dirt followed me as I nearly collided with Scott.

"Zelda," I said, "where is she?"

He gave a sharp gesture down the back lawn near the garden and pulled me away from the house.

"She started it," he said.

I put my hands to my mouth. "No. On purpose?"

"She says she was burning the past in the fireplace," he said, his voice quavering. He placed his hand on his forehead and suddenly lost all of the color from his face. I helped him to sit on the front lawn while the firefighters attacked the blaze. Smoke began to billow out of the house.

"She will be the death of me, Anna," he said.

I could not disagree with him.

"Were you able to get out your manuscript papers?" I asked.

"Yes." He pointed to the messy stacks near us, damp from the morning dew.

"Shall I get you some water from the Turnbulls' house?"

"No," he said. "Just see to her."

I looked him in the eyes and put my hand on his shoulder. His pallor was so ghastly he looked like he needed to return to the hospital. Suddenly I saw Zelda. She stumbled toward us, her eyes on the house and red rimmed from crying, alternating between laughing gasps and wails. When she reached us, she collapsed at Scott's side, throwing herself into him. I was surprised to see him wrap his arms around her and put his lips in her hair. He had no fight left in him.

"I'm so sorry, Goofo," she said. "So very sorry. I am a fool. I will be the death of us."

He gave an ironic laugh and wiped his eyes with his free arm.

We stayed there watching the men extinguish the fire amidst a wreck of charred furniture and papers, paintings, and trunks. It looked as if the lower floor of the house would be okay, but the upper floors were blackened and exposed. Scott stood, straightened his bathrobe, and lit a cigarette. Zelda sat on the nearest chair. A small crowd had gathered, including the Turnbulls, the family who had rented La Paix to the Fitzgeralds.

"We'll take care of this," said Scott.

Mrs. Turnbull shook her head, dumbfounded, as a car pulled up carrying a newspaper reporter. I was shocked at how quickly the news had traveled. The reporter went immediately to the famous couple, eager to add this story to the volumes of legend surrounding the retired flapper and the alcoholic writer. Scott spoke to him while Zelda looked on, her face a mixture of adoration and remorse.

I saw the flash of the reporter's camera go off, and noticed the wilted feathers of

Zelda's blue ostrich feather fan in the wet grass.

I slipped over a puddle that had grown on the spotted wooden floors of the foyer of La Paix and grabbed the banister to steady myself. When I pulled my hand away it was covered with black soot. The wet, charred smell was unbearable, and I couldn't believe that Scott had negotiated another month of rent to stay in the house so he could finish his novel.

There was a lot I would never understand about writers.

The sounds of Zelda's opera music moaned from a nearby room, and I could hear Scott's voice dictating dialogue aloud from his study down the hall, while Isabel typed furiously to keep up with him.

The thunder rumbled outside, and the whole house was so impossibly gloomy I felt as if I could cry.

Poor Scottie.

I walked through the back door of the kitchen toward the sound of the wind chimes, which played an especially melancholy tune in the quickening air. I saw Scottie's silhouette on the lawn watching the approaching storm. She looked so small and alone. I decided to take matters into my own hands.

"Scottie," I said.

She turned to me and her face lit with a smile that tugged my heart. I didn't think I'd ever seen such a lovely child, and thought, not for the first time, that she deserved better.

"Hello, Nurse Anna," she said, followed by a little cough. Her poor lungs must have been lined in ashes.

I stood next to her and placed my arm around her side.

"Would it be okay with you if I asked your parents if you could stay with a friend for a while?" I asked.

I saw a flicker of relief and longing pass over her face, and then she rearranged her features.

"Oh, yes, please," she said. "Daddy is so busy with his novel, and Mother is . . . Mother, so maybe I could stay with my friend Peaches."

"Why don't you go ahead and pack some things, and I'll speak to your father and make some calls."

"Should I wait to see if he says it's okay?"

"I'm sure it will be okay."

She gave me a hug and skipped indoors as thunder rumbled over the reservoir.

■ ■ ■ ■

I stood in the driveway and waved at Scottie as her friend's father drove away. A blast of hot wind on my face warned me that the coming storm would be severe, so I picked up the mail and turned back to the house. When I looked up, there was a dark form in the front room window, but it disappeared. It was probably Zelda lurking and watching: two of her recent unsettling habits. In spite of the summer's heat, I rubbed away a chill on my arms.

Once I shut the front door behind me, I felt the isolation press into me. With Scottie gone, all the light had left the house, and I felt her absence acutely. It was difficult watching a child become lost in the shuffle of her parents' misery. I found myself wanting to hug her, talk to her, brush her hair. She was remarkably independent, however, and I reminded myself that my place in the house was at her mother's side. After all, Zelda needed the attention just as much as Scottie did.

A flash of lightning lit Zelda's form as she crept up the top half of the split staircase.

"Zelda, come down," I said. How many times had I reprimanded her to stay away from the charred upper floors? Half of the hall looked as if it would collapse.

When she did not respond, I walked over to the staircase and started to climb after her. When I reached the top, I peered down what was left of the hallway, but did not see her.

"Zelda," I called. "Come here at once."

I heard a creak on the stairs below me, and looked back over my shoulder. I was horror-struck to see Zelda staring up at me.

"Who are you talking to, Anna?" she asked with the voice of an insolent child.

I felt my heart race. I was certain I'd just seen her go up the stairs. I looked down the hallway again and saw nothing, but had the worst feeling of dread. When I looked back at Zelda, she was smiling at me in the most unnatural way. I slowly turned and started down the stairs, and when I reached the small landing at the bottom, I stood eye to eye with her.

Lightning crashed and rain began to pelt the front of the house. I looked past her out the windows and saw trees bent in the storm, and leaves blowing in the wind. When I looked back at Zelda she was not smiling, but rather had a look of fear on her face as she stared up at the second floor. She laced her arm though mine and pulled me into the front room.

"This is a bad house," she said.

I felt inclined to agree with her at the moment and desired to break the spell the storm had cast. I pulled free from her claw-like grip to turn on the parlor lights.

"That's better," I said, still on edge.

It was then that I realized I still held the mail in my hands. I looked down to see whether there were any envelopes for Zelda before giving the rest of the pile to Isabel. Near the bottom of the stack I found a letter from Zelda's mother, Minnie Sayre.

"Can you read it to me?" said Zelda as she rubbed her eyes, which had been giving her more trouble than usual. She had to take frequent rests from reading because of how poor her sight had become.

"Certainly," I said.

July 14, 1933

My Dearest Zelda,
I received your letter, my dear, and though I'm sorry to hear the reading of your play was not as much of a success as you'd hoped, I'm proud of you for writing a whole play all by yourself, and you should be, too. I'm glad to hear that Scott invited so many of your friends

down to see it. He must have thought highly of it to do so.

I do have some sad news to report. It seems your brother, Anthony, is not well. His nerves are under some strain and his mind isn't quite right. I'm sure it's because he hasn't been sharing as much with me as he should. I could help you children if you would just confide in me. It would make everything okay.

Anthony is getting treatment in Asheville. I hope he is well by the autumn so you can possibly come for a visit. He writes of you often and wishes to see you, as do I.

I'll write you once he's well. I hope you are taking rest for yourself, dear, and not overdoing anything.

Your Loving Mother . . .

Scott walked into the room while I read. When I finished, I looked from him to Zelda. She spoke first.

"I need to go to him," she said.

"Absolutely not," said Scott.

"He needs me."

Scott laughed. "Oh, and how will you help

him? You can't even help yourself."

"Enough," I said.

He looked at me with surprise at my tone. I didn't often interfere in their quarrels, but his meanness had reached new levels, and I could no longer tolerate it without intervention. My position as his hired employee had prevented me from speaking up much thus far, but I now felt that my duty to protect and care for Zelda called for it. Especially because I knew he couldn't get on without me.

"Am I wrong?" he asked.

"Yes," I said. "In spite of Zelda's fragile mental condition, her ability to work with others who are troubled has always been exemplary, even at the Phipps Clinic."

"Thank you, Anna," she said.

"So you think she should be allowed to travel south to see him?" said Scott.

"It's worth considering," I heard myself say, though I was aware that it would be highly risky for her to make the trip. I wondered whether my desire to get away from La Paix was influencing my words.

"Fine, go," he said.

Zelda and I looked at him in shock.

"Oh, Goofo!" she cried, lunging into his arms. He moved his arms up and stiffly hugged her. He pulled away after a moment.

"I just ask this," he said. "Let me finish this novel and I'll go with you."

She nodded her head up and down, like a child who'd been promised a trip to the candy store.

"I'm so close, Zelda. So close."

"Yes," she said.

"I'll write to his doctor to see if I can get any more information," he said, "and then we'll see about arranging a visit."

"Thank you," she said.

"It's best we wait until the fall, anyway, after the worst heat of the summer has gone."

"Yes," she said.

The front door suddenly blew open on a gust. I ran to close it, with some difficulty, and when I returned to the parlor Scott and Zelda were locked in a passionate kiss. I stood in the shadows of the hallway, perplexed though not unhappy about their exchange. I never could have anticipated such an event following the terrible months preceding this moment, but I also knew that the only thing predictable about the Fitzgeralds was their unpredictability.

Scott wrote to Anthony's doctor in Alabama, where he'd returned to see a nerve specialist. His suicidal and homicidal thoughts had worsened, but his doctor mentioned that he didn't feel Anthony was a real risk to his family or himself.

"He wrote that the condition might indeed run in the family," said Scott, "which I can certainly confirm on this end."

As I prepared a cup of tea for Zelda, Scott sat at the kitchen table telling me about the letter. Zelda bathed herself in the unburned bathroom upstairs, with her record of *La Gioconda* at full volume. I looked at the ceiling and then back at Scott with raised eyebrows. He drained what remained of his sixteenth can of beer that day, put his face in his hands, and rubbed his eyes.

"What did he mean by 'homicidal' thoughts?" I asked.

Scott hesitated a moment, then spoke. "He's had thoughts of killing his mother."

I put my hand to my mouth.

"He is distressed by these thoughts and says he'll kill himself before killing someone else."

"Do you think we should still attempt a visit with Zelda?" I asked.

Scott looked back up at me, and he appeared to be so ill, I felt my heart reach out to him. As mean and difficult as he could be, he also hadn't given up on his wife, his daughter, or his work. I knew that his alcoholism was a major factor in his attempt to cope, though it had the opposite effect. He was a sick man.

"I don't know," he said. "His doctor mentioned that Anthony begged to come to Hopkins to be near Zelda. The Sayres don't have the money for Phipps, though, and I sure as hell don't either. I can barely afford to keep up with Zelda's therapy sessions there." He stood, lit a cigarette, and began pacing the kitchen. "Once I publish *Tender Is the Night,* our financial issues will be solved. It's my finest work yet."

I was glad to hear this. His popularity in the short-story market had been waning, and I knew from Isabel that their bills were piling up. I felt a small ripple of panic at the thought of being financially dependent on them, but felt better that Scott was so sure his novel would be a success.

"Anna!" Zelda called from upstairs.

"Excuse me," I said, and turned with the tray to leave.

Scott put his hand on my arm and looked up at the ceiling. "I'll take it to her."

I worried that Zelda would be angered if Scott showed up instead of me, but I couldn't refuse him.

Zelda's paintings now lined the perimeter

of the front parlor. I had used a cloth to wipe the smoke and ash from as many of them as I could, but some were beyond help. Zelda expressed that they accurately reflected her mental state and should remain, but Scott had insisted we take those paintings to the junkyard. I stacked them in a pile and would have Zelda help me remove them from the house after convincing her how depressing they were.

The other canvases reminded me of a funhouse with moving walls. Motion was a theme, and though the pictures were strange, they were captivating. Contorted ballet dancers with bulging muscular legs, enlarged feet, agonizing positions. I had wondered whether these compositions were the result of her poor eyesight until she told me, one day, about the technique of enlarging parts of the human body for thematic emphasis.

The hue of red paint she used reminded me of blood, and I didn't know whether that was deliberate or just my own morbid take on her palette. The Chinese acrobats were splashed in red, the dancer in arabesque, and finally, a portrait of Scott. There were two portraits of Scott, actually, and the one that struck me most showed him with a crown of thorns. I couldn't decide whether it was out of love or irony that she had drawn him in such a way.

Behind Scott's crown-of-thorns portrait was an unfinished painting I hadn't seen before. It appeared to be a woman, eyes facing heaven, with her breasts exposed. It was such a collection of arcs and circles that I initially had a hard time discerning the infant at her breast. Was it a picture of Mary and the child Jesus? Was Zelda becoming more religious?

The grandfather clock in the hallway bonged the six o'clock hour, and thus time for me to catch the bus home. I took one more look at the canvas, uncertain about what drew me to it but intensely interested in it just the same. Then I went up the stairs to bid Zelda good-bye.

The recording of *La Gioconda* had reached the beautiful lovers' song, and I felt chills rise on my skin at the passion it conveyed. I wondered whether playing the piece on the piano would do it any justice. When I reached the top of the stairs and turned toward the bathroom, I stopped in my tracks.

Scott was kneeling at one end of the bath, behind Zelda, pouring water over her shampooed hair and rinsing the suds away. Her face was tilted toward the ceiling and her eyes were closed. It was the loveliest expression of tenderness I had ever witnessed.

When he finished rinsing her hair, Scott placed the pitcher on the floor and eased Zelda back to recline against the side of the bathtub. He ran his hands over her shoulders and massaged her for a moment, until he slipped his hands down farther to her breasts.

I felt my breath catch in my throat and tiptoed down the stairs, careful not to make any noise. I stood at the bottom until my heart stopped hammering and walked to the kitchen, where I left a note sending them wishes for a good weekend.

For once, I felt certain that it would be so.

NINETEEN

August 1933

But peace never stayed long in the Fitzgerald house.

In August, Zelda's brother Anthony committed suicide by leaping from the window of his psychiatric hospital. No work, no money, and his terrible murderous thoughts had pushed him too far.

"No!" screamed Zelda. "He needed me, and I didn't go to him. This is *your* fault!"

She pointed her finger at Scott and he stared at her, his face aged and racked with guilt, his mouth half-open in disbelief.

"We said we'd wait until the autumn to visit," he mumbled, almost to himself.

I felt the need to step in. "Zelda, it was not because you did not see him. He was sick beyond anyone's help."

"No," she said. "If he could have seen me it may have made him better. Scott had to finish that damned novel —" She grabbed a stack of papers from his writing desk and threw them all over the floor. Scott's face changed and he lunged toward her.

"How dare you!" he shouted.

I pressed him back with my hand and then took him by the arms. He turned his face toward mine and I pleaded with him with my eyes to have some understanding. Her brother had just killed himself. This would be horrid for even the sanest person to face, and Zelda was so fragile. He seemed to understand and turned away, crouching down to pick up the papers. After a few moments, he spoke softly. "Zelda, I am very sorry for you and for him."

She cowered in the corner of the room with her eyes squeezed shut, shaking her head from side to side, as if trying to keep the terrible vision of her brother's death from her mind. I crossed the room and took her in my arms. She allowed me to hold her while she wept.

After that awful afternoon, Zelda clamped shut. She refused to write or speak at the house, and would only paint. She developed a twitch on her face, and began to contort her mouth in strange ways and laugh at inappropriate times. She didn't even want to spend time outdoors, which had always been her favorite release. I tried to lure her outside by opening the window to the sweet beckoning of the September breezes, but she would not come.

After Zelda's episode with Scott, he again retreated from her. He was immersed in revisions and lived inside of his writer's mind, which must have been the only place where he felt safe and in control. Mercifully, Scottie was busy with the start of school and friends, so she continued on, the third piece of this broken family, each inhabiting separate spaces from one another.

Once November arrived, they finally moved from La Paix to a house not far from mine in the city. Moving into Baltimore made more sense for them, since it was closer to Hopkins and felt less isolating for Scott. Scottie elected to spend most of the week with the family of her friend nearer to her school, and they seemed delighted to keep her. I accompanied Scott and Zelda to weekly therapy at Phipps, and noticed that Scott was becoming more hostile to Dr. Rennie and Dr. Meyer under their scrutiny.

"Are things any better now that you are away from La Paix?" asked Dr. Rennie.

"And the writing is complete," murmured Zelda.

Scott shot her a piercing look.

"Shall I stop writing?" he spat. "Shall I paint pretty pictures like you all day and see if that will support us?"

"You know painting is therapeutic for me," said Zelda.

"Yes, and we wouldn't want to take anything therapeutic away from our dear, fragile Zelda."

"What is that supposed to mean?" she said. "You've taken everything else from me in the world; now do you want me to stop painting?"

"I don't know what I want," he said, trying to light a cigarette. His hands shook so badly that he could not do it. Zelda's face suddenly softened and she looked at him with pity. She reached over and lit the cigarette for him, and then placed her hand on his knee.

"You are worn out, my husband," she said.

He coughed and laughed a little. "Just noticing?" he said, not unkindly.

She reached up and ran her hands over his hair and down the back of his neck. It was an intimate gesture, and I noticed Dr. Rennie shift in his seat. He looked stiff and uncomfortable. Was he jealous?

Living with the Fitzgeralds, I'd seen moments of tenderness, but this was the first time Rennie or Meyer had ever witnessed the depth of their feeling for each other. They were spellbound as Zelda leaned in and kissed Scott softly. They let their foreheads rest together.

"These battles are destroying us," she said. "We must stop. We don't want to kill each other."

Zelda folded her arms and leaned on them in Scott's lap.

Dr. Meyer spoke. "I have never seen you treat each other so kindly." His voice was gentler than I'd ever heard it. "Perhaps you should go away together."

Zelda sat up slowly and faced him. "Yes."

"A holiday for you to find each other again."

My spirits lifted. It was a good idea — though I worried whether Scott would be able to handle her alone.

"Do you think she could?" asked Scott, with eagerness.

"It would be a risk," said Meyer.

"Perhaps Anna could go with us," suggested Zelda.

"I don't think a romantic holiday should include a nurse," I said, smiling.

"Well, you don't have to come to bed with us," said Zelda. Dr. Rennie gave a nervous laugh. I blushed.

"Yes," said Scott. "Anna, you have a way

of floating beneath the surface until you're needed."

Another reference to my blandness frustrated me. He must have seen my displeasure, because he quickly elaborated.

"I mean you fit so seamlessly into our lives and reinforce us when we need you. You are perfect for us."

Better, I thought. He was smooth.

I finally spoke. "If Dr. Meyer and Dr. Rennie think it is a good idea, I will fully support you the best way I can."

"Oh!" Zelda clapped her hands together. "Where shall we go, Goofo?"

"How about Bermuda?" he asked. "We've always wanted to go there, and it's not too far."

"Yes, some island sun would do us well," said Zelda. "November is such a dreary month."

I was delighted at the thought of spending a holiday in Bermuda. I'd never been there, and while the Fitzgeralds learned to love each other again I could do some sightseeing and sunbathing.

It was the first time we'd ever left therapy with Scott and Zelda holding hands, and it suddenly felt as if everything might turn out all right for them.

TWENTY

November 1933
Bermuda
Rain.

Dreadful rain soaked our skin as we ran to the hotel lobby. It raged outside the window while we unpacked. Whispered along the terrace where we drank sherry. Drenched us as we walked along Elbow Beach. Lulled us to sleep at night, but woke us in the morning.

The rooms were beautiful but damp, and soon Scott began to cough. He claimed to have suffered from recurring bouts of tuberculosis throughout his life. I did not know whether this was true, but his cough grew wetter and thicker with each passing hour. It sliced through the atmosphere and tensed our shoulders. The more he tried to stop, the worse it became, and I grew worried.

"I'm so sorry," he wheezed. "This damned rain!"

"Perhaps we should call a doctor," I said.

"It will clear up soon," said Zelda.

"My cough or the rain?" asked Scott.

"Both," said Zelda.

"I don't want any doctor. I want a vacation from doctors."

"At the very least," I said, "you should rest."

"Yes, rest," said Zelda. "Anna and I will go biking."

"In the showers?" he said.

"What do I care?" asked Zelda. "I didn't come all the way to Bermuda to memorize the interior of our hotel, splendid though it is. I came here to make love to you and see the sights, and I intend to do both."

He smiled a bit until he fell into another coughing spell. We left him on the bed, spitting mucus from his lungs into his handkerchief and drinking rum.

Once we resolved to spend time outdoors in the rain, it took on a thrilling, surreal quality, and that was how Zelda and I passed the rest of her and Scott's vacation. We slipped over slick cobblestone roads and pedaled over the sand on our bikes in a state of near euphoria. Zelda laughed and sang and pointed at the places on the island that would have been beautiful under a full sun, yet were still interesting under the cover of clouds: vine-covered rock outcroppings, shallow tidal pools teeming with fish, sulking palm trees, endless stairways, pastel-painted houses, lush bougainvillea, bulky shipyard workers.

Zelda became fixated by the workers.

"Look at their musculature," she said. "They move like dancers."

We watched the island men as they wrapped coiled ropes on wood beams, and laughed and called to one another in the downpour. Then we pushed our bikes down to the beach, removed our shoes, and walked along the shore in the wet curve of sand. The beach held us like infants in its arm while we sat, still soaked, and watched a group of island girls and boys playing in the surf. Their sweet voices and laughter reached us between the raindrops and wind.

"These are the happiest children in the world," said Zelda. "I envy them."

"They are a snapshot of perfection, aren't they?" I said.

One of the smaller girls cried out and limped out of the water. The other children ignored her. She plopped onto the sand and pulled her foot in toward her to see what had caused the hurt. I stood, walked over to her, and crouched next to her. She brushed her arm over her eyes to remove the rain or tears.

"Are you okay?" I asked.

"I stepped on something," she said.

There was a tiny dot of blood on the bottom of her foot. She had probably hopped on a piece of shell or rock.

"Let me have a look," I said. "I'm a nurse."

She stuck her small foot up in my face, nearly kicking me, and I pretended to fall over. She looked scared until I laughed, and then she pretended to kick me again. We played at this for a bit until she stood and started running around me in circles, encouraging me to chase her.

"I thought you hurt your foot," I teased.

"It's good now," she said.

"It had better be, because I'm going to get you!"

I pretended to lunge at her and she squealed in delight and ran back to her friends in the water. I waved at her and returned to Zelda, who was now standing.

"You would make a good mother," said Zelda.

I looked at the girl and tried to form the words in my throat. They stuck a little, but it was the right time.

"Zelda, I never finished my story with you

that day. About my past."

She looked at me, her face serene and inviting. "You are a mother," she said.

I could not hide my shock. "How did you know?" I stammered.

"We've dressed together before, Anna," she said. "The line on one's stomach never fully fades, does it? The children mark us. We're forever tethered."

"Yes," I said. "Are you upset that I've never spoken of it?"

"No," she said. "There's a right time for telling things."

She looped her arm through mine and we began walking back to our bikes.

"Can you tell me what happened?" she asked.

The heavy thing in my heart suddenly became loose.

"Yes," I said. "I lost her to pneumonia when she was five. Katie. Her name was Katie."

"How sad, Anna. How terribly sad," said Zelda. "And yet here you are. Upright. A pillar. A post. A trusty sidekick."

"I wish I could agree with you. I seem to have a penchant for holding on to the past."

"Maybe that's why you cope so well," she said. "Remembrance allows them to live on."

"Maybe."

Remembrance. Even more, confession. It did always made the heavy things come loose. Why did I always forget that?

We retraced our old footsteps in the sand, and Zelda took care to step into each of her old footprints.

"What are you doing?" I asked.

"You've inspired me. I'm going back in time," she said. "It makes me sad to see my old footprints in the sand from earlier, when I was younger."

"It was mere minutes ago," I said.

"But that was then, and this is now, and time soldiers on."

"But now you are wiser. Wisdom is the gift of age."

"Madness seems to be the only gift in my stocking," she said.

"And beauty, and creativity, and a legacy," I said.

"And Anna," she said. "My greatest gift. A true friend."

I squeezed her closer, and kissed her on the cheek.

When we reached our bikes I turned back to the beach, inhaled the saltwater smell, and threw back my head to take in the elements, feeling invigorated. When I opened my eyes, I saw Zelda smiling at me.

"Look at you," she said. "Opening like a magnolia, spilling out sun instead of taking it in."

That was just how I felt.

The three of us sat around our table of emptied cups and crumb-covered plates, captivated by the couple across the room.

The woman had the deepest shade of red hair I'd ever seen. The man had slick black hair and warm olive skin. Their feet rested between each other under the table. She held her face in the palm of her hand with her elbow on the table. He toyed with her hair and stole kisses from her between nibbles of tea and biscuits. She laughed — high and lilting — at everything he said.

"Do you see how their untarnished wedding bands catch the light?" said Zelda. "They haven't yet lived in 'for worse.' "

"Or in sickness, or poverty," said Scott. He reached across the table and took Zelda's hand.

"Half of me wants to run over and warn them," said Zelda, "while the other half of me wants to erect a moat for them."

"And plant giant arborvitae to block out the rest of the world," I said.

"And poplars and sturdy oaks," said Scott.

"We should have done that, Goofo," said

Zelda, cupping his hand with her other hand.

"We tried here and there," he said.

"Exactly," she said. "Here and there. Damn us for being so careless with the perfection we had."

"But you can't build a moat to keep out mutability," said Scott. "Time knows no barriers."

"Then we should have killed ourselves in youth, like we'd promised."

"And leave Scottie?"

"Everyone loves her," said Zelda. "Someone would have raised her up right and well."

I hated Zelda's talk of suicide. She spoke of it so freely that I'd stopped being ruffled by it, and that frightened me.

The couple across the room began to kiss passionately, and the man slid his arm down her back and pulled her closer to him. In spite of my embarrassment, I couldn't stop watching them. Neither could my company. Finally, the man grabbed a wad of bills out of his pocket, dropped them on the table, and practically carried the woman out of the room and up the hotel stairs, where they would, no doubt, spend the rest of the evening in their room.

Zelda looked at Scott with open longing,

287

and I did what I did best — slipped away from the table and faded into the wallpaper so that Mr. and Mrs. Fitzgerald could be alone.

The rain ceased that night.

Eager to escape the solitude of my room, I went to the bar. It was nearly empty at ten o'clock, except for a lone bartender, an island woman sweeping between the tables, and an aged man in a crisp suit smoking a cigar. The night and the bar were one in the open air, and moonlight spilled in through the porch.

I ordered a rum swizzle and read from a book Scott had recommended to me, Ernest Hemingway's most recent volume of short stories, *Winner Take Nothing*. He had made me promise not to tell Zelda that he'd given it to me. He didn't want to get her started on Hemingway again.

I read "A Clean, Well-Lighted Place," a story of an old man and two waiters at a café in the night. The young waiter was impatient to get home to his wife. The old waiter sympathized with the old man, a lonely projection of faded youth.

Mutability. The passage of time, or rather, the inevitability of the passage of time.

The story held shocking significance to

me in light of my earlier conversation with Scott and Zelda and my current surroundings. I looked at the old man sitting at the table across the room, and wondered whether he did not want to be alone in his room the way that I did not. He did not look at me, but rather at the piano in the corner that sat silent.

In the Hemingway story there was no music, and because I was a little drunk and strongly wished for the story to not be about me and these people, I walked over to the piano bench and sat down. Also, since I was a newly opened magnolia, I wanted to play the piano just for the pleasure of the music and the living, and in no way because it connected me to the dead.

I looked at the old man and raised my eyebrows. *Is this okay?*

He nodded and smiled a little.

Good, I thought. He made a wish for music and I made it come true.

The atmosphere was so sad from the dark and the solitude that I decided to play something quiet and pleasant. I settled on "Clair de Lune." Once I was halfway through the song I realized the sadness hiding in its beauty, but it was too late to turn back. When I finished, the old man raised his drink to me. The bartender wiped the counter and did not look up. The woman sweeping had stopped to listen and stared out into the night at the dark sea.

In the magic of the moment, I stood from the piano and walked out onto the balcony overlooking the water, mesmerized by the waves reflecting the moonlight. While it was beautiful, the dark water filled me with dread. I thought that Zelda would agree that darkness always lurked just beneath the surface of beauty. I hoped she and Scott were finding comfort in each other's arms, if just for a short time, and experiencing no darkness or dread tonight.

I returned to my room feeling the empty, exhausted relief of one who has had a good cry, though I had not cried. I slipped easily into sleep, and imagined waking tomorrow to the novelty of sun. I saw the golden rays warming the rocks and sand, the aquamarine translucence of the water in the light. I dreamed of swimming bold, vigorous strokes in the water, waking up my body after years of too much quiet. In my dream I floated on the surface with the heat of the sun on my skin and the cool of the water under my back, until suddenly I was dragged under.

I woke up with Zelda over me, shaking my arms, a look of frantic agony in her eyes.

I sat up quickly in bed with my heart racing.

"What is it? How did you get in here?"

"We have to go home," she said.

I looked at the clock on my nightstand.

"Zelda, it's three in the morning," I said. "Has something happened?"

She scratched at her neck and sat, rocking, on the side of my bed.

"His coughing is giving me asthma," she said. "I can't breathe. He's taking up all the space."

"He can't help it," I said.

"He won't," she said. "We have to get him home and get me away from him. I don't want to be one with him anymore. I just want to be alone. I don't ever want to go anywhere with him again."

I pulled her arms away from her neck and held her hands. The skin of her hands felt like it was on fire, but her forehead was cool and clammy.

"Zelda," I said, "aside from his illness, you've enjoyed yourself here."

She shook her head.

"Yes, you have," I said. "Remember the shipyard workers? The children in the surf? Scott holding your hand on the table?"

She pulled her hands out of mine and began twisting them over each other. She

291

continued to shake her head. I worried that I might need to sedate her if she didn't calm down. She was dangerously close to an outburst, but I wanted to try everything possible before resorting to sedation.

Moving. I had to get her up and moving.

"Zelda, let's go for a walk in the moonlight," I said. "The clouds are almost gone. The whole island will be lit tomorrow."

She stood and walked to the door, and I was able to wrap a robe around her. I quickly threw on my own robe and grabbed my key, then hurried to catch her in the hallway. As I passed their room, Scott's cough seeped out and followed me down the stairs.

Zelda strode toward the water through the moonlight, shedding her robe when her feet touched the sand and her nightgown as she waded into the waves. She dived forward and started swimming, naked, straight out to sea.

I didn't want to scream and alarm anyone, but I was horrified that she wouldn't stop swimming, like the dissatisfied wife and mother Edna Pontellier, from *The Awakening.* I knew I could never catch Zelda, so I watched in agony, thankful that at least I had the moonlight to show me her form in the sea.

The dark water filled me with dread, as it had when I watched it from the bar. I began imagining sharks and barracuda looking for prey. I imagined currents from the stormy waters dragging her under, or fatigue overcoming her. A lone cloud passed the moon and I lost sight of her. I thought of having to explain to Scott, "Yes, I watched your wife commit suicide and did nothing to intervene."

I was going to have to go in there after her.

I tore off my robe and nightgown and started forward. The water was shockingly cold and I shivered from the temperature and my fear. I took a deep breath and began to swim. This was in no way the blissful swim from my dream, but rather a test. Zelda wanted to see whether I would go after her. It was like her night on the dance floor with her aviator. Scott watched as she destroyed them. I could not do the same.

I came up for air and couldn't see her anywhere. I spun in circles, in water too deep for my feet to touch the ground. Something brushed my leg and I couldn't help but scream.

The cloud passed and I could again see

all around me, giving me a moment of peace. I noticed a splash farther out and thought I saw Zelda's arm. I had to follow, so I took a deep breath and began swimming farther away from the beach. When I surfaced, another cloud covered the moon, and all trace of Zelda was gone. My breathing was labored, my heart felt as if it would pound out of my chest, and the strength in my arms and legs was beginning to fail me. I knew I'd have to swim back.

Oh, my Lord, I lost her.

I felt tears form in my eyes and a sob in my throat. How could I tell this to Scott? How could I live with this? If only I'd started after her sooner! If only I'd sedated her.

I began the slow, miserable swim back to the beach, my tears mingling with the salt water. When I came up for air and to see how much farther I had to go, I was horrified to see that I'd made almost no progress. I must have been caught in a riptide, and now I thought we'd both die out here and Scott would be alone.

But I didn't want to die. I was just learning how to live again. With renewed panic and a burst of energy, I pushed myself harder through the water, determined that I would get back, but when I resurfaced, it seemed that I was even farther out. I realized then that it was futile. I had no more strength. This made me unbearably sad.

Suddenly Zelda was beside me, her face ghostly but peaceful in the moonlight.

"You came for me," she said.

She was barely winded.

I cried out in relief, and she looped her arm around my waist and began to pull me back to the beach. I was astounded by her strength. She took me to a place where we could stand and set me down.

Before she walked away, she said, "That" — pointing to me and then out to the water — "that is how I feel all the time."

TWENTY-ONE

November 1933–February 1934

We were forced to return home from the trip early, and Scott was diagnosed with pleurisy — inflammation of the lungs. He was confined to bed, where he finished his revisions for *Tender Is the Night*.

Zelda was a wreck.

Her moment of lucidity in the moonlight on Bermuda was the last I had with her for a very long time. Our journey home to the city was a series of nervous incidents, alternating bouts of manic tears and laughter, angry eczema, fits of asthma, weeping and accusation. She was like a woman possessed. At one point she even mentioned the attacking demons, and I nearly called Peter for help. Instead, I sedated her — a practice I was engaging in more and more often.

My chief objective became keeping Zelda from harming herself or disturbing Scottie, which left me exhausted each day and often resulted in my having to spend the night at their house. I hadn't seen my family in weeks, but I was afraid of what would happen if I left Zelda alone. I began to look for a good opportunity to recommend that she recommit herself to the clinic.

Zelda did experience a burst of creativity during her increasing horrors, which resulted in many disturbing and fascinating paintings reflecting her emotional turmoil. She insisted that I arrange and rearrange the paintings ten times a day around the study. She wanted them by subject, then by medium, then by range of emotional intensity reflected in the color scheme. Sometimes she wanted arbitrary assortments of large and small canvases. Other times we had to order them in increasing or decreasing size.

She blared her ballet music and punctuated her exclamations on organization with dance, and in the midst of the chaos, Scott would come through, drunk out of his mind, and encourage her bizarre behavior. I would send him back to his writing and try to get her to sit still and eat a full meal. She'd leave her plate and call to him to come see her new gallery design idea. It was a grotesque circus with mad performers, and I could feel the bottom falling out with each passing minute of every passing day.

Then the bottom did fall out.

On a terrible blustery February day, Scott's friend Cary Ross blew in from his New York gallery to see the paintings. I pulled Scott into the kitchen while Zelda showed Cary her work.

"Who is he?" I asked.

"He owns a gallery," said Scott. "I invited him down to see about showing Zelda's paintings."

"Do you honestly think she's in any state to travel to New York for a gallery showing?" I asked. *Have you completely lost your mind?* I wanted to say.

"I think it will do her good," he said. "Finally, she can express herself without having to compete with me."

"I'm very pleased that you are encouraging her creative expression, but she needs to stabilize her emotional state before we attempt anything so large."

Scott gave me a patronizing smile and downed his beer. "Nurse Anna, you are adorable when you're agitated."

He kissed me on the forehead and rushed out of the room. I heard him making all sorts of exclamations on Zelda's talents for Cary, punctuated by Zelda's laughter. Then

I heard a sneeze from the top of the stairs. I looked up to see Scottie staring down at me from the dark. She walked down and I met her in the hall, where we watched Scott twirl Zelda around for Cary, motioning at her work with his cigarette, and all of them talking gaily about the exhibit.

"It's nice they're so happy," said Scottie. She looked at me with large eyes and no smile. She could sense impending disaster in the shrill tone of her mother's voice and her father's intoxication.

"Yes." I attempted a smile for her. Then I tried diversion, which seemed to be my only trick these days. "Did you finish your homework?"

"Yes," said Scottie. "And I wanted to see what all the fuss was about."

"Your mother's paintings might go on display in New York," I said. "Isn't that swell?"

Scottie nodded and allowed me to lead her back up to her room, as Zelda started the record over and turned up the volume.

When we got to Scottie's room, she crawled into bed. I pulled the sheets and comforter up to Scottie's ears, and pressed the blankets around her, hoping the coverings would muffle some of the noise from downstairs.

"My mom used to tuck me in up to my ears," I said. "Snug as a bug."

Scottie smiled, her sweet face framed by the pink flowers on the bedding.

"You're not too old for tuck-ins, are you?" I asked.

"No," she said. "I love tuck-ins."

The music downstairs came to an abrupt halt, and I heard Zelda's voice flare in anger, though I could not make out her words. Scottie's smile vanished. Scott's voice came in a yell up the stairs.

"Oh, dear," said Scottie. "We knew this was coming."

I looked at her for a moment, shocked by her maturity. I made a decision to stop trying to distract her from Zelda's madness. It somehow seemed worse than facing it head-on. Perhaps it would help her deal with her mother as she got older if she understood the warning signs.

"We did," I said. "I saw your mother's rash on her neck. It's a warning flag."

"And her trouble breathing," said Scottie.

"Yes, and her feverish activity," I said.

Zelda was now crying and screaming, and I knew I'd have to go to her, but it was important that I finish this talk with Scottie.

"I hate when she gets like this," said Scottie. "Especially around other people, outside of us."

"It's okay to feel embarrassed," I said, "but I want you to remember something. Your mother is ill. Her mind has a sickness, just the way someone's lungs or heart get a sickness. Illness makes symptoms, and sadly, when your mind is sick, the symptoms are more disturbing than with other parts of the body, because it makes people think the one who's ill must have some control, but she doesn't. We have to watch for her symptoms, and then treat them the best way we can."

Scottie nodded, though I didn't know whether she understood.

"It's important for you to know how much she loves you," I continued, "and how much she wishes her mind weren't ill so she could be a better mother."

The distinct sound of a vase shattering pulled me to my feet.

"I have to go. Try to sleep, Scottie."

"I will," she said.

I closed her door and hurried down the stairs, bracing myself as if entering a war zone. When I reached the bottom of the stairs and stepped into the front room, Zelda stood in front of a pile of her paintings with her arms out as if protecting them from Scott and Cary. Her eyes were wild and her hair unkempt, and she had removed all of her clothing.

"I will not allow the two of you to rape me for profit!" she shouted.

"You wanted this!" yelled Scott.

Cary backed to the doorway and drained his glass. "I thought you'd agreed on this," he said. "If Zelda doesn't want to do it, I don't want to force her."

"This is an outrage," said Scott. "I had Cary come all the way down here to schedule the showing that *you* wanted and now you're changing your mind? That is not how a professional behaves."

"Oh, please," she said. "And are you supposed to be the professional, you sniveling, hacking, drunken scribbler?"

"A fine insult coming from you, a dried-out, washed-up, wrung-out lunatic!"

Zelda grabbed a plant on a stand near her and heaved it at Scott, narrowly missing his face. The pot shattered and sprayed dirt and glass all over the wall and rug. Then she crumpled to the floor and began to sob. I hurried across the room, throwing a blanket on her from the couch nearby, and trying to persuade her to go to bed.

She suddenly turned and stared at me with eyes blackened by enlarged pupils.

"You should have let me drown," cried Zelda. "Then I could have gone to Ben and Katie."

It seemed as if all sound ceased, and I could hear only the noise of my heart pumping blood through my body. Zelda was mocking me like someone possessed, pretending to speak in my voice, ridiculing my deepest hurt. I stood and backed away from her, and the sound returned in a rush with her cruel words.

"If I'd died, I could have been with them," Zelda continued, in her grotesque ridicule of me. "Instead of living this miserable, hollow life with only a madwoman and an out-of-tune piano for company."

I was vaguely aware of Scott begging Cary not to leave and promising they'd be ready for the show in March. The door closing. Scott coming back in the room, trying to drag Zelda to her feet. Yelling at me to get the sedative. Zelda continuing to howl, suddenly screaming apologies to me.

I stumbled to my bag and grabbed the needle, removed the top, and allowed the sedative to fill the syringe.

I returned to the scene where Scott sobbed over Zelda. I pushed him away and then jabbed the needle into Zelda's thigh.

■ ■ ■ ■

I pounded on the door of the rector's quarters behind the cathedral, shivering in the cold, keenly aware that it was three o'clock in the morning and I was alone on the streets of Baltimore.

"Dammit," I said, and banged harder, ignoring the pain in my knuckles from the freezing door and the below-freezing air.

I noticed a rat dart from a nearby bush to the alley and wrinkled my nose in disgust.

As I began to pound again, the door opened and I nearly fell in. Peter stood before me with his hair unkempt and dark hollows under his eyes.

"Jesus," he said. "If I didn't answer, the dead cardinals surely would have."

He pulled me in and wrapped me in a hug. He smelled of sleep, of nicotine, and faintly of incense. I inhaled and allowed myself to cry for the first time that night. He closed and locked the door, and led me through the ornate foyer to the kitchen in the back of the house.

"Sit," he said, while he filled a teapot with water and lit the burner. "What happened?"

"Zelda is back at Phipps."

He placed the pot on the burner and

looked at me. "Oh, shit. What happened?"

"I don't even know where to begin," I said.

"How about you start with Bermuda? You never did fully explain your trip."

"It was such a tease," I said. "Everything seemed to be going well. Then Scott got sick and Zelda started slipping."

"Then you returned and she lost it."

"A little more each day," I said. "It came to a head tonight, when Scott had his New York gallery owner friend over to discuss an exhibit of Zelda's paintings. She changed her mind and said they couldn't use her work. It would expose her too much."

"I can understand that," said Peter.

"Well, yes, but she's been pushing for it for so long, it was a rather abrupt about-face."

"Ah."

"So she and Scott began to quarrel, and Cary left, and she lost it."

"What exactly does that mean?" he said.

"Screaming, crying, throwing things. But something else happened tonight that really disturbed me. It was as if she were possessed."

Peter's eyebrows knit together. The tea-kettle started to whistle, making us both jump. He placed two tea bags into two teacups and poured hot water over them;

then he joined me again at the table.

"How so?"

"It makes me sick what she said. It was like she was pretending to be me."

His face grew even more horrified. "What did she say?"

I explained to Peter how I'd told Zelda about Ben and Katie, and that night when I almost drowned in Bermuda. Then I told him what Zelda had said.

"Anna," he said gravely, "are you okay?"

I wrapped my hands around my teacup and let the warmth seep into my hands until my shivering stopped. "I think so," I said.

"I wish I could have been there. At least to see what we're dealing with. At most, to put a cork in her mouth and douse her in holy water."

"I think her problems require more than holy water," I said.

He did not reply.

"Deep down," I said, "I know that Zelda didn't have any control at that moment."

"That doesn't change how awful it must have been for you to hear her say that."

"No," I said.

"And did you agree with her?" he asked. "Did you think that about drowning? About seeing Katie and Ben again?"

I thought back to the water, to the moonlight, to the panic. I remembered how badly I wanted to live.

"No," I said. "Not even for a moment."

He exhaled and leaned back in his chair. "Will you go back to them?" he asked.

I hovered over the steam lifting off my tea and blew gently on it, weighing his words, though I knew the answer in my heart.

TWENTY-TWO

March 1934

Zelda was my purpose. I could not turn away from her.

But once she was admitted back into Phipps, she was placed on suicide watch, and I was shut out of her life.

Alone and unemployed, I felt as if I'd lost my way. Although ashamed, I begged Meyer to give me back my job. He was apologetic but firm. He took no pleasure in turning me away, or in recommending that I take some time to myself to get on "stable footing," but he would not yield.

I decided to go and see Scott. I went to the Fitzgeralds' place on Park Avenue at my regularly scheduled time, but Scott was not there. Isabel greeted me.

"I don't know when he'll be back," she said. "But he did leave this copy of *Tender Is the Night,* inscribed for you. He said he couldn't have finished without you."

She stepped out of the room and returned with a photograph that she handed to me. "Scott also wanted you to have this," she said.

It was a picture of Zelda and me sitting on the beach between rain showers in Bermuda. We had our arms around each other's waists. The photo moved me and it trembled in my hands.

"Do you think he'll have any use for me?" I asked. "To help him or look after Scottie, or be here if Zelda gets discharged?"

"I'm sorry, Anna, but to tell you the truth, he's almost out of money."

"What?"

"He's confident that *Tender* will put him on solid financial standing, but I'm worried. He's not getting nearly as much for his short stories as he used to, and the reviews of the book are mixed. I'm afraid he's gone out of fashion."

It was bad enough keeping Zelda safe when he had money. Now, without money, what would he do? Lock her in a public institution? *My God.*

"What will he do with Zelda? Or Scottie?"

"He is very committed to giving both of them the best possible care and education, thank goodness."

I nodded and looked around the room.

The study felt empty.

"Where are her paintings?" I asked.

"They're going to New York for the gallery opening next month."

"You can't be serious," I said.

"Sadly, I am," she said. "And I think Zelda's moving, too. Scott is sending her to a private mental care facility called the Craig House. It's extremely expensive. I don't know how he'll afford it."

I suddenly felt cold and light-headed, and sat down on the nearest chair. I was losing her. Maybe forever. I was embarrassed to find myself in tears. Isabel fidgeted uncomfortably.

"Anna, I'm sorry," she said. "You have been very good for her. And for all of them."

Was I? Zelda was on suicide watch. Scott was shipping her away. I had no job. I'd tricked myself into thinking I was living again when I was simply living through another person. I'd spent more than a decade with a misplaced self, transferred from Ben, to Katie, to Zelda, stretched thin as trapeze wire but with no solid anchors.

What had I allowed myself to become?

I stayed at the house until late that afternoon, when Scott stumbled in from the bar, and persuaded him to let me pack up some of Zelda's things to send to her. In the passing days, I needled him for details from his therapy sessions with Dr. Meyer, and wrote letters to Zelda that weren't answered.

Day after day, for no pay, I went to the Fitzgerald home, organized and reorganized as much as I could, and trudged home to my apartment building, where now only dust lay in the front window that used to frame Sorin's silhouette, and only silence greeted me from overhead, where the ballerinas had long since graduated and no one had filled their space. I renewed my fantasies of traveling, of trying to find Zelda's diaries, but with no money and no car, that was impossible.

I realized this couldn't go on. I had to stop going to the Fitzgeralds' house, and start looking for a real job. I'd saved a decent amount of money while I worked as Zelda's private nurse, but without any income to replenish it, it was disappearing at an alarming rate.

I'd also reached a new level of disgust with Scott.

I'd been reading *Tender Is the Night* and was horrified to see how he exposed Zelda, like a butterfly pinned on a corkboard. Her madness, her fits, letters she'd sent from the psychiatric clinic in Switzerland copied word for word, conversations with therapists; it was all there, in black and white, for all of their friends and enemies to read and to judge.

In a fit of drunken hysterics one evening, Scott confessed to me that he knew *Tender* had driven Zelda to new depths of despair. He alternated between justifying himself to me and begging me to call Peter so he could make a confession. The next day I went to the house early and officially resigned, while he was sober. He answered by pushing twenty dollars into my hands and begging me to help him escort Zelda to New York, where he would transfer her to the Craig House, an exclusive and progressive psychiatric facility in Beacon, New York, where there were no locks on rooms, no bars on windows, and a country club atmosphere. She would get plenty of rest and exercise.

I had no idea how he could afford the Craig House, but I hoped it was because his novel's sales were strong and not because he had borrowed from his agent or editor again. I could tell by the look on Isabel's face that the latter was probably true.

On March eighth, I escorted Scott to the Phipps Clinic to help with Zelda's transfer. As I walked through the doors of the clinic, I was filled with overwhelming sadness. I'd worked there for five peaceful years. Zelda's admittance had shaken me loose from a secure nook in which I'd burrowed myself, and now I could not fit back in.

While we waited for Zelda in Meyer's office, he would not meet my gaze. He spoke to Scott of Zelda's condition, his expectations, and his advice for the future. The men were not parting on good terms. Scott still resented Meyer's insistence that he stop drinking. Meyer was frustrated that he'd not made more progress; his authority had been challenged and he'd lost a nurse.

I watched the door, eager to see Zelda again, while trying to caution myself that she would be very changed, and might not acknowledge me. When she came around the turn, my deepest fears were confirmed. Her skin had lost its color. Her tawny hair was dull, her eyes blank. She was extremely underweight, and her motions lacked their usual grace. She refused to sit down or make eye contact with any of us.

She broke my heart.

I stood and placed my arms around her. "Come on, Zelda. We have a train to catch."

She did not act as if she understood what I had to say, but she allowed me to guide her out of the doors of the Phipps Clinic for the last time.

■ ■ ■ ■

During the entire train ride from Baltimore to New York, Zelda didn't say a word. She alternated between sleeping and staring out the window at the passing landscape. Scott paced from our seats to the bar for drinks, and passed out somewhere near Philadelphia. Zelda fell asleep shortly thereafter against him.

In sleep, without emotion, hysteria, intoxication, or motive, their faces softened to what their youthful countenances must have once been. Their long eyelashes rested below their eyes, their wrinkles disappeared, and their mouths pursed into little bows. The afternoon sunlight that glowed through the window lit their golden heads and put a touch of pink in their cheeks. They looked like two dolls, and watching them at rest, I was moved.

It was he who woke first. He gazed at her for a moment with great sadness and tears in his eyes. He traced the curve of her face with his fingertip and kissed her mouth. She stirred and met his gaze, offering her face to him, prolonging the kiss. He slid his hand in hers and they rested on each other for the remainder of the trip.

For just a moment, they could have been any other married couple on a train.

Theirs was a tender parting, yet she did not acknowledge me. She kissed him passionately and promised him she'd try her hardest to get better so she could come home. He was emotional on the return train and tried to cry on my shoulder, but I was in no mood to be a prop for him; nor did I want to spoil the beautiful image I held in my heart of the two of them sleeping.

He drank on the train ride from Beacon to New York City, where he got off to meet with Cary to complete plans for the gallery opening to which I would come back up and accompany Zelda at the end of the month, if she was well enough to attend.

I didn't get home until very late that night, and I was so weary that I didn't even undress before getting into bed, where I had nightmares all night of Ben and myself, and the train station in the war.

At Scott's instruction, I escorted Zelda to An American Place, a gallery on Madison Avenue showing the work of Georgia O'Keeffe. I led Zelda past the haunting paintings of enlarged flowers, empty skulls, and landscapes that adorned the walls. We reached a painting of black water in the dark that made me shiver as I recalled that night when Zelda had saved me. We stood before it for many minutes, but Zelda did not address me. She had not spoken to me since that terrible night when she'd mimicked me and I had sedated her. How I longed for her to speak to me.

"It's like that night in Bermuda," I said.

Silence.

"When you saved me," I said. I turned to look at her, but she would only stare straight ahead at the painting. I noticed her trembling, and saw that two small red hives had appeared at the base of her neck.

"Zelda, please talk to me. Acknowledge me. I'm so sorry if you've felt . . . abandoned? Hurt? I don't know, because you won't tell me. Please speak to me."

She began to blink rapidly, and turned away from me. A wave of such pain and sadness engulfed me that I felt light-headed. Her coldness was torture. I wrapped my arms around myself and watched her walk through O'Keeffe's bizarre garden. Though Zelda moved slowly, she grew breathless. When I heard the wheezing begin, I knew she was too troubled to stay.

She allowed me to guide her out of the showing and back to Cary's gallery, several

316

blocks away, which was now full of people. As we walked through the door, Scott removed himself from the company of a woman, ran to greet us, and nearly drenched our coats with the contents of his glass of gin.

"You were gone so long," he said, kissing her on the cheek and tugging off her coat. "All of our friends are here. Come, Zelda! Dorothy Parker! The Murphys!"

He pulled her away from me and she was swallowed by the crowd.

For hours, Zelda tried to pry herself from conversations with people who seemed so important to Scott, but who only confused Zelda. She walked to the door several times, but Scott kept ushering her into new groups. I finally overheard Scott say that Ernest Hemingway would be arriving soon, and Zelda gasped aloud. She pulled away from Scott and hurried over to where I stood. My heart raced at the thought of her finally speaking to me, but she would not. I could see a lacy red rash tearing up her throat, and without a word I knew she had to leave immediately. Scott tried to guide her back, but I put my hand on his arm.

"Look at her," I whispered to him.

He glanced at her face and then her neck.

"I'm taking her back," I said.

He gave me a little nod and helped me with her coat.

I pushed her out the door and we nearly ran into a man I recognized as Ernest Hemingway, with his strong build, mustache, and penetrating eyes. He smiled wryly and put out his arms as if to embrace Zelda, but she rushed out onto the street without acknowledging him. He raised his eyes at me, gave me a wink, and walked into the gallery without a second glance.

Though we had only a couple of blocks to go, it felt as if I would never get her to the train station. Then she was shaking her hands and pacing beside the track while we waited, and I feared the conductor wouldn't let her on in this state. I guided her behind a pillar and talked quietly to her until our train pulled up, whereupon I promptly shoved her into her seat and sedated her.

One week later, I received an envelope from the Craig House addressed only to "Nurse" in Zelda's handwriting. Inside were two slips of paper. One torn sheet said, "Burn." The other said this:

AUCTION: ART GALLERY — 1934

It started as my idea, became his idea, and returned to my idea: a showing, an art sale, a way to earn some money for my "hobbies." But when the paintings went on display I realized what it was: an auction of the fragmented bits of my soul — shards of jagged emotion chiseled like sparkling limestone from cave walls, a palette of my moods from the dullest, creamiest days to the most red-violent nights.

He was to invite our friends, or rather, those who were in our acquaintance, a smart set of poets, artists, writers, mistresses, and misogynists. The room suddenly became too tight, so I drifted down the avenue to a gallery showing a fine flower woman, a real artist, whose tender, rounded magnifications caused my nerves to stand on end and my heart to ache with their beauty and my envy to burn green at the thought of her in the desert in solitude, in full creative power and in full control of it.

Then I returned to my exhibition in time for the sales.

See here, a fine oil on canvas, *Chinese Theater.* Can you imagine the acrobatics? Can you feel the swollen muscles in symphonic concentration? Twenty-five cents from the couple once in charge of orchestrating all of us. Sold.

Look at this here, *Arabesque,* dancers at the barre — no, not the bar, Mr. Fitzgerald, a ballet barre. You there, Parker, mistrustful woman of words, how much say you? Fifty cents. Sold. And why don't we throw in this lovely art of Scott disguised as a coronet player so you may admire him even when he's not sharing your bed.

And oh, the crowning glory, the portrait of the man with the crown of thorns. Not the historic man, but rather, the one who wishes to be historic, who betrays his wife with a kiss and exorcises her demons just enough to hold him over until next time. Do you want it? One dollar. Sold.

Thank you all and good night.

I read her piece twice, stuffed it back in the envelope, and placed it on my bedside table. It was the only attempt she'd made at communicating with me in so long that I hated the idea of burning her writing. I sent her a letter telling her how much I missed her and how much she meant to me, and each night I reread her piece, but soon it kept me from sleeping. My guilt over not burning it blurred into my dreams turning them to nightmares. After a week of insomnia, I finally got up at two in the morning, crept down the stairs of my chilly, half-abandoned building, and pried open the door to Sorin's old apartment. I placed Zelda's papers in the sooty fireplace, lit a match, and watched the edges curl inward with fire until everything was erased.

TWENTY-THREE

April 1934

The spring was stubborn in its arrival that year, and maintenance at my apartment building was scarce. The landlord tried to keep up with the peeling paint, crumbled front stoop, and wiring issues, but with no other boarders, it was hard on him. The depression was drowning everyone, and I was going down the drain with it.

One Sunday night, just home from my parents' house — where I now went every weekend to escape the empty misery of my life in the city — I sat in the fading light at the piano, playing "Anii" and working myself up for a good cry, when there was a knock at the door.

I was alarmed. I hated being alone in the building, and thought, more than once, that I should consider moving back in with my parents, where I could at least be of help to my mother. Of course, I'd mentioned this to her last weekend and seen the worry etch her forehead. She had gently explained that while I was always welcome, I needed to keep living my life outside of them. She was probably right.

The person knocking tried again, and I wondered whether it was Lincoln. Maybe I had left something in his taxi. I knew it wasn't Peter, because he would have made a song out of his knock. I crept over to the door and finally raised my voice.

"Who's there?" I called.

"Anna," said a male voice. "It's Will."

I was confused for a moment and about to say, *Will who?* when it occurred to me who it was.

"It's Will Brennan," he called.

"Yes, Will!" I said, and began to unlock the chains when I caught sight of my dark-circled eyes, limp hair, and gaunt frame in the mirror by the door. I hated for him to see me like this, but what could I do? Turn away an old friend after years and years? I quickly ran a hand through my hair and pinched a little color into my cheeks.

When I pulled open the door, he stood before me, looking as awful as I did. He had an overgrown beard and his shirt hung on his frame as it would on a hanger. I couldn't help but laugh. He broke into a smile so wide I could see the boyish face beneath the beard and saw the light in his blue eyes.

"Haven't changed a bit, have I?" he said.

"Nor I," I said.

He stared at me for a moment, then dived into me with a hug. It took my breath away.

We sat over a dinner of toasted cheese sandwiches and tomato soup, and talked as if not a day had passed.

"I'm sorry about the dinner offerings," I said. "I don't go to much trouble for myself these days."

"This is gourmet to me," he said. "I've lived on soybeans and peanuts for the past three years. Now that I've sold the family farm I'm hoping to enjoy a better standard of eating."

"You sold it?"

"Yes, my dad died at the end of the summer. I sold the farm and the store, passed around the measly profits with my brothers, and came to the big city to follow my dreams."

"I'm so sorry to hear about your dad," I said.

"He was a good guy," said Will. "Died of cancer. I'd swear it was those cigarettes."

"Maybe," I said.

I wondered about Will's wife, but he

didn't bring her up, and I didn't feel comfortable asking. "What kind of dreams are you pursuing in Baltimore, exactly?"

"Newspaper reporter. The *Baltimore Post*. I'm hoping to get an interview there and find a place to live in the city."

"Really? The rooms above and below me are vacant. My landlord would kiss you."

"That would be heaven." He blushed bright red while I laughed. "Not your landlord kissing me, but living so close to a friend."

"Ah."

Stillness settled around us. I continued eating my soup until he cleared his throat.

"You're too polite to ask, so I'll just tell you," he said. "My wife, Betty, left me two years ago."

"Why would she do a stupid thing like that?" I said, dragging my spoon around the bowl.

He smiled. "We couldn't have kids. She thought it was because of war injuries or gas exposure. I told her I only got shot in my leg and not my . . . you know. Hell, I don't know. It was a strain on her, seeing all of her friends getting pregnant, having babies. She started feeling suffocated in the small town. She was granted an annulment on account of our being so young and in a hurry to get married after the war. Can hardly blame her."

"You seem to be coping pretty well," I said.

"Well, it's been two years," he said.

And here I was, far more years later, forever tethered to my missing husband and deceased daughter in an arrested state of grief. I was ashamed that I hadn't done more for myself.

"I was bad to start," he continued. "But after the sting wore off I realized I was better off. She wasn't the kindest person. Honestly, I don't think she would have made much of a mother. Not like you."

My eyes flicked to the frame with Katie's sweet, round, four-year-old face. The picture was taken at the shore. She held a seashell, and the wind blew her dark hair. I could still smell the seawater and feel the warmth of her plump hand in mine. Tears blurred my eyes, but I didn't wipe them away. God knew Will and I had cried together before.

I met his gaze and he reached for my hand. I took it.

Three days later I opened my curtains to see his shabby blue pickup truck pull up to the front stoop, loaded with boxes and furniture. He hopped out of the driver's side and looked up at the building, breaking into a grin and waving like a fool when he saw me glancing down at him. I hurried down the stairs and opened the front door.

"I'm sorry, sir, but we don't want your kind here," I said.

"I thought that might be the case," he said, "so I packed a case of moonshine to offer to the neighbors as a bribe."

"I can get that any old place now that the world is wet again," I said. "But I suppose it's a start. Just don't let my brother find out, or he'll fight me for it."

The morning air still had a nip in it, so we made quick work of the boxes. I noticed that Will walked with a slight limp from his war injuries years ago, but he didn't need a cane. The only thing I couldn't help him lift was the couch, but luckily the landlord stopped over to collect the first and last months' rent, so he did. Before he left he gave us a strange look, but seemed happy to have a new boarder.

Will had chosen Sorin's apartment, which I had to mentally instruct myself not to say aloud many times, for the beautiful front window that provided lots of natural light. He set up his writing table and typewriter in front of it and his couch on the wall behind it, exactly where Sorin's couch used to stand. I shuddered a bit at the thought of the night I was attacked, so long ago. Will noticed.

"It is a little chilly in here," he said. "This window's drafty. I'll have to seal the edges." He looked around the apartment and nodded. "I like it."

"I like that you're here," I said. "Imagine if I'd told you what would happen to us those many years ago, and that after all of it, we'd be right here, like this. Would you do it over again?"

"Yes," he said. "As long as I could be standing right here, just like this."

"Well, welcome to the neighborhood, Mr. Brennan."

That following Thursday night, at Peter's invitation, I took Will to the Owl Bar, which, now that Prohibition had been lifted, stood as a symbol of the past.

I was on edge when we arrived, but after a quick scan of the room, I was relieved to see that Scott was not there. Peter had already gotten us a table and a round of drinks, and seemed half in when we greeted him.

"Will! It's been years!"

My brother and Will had met briefly while I nursed at Walter Reed. Now they bonded instantly over music, and Peter monopolized the conversation with his talk of jazz and how the big-band sounds were about to blow the lid off music as we knew it.

"That's what Anna should be playing on that piano of hers," said Peter. "Instead of moody music by dead white men."

I rolled my eyes and then watched the door.

"Anna," said Peter. "Hello, Anna. What, are you afraid he'll come here?"

"Who?" asked Will.

"Her boyfriend," said Peter.

I punched him on the arm when I saw the look on Will's face.

"Oh, can it, Peter," I said. "I don't have a boyfriend, but yes, I'm worried that Scott Fitzgerald will come here."

"Why are you worried?" asked Will.

I had written briefly about my work with Zelda in my letter to Will, but I quickly filled him in on some of what had happened since.

"I see why you're worried," he said.

"And, Peter," I said, "do not call Scott over if he comes stumbling through the door."

"Yes, ma'am," he said with a salute. "Now, Will, have you found a job in the city yet?"

"No. I've got an interview coming up soon, though, with the paper."

Peter wrinkled his eyebrows and cleared his throat. "Um, how soon are we talking, here? That beard is . . . intense."

I kicked Peter under the table.

"Ouch!"

Will laughed. "No, he's right. It's coming off before the interview."

"Thank heaven!" said Peter. "Oh, which leads me to you, Anna."

"I know. I've let myself go this winter. I'm getting my appetite back already."

"That's good, but I wasn't thinking of that," said Peter. "I have an actual reason why I invited you here."

"I know," I said. "To get you drunk within walking distance of a bed where you may lay your head without scandal."

Will laughed.

"Yes, that," said Peter. "But actually, I have a job offer for you."

He had my attention.

"It's not glamorous and it doesn't pay much, but we need an organist at the cathedral, starting in mid-May. You'd have to work Sundays, holy days, weddings, and funerals. What say you?"

I began to stammer some kind of rejection, because I didn't know whether I could handle playing an organ, and in front of a crowd, when Peter cut me off.

"No one would see you except for the choir," said Peter. "You'd be in the loft. Your beautiful music would come from above — as if from heaven."

I had the strangest sensation at that moment — one I couldn't identify at first because I hadn't felt it in so long. The more I thought about it, though, the more clearly I realized what it was.

Relief.

Peter could see it on my face, and reached for my hand.

"Is this a ploy to get me to attend mass more regularly?" I asked.

"Yes," he said.

I smiled and squeezed his hand. He kissed it and motioned for the bartender to bring us another round.

"Of course, I'll still be playing music by dead white men," I said.

"I thought about that," said Peter. "We'll see if we can find some old spirituals to add to the lineup, though. Shake the congregation up a little."

I heard myself laugh as the music rose around us.

Will and I escorted my dear, drunken, holy brother back to my apartment, but after a few minutes, Peter was snoring on the couch so loudly that Will and I could barely talk over the racket. We closed him into the room and went down to Will's apartment, because he wanted my advice on what to wear to his interview the following week.

I'd had a little too much to drink and stumbled on the bottom step, but Will caught me and we went laughing into his apartment.

"I don't know if I'm the best judge of this at the moment," I said. "Everything's tilting a bit."

"You'll be just fine."

I sat on his couch while he flipped on the light and started music on the gramophone — Gershwin. "Embraceable You," an instrumental version.

"Very nice," I said.

He called to me from the bedroom. "I just picked it up for a steal. Isn't it swell?"

"Yes," I said. "Maybe I'll learn to play it, to at least catch up my musical tastes to this century."

I leaned back on the couch, closed my eyes, and allowed the music to fill my ears. It was slow and sweet, like a long walk on a first date.

In a moment, Will was before me holding up two new suits on hangers — one a double-breasted gray, the other a crisp navy with a thin pinstripe.

"Ooh!" I said. "Where did you find them?"

"City consignment shops have much better merchandise than country shops. All I could find in southern Maryland was a pair of overalls without a hole and one with a hole."

I laughed and squinted my eyes, trying to decide which suit I liked better. I stood and moved the navy suit in front of him.

"Honestly, I'm having a hard time envisioning you in either with that beard," I said.

"I know. It's awful. I'll shave it tomorrow."

"No," I said. "Come on; it's coming off now."

I walked into the kitchen and dragged a chair from under the table to the sink.

"Where's your razor?" I asked.

"In the bathroom," he said, giving me a strange look. In a moment he disappeared around the corner and returned with a razor, shaving cream, and a towel. I guided him into the chair and placed the towel around his neck. When my hands brushed his skin, I saw goose bumps rise.

"Are you sure you can handle this, Nurse Anna?" he asked, sounding very much like the young, cheeky man from the hospital all those years ago.

"Are you sure *you* can handle this?" I

teased, giving him a little shove on his back.

"I'm absolutely aces," he said. "Though it's been a long time since a dame's been so close to me. This isn't going to embarrass you, is it?"

"Please, I had to shave more than your face in the hospital."

He laughed. "There's my Anna."

I filled the bowl with warm water and placed it on the counter. Then I squeezed shaving cream on my hands and worked it into a lather.

My Anna.

At first his words had passed me by, but once I caught them from the air I realized I liked the sound of them. I also realized that both of us were tipsy and therefore loose with our commentary.

When I touched his face, he closed his eyes and tilted his head. I worked the cream around his cheeks, chin, and mouth, and paused to consider his lips — the little upturned corners, the thin upper lip resting on the full lower lip.

I warmed the razor in the water and began the slow scraping motion down the left side of his face. I didn't get far before I had to clean off the blade and continue, due to the thickness of his beard, but it didn't take long for me to finish the left side, and most of the right.

The record stopped, and suddenly the room seemed very warm and close. He opened his eyes, and in a husky voice said, "Start it over." I nodded and left the room for a moment. When I returned, his gaze pierced me and I suddenly felt unsure. My confidence seemed to have slipped out through the draft in the front room window. He must have sensed my hesitation. "Do you want me to finish?" His voice was very quiet.

I shook my head. *No.*

I walked back to the sink and rinsed out the bowl. The steam rose around my face and I fanned it away, then returned to him.

"Close your eyes," I said.

"Why?"

"I don't want to get any shaving cream in them."

He gave me a devilish smile, held my gaze for a moment, then very deliberately closed his eyes and again tilted back his head.

As I scraped the razor down the rest of his face, I was suddenly struck by the emergence of the young Will I'd once known, when we had teased, and played, and life was so, so easy. I felt my confidence return, and with it an undeniable desire to kiss him.

Clearing the rest of his face didn't take

nearly as long as I wanted it to, so I took my time. Finally, as I leaned over him to shave the last place on his chin, he opened his eyes. We stared at each other and I reached up with my fingers to clear away a dab of shaving cream under his lips.

"There you are," I said.

He gently pulled me into his lap and kissed me.

Our kiss was long and slow and sent heat down to my toes. As it intensified, I felt overcome and completely out of my senses.

Until the record stopped.

I pulled back, breathless, and put my hand on my mouth. He opened his eyes and stared at me with such longing that I had to stand up and step backward to the wall.

In a moment he was before me, his lips on mine again, his body pressing into me. I responded, but then pulled away and walked into the front room. He reached for my arm and brought me close to him, pressing his forehead into mine.

"Anna, don't go."

I closed my eyes and allowed myself just a moment of imagining what would happen if I stayed, but then reality, or what I'd made my reality, came pushing in. Peter was upstairs. Will and I weren't married. But maybe I was still married.

No, I wasn't. Suddenly I knew that for sure, but all of the other thoughts won and I pulled back.

"I have to go," I said.

He released my arm and let me walk to the door and halfway up the stairs before he called to me.

"Anna."

I stopped and gazed down at him, sweet Will, bursting with emotion, and desire, and what I hoped was love, because I knew I felt it for him and I knew it wouldn't go away in the morning, which made it all the more important to me that I continue up to my apartment.

"Anna, I'm not going anywhere," he said.

I looked at him for a moment and then felt a smile start. He grinned back, ran his hands through his hair, and groaned.

I turned and continued up the stairs, but when I got to the door I looked down at him and pressed my hand to my lips and then toward him.

He put his hand over his heart.

Twenty-Four

I awoke to rain, but it did not oppress my spirits. It felt fresh and cleansing, so I opened my window and inhaled the pure smell of spring.

Peter had awoken early and left a note.

Swing low, sweet chariot, a taxi came to taketh me home. Come by anytime to practice for your big church debut. I love you and I think you should marry Will.

All my love,
Peter

I laughed and hummed my way through breakfast, acutely aware of the man occupying the space in the apartment below me, and somewhat surprised by how eager I was to see him. I was not at all embarrassed about our kiss. How different I would have felt this morning if I hadn't left his apartment when I did.

Or maybe not.

I bathed and washed my hair, and looked forward to a day of organizing my apartment, writing a letter to Zelda, though I knew it would go unanswered, and practicing the piano, when I heard a knock at the door.

I went to greet who I was sure was Will, but when I pulled it open, I was shocked to see Scott standing before me, wet and sobbing, his skin the color of weathered slate. He stumbled in, and I nearly had to carry him to the couch. I went back and shut the door and returned to him.

He buried his face in his hands and continued sobbing, and I could feel myself recoil. I'd been reaching out to the Fitzgeralds for so long that it was a strange sensation to want to pull away, but I thought that might have something to do with the warmth that had been in my apartment before he'd come in with his terrible coldness.

I recalled that Peter had warned me about how famous people had a way of absorbing others into themselves, and not to allow myself to be swallowed by the Fitzgeralds. It was presumptuous for Scott to find me at my apartment and bring his troubles to my door. Of course, I'd been nearly begging him to let me help with Zelda for so long, I could see why he'd do it. Clearly he needed me, and yet here I was resenting the intrusion and wishing to soak in my own joy without disturbance. I forced myself to sit next to him on the couch.

"I can't do it anymore," he said. "I can't support her."

"What's happened?" I said.

"*Tender* isn't selling enough. My best work yet — my soul splayed open for all to feast upon — and the readers simply do not care."

I nearly laughed aloud. *His* soul? I could not find any words to answer him.

He looked up at me and then stood as anger flashed over his face.

"I know what you're thinking," he said. "It's *her soul* — her soul that was used. But don't you see? Her soul is my soul, and not because it belongs to me but because we share it."

His notion was a romantic one, but I worried that he, too, would succumb to madness with thoughts like these. I decided to steer the conversation to the book, since I could not speak of their souls, joint or separate.

"Scott, low sales are a factor of the depression, not your work."

He shook his head.

"Is the situation so dire that Zelda cannot stay at Craig House?" I asked.

"Yes," he said. "If I didn't have Scottie's school tuition to pay, I could keep her there a bit longer. Zelda begs me to send her to a less costly establishment, but I can't bear to stick her in a state institution. She's better than that. She deserves more."

He crumpled again on the couch and renewed his sobbing. I was alarmed at the condition of his emotions and his inebriation, and felt real panic rising up at the thought of Scott sticking Zelda in a state-run mental institution. At least he knew she didn't belong there. We would figure something out.

There was a knock at the door. I stood and went to open it, only to find Will before me with a massive bouquet of daffodils. His smile froze when he saw the wet, sobbing man inside.

"Is now a bad time?" he asked.

I slipped into the hallway, closing the door behind me, and kissed him. Then I pulled away and whispered, "Yes."

"Who is that?"

"It's Scott Fitzgerald."

Will made an O with his mouth. "So I should come back later to take you to lunch in the rain, instead of breakfast?"

I smiled at him. "Yes."

"Are you okay with him in there?" Will suddenly narrowed his eyes. "He's not trying anything with you, is he?"

I nearly laughed aloud. "No. Not at all. But I do fear for his health, so I'll have to fill you in later."

Will wrapped his arms around me and pulled me close for another kiss that took my breath away. When I pulled back he put his lips to my ear.

"You are going to drive *me* crazy, Anna," he whispered. "But then maybe that would be good so you could take care of me all the time."

"I would like that very much," I whispered back.

I reached for his smooth face, again marveling at the transformation. He kissed me one last time, pressed the flowers into my hands, and left me on the stairs.

Once my heart rate returned to normal I walked back into my apartment, quickly put the flowers in water in the kitchen, and entered the main room to find Scott at my piano. He had composed himself and was looking at pictures of Katie and Ben. He gave me the saddest smile.

"I have to apologize," he said.

"Why?"

"Because you have a whole life outside of me and Zelda, and I know nothing of it," he said. "Who are they?"

Taken aback by his notice, I hesitated a moment.

"I'm sorry to interfere," he said, placing the photographs back on the piano.

"No," I said. "It's okay. I was married to him, to Ben, but he never came home from the war. Katie was my daughter, but she died at five, of pneumonia."

"Oh, Anna," he said. "I'm so very sorry."

I looked down at the floor, suddenly wishing with all of my heart that he would leave. He felt like an illness, and I did not want him to infect me.

"And here I am, giving all of my problems to you," he said. "I should go."

He started toward the door, but stopped when he got to me.

"I just have one more request," he said. "When it's time for me to move Zelda, wherever that is, will you help me escort her?"

"Yes, Scott, of course."

"Thank you." He hugged me, overwhelming me with his embrace and the odor of gin. Just as I felt I was about to suffocate, he pulled away and was gone.

TWENTY-FIVE

May 1934

I waited anxiously in front of our building for Will's arrival. I'd worked out Zelda's travel arrangements with Scott's secretary, Isabel. Zelda would return to Baltimore, but this time to the Sheppard and Enoch Pratt Hospital, a step down from Phipps, but not as bad as some other places. My stomach had been roiling about it, and I worried for Zelda. I prayed she'd thrive so she could eventually leave, but I tried not to set my hopes too high.

I spent the rest of the day painting the trim on the hall moldings. Now I stood pacing on the newly bricked front stoop that Will had repaired just last week. Will was handy and had worked out a deal with our landlord for a break on the rent in exchange for his services around the house, the way I had with cleaning. I found myself enjoying the time we spent together fixing up the building. With just the two of us living there, Will could leave open his door and blast his music into the stairwell while we worked.

We now had fresh paint in our rooms, in the hallways, and on the wrought-iron railings down the stairs; newly polished floors, reliable heaters, and electric lighting that didn't flicker. I'd replaced the light fixtures and switch plates with more modern coverings, and found some inexpensive prints that reminded me of Zelda's or O'Keeffe's flowers for the walls around the entrance.

I went back inside for a moment, grabbed a watering can, and took it outside to soak the phlox and irises blooming in the front flower boxes and beds. The evening sun warmed my back, and the laughter of children at the newly erected playground across the way eased my anxious anticipation.

It wasn't long before I heard Will's truck. He screeched to a halt in front of our building and was nearly out the door before the vehicle stopped. I turned in time for him to pick me up and swing me around in a circle.

"You got the job," I said.

"I got the job!"

He swung me again, and kissed me. I could feel his heart pounding.

"I'm so proud of you," I said.

He kissed me again, and then set me on

the stoop. He suddenly looked very serious.

"What is it?" I asked.

"I just want to freeze this part, you know. This good feeling, here, with you. I haven't had this in so long. I need to savor it."

I knew what he meant, the dreadful shadow behind the good days we'd had. The threat of the passage of time. I shook my head. "No, this is our reality now. Don't worry about a thing. Just enjoy this moment and be thankful for it."

He nodded, but the sadness remained in his eyes, and I could see him thinking.

"What is it?" I asked.

He shook his head and smiled. "Nothing. This. I'm going to enjoy today."

"Good," I said. "Me, too."

I put down the watering can and we sat on the front step, resting against each other, watching the children climb and swing. The playground seemed to have bloomed almost overnight, and now it was often filled with laughter and happy shrieking. I loved its beautiful music.

A little girl walked on the balance beam near the edge of the playground. I saw her there often, with her older brother and her young, worn mother. When the girl looked up at me, I waved to her and she waved back. She reminded me of Scottie.

"Tomorrow's the day I'll have to go to New York," I said, "to help transfer Zelda to Sheppard Pratt."

"I bet you'll be relieved to have her so near to you again."

I didn't know how to respond. In some ways, yes, I felt connected to Zelda and wished to have her near me, but on the other hand, I worried that I would again allow myself to become consumed. I knew it was unlikely, since I did not work at the hospital and she wouldn't speak to me, but I also knew that when it came to Zelda, I seemed to lose all reason.

"We'll see," I said. "I don't know if this is the best move for her, but I think it's the best he can do right now."

"And how about you?" Will said. "Are you ready for your debut at the cathedral?"

"I think so," I said. "I'm just playing traditional hymns this weekend. We'll try to shake them up some other time. But enough about all this. Tell me about your interview."

I let Will's voice fill my head, with the chorus of children behind it, and pressed into him and listened to him talk about his new boss, and the paper, and his first assignment, while the sun set over the city.

I was up and on the train headed north,

with Scott, before the sun rose the next morning. I sipped coffee and tried to read the paper while we traveled, but I found it impossible to concentrate on the words. I eventually gave up and watched the cities slip by while my sense of unrest grew.

Scott was a mess. He'd warned me about Zelda's recent erratic and unusual communications. I steeled myself for a vacant, agitated, and possibly excitable woman, and tried not to think of Zelda, my friend, whom I desperately missed. I missed her unique views, her gorgeous poetic narratives, the way she made a sensory experience of every description, the way she spoke of art and dance as naturally as the weather. I missed her large gray eyes, her moments of clarity that outshone the rest of us, her grace.

And as I knew and had prepared myself, my Zelda was not there.

It was a blank woman whom we moved down the East Coast that day. I got nothing from her, not even a moment of time to spend with my friend. And yet her blankness, her nothingness seemed a construct, a dramatic stage of denial, a bizarre form of self-preservation. It was as if a barren tundra existed between us. I felt deeply that this woman gave us no access to her so that she had nothing to mourn at our parting.

Scott twitched with nervous energy, but to his credit he remained sober, and did not disturb her. He and I escorted her into the sterile ward that would become her home. There was no charm to the building, no kindness in its nurses, and no color anywhere. It was all I could do not to weep.

Scott took well the instructions that he was not to visit her for at least two weeks while Zelda acclimated, but by the time we'd kissed her stony face and walked out of the gray doors, we were both in tears. Once the doors shut, we cried in each other's arms under a willow tree.

I didn't get home until seven o'clock that night, and when I opened the door to the building, sad opera music filled the foyer. For a moment I felt confused and then chilled at the thought of the ghosts of my ballerinas whispering and practicing upstairs, but the warm spill of light from Will's room where his door was opened to me reminded me of my new building mate. As I shut the front door, he walked out of his rooms and opened his arms to me.

I gave up any thought of trying not to cry and let him hold me while I wet his shirt with my tears. Once I pulled myself together, I looked up at him and apologized.

He wiped my face and led me into his apartment, where a plate of cheese, bread, and fruit and a glass of red wine waited for me at the place where I liked to sit at his table.

"What do you have to be sorry about?" he said.

"I didn't want to be a mess when you saw me."

"It would be strange if you weren't a mess," he said. "She's your friend."

I nodded and wiped my eyes, suddenly aware of how very hungry and tired I was. He saw me eyeing the plate and smiled. "I know it's not much, but I wasn't sure what time you'd be home, and I didn't want to make anything that would spoil. Oh, and also, I can't cook for shit."

I laughed for the first time that day, and sat at the table.

While I began to eat I noticed that Will didn't sit down. He darted around the apartment making meaningless adjustments to the couch, straightening his writing papers, hustling empty cups to the kitchen, washing dishes. I couldn't catch his eyes, though he attempted small talk about the train ride, the weather, baseball, the price of milk.

I felt a coldness begin in the pit of my stomach.

Something was wrong.

I took a healthy sip of wine and dabbed my lips while he straightened a picture on the wall and arranged a stack of magazines on his bookshelf.

"Will."

He stopped, but still wouldn't look at me. It took every ounce of courage I could summon to manage two words to which I couldn't imagine the answer.

"What's wrong?"

He turned slowly toward me, his face a mask of pain. I stood, crossed the room, and grabbed his arms. "What is it?"

He moved away from me toward his writing desk, where a single envelope rested on the windowsill. I could see it had my name on it and it was not opened.

"That came in the mail for you today," he said. His voice was very quiet.

I walked over to the window to see why he was so shaken, and knew once I saw the sender.

United States Department of Defense, Prisoner of War/ Missing Personnel Office.

It suddenly seemed as if all sound was silenced and I could hear only my pulse in my ears. The coldness in my belly had spread to my fingertips. I had an urge to take the letter and run up to my apartment, where I could be alone with it, but no part of my body would do what I wished of it, so I just stood there, focusing on controlling my breath.

After a moment, I became aware of my surroundings again: the melancholy song on the gramophone, the shush of tires on the road outside the house, Will standing just inches away from me. I also became aware of how quickly the cold in my body turned hot and rose up through me. I could feel the color hit my face as if I were a thermometer, and my hands began to shake.

"Anna," he said. "Would you like me to open it?"

I knew he wanted to be there for me. I could feel his desire reaching out to me from the atmosphere between us, but I had to be alone.

"No," I said, quickly grabbing the letter while my senses were in obedience of my mind. "No. I have to go."

I turned toward the door and tried to leave, but he grabbed me by the arms and started to hug me.

"Anna, you shouldn't be alone."

I pulled myself from his grasp and continued to the door. He moved in front of me to block my path. I looked him in the eye and saw that there were tears. *No, not his grief again* — I couldn't take the weight of his grief. Suddenly I felt as if we were back at my parents' home all those years ago while he sobbed over Ben. I couldn't console him again. I just needed to be alone with my own pain.

I knew my feelings were cold and savage, but I was in the midst of such a tumult of emotions that I couldn't separate the anger — no, the rage — I felt at the Defense Department, Scott, Zelda, and Ben himself for shattering this thin, fragile happiness that I'd been trying to create. And then it dawned on me that I was most angry at myself for allowing myself to think that things could ever be okay, that just yesterday I could counsel Will into believing that everything would be all right when it never, ever would. The past would haunt when the present let up, and always, always the future would loom with its certainty of tragedy and pain.

But none of these thoughts made any sense, and I knew Will was hurt because he must have felt like a target of my anger. Maybe he was, because I resented him.

"Don't tell me that I shouldn't be alone," I said. "I was doing just fine alone before all of this painting and hammering and organ playing and busyness tried to trick me into thinking *together* was better than alone."

He turned bright red, and I knew I had hurt him, but I persisted in my mania and tore the letter open.

"Okay, Will, here I go. We both know what it says, but I'll read it with you so I don't have to be *alone.*"

"Stop," he said.

"No, according to you, this is what I need. I need to not be alone when I read this," I said. " 'Dear Mrs. Howard —' Ha! Mrs.! See, I am still married."

"Knock it off, Anna. You're making it worse."

"No, you should hear this. God knows I'll burn it when I finish reading it, so now's your chance to hear it. 'We regret to inform you that on April the second day of 1934, French nationals fishing on the banks of the Meuse/Argonne River found a single set of human remains.' "

"Damn it! Stop," said Will as he stormed to the kitchen and stood at the sink with his back to me, clutching the counter.

I raised my voice.

" 'There were dog tags and other identifying materials with the remains, and after comparisons, it was determined that the remains were those of Sergeant Benjamin Howard of the U.S. Army, of Maryland.' "

My voice broke, but I continued. " 'He was killed during the Meuse/Argonne offensive and died bravely defending his country. He will be returned to you for burial with full military honors.' "

God help me, but I threw the letter on the floor and pushed over the gramophone with all of my strength to stop that horrible opera music, then crumpled to the floor and sobbed. Within moments, Will was there, his arms wrapped around me, holding me.

TWENTY-SIX

June 1934

On June 12, 1934, Will, my parents, and Peter were at my side to bury Ben's remains next to Katie's at Baltimore's Green Mount Cemetery. Ben was eligible for burial at Arlington National Cemetery, but I wanted him with Katie, where I could visit them both.

It was the fairest of June days. The world was fresh and soaked from an early morning shower, and the warm, pure scent of earth and flowers hung in the air. As much dread as I'd felt leading up to the service, I walked away with a sense of peace and stillness.

It was finally over.

Will drove Peter and me to my parents' house for dinner that evening, where we sat amidst the wind chimes around the porch, overlooking the walk to the woods. My mother had taken out all of her candles and best china, and played her recording of John Field's Grand Pastorale in E Major for us while we dined and watched the fireflies wink from the lawn and trees.

And so began our new weekend tradition. Will drove Peter and me to my parents' house for Sunday dinners, which grew to weekend stays. Will taught me to drive on the back roads. He prepared oysters for us, entertained my mother with his reporter stories and city gossip, and sat at my father's side learning to make wind chimes. I loved watching them together week after week in the wind shed, heating, cutting, and threading copper to blocks of wood, with my mother sitting nearby reading in her wheelchair. I grew to love playing my piano for them after dinner, especially when I'd look up and Will would be watching me with a burning intensity that reached across the room and made it harder and harder for me to stand sleeping just one room away from him at the house, and even harder at our building in the city without a priest and parents snoring nearby.

It was on a warm July Saturday morning, just days before my thirty-eighth birthday, when I learned I would not have to continue to wait much longer.

The aroma of coffee and pancakes coerced

me out of bed and into the kitchen, where Will, Peter, and my father had cooked enough breakfast for an army. They whistled around one another, fully dressed and coiffed, while I stood, pleasantly surprised, with my robe wrapped around me and my hair, loose and disheveled, on my shoulders.

"What is going on?" I asked. "This isn't the usual morning protocol. And why is Will allowed near the stove? That's extremely dangerous."

"I'll have you know that I've cooked about three dozen blueberry pancakes, and at least a dozen of them are edible," Will said.

"Wow!"

"Yes," said Peter. "So you just go and primp yourself presentable, and leave the cooking to us."

I raised my hands in surrender and left the room, happy to be off kitchen detail and with a growing feeling of anticipation. I dared not allow my imagination to take me to the place where I wanted it to go, though I knew in my heart what was coming.

I put on a pink tea-length dress with capped sleeves, and pinned my hair into a loose chignon. With a little makeup I felt much younger than a woman pushing forty. I thought I looked it, too.

When I stepped out of my room, I met

my mother in the hallway. She leaned against the walker she used inside the house, and had clearly taken care with her dressing and hair. When she saw me, her eyes glistened with tears. Holding back my own, I hugged her and placed my hand on her back while I helped her out onto the porch, where I could hear the men talking and laughing. When we stepped outside, Lincoln was on the back porch in brown slacks and a white collared shirt with a slim, smiling woman at his side.

"Lincoln!" I gasped and ran to hug him. I'd missed him since I had found my own personal chauffeur, though I did see him every now and then driving through town. He gave me a squeeze and then pulled back and introduced me to his wife, Nellie. Seeing Lincoln and Nellie confirmed what my heart had suspected, and I scanned the group until I found Will. He stood by the door on the far side of the porch. His face was drawn with emotion, and my heart began to pound.

"Everyone," said Peter, "please enjoy a drink while Will and Anna take a stroll. Then we can all enjoy breakfast together when they get back. *If* they come back."

A ripple of laughter went through the small group, and I walked over to Will. He took my trembling hand and led me to the backyard.

The sun's warmth rested on our heads like a blessing, and the aroma of honeysuckle drifted on the breeze from the forest edge. Mourning doves cooed from the branches overhead, mingling with the music of the wind chimes. When we got to the wind shed, he led me in, turned to me, and held both of my hands in his.

When Will started to speak, his voice broke and he looked away. I reached up and turned his face toward me. I hoped that if he saw my tears flowing freely he'd feel more at ease. He smiled at me and cleared his throat.

"I'm sorry," he said.

"Oh, no, you have nothing to be sorry about." I beamed at him.

He took a deep breath. "Okay. Anna. Anna, Anna."

"You're stalling," I said.

He laughed and squeezed my hands.

"Yes, I am," he said. "Because I want to live in this moment for a long, long time."

He closed his eyes, then opened them and began to speak. "Since the time you started nursing me after the war, I was smitten. But back then, I had promised myself to another, so I had to suppress my feelings. And

360

then you fell in love with my best friend, and that actually helped me, because it made me so happy to see you both so happy, and I could accept my fate.

"But then he was lost. And while I mourned him hard, what killed me was coming to see you and that sweet baby, alone, while I was married and couldn't do a damned thing about it." His voice failed again, and he took a moment to gather himself. I was overwhelmed by his confession. I thought he'd just been crying over Ben all those years ago. I'd had no idea that he was also crying over me. I reached up and wiped my tears, overwhelmed by my love for him.

Once he steadied himself, he began to smile again. "But I was given a second chance with you. And I can't stop thanking God every day. Your father has given me his blessing, and I don't want to wait any longer."

Through my tears I could barely see him get down on his knee or lift the ring.

"Will you marry me?"

My hands were shaking so badly, it was hard for him to put the ring on my finger, but he managed. I reached down and pulled him up, and kissed him with every ounce of passion I'd felt growing in me, while whispering my yeses between the kisses. I had never known such happiness.

Once we could tear ourselves away from each other, we hurried back to the house. As we approached, Will yelled, "She said yes!"

Our loved ones clapped and cheered from the porch. I'll never forget that perfect moment of heaven on earth. When I think of it, I know I'm the luckiest woman in the world.

Peter married us two weeks later, on our crazy, mixed-up wedding month, where we got engaged at dawn and had a reception brunch that day, followed by a ceremony at the cathedral two weeks later, and ending with a honeymoon in the home we already shared.

The night after the ceremony, we arrived at our building. Will opened the door of the truck, swept me into his arms, and carried me over the threshold. He placed me on my feet in the foyer and looked at me in the dark. I suddenly felt butterflies in my stomach. It's quite a thing to have all of your dreams come true over the course of a single month.

He ran his hands over my hair and face and kissed me. Then he led me into the front room and turned on the gramophone. "Embraceable You" began, and he held his hand out to me. We began to dance to the music in the darkened front room, and he leaned his face close to my ear.

"Do you remember the night this played when you shaved me?"

"How could I forget?" I said.

"I have been burning for you ever since, plus all of the years I loved you but couldn't love you."

I met his gaze and we again kissed each other, the heat growing between us until we could stand it no more. We managed to stumble upstairs to my room, which was now our room. The moonlight shone in through the window on the bed. Within moments, he had removed his shirt and tie. Then he turned me away from him and unzipped the back of my dress while he kissed my neck. I finished removing my clothes and lay across the bed, waiting for him to finish undressing. He stared at me for a moment, and then climbed into bed with me, where we made up for all the years we'd waited for each other.

As Will lay sleeping with his arm across my waist, the unearthly shaft of moonlight had moved from the bed to my photograph of

Zelda and me on the beach in Bermuda. We were wet from the rain and humidity, bulbous clouds over us, a tumultuous sea behind us. Our arms were wrapped around each other like we were holding on for dear life.

We were, really.

But now I'd found my life. I had learned how to love and take risks again because of the strength and confidence I'd found in being needed by Zelda. While my new life gave me a frightening amount of happiness, there was turmoil beneath it. I knew I would always carry the guilt of moving on. Lurking beneath the surface of the beautiful years to come would always be the worry that I'd used Zelda the way Scott had.

■ ■ ■ ■

SECOND ACT

■ ■ ■ ■

"There are no second acts in American
lives."

— F. Scott Fitzgerald

TWENTY-SEVEN

February 1948

I had the dream again — the dream in which Zelda and I are swimming in Bermuda, the night she saved me. Only, in the dream, after she places me on the beach, Zelda goes back out into the water and swims until the sea claims her.

I awoke in a panic, covered in sweat, and felt a tugging at my arm. It was my twelve-year-old daughter, Sara.

"What is it, honey?" I asked.

"I heard something," she said. My daughter's large gray eyes were so like mine, it startled me. Like Zelda's, when I first met her. I thought for a moment about that day, all those years ago, and how drawn to her eyes I was because they mirrored my own. I glanced at my bedside table at the picture of Zelda and me.

"Mommy," said Sara.

I shook my head, clearing away thoughts

of Zelda, which had been coming with more and more frequency. I was starting to worry that it was a sign. Peter would undoubtedly think so.

"I'm sorry," I said. "What did you hear?"

"Listen," she whispered.

Will adjusted himself in his sleep, but didn't wake. I slipped off the covers and took Sara's hand. We walked into the hallway and I glanced around, half expecting to hear Romanian violin music or the pounding of ballerinas. Why did I still think of them all as ghosts in this house? Especially since Will and I had owned it for years, and I'd remained in contact with Sorin. I'd even taken Will to a concert several years after we got married, when Sorin came as a guest violinist to the Baltimore Symphony Orchestra.

I did hear something. It sounded like voices in the front room. I stopped and listened.

"Oh, it's just the radio," I said. "We must have forgotten to turn it off when we went to bed."

She smiled and I led her back to what was now her room — the former living room of my apartment that Will had built into a private bedroom when the babies started coming. She crawled into bed and I tucked the covers up around her ears.

"You're not too old for tuck-ins yet?" I asked.

"No, Mommy," she said with a sleepy smile.

I pulled the covers up around her ears. "There. Snug as a bug."

Sara closed her eyes and I sat at her bedside, smoothing her hair until she drifted off to sleep. My heart was full of love for her and for her sleeping thirteen-year-old twin brothers, Ben and Will Junior, in the rooms above us that used to hold the ballerinas.

The grandfather clock in the foyer bonged the two o'clock hour as I walked down to the front room. I switched off the radio, but was thoroughly awake, and did not relish the prospect of going back to bed and staring at the ceiling through the dark, dwelling on my dream.

I glanced around the room at the mess of my family with half a sigh and half a smile. Sara's little scrunched-up tubes of paint were scattered about the corner where her easel held a painting of the beach at the Eastern Shore, where we now took the children every summer. I could make out the faint sketch of a horse at Assateague Island to which she intended to add color tomorrow.

Will Junior's sheet music lay scattered on the floor around the base of the piano, where we'd moved it to the front room years ago. I bent over and began to straighten the pages, leaving his recital piece on the stand, but shoving the rest in the bench. Just as I was about to lower the lid, I noticed Sorin's "Anii" peeking out of the bottom of the pile. I slipped out the old, crumbled paper and smiled to myself. The haunting melody stirred my memory, urging my fingers to play. I knew I could not or it would wake everyone, so instead I placed the sheet back on the top of the pile in the bench so I would not forget to play it another day. Maybe I'd play it for one of my patients.

For the past three years, I had worked part-time as a music therapist with shell-shocked soldiers at Walter Reed, the army hospital where I'd met Will all those years ago. Once the kids were in school, my passion for helping wounded veterans had led me back to Walter Reed during the recent World War. When Will wasn't working at the paper, he also spent a great deal of time with the soldiers. He knew how lonely recovering from the physical and mental wounds of war could be, and he wanted to help in the effort any way he could. I had thanked God every night that his leg injury from the first World War had prevented him from joining the action, but I knew there would always be a part of him that regretted he couldn't help in the fighting. I felt the same about my nursing.

At Walter Reed, I worked in the music therapy program under the training of Miss Frances Paperte — a pioneer in the field and a former singer with the Chicago Opera. I played the piano for soldiers at all stages of recovery, and was making wonderful progress with many of them. It was a beautiful thing to witness the healing power of music, the way it could lift a man out of his present and his past and let him exist in a totally separate and peaceful place, a place he could learn to access when the nightmares, memories, and terrors became too much to handle.

I hummed the melody of "Anii" as I collected little Ben's baseball bat and ball, and placed them in the basket by the front door. When my oldest twin wasn't in school, no matter what the weather, Ben was outside from dawn until dusk, covered in dirt, with only his quick white smile flashing for us.

They were good children, and I reflected as I often had on my gratitude for this second chance at life I'd been given. Immediately following my thoughts and prayers of thanks, however, came the nagging guilt of being away from Zelda, and the painful remembrance of my time caring for her, when I never really felt as if I'd helped her. In my obsessive looking back I couldn't help but think it was my support of Zelda's transfer out of Phipps that did her real harm. At the time I'd thought it would be good for her family and would help her adjust to life. I realized that I had been gravely mistaken. Of course, Scott's financial trouble and his hatred of Dr. Meyer had played a large part in his pulling her out of Phipps, but as her nurse I should have pushed harder for her return.

With heaviness in my heart, I walked over to the bookshelf, pulled out the box containing letters from Scott and Scottie, and sat on the sofa to read them. Scott had corresponded faithfully with me until his death in 1940 of a heart attack at age forty-four. He had abused his body too long with alcohol, and I prayed that his soul was at rest. Scottie had been good enough to pick up where he left off a few times since his death to fill me in on Zelda's progress.

As I flipped through the letters, my mood darkened. The pages told of Zelda's stay at Sheppard Pratt, where she would not allow my visits and where Scott had written that she'd tried to take her life by running out in front of a passing train. They described her sudden religious fanaticism and belief that she could talk to the dead. The letters took a more positive tone once Zelda had been transferred to Highland Hospital in Asheville, North Carolina. Their rigorous regimen of outdoor exercise seemed to suit Zelda. Scott had written that her letters had become less erratic, and she was even able to attend Scottie's graduation from the Ethel Walker School in 1938.

The next year, Zelda's silence had been particularly painful to me, since that was when I'd written to her about the death of Lincoln, and then my mother. Within one week of each other, I had lost my dear friend and my beloved mother, and it made me so sad that my children would never get to know her well. She had contracted a terrible kidney infection that had led to blood poisoning. We had taken her to the hospital, but once it was clear that the infection was beyond the doctor's control, she had asked to go home. I had spent her final days at her bedside with my brother and my father, while Will kept the children at home. The end was mercifully quick for her, but left us all numb and stunned. I couldn't believe almost ten years had passed since then.

I realized I was crying when a tear wet the last letter I held from Scott. It was dated November of 1940, one month before his death. It was from Hollywood, where he had spent his final years, and in it he spoke of his pride in Scottie and his new novel, which he thought would resurrect his career and help his finances.

The last few letters were from Scottie. She told of her marriage and children, and of how Zelda lived with her mother in Montgomery between hospitalizations at Highland in Asheville. It did appear that Zelda experienced more calm than upset in recent years. Her paintings were shown in art museums, Scottie continued to write, and she had even helped at the Red Cross at home during the Second World War. I often wondered whether Scott's death had freed her in a way so she could live on her own, according to her own wishes, and preserve the memories of the good time they had had together.

I put the letters back in the box and on the shelf while I thought of Scott's funeral. I had attended the burial in Rockville, Maryland, to honor him, but mostly because I longed to see Zelda. I'd imagined running to her, embracing her, and our tearful reunion being full of apologies, sadness at Scott's passing, and news of the years gone by. But my fantasy was never realized. Zelda was not stable enough to attend the funeral.

As I moved to turn off the light and head back up to bed, I noticed a pile of mail on the floor next to the coatrack. One of the children must have brought in the mail earlier and dropped it there. I leaned over to pick it up, and quickly flipped through it, when the third envelope almost made me faint.

Zelda!

I tore open the envelope from Highland Hospital and raced through the words as fast as I could.

My Dear Anna,
Listen to me.

I must begin with apologies. I can never say sorry well enough for my silence through these years.

How can I explain? I was so raw and injured when I entered Craig House that I felt like I'd been skinned. I literally felt like all the flesh had been torn from my body. Even the wind hurt. How could I let anyone in until the scab formed?

Then it fell off over and over again while

I was at the hell of Sheppard Pratt, and even the years after, and — Oh, enough of that bloody metaphor.

All is not well.

I've lost my face and my grace, and all that's left is the faded, bloated lapel flower.

It occurred to me today that all trace of my youth is gone and will never return to me. The hall clock ticks so loudly, taunting me about the damned relentlessness of time. The sweet nights on the Riviera, dancing with my ballet instructor, dinners with the Murphys, fights with Ernest Hemingway, the party that lasted for five years and ran from New York, to Paris, to Italy, and back — it's most definitely over. Hemingway is on his fourth wife, Scott's old editor (and mine!) Max Perkins has died, and Katy Dos Passos was decapitated in a terrible car accident. It's all I can see when I close my eyes.

Scott often comes to me in the drain-pipes or on things ice-green like his eyes — I see his eyes everywhere like T. J.

Eckleburg's, watching me, judging me, crying for me. I'd do anything not to see his eyes on a snatch of leaves or a dinner napkin, and just see them as they were, looking out from his pale face over lips that would press into me.

Oh, God, I didn't mourn him this hard just after he died, but now I feel like I'll burst over it.

Anna, you must find me those damned diaries. Scott told me. He said if I just hold them and burn them I can get fixed up. I keep trying to remake them but I can't. I need the real thing. When I ask, he won't tell me where they are, but they must be in Delaware, or New York, or Connecticut. Somewhere.

I know I ask an impossible task of you. If you can't find them, just bring me yourself. Even if just for a day. I need one pure face from my past with no stain to show me that life isn't all misery.

Write and tell me when you'll come.

Please come to me.

Zelda

I didn't realize how tightly I was clutching the paper until the words ran out, and it was just me, alone in my front room, in the middle of the night. I began pacing. After all these years! Zelda had reached out and grabbed my heart with her fist and I didn't know how to separate myself from her, or whether I even should.

The creak of the floorboards called my attention to the doorway, where Will stood, rumpled from sleep, with a look of concern on his face. "What is it?" he asked.

I couldn't speak, so I handed him the letter from Zelda with a shaking hand. His eyes darkened as he read to the end of the page. He sighed when he finished and looked at me.

"I have to," I said.

I could see he wanted to protest. He glanced around the room at all of the kids' things. It would be hard on him working, taking care of them alone for a little while, worrying about me. I knew he also resented Zelda, in spite of my excuses for her silence. He knew how much pain she had given me over the years, and Will only wanted to protect me.

But just the same, he looked back at me and nodded.

TWENTY-EIGHT

March 1948

The night before my trip, after my father had left, Peter and I sat with candles and tea between us at the dining table, while Will and the children slept upstairs.

"I've prayed for you and for Zelda," he said. "What you're doing is important."

"I'm glad you think so. I feel a tremendous amount of guilt for leaving my family for this fool's errand."

Peter wrinkled his forehead in surprise. "Did Will say that?"

"Heavens, no. I'm saying it."

"Well, stop saying it, or even thinking it. What you're doing is charity, and charity is goodness, which is God."

"It's *God* to leave your family to embark upon a fruitless search to find the hedonistic ramblings of a flapper? A flapper who hasn't spoken to me in years, and who is acting on the advice of her dead husband?"

"Yes."

I rolled my eyes, and he continued. "Zelda doesn't deserve what you're doing for her."

I began to protest, but he held up his hand. "The way that none of us deserve the price of our salvation. But it was given out of love, so it is ours to have. A gift."

I began to understand him, and this time I didn't roll my eyes over his spiritual musings.

"You are giving Zelda a gift," he continued, "and whether or not you find the diaries, it doesn't matter. No one has ever done anything like this for her. Your sacrifice on her behalf will restore hope in her. And if that isn't healing, I don't know what is. Remember the line 'There is no greater love . . .' "

" 'Than to lay down one's life for one's friends,' " I said. "I'm just so worried about leaving the children. And Will."

Peter hesitated for a moment, and then looked upstairs as if he expected someone to come down. He cleared his throat. "This trip will be good for you, too. It's time to go out on your own. The kids are bigger and you still baby them. Especially Sara."

"She has always been shy . . ." I said.

"Babied."

I began to protest until I realized that he

380

was right. Given my past, however, could he really blame me? I understood how fleeting life could be. I never took time with my children for granted, and felt gratitude for them every day — even when muddy boot prints were sloshed across the foyer, or incessant piano practice made conversation impossible, or the shrieks of sibling confrontation sliced through the house. I was well aware of my blessings, and in no hurry to be separated from them.

"It will be good for all of you," he concluded, reaching for me.

I nodded and squeezed his hand, and we finished our tea in silence.

When I climbed into bed well after midnight, Will was still awake. He wrapped himself around me and we whispered all night about my travel plans, what I'd find and wouldn't find, and most important, what I would give to Zelda when I saw her. It had been Will's idea to photograph the places I visited and put them in a scrapbook. If I could not find her real diaries, I would create them.

I had in my possession a model of the new Polaroid Land Camera, due out later in the year. Will had paid a photographer at the paper an ungodly sum for it once he saw how it produced a picture in less than one

381

minute. It was the most spectacular thing I'd ever seen, and we had taken several pictures of the kids and each other when we'd first gotten it. I would bring it with me on the trip so I could work on Zelda's new scrapbook a little each night, and present it to her when I saw her.

"This will be good for you," said Will. "I know you've felt guilty all these years for moving on after your time with Zelda, though I don't think you should."

"I've always felt her shadow," I said. "We were so intensely close for so long, and then she was suddenly ripped away. I've never had peace with that."

"I know." He kissed me and pulled me closer.

In the darkness, we made love and slept in each other's arms until the morning light awakened us. It was terrible getting out of bed that morning, leaving the warmth I felt wrapped up in Will. When we heard the kids in the hall, we finally forced ourselves to arise.

I hurried about getting ready, swallowing the lump in my throat while Will made breakfast. Peter hummed jazz songs and caused mayhem, but he did pause from chasing the boys around to help me carry my bags to the foyer. When it was finally

time to go, Peter placed his hands on my
head to give me his blessing. I couldn't stop
the tears any longer. Sara lunged at me with
a hug.

"My little shadow," I said. "I'll be back to
claim you before you know it."

"How long will you be gone?" she asked.

"It all depends," I said.

"On which way the wind blows and which
way the road goes," said Peter. "Don't
worry, kids, Uncle Pete and Poppy will
come over often and give you more candy
than your mother would allow, and let you
stay up very much past your bedtime."

The boys cheered, but Sara still clung to
me.

"We'll be fine," said little Ben. I rumpled
his hair.

Will stepped forward and hugged us both.
Then he kissed me and put his forehead on
mine.

"Call when you can," he said. "I don't
care about the cost. Write, telegram often. I
want to feel I'm with you."

"You will," I said.

After I pried Sara from my waist, I hugged
the boys again. Then Peter grabbed my
suitcase and I took my purse, and we all
went outside to load up the car. The winter
wind hit us with force and I shooed them

back inside, worried they'd catch their death out here. I put on my gloves and closed myself in the car before looking back at the house, where the front window framed my family. Will couldn't seem to manage a smile. The boys and Sara waved furiously. Peter winked at me, and I could still feel the weight of his hands on my head as he blessed me. I waved once more, blinked away my tears, and began the journey.

The thing about trips is that all the trouble is in the anticipation. Once I was under way, I was able to tuck my family into a quiet place in my heart and focus on my task.

I'd placed the photograph of Zelda and me on the passenger seat so I could look at it often and remind myself what I was after for her. Will had filled up the tank in our black Plymouth P15. We were lucky to have a car in postwar America, with factories continuing to transition back to civilian use and materials still scarce. I was reluctant to take the car, but there really wasn't another way. Will and the kids could use public transportation or my dad's car, but if anything happened to the Plymouth we'd be in a bind.

The first leg of the trip, however, went smoothly, and a couple of hours later on the banks of the Delaware River, I pulled up to the mansion where the Fitzgeralds had lived all those years ago.

Ellerslie.

The house looked exactly like the oil painting Zelda had made of it — stately white columns at the end of an imposing drive; the hard, square lines of the windows and porches crossed by the empty arms of naked winter trees. I noticed a cardinal hop down some nearby branches like stair steps and fly away, toward the river, and imagined how beautiful it would have been here in the spring with newly opened buds and birdsongs.

The Fitzgeralds had lived at Ellerslie from 1927 to 1929. Scott had wished for it to be a retreat where he could write, but the gin-soaked crowd penetrated the stillness and scattered it about in pieces on the lawn. I snapped a picture of the facade of the house, the cardinal that had made its way back, and the faraway banks of the river, but I stopped taking photos when the hair on the back of my neck stood. I had the most dreadful feeling of being watched. I looked up at the windows of the second floor and searched the glass, and could have sworn that I saw a shadow move away from the windows just above me.

My mouth went dry and I wondered why I was doing this at all, when I noticed a simple trapeze swing, swaying in the wind from a branch in a nearby tree. I had remembered a photograph of Scottie hanging from it, laughing gaily, with Scott standing next to her, hands on his hips, looking young and dapper and wearing an easy smile.

It was for them — the Fitzgeralds — all of this. I had to help Zelda honor the sweetness in her former life and who she was before they came apart.

With renewed courage I continued onto the front porch, stepping over peeling paint and warped boards, and knocked on the cracked wood door. I imagined that if I were there years earlier, the suave writer or retired flapper would greet me and pull me into a tumble of partygoers and entertainment for the weekend. I knocked again and waited, but only silence greeted me.

I walked to a nearby window to peer in, but instead encountered the remains of a huge spiderweb. Gasping, I swatted it away and brushed it off my face. I turned to go back down the step, and almost ran into a scraggly man. He startled me so much that I nearly screamed. His eyes were pale and hollow, and his cheeks were sunken into his face. He had long, greasy hair and his chin was covered with stubble. A cigarette burned between his chapped lips, and he spoke without removing it.

"Ain't for sale."

"Excuse me?"

"The house ain't for sale."

He had an ax slung over his right shoulder, and must have seen my wide eyes, because he put out his free hand for me to shake. I took it and smiled, though I did not feel relieved.

"Just choppin' wood. Nothing to be scared of," he said. "I'm the caretaker here."

"Oh, doesn't anyone live here?"

"No, ma'am," he said. "No one can stand to stay here long."

"Why?"

"The haunts."

Chills rose on my arms. I remembered Zelda mentioning the haunts of Ellerslie, but I'd imagined she was referring to her marital or emotional troubles.

"That factory upriver owns the house and land."

"Such a beautiful place."

"You wouldn't think so if you lived here awhile."

An icy wind reached its fingers into my coat and gave me a chill, as winter clouds grew, threatening precipitation. I wanted to get through the house before I lost the light.

"Sir, if it wouldn't be too much trouble, may I go into the house and look around?" I asked, trying not to appear too eager. "My dear friend used to live here, and has spoken of it so fondly. I was in the area, so I thought I'd try to see it."

"Why did she leave in the first place, if she liked it so much?" he asked. "Ghosts scare 'em off?"

"You could say so."

He pulled the cigarette stub out of his mouth, tossed it on the ground, and crushed it with his scuffed black boot. Then he looked up at the second floor, where I thought I'd seen the movement earlier. His eyes seemed to darken at something he saw, and I suppressed the urge to go tearing back to my car and down the drive. He didn't say anything, but walked up to the door, unlocked it, and gave it a shove. It stuck on its frame.

"Don't use this entrance much," he said.

I followed him into the foyer and then walked ahead of him, taking in the grand staircase, ornate moldings, and dusty chandelier. It wasn't hard to imagine how spectacular this place would have been under the layers of neglect. I could almost hear the strains of an old jazz record emanating from the gramophone in the sitting room, Zelda dancing with fine, sleek-haired gentlemen and smoking long cigarettes with her red-painted lips.

The caretaker slammed the front door, calling me out of my reverie.

"Your friend isn't that writer, is it?"

"Yes," I said. "Well, his wife."

"They had all this big furniture made to fill these rooms, since they're so huge. Then they just left it all here. Can you imagine the waste?"

How could I explain to him how ill equipped they were to handle their wealth? How they were always in motion, and even tons of furniture filling up gilded rooms couldn't anchor them? Maybe if it had, they wouldn't have been in so much trouble.

Sheets covered massive sofas and tables, their legs sticking out below like glimpses of hibernating giants. I stepped farther into the room and saw a huge mirror covering the far wall, cut through the middle with a ballet barre — its edges tarnished with black spots like a faded photograph. My chest grew tight and I had the most unusual feeling that Zelda was there with me. I could see her moving through her warm-ups at the barre, wearing her delicate tutu, playing her records over and over again.

What else could I do but dance? I remembered her saying about her time at the house. *He wouldn't let me take care of the child. He wouldn't let me write. How else could I express all those things that needed to come out?*

The man released a phlegmy cough and spit in his handkerchief, and my thoughts of Zelda scattered. I knew I wasn't going to make much progress with the caretaker at my heels.

"Sir," I said, "if this is too much trouble, I would be happy to explore alone and come find you when I'm through. I won't be too long."

He smiled his rotten smile at me and again spit into his handkerchief. Then he looked out into the yard and back at me.

"You want to be alone in here, huh?" he said. "I'll be around back chopping wood. You come out the back door and check in with me when you're done. I don't imagine you'll be too long at all."

He started toward the back of the house, but stopped and turned to me.

"This place is a whole lot scarier without me than it is with me, but suit yourself."

He turned away, and after a few moments I heard him slam the back door, leaving me alone. The silence intensified without another person there with me to occupy the space, and the air seemed to grow colder. I pulled my coat collar up around my ears and shook off the chill. I then returned my attention to the room and snapped several pictures of it, including the mirror. When I finished photographing the first floor, I slipped the covers off the furniture to check drawers and cushions just to be sure, though I knew I wouldn't find anything. My search turned up empty, of course.

The steady chop of the man's ax outside began and gave me some comfort that he was nearby. I laughed at the irony of the presence of a gnarled old armed stranger giving me comfort, and wished Will were with me instead.

With renewed determination I continued my explorations downstairs, snapping photographs and inspecting what furniture and shelving I came across. The coming storm made shadows cover the rooms like a blanket, and I decided to hurry upstairs to see whether I could find anything of interest or value for Zelda.

The upstairs loomed dark and foreboding, so I began to hum Gershwin's "Summertime" to myself to keep my mind off the house haunts, but they wouldn't be ignored.

The unmistakable sound of an old door creaking on its hinges stopped me midstaircase. I waited for a moment and, when I heard nothing else, continued up more slowly and without singing. My ears were alert and my heart pounded. The blood in my veins seemed to freeze as a gust of cold wind blew down the stairs and through me.

I stopped again and tried to tell myself it was just a drafty old house, but I was suddenly overcome with a feeling of great sadness and fear. Had Zelda felt this way here, in this place? She'd always had a terrible sense of the inevitable passage of time. Could she foresee the ruin of the house, empty, abandoned, once grand and now forgotten and crumbling?

The melancholy was so sudden and intense that I had to sit on the staircase and reorient myself to my own thoughts and feelings. The steady chop of the ax brought me back to the moment and reminded me of who I was and what I was doing. I looked back up the stairs and stood, desperately wanting to leave but certain there was something up there that I should see, even if some*thing* didn't want me to see it.

When I reached the top of the stairs I saw it. A shadow slipped into the room down the hall. Everything in my body said to run, but instead I strode toward it and opened the door. I gasped when I saw what was inside.

A grand dollhouse nearly filled the room — layers of painted papier-mâché crafted intricate doorways, staircases, beds, lamp shades, chairs. It was the most magnificent thing I'd ever seen, and I knew that Zelda had made it for Scottie. I remembered when Zelda had told me about the dollhouse. I could almost hear her whispering again.

For Christmas I made Scottie a dollhouse. When your husband thinks you unfit to care for your daughter you must find ways of staying in the child's life. I crouched on the floor for months like some manic elf at Santa's toy shop with the single-minded task of creating a world away from our world where Scottie could safely play. A place to preserve the sweet-hearted innocence of her imaginings, where I could meet her as if in a garden removed from our lives here, where no one could touch us, and where we could communicate as if through secret notes passed in class.

I photographed the dollhouse from every angle, overcome by the sheer enormity of Zelda's expression of love for her daughter. It would be very good for Zelda to see this and to remember it.

But the bad thing in the house was back. Every nerve of mine stood on end, and the air felt . . . wrong. I heard a faraway door slam again, and my courage failed. I started walking swiftly from the room but felt the thing at my back and broke into a run down the stairs, through the hallway, through the kitchen, and out the back door of the house.

The old man with the ax seemed amused to see me run out of Ellerslie, breathless and troubled, but he didn't have to ask why. I thanked him for allowing me access and he nodded and waved me off. I went back to the car while an icy rain began, and started to pull away when I noticed the man stacking the logs between two trees. His coat was threadbare, and he had no umbrella. I had only one myself, but I felt I needed to make some kind of offering to him for letting me look around the house. I drove the car closer to him and got out while I left it running.

"Here," I said, thrusting my umbrella at him. He looked at it for a moment as if he didn't know what it was; then his eyes flickered with recognition and grew soft.

"No, thank you, ma'am," he said. "I've got too much to carry to mess with that. I'm not worried about my hair." He chuckled while he ran his hand over the greasy strands on his head.

I opened the umbrella over myself and started back to the car. I tried to think of something else I could give him for his time, and decided to offer him a little money.

I returned to him and held out a couple of bucks. "Here, at least take this for your trouble."

He eyed it a moment, then looked back at me. "You sure?" he asked.

"Yes."

He took the money and stuffed it into his pocket. "Thanks."

I nodded and hurried back to my car, eager to get out of the rain and away from Ellerslie forever.

Twenty-Nine

Within an hour, the icy rain turned to sleet, and finally to a gusty snowstorm. As I made my way out of Philadelphia, the car began to slip on the road, and I could barely see through the steam on the window and the assault of the flakes on the windshield. I'd planned on driving into New York City that night to stay, but knew I wouldn't make it that far safely, and began to search for lodging.

As I passed into New Jersey, evening dropped and the storm let up a bit. It wasn't long, however, before it returned. I was hungry, my back ached from driving and tension, and I desperately wanted a hot bath and to call home, but I wasn't familiar with any of the town names I passed and was afraid to stop.

My windshield wipers froze and I slammed the steering wheel. "Dammit! You fool, you should have turned around after that dreadful house and gone home." I spoke aloud to release my fear and anxiety, and to stay awake, since I was tired to my bones, but I realized how odd it was to talk aloud to myself. I slammed the steering wheel again, and then used my glove to wipe away the steam, but it was no use. The wiper had frozen and I couldn't see a damned thing. I had to pull off the road.

The Plymouth slipped when I applied the brake, but I was able to steady it and come to a stop under a street lamp. I opened the car door into the swirling, freezing black night, bundled my coat tightly around my body, and walked to the front of the car. The snow had been falling here for hours, and it slid into my shoes, making my feet wet and numb.

The driver's-side wiper was frozen in a mound of ice and snow, so I began to pick at it with my gloves. That wasn't getting me anywhere, so I trudged through the snow, certain I could feel frostbite beginning on my toes, and hunted through the brush until I found a stick. I walked back to the car through my path, but tripped on a rock and landed in the freezing mud. I stood up and poked my knee through my coat, where I could see a cut bleeding through my ripped stockings.

I wanted to cry, but I tried to think calming thoughts: I would find a hotel. I would have a warm bath. Will and I would laugh about this on the phone. The boys would love to hear about my adventures. Sara would think I was so brave.

Thoughts of Will and the children made the tears fall fresh and fast, however, and I decided that after tonight, I'd head south to North Carolina and call off this whole dreadful business of bringing the past back to Zelda. I'd just try to bring myself to her — alive and in one piece — and see if that helped her.

As I got nearer to my car and the road, I noticed a sign on the other side of the highway and stopped short.

Princeton.

I began to laugh a wild, almost maniacal laugh. If anyone had been nearby, they would have dragged me — a frozen, wet, muddy, laughing mess of a woman — off to the sanitarium. I could almost imagine Scott's ghost leaning casually against the sign with his hands in his pockets, his feet crossed, and a cigarette hanging out of his mouth.

"Thank you," I whispered to no one.

A sharp wind reminded me that I needed shelter soon, so I hurried back to the car, used the stick to chisel the wiper out of the ice, and snapped a picture of the road sign for Princeton. I hoped it would turn out so I could tell Zelda how it appeared like a light at the end of a dock, leading me back to safety.

Hot water surrounded me like a hug in the pristine tub of the Nassau Inn at Princeton. The inn was just across the street from the university, and the staff had checked me in with the kindest of manners in spite of the fact that I must have appeared from the storm like some kind of female yeti. I'd spent more than I wanted to for the room, but what could I do? I was too cold and shaken to search for another place, and I had no guarantees that I'd find something with a vacancy that cost less money.

I allowed the heat to thaw my skin to the bone and, once I'd relaxed and finished my bath, wrapped myself in my nightgown and a thick robe hanging in the closet, and went to use the telephone in the hallway. It was seven o'clock, so all of the children would still be awake. Will sounded frantic when he answered.

"Anna, thank God!"

"I know," I said. "It's been quite an adventure."

"Are you okay?"

"I am," I said. "I'm sorry to have worried you."

He was quiet for a moment; then he replied in a tumble of words and nervous energy. "If you are going to be away from us in poor weather for the next few weeks, you're going to need to communicate a little better."

I was taken aback by his tone. Will was usually so even-keeled. It was jarring to hear him speak this way after I'd just calmed myself down. I felt my defenses rise, and in spite of a nagging feeling that I should just stay calm, I couldn't help but snap back at him.

"I've just been driving in a blizzard for hours, by myself, on roads I don't know. I had to pull off into a snowbank to chisel ice off the wipers. I fell in mud, bloodied my knee, and ripped a pair of stockings. Oh, and I walked through an abandoned haunted house this afternoon with a scary man with an ax. I haven't eaten anything all day except for some smashed-up crackers I found at the bottom of my purse. And I haven't even been gone for twenty-four hours!" My voice had risen, and I hoped no one would come out in the hallway to see the madwoman with wet hair yelling into the phone.

"You should have turned around and come home," he said.

"You encouraged me to take the trip!"

"Was there really anything else I could have said?"

I was about to strike back at him when I realized that what he said was true. I would have gone either way. He'd encouraged me to go because he knew it was something I needed to do, but not because he'd wanted me to go. Not at all.

There was a scuffling sound and Sara got on the phone. "Mommy, Ben refuses to take a bath, and Daddy said he's not fighting with people about baths while you're gone, but Ben stinks because he was in the snow all day —"

Her voice cut off, there was more scuffling, and suddenly Ben was on the phone.

"Hi, Mom. I don't stink. She's just weird. I'll take a bath one of these days."

"Benny," I said, "please don't cause your father any stress while I'm gone."

"Okay," he said. "See ya!"

Then Will Junior was on the phone.

"Hi, Mom," he said.

"Hi, honey. Could you please help Daddy with those two?"

"Yes," he said. "I practiced my piano for

forty-five minutes after school today."

"Wonderful," I said. "Thank you. I love you."

"I love you, too."

"Mommy." It was Sara again. "Can I go and live with Poppy while you're gone? The boys are driving me crazy."

"Sara, I need you to help Daddy. Can you do that? He's a little frantic because I'm gone. Please."

She was quiet for a moment, then replied, "Okay. I love you. When are you coming home?"

"I don't know exactly when, but hopefully in a couple of weeks."

She exhaled loudly. "Okay. I'll help."

"I love you," I said.

"Me, too."

There was another pause until Will got back on the line. "Anna, it's me."

I was filled with guilt. The three kids were a handful to manage even when I was home. I should never have gone on this trip.

"Will, I'm sorry. I'm going to come home tomorrow and forget all of this. I didn't think it through enough. This is madness."

"No," he said. "I'm sorry. I didn't want to do this. I told myself I could handle them and I wouldn't let you know if it was otherwise, and I've failed already on day one."

"Please don't apologize," I said. "I'm sorry."

"Well, you can't come home yet," he said. "This was just a bad start. Keep at it and we'll reassess after a few days. Where are you?"

"Princeton."

"Princeton?" he said.

I proceeded to tell him the whole story, from Ellerslie, to the drive, to the sign appearing in the darkness. He laughed.

"I might believe in ghosts now," he said.

"I sure do, after that god-awful house."

"It sounds like it was worth it, though, for those pictures you got of the dollhouse," he said.

"I wish you were here with me."

"Me, too," he said.

"Especially because I was all alone in a bathtub."

He whistled through the phone. "Stop it, woman; you're killing me."

I laughed.

"Listen," he said. "In all seriousness. You need to do this, and I can handle them back at home —" He cut himself off and must have covered the phone with his hand, because I heard his muffled yelling at the kids.

"Pardon me," he said. "As I was saying, I can handle them. I might have to start spanking them again, like when they were little ones, but we'll come through. Please, though, please be more careful. Please try to keep out of danger."

"I promise," I said.

"Good," he said. "And I'll try to relax a little more. It felt like midnight when the phone rang. I couldn't believe it was only seven."

"If we talk every night it could get expensive, so I'll try to call around this time every other night," I said. "That way you should be done with dinner and I should be done with my explorations."

"Deal," he said. "I love you, Anna."

"I love you."

"I'll be thinking about you and that tub later," he said.

"Good."

After I hung up the phone, I went back into the room, set my hair, crawled into bed, and slept like the dead.

The arches of Princeton framed the snowy paths in and out of the campus with all of the romance and tradition I'd imagined from Scott's novel *This Side of Paradise*. Young men in smart coats and orange-and-black scarves hurried over the cobbled paths, singing, tossing snowballs at one another, and making general mayhem as young men tend to do.

On a recommendation from the woman at the front desk of the inn, I found a little shop where I bought a pair of warm winter pants and a pair of well-lined boots. She told me the afternoon was expected to warm up and the snow might melt from the roads by as early as tomorrow. After my shop visit and some internal debate, I decided to send Sorin a telegram in New York City telling him that I would be in town soon. It would be nice to see his friendly face after all these years.

It felt good to tromp through snow in pants and boots, and I decided to take a walk around campus to try to understand Scott's world a little better. This trip was about Zelda, but when Scott fell in love with her and when she controlled the relationship, he was a product of this environment. I wanted to remind her of the time before the power shifted, which Zelda probably considered the good times. It occurred to me that they never managed to balance the power in their marriage, and maybe if they

had, neither of them would have deteriorated so much.

The impressive Gothic buildings covered
in dried, snow-covered ivy inspired awe in
me, and a feeling of old money hung in the
air about the lawns, spires, and cloisters. A
group of young men walked by, turning as
they passed to see me better. I didn't
imagine females frequented the campus
much. When they noted my age, however,
most of them lost interest, except for one
very tall young man at the front of the pack
who tipped his hat at me, winked, and then
continued on. I smiled to myself and
snapped a picture of them as they walked
away. Then I turned and took pictures of
the buildings and winter trees looming over
me. I shivered, and thought I should have
brought a scarf.

When I reached a courtyard with a central
feel to it, the carillon bells in the Princeton
University Chapel began to play and filled
the outdoor space with their beautiful
music. I wished I could have recorded it for
Zelda, but I could not, so I simply took a
picture of the chapel.

"Inspiring, isn't it?" A young man stood
at my side, and when I turned to him, I was
surprised to see that he was a Negro. I
didn't know that Princeton admitted col-

ored students.

"Yes," I said. "Though I'm afraid my camera can't quite capture the beauty."

"Are you here writing a story about Princeton?"

"No. I'm just trying to bring a little of the past to a friend of mine. Though if I were going to write a story about the school, I would like to talk to you."

"And how I got here," he said.

"Yes."

The bells ended, and we fell into step together.

"Yes, there are many Southern supporters of Princeton," he said. "President Wilson being the head Southerner, if you understand my meaning."

"I do," I said. "Mr. Wilson was known for many things, but racial tolerance was not one of them."

"Yes, ma'am."

"Please call me Anna," I said. "What's your name?"

"Pete."

"I have a brother named Peter," I said. "I'm very fond of him."

Pete smiled and looked down at his shoes.

"So are there many other colored students?" I asked.

"No," he said. "Though I'm not alone.

They opened a Naval Training School here in 'forty-two, during the war. That started the new admission policy of allowing Negroes. Princeton was one of the later schools to allow us."

"How has it been for you?" I asked.

He was quiet for a moment. Then he said, "I'd say it's been satisfactory. I mostly keep my nose in the books. I don't have any illusions about being welcome in the popular eating clubs on campus, so I'm in Prospect, but I enjoy myself."

"I'm glad to hear it," I said.

We walked in silence a bit more, and then ended up at the library.

"It was nice talking to you," he said. "I wish you success in bringing the past to your friend, though I'd personally like a bit more of the future."

"Very young people say that," I said. "Though for someone like you here, I can understand why. I wish you a lot of success, Pete."

"Thank you," he said. "Would you like to come into the library and warm up? You look like you're freezing."

"No, thank you," I said. "I'm going to find a place to eat and write a letter to my friend. But it was nice talking to you."

He smiled and nodded. Then he thought

a moment, unwound his Princeton scarf from around his neck, and held it out to me.

"Would you like this?" he asked. "They're pretty easy for me to come by around here."

I was touched by his offer and glad to accept it, for myself, and as an artifact later for Zelda.

"I would like that very much, thank you," I said, wrapping it around my neck.

With that, he disappeared into the library.

Later that evening, after I sent a telegram home updating Will on my progress, I stepped into the bar at the Nassau Inn with my book and my camera. There were many smartly dressed young men and women laughing and carrying on. I was out of place amid all of the youth and carelessness but was very charmed by them, so I found a table out of the way where I could observe.

I was a horrid cliché, sitting there reading *This Side of Paradise,* sipping beer, but I had reached the age of not caring what those around me thought. I opened the book and had just come to the moment when Amory Blaine had begun to think of others outside of himself, when someone walked over to my table and cleared his throat. I looked up and saw the tall young man who had tipped his hat at me earlier that day.

"Required reading for all us Tigers," he said, pointing at my book. "May I join you?"

"Please," I said. I noticed his friends sniggering in the corner, watching us. "Though you might be the butt of many jokes following our chat. I am probably old enough to be your mother."

His face was flushed from the warm bar and the cocktail in his hand, and he laughed. "I am the butt of all the jokes anyway," he said with a great deal of charm. "But this is no joke. They are all jealous that I have the courage to approach the lovely woman we've seen around campus, who has a great air of mystery and romance about her."

I laughed aloud at his description of me, and he seemed pleased. He smoothed a lock of his light brown hair out of his blue eyes and held out his hand.

"Wallace," he said. "Charles Davenport Wallace the Third."

I reached for his hand. "Nice to meet you, Charles Davenport Wallace the Third. I'm just Anna."

"Well, just Anna, what brings you to our fine campus, with your camera and your snow boots?"

"And my great air of mystery and romance."

"That especially."

I drank more of my beer, and because I was emboldened by the alcohol and the admiration of young Wallace, I spoke without censor. "I am traveling on behalf of my dear friend, Mrs. F. Scott Fitzgerald, who is unable to travel, in order to bring her a remembrance of her past."

His face suddenly became very serious. "Is that true?"

"Every word of it."

"You're friends with the Fitzgeralds?"

"Yes. I was once, anyway."

"How wonderful." He looked very wistful and tragic, and his forehead wrinkled. "I wish I had known him, and her," he said. "Would you tell her we all remember the Fitzgeralds often and think highly of them? I know she's not well, but tell her she still has many admirers, and many of us came here wanting to be like him and find a girl like her. But to do it without all of the trouble, of course."

"I'll tell her," I said.

Wallace turned to his friends and motioned them over, telling them who I was and what I was doing. I was suddenly flooded with introductions, handshakes, and drink offers. One of them asked me to

411

dance, which I politely declined, but I did accept another beer, and listened to all of them discuss their favorite passages from Scott's work.

"I know you all know Scott's novels, but have you read Zelda's?" I finally asked. "Or did you know that he used passages verbatim from her diaries and letters in his stories?"

There was a general uproar when I said that.

"She wasn't a writer," said one of the young men. "She was a drunk and a nymphomaniac."

"And a wacko," said another.

Wallace smacked both of them on the shoulder. "Watch it! This is Zelda's friend."

"I know all of the popular views of Zelda," I said. "But before you spout them off in bars, you need both sides of the story. Read *Save Me the Waltz,* and then form your judgment."

"I've read it," said one of them. He was the quietest in the group, and the smallest. His neat blond hair parted in a wave, like Scott's, but he had big brown eyes and loads of innocence.

"What did you think?" I asked.

"I think she gave up a lot for him. I think she could have been a swell writer, too."

The uproar began again from his companions, but he ignored them and smiled at me. Wallace put up his hands and silenced the group.

"Just Anna," he said, "I pledge that I will force all of them and myself to read *Save Me the Waltz.* You have certainly piqued my curiosity."

I smiled and finished my beer. "Good. If you'll excuse me, I'm very tired, and I have to leave tomorrow, but tonight has been very interesting. Now please go and pay attention to the beautiful girls at the bar whom you've been ignoring for far too long."

Wallace eyed my camera. "Would you like a picture of us for Zelda? You can tell her we're her admirers."

"I think she would like that very much," I said.

They all put their arms around one another and smiled their winning, charming smiles, and it suddenly seemed as if I were looking into the past at a group of young soldiers on a dance floor, vying for Zelda's attention.

Yes. She would like it very much.

THIRTY

There is a unique solitude found in cities that I crave.

The shadows of New York's buildings cloaked me with a pleasant anonymity. It felt good to blend in, to become indistinguishable from the patter of many moving people, where no one would notice me.

After living in Baltimore for so many years, I had become suited to urban living. It was as if all of the motion from the taxis, people, business, and culture had nudged me along and kept me afloat during the dark years, when my impulse had been toward stagnation. But in that motion, I was able to bob along, undetected.

Now I began to believe I might actually succeed on my journey, and it was right for me to take it. The last time I was here, Zelda was at my side, crumbling in my very grasp as we looked from her paintings to O'Keeffe's. How I longed for the young flapper Zelda to be at my side now, calling taxis with a whistle and a slit skirt, riding on cars, splashing through fountains, moving from party to party full of waxy-haired men before the wars burned us all out and left us dried up and lost.

I soon arrived at the Biltmore Hotel on Madison Avenue, where Scott and Zelda had lived after their wedding until they were asked to leave for their antics. As I checked in, I was greeted with a wonderful surprise. Sorin had received my telegram and left me a message at the front desk asking me to meet him in front of the Plaza Hotel for dinner at six thirty. Now I would have something to look forward to after my day of searching.

Since I had a lot of ground to cover, I quickly bathed and put on my sharpest dress. Snow boots and orange scarves would not do for New York City. The dress was one I'd worn to a holiday charity ball Peter had arranged. It was dark green and crossed at the neck, and the A-line skirt extended just below the knee in a quiet green-and-black plaid. It was perfect for wandering in and out of posh New York hotels, asking to see the lost and found.

As it turns out, however, lost items — even in posh New York hotels — are often found by going down creaky cargo elevators with strange men to moldy, rat-filled basements. After sneezing my way through dozens of basement boxes and crates in the Biltmore, the Commodore, and the Plaza, I was not only forlorn because I had not found the objects of my searching, but I was distressed over the amount of cobwebs and dirt covering me and my beautiful dress.

I caught sight of myself in the lobby mirror of the Plaza and groaned. I did not want to meet an old friend looking like this, so I stepped into the opulent bathroom in the lobby, smoothed my hair, wiped a streak of dirt off my face, and fixed my makeup. Thankful for modern conveniences and good lighting, I continued to the entrance, and pushed through the swivel doors into the bitter winter afternoon.

The round clock on the corner showed that it was nearly six thirty, so I was right on time. I was thankful that I had reached out to Sorin, because my mood would have been low after my day of fruitless, uncomfortable searching for Zelda's diaries. I walked over to the fountain, but it was nearly empty of water except for a thin, frozen sheen of leaf-covered scum in its base. I snapped a picture of it as I imagined Zelda frolicking in its spray, and couldn't help but smile.

I felt someone watching me, and turned to face Central Park. My heart lifted when I saw Sorin. He had trim dark hair, a tailored wool coat, and small neat glasses. He carried a violin case in his left hand. We hurried to meet each other, and I couldn't stop myself from hugging him. He seemed bashful when I pulled away.

"I'm sorry," I said. "It's been a long couple of days and it's so nice to see a friendly face."

"I knew you immediately," he said. His accent hung only faintly about the corners of his words, now, no doubt smoothed out over the years of living in the United States. "You have barely changed."

I laughed aloud. "I don't know if that's good or bad," I said. "I've been poking around in hotel basements all afternoon."

"It is very good," he said.

"And you," I said. "So sophisticated. Where is the mad violinist from the bottom apartment who rescued me from the criminal?"

It was his turn to laugh. "Did I really do that?" he asked.

"You really did," I replied. "Doesn't it seem a lifetime ago?"

"Yes," he said.

He held out his arm and led me back toward the Plaza Hotel.

"I'm so glad you received my message," he said. "I'm taking you to the Oak Room here. It's quiet."

"Are you sure?" I asked, cringing inside at the thought of how expensive our meal would surely be. I had already spent more than I'd budgeted by stopping in Princeton.

"Yes. I insist. My treat."

I began to protest, but Sorin shook his head, walked me back into the Plaza, and to an intimate restaurant with dark paneling and detailed murals on the walls. The host greeted Sorin as "Mr. Funar" and led us to a table in a back corner of the room.

"The usual, Mr. Funar?" asked our server.

"Please," said Sorin.

"And for you, ma'am?"

"I'd like some Irish coffee, please."

"Right away."

"Caffeine and alcohol?" asked Sorin with a smile.

"It's been a long day," I said. "A long couple of days. And you — 'The usual, Mr. Funar'?"

He smiled as I teased him, and raised his hands. "What can I say? I do not cook much and this place is convenient."

"Clearly you've done well for yourself," I

said. "I'm so happy for you."

I glanced at his ring finger and saw nothing. He caught my gaze.

"Never married," he said. "Close, several times, but it never worked out. Musicians are fickle and tempestuous."

I laughed and placed the napkin on my lap as the waiter arrived with our drinks and to discuss the menu. We listened and ordered: tomato and fennel soup and lamb for me, bisque and the fish of the day for Sorin. When I looked back at him he was staring at me.

"I was happy and surprised to get your telegram," he said.

"I wanted to see a friendly face in the city, so I had to try."

"You are still married to Will?"

"Yes. We have three children." I could not hide my smile.

He raised his eyebrows and looked me over. "How can that be? I would never guess."

I laughed at his flattery, and we began catching each other up on our lives.

For the first time, I told him about everything: about Ben and Katie, Zelda at Phipps, Zelda at La Paix, and life without Zelda. Then how Will had shown up at my door, and we had married, and how I had learned to live again. I spoke to Sorin of my work in music therapy with shell-shocked soldiers.

"You deserve every happiness, Anna."

"I don't know if I deserve any of it, but I'll surely take it. It's such a strange thing to have lived two lifetimes."

"In some ways," said Sorin, "I think perhaps I have not started living."

"Why do you say that?"

"It has always been me and the music, but no one constant to share it with. When I spoke of tempestuous musicians, I was also speaking of myself. I have never been able to balance the art and my life outside of it."

The waiter brought our dinner, but instead of eating, I listened.

"Art is a form of madness, I think," he said.

I felt his words wash over me, but I hadn't yet achieved full connection to and understanding of what he was trying to say, or how I could use it to help Zelda.

"I am sorry to go on like this," he said.

I placed my hand on his arm. "No, please. Keep going."

He nodded and took a sip from his wineglass before continuing. "When I am in the creative place, I am outside of this time and space. It is jarring to come back — almost painful sometimes. I feel hollow and exhausted, and as if I need to return to it to feel complete again. Almost no one, not even another musician, has been able to understand that or live with it. Or if she has, our creative cycles were off and we were forever hitting each other at highs and lows in the process."

"Then art is addiction," I said.

"Yes. Yes, it is an addiction. And just the way that some are able to handle their liquor and others are not, some can handle their art and others cannot."

I shook my head. "But then, for someone like Zelda, does this mean that she should not create because of what it does to her? I can't believe that is so. The act of art is so important. It is expression, identity. It helps others cope. I use music therapy with war veterans. Sometimes it is their only sanctuary. It's a safe place where they can confront their demons and conquer them."

"That is beautiful, Anna."

Sorin was leaning across the table, gazing at me with adoration, and I suddenly felt wary. We were wading in too deep, and I could see and feel that he thought someone like me would understand him. I had to pull back. It wasn't fair to encourage him, though I could not pretend that his admiration did not warm me. I sipped from my Irish coffee and began to eat. Sorin seemed to sense my retreat, and started on his dinner.

We didn't say much after that. How do you talk of the weather and other small matters after you speak as we had spoken? As our meal drew to a close, Sorin wiped his mouth and cleared his throat.

"Tonight is our final rehearsal for this weekend's performance of Mahler's *Kindertotenlieder,*" he said. "It is a powerful composition that I think would particularly touch you, in light of what you have told me about your own past."

"Why is that?"

He hesitated for a moment, as if he were worried that he had said too much. "It is about the loss of a child."

I flinched. Though I would always hold sadness in my heart for Katie, I had experienced true peace after Ben's burial next to her. But now, forever lurking beneath my life was the deep, wrenching fear of losing another child. It made me wary of cold winds, sickness, and separation. And here I was, so very separated from them. Offering them no protection.

Sorin reached for my arm. "I have upset you. Please do not worry about coming tonight."

I shook my head. "No, I am already here. Just tell me, is there hope in the song? At the end?"

He smiled broadly. "Yes, Anna. A peaceful, resigned hope. A letting go."

It is quite a thing to sit alone in a darkened theater, with an entire symphony orchestra playing a message that you need to hear.

The exquisite irony of the music therapist finding healing through a symphony played by a friend did not escape me, and it was at that moment, more than any other in my life, that I was convinced of the existence of God and great goodness. Peter would be so glad.

When his rehearsal was over, Sorin came to me and held me. I tried to send him many words I could not say aloud but hoped to convey in my embrace — words of his extreme worthiness, his beauty, and his good soul. I think he understood.

I was still caught up in the music as I returned to my hotel that evening, taking an extra spin or two in the revolving door in honor of my darling Zelda and her beau, Scott, and returning to my room, where I got a deep, restful sleep.

I had no idea how much I'd need it for
the rest of the journey.

THIRTY-ONE

As I passed out of New York and into Connecticut, the buildings transitioned to houses, which stretched farther apart, until nature became the view out my window. I felt united to myself again, specific, no longer anonymous, and somehow complete. I wished I could talk to Peter and tell him of revelations and inspiration and catharsis, but that would have to come later.

So off I went to Westport, Connecticut, my last stop before Highland Hospital in Asheville, North Carolina, to the house where they'd lived, and the final place where Zelda remembered the diaries.

I soon noticed blue-and-white hyacinths peeking out of the ground around well-tended houses and on tidy yard borders, and realized that it was March, and had been for several days. Soon it would be spring and Easter. The world reborn.

Before long, I pulled up to the house: 244

Compo Road South.

It was charming and tidy, almost rigidly so, with a trim lawn leading to a freshly painted gray-shingled colonial. The trees possessed manicured symmetry, and an American flag waved in the breeze. Neat clusters of daffodils were spaced about the yard in an orderly fashion. It was so ordered, in fact, that I could not imagine Scott and Zelda ever living here.

I was suddenly overcome with melancholy. This house could not possibly hold any of Zelda's spirit in it, and most certainly would not contain her diaries. I gripped the steering wheel and stared at the house, searching for a sign of life or something that would let me know it was okay to disturb the quiet with my knock and my strange queries. With a heart full of trepidation, I forced myself to get out of the car and walk up the front path. This was, after all, the entire point of my trip. I couldn't stop now.

The door was painted crimson and shone in the morning sun. It did not look as if it had ever been touched by human hands. Did Zelda really run in and out of this front door, half-clad in bathing gear with revelers and critics at her heels, hoping for a bit of her attention? Did Scott really make a fool of himself with drunken friends in front of her parents here?

I abandoned my musings in favor of action and knocked on the front door. In a moment, a tall, slender man with a crew cut stood in front of me. He had an air of distracted efficiency that his polite smile did not quite hide.

"May I help you?" he asked.

"Yes, sir, I'm Anna Brennan. I'm afraid I have a rather strange request. . . ." I let my voice trail off and waited for him to invite me in, but he did not extend an offer, so I continued. "A friend of mine lived here many years ago, and I think — while this will sound very strange — she might have left something of sentimental value here. In the basement."

For some reason, I did not wish to speak of Zelda with him. It felt like a violation of her privacy. I also didn't want him to think I was some crazed fan of Scott's, so I held back.

He looked perplexed. This was clearly not a man used to strangers appearing on his doorstep. I imagined anyone who wanted to see him made an appointment. I could almost see him processing the information and imagined him trying to find a suitable way to turn me away.

"I'm sorry," he said. "I'm certain there is

nothing in the cellar but a few boxes of my old military artifacts. Everything else has been cleaned out and swept away. There was an old record collection, but we gave that away years ago."

"Is it possible there are some unexplored corners where something might have been overlooked?"

He gave me a patronizing smile, as if I were a child. "No, I'm quite sure I haven't overlooked anything. I'm sorry I couldn't help. I hope you haven't come a long way."

I felt my hopes sinking. I had come so far and couldn't let him turn me away so easily. As he nodded and began to step back to close the door I again spoke.

"Please, sir, I actually have come a very long way, and it would mean so much to me to at least be able to tell her I checked for her. You have no idea how it would buoy her spirits."

"I'm sorry, ma'am," he said, all trace of a smile leaving his face. "I keep a very neat home, and I would know if there was something in the basement that did not belong to me. And if it is in the basement, then it actually does belong to me, because I own this house, so there is still no need for you to poke around. Now, good day."

He began to close the door but I shot out

my hand and stopped it.

"It is nothing of monetary value, I assure you," I said, losing my polite tone, "but of a very sentimental value. It's just the diaries of a young woman, but if I could give them back to her it might help her with her rehabilitation."

His face turned red and I saw how shocked he was that I would put my hand on his door and prevent him from closing it. I drew it back to my side and tried to appear less aggressive.

"Look," he said, "I have no idea who you are or what you're looking for, but you certainly are not welcome to coerce your way into my house and go prying around in places where you will not find anything."

My frustration crystallized around my heart and head, making me feel stiff and frantic. I couldn't force myself into his house, but he had to let me look. I could not bribe him as I had with the caretaker of Ellerslie, or flirt with him as I had at Princeton, but my God, I had to get down in that basement. I began having wild thoughts of sneaking back at night and breaking into the house, but I realized how crazy that was and that I just needed to accept that I was not welcome. It wouldn't matter even if he did let me inside. I would not find her diaries.

Not ever.

My eyes misted over with tears and I looked down at my hands. I had to try once more, and then I'd go. I could feel Zelda's need for me, with or without her past, and I knew it was time to answer her call. I cleared my voice and tried to steady it before I spoke.

"My friend is Zelda Fitzgerald. She was married to the writer F. Scott Fitzgerald, and they lived here for a time, many years ago. She is schizophrenic and alone, and would like to see some of the memories she preserved for herself on the pages of her diaries. The last place she remembers anyone seeing them was in this house. In the basement. In an old box. I know they probably are not there, but it would be a real act of kindness if you would just accompany me into the basement, allow me to walk around and then leave."

I heard a sound in the hallway leading to the front door, and saw a woman about my age holding a vase of cut hyacinths. She set the vase on the hall table and walked up behind the man, placing her hands around him and smiling out at me.

"You are a friend of Zelda Fitzgerald?"

she said.

"Yes, ma'am."

"How sadly it all turned out for the Fitzgeralds," she said. "I believe my father rented this house to them in the twenties. Please come inside."

The man began to protest, but she gently placed her finger on his lips and winked at him. He seemed to soften from her touch and moved aside for me to step into the foyer.

"I can't thank you enough," I said. "I'm so sorry to disturb you. I know how strange this must seem."

"What, a friend helping out a friend? It doesn't seem strange at all. Follow me."

We walked in a line, the woman at the front, followed by me, followed by the reluctant doorkeeper. We passed a handsome office and a feminine sitting room before ending up at a slim door on the back underside of the staircase. The woman opened the door and pulled a beaded cord, illuminating the steep wooden stairs with the yellow light of an ancient bulb. The smell of earth and moisture rose from beneath us, and we started down the stairs.

To the credit of the man, the cellar appeared empty except for three crates, which I presumed were his "military artifacts." The dirt floor and walls were packed solid. An old sewing machine sat in the far corner of the room near the foundation of a chimney, and along the wall to our left was an impressive shelf of wine bottles. I wondered whether the man had been reluctant to let me in because he thought I'd steal from his wine collection. I met his eyes and he looked away.

"You see," said the woman. "Though my dear husband was being very rude, there isn't much in here. We hope to finish the basement someday in the future, but it's mostly dirt for now."

"The old records were on the floor where the sewing machine is now," he said. "But that's all we found."

I gazed around the space and tried not to feel overwhelmed by the sinking feeling growing inside me. I walked over to the sewing machine and looked behind it, but there was nothing of note to observe. I gazed up at the ceiling and around the wine rack, but it was just as the man had said. There was nothing else.

I thought back to Zelda's story about the diaries. A man with whom she'd developed a serious flirtation, a theater critic named George Jean Nathan, had found and read the diaries during one of their drunken parties late one night. He'd told Scott he wanted to publish them, inciting a rage from Scott that caused him to tear the books away from Nathan, and began a rift that eventually destroyed their friendship. From that point on, Scott told Zelda he had hidden the diaries, but perhaps he destroyed them. After all, by that time he'd used most of the material he'd needed from her early life. He might not have had any more use for them.

I shook my head. "Thank you for allowing me to come down here. I am very sorry I disturbed you."

"It's no trouble," said the woman. "I wish we could have found something for you to take to her."

"May I take some pictures?" I asked, holding up my camera. "I'm making a new scrapbook for Zelda of places from her past. I think she would enjoy my amateur detective work."

"That would be fine," she said. "We'll just be upstairs. Come on up when you finish."

The couple went up the stairs, leaving me alone in the cellar. I snapped several pictures of the basement, including the wine rack and sewing machine. I turned to snap one more picture of the staircase when I felt a draft coming from behind it. I peered around the back of the stairs, and though it was dark, the bulb at the landing above gave me enough light to illuminate a hole in the wall where a piece of plywood rested half across it on a ledge under the opening.

My heart began to pound. I thought I should call the couple upstairs, but then I decided not to. I moved slowly toward the opening, praying that I wouldn't stumble across any rodents. I took a deep breath and pulled down the board, a little surprised by its weight.

I could see only a couple of inches into the hole, and the rest was covered in shadows. I didn't want to reach my hands around what appeared to be a crawl space, so I lifted my camera and, using the flash, took a picture of the hole.

I pulled the film from the camera, watching the empty space seep forth from the film paper, eager to see what it would reveal. Amazed as I'd been about the instant developing in this new-fangled machine, it could not develop fast enough. I shook the paper in the air, hoping it would somehow speed the process and show me what was in the crawl space.

I looked again. Ever so slightly, I saw the shape of the plumbing at the top of the crawl space taking form. That and something on the floor.

It was a box.

I dropped the picture, put the camera roughly on the ground, and lunged forward, thrusting my hands into the black, no longer caring about rodents or dirt. The box was moist and wanted to give in my hands, but I dragged it toward me and hefted it to the center of the cellar, where I could see what was inside it.

When I saw, I sat in the dirt, unable to support myself. I must have gasped, because the woman was at the top of the stairs in a moment.

"Are you all right?" she asked.

I looked up, her form blurred by my tears, and shook my head.

She walked slowly down the steps and stopped at the last one. "Is it . . . ?" she whispered.

"It is."

THIRTY-TWO

The trip from New York to North Carolina took two days due to an overheated engine and a flat tire. These both occurred in Virginia, and, mercifully, within a mile of a gas station. I was able to get the car towed and worked on overnight while I stayed in a motel that, though quite shoddy, allowed me to take a hot shower and call my family.

Will Junior answered the phone, and we spoke of the kids' fun in the big snow in Baltimore. It wasn't long before Ben wrested the phone from him and said that he couldn't wait for springtime and baseball. When it was Sara's turn, she told me she was being a wonderful help to Daddy and that he'd bought her flowers for cleaning up the downstairs. I sent them all hugs and love and promises that I'd see them soon.

Will finally got on the phone and I told him that I'd found the diaries, though they were as badly decomposed as old corpses.

"I'm sorry to hear that," he said.

"I know. I feel foolish for thinking it could have been any other way. The pages are so moldy that they crumbled in my fingers."

"Were you able to decipher any of it?"

"At first I thought I would try to, but as soon as I read the first date on the page in Zelda's sprawling, girlish penmanship, I closed the book. It felt like a violation of her."

Will was quiet for a moment; then he spoke. "Anna, you are the bravest person I know."

I laughed aloud. "I don't feel that way."

"You are," he said. "You've done it. No matter what the state of the diaries, no matter what you find when you go to Zelda, you've done something beautiful for her. And even if she's not of a mind to grasp it right now, one day she will."

"Thank you for saying that. And for doing so well with the children. It is a great relief to know you all are well. It won't be much longer."

"I won't say we don't miss you terribly," he said, "but we're managing. Take as long as you need with Zelda."

As long as I need.

His words stayed with me as I pulled up

to the Inn on Montford Avenue in Asheville, North Carolina. The warm glow from its windows welcomed me, and I felt peace envelop me. The twin peaks at the roof of the house, underlined by the wrap-around porch, made the inn look like a large, smiling face, and even reminded me of La Paix. From the outdoor gardens to the lobby to the rooms, one had the sense of continuity, stability, and unity.

I slept well that night.

The next morning, I awoke early to the aroma of eggs, bacon, and coffee drifting up from the dining room. My stomach growled in response, and I hurried through washing and dressing so I had enough time to eat and finish assembling the photo book I'd been working on before my visit to Highland.

A middle-aged woman with a loose bun and the most arresting blue eyes I'd ever seen greeted me when I entered the dining room.

"I'm Amelia," she said in a soft Southern drawl. "I hope you're hungry, because we only have one other boarder this morning, and he left before dawn to do some hiking nearby."

"I'm starving," I said. "It's been a while since I enjoyed a home-cooked breakfast."

"Have you been traveling long?"

"Only about a week," I said. "Though it feels like much longer."

"Are you away from family?"

"Yes," I said. "My husband and three children. I miss them very much."

"Well, we'll take good care of you while you're here," said Amelia. "Start with breakfast, and then I can help you make plans for the day if you've never been to the area."

"Actually, I'm here to visit a friend at Highland Hospital. I wonder if you could find out visiting hours for me."

"Certainly," she said. "I'll do that. You help yourself."

Amelia disappeared around the corner while I fixed myself a plate from the buffet on the dark cherry sideboard. After I piled my plate with fluffy eggs, warm biscuits, and crispy bacon, I took my seat. A young Negro woman in a maid's uniform entered the room from the kitchen, bearing a tray with a mug, a bowl of sugar, and a small container of cream.

"Would you like coffee or tea, ma'am?" she asked.

"Coffee, please," I said.

She returned shortly with a small pot of coffee, a trivet, and the morning paper.

"Thank you."

She disappeared again into the kitchen, leaving me to take in the beautifully carved wood panels, wallpaper with tasteful, muted floral designs, and thick rugs. Amelia came in with a piece of paper and placed it on the table in front of me.

"The hospital visiting hours are just after lunchtime, from one to four o'clock," she said. "I wrote down the times for you, and the name of the street where you'll find it, Zillicoa Street. It's a short walk from here, or we can have our driver take you over and pick you up."

"Thank you for the information and the offer," I said. "I'll walk, if it's nearby. I've been in a car more this past week than in my entire life."

"Very good. If you need anything while you're here, please don't hesitate to ask."

"I won't. Thank you."

After she left, I ate my breakfast and returned to my room to finish assembling the scrapbook I'd made for Zelda, adding captions and anecdotes I remembered from her stories and my time on the road. It took me several hours, and I was pleased with the book when I finished. I hoped Zelda would enjoy it.

Much to my dismay, it still wasn't time to

visit her. Every minute passed like an hour, and I decided the best thing to do was to begin walking to Highland Hospital and enjoy some of the sights nearby. Amelia gave me a map and told me the best historic homes to see on the way, and also the location of a pretty park in the middle of town where I could eat lunch. She had the cook pack me a sandwich and some fruit, and gave me a large canvas bag to hold the food, my camera, and the diaries. I know she was burning with curiosity, but while I didn't mind telling her why I was here in theory, the story seemed too long, and I was impatient to see Zelda. Perhaps I would share more with Amelia later that night.

The difference in weather and atmosphere between the North and the Southeast was remarkable. Springtime was in full bloom here in Asheville, and I admired the weeping cherry blossoms, newly opened tulips, and magnolias. At various points in town I could see all the way to the distant mountains, which were still covered in snow. I inhaled the air deeply and shivered a little, knowing Zelda was also breathing this air nearby. I hoped it made her feel as fresh as it did me.

The bag was beginning to weigh me down, so I switched shoulders and removed

441

the camera so I could begin taking more pictures. These pictures would be for me and for Will, and I hoped I could come back with my family sometime.

I passed rows of gorgeous old homes, some stately and traditional, others like small stone castles. The mingling of Victorian homes with wraparound porches and châteaulike architecture stimulated my imagination, and made me think of those who had lived here long ago. What would they think of us now with our fast cars, telephones, and cameras that made instant pictures? What did Zelda think of it all?

When I arrived at Montford Park, I found a bench under a willow tree and enjoyed the blooms around me while I ate a delicious cold ham-and-cheese sandwich on crusty French bread. The cook had wrapped up a pickle for me, and had even slipped in a chocolate cookie and a bottle of soda. It felt good to fill my belly, and I hoped it would add some color to my thin winter face.

I glanced at my watch and saw that it was a quarter to one o'clock. Finally, I'd get to see Zelda after all these years. My stomach was in knots. I vacillated between unbounded excitement and extreme nervousness. What if Zelda was incoherent and frenzied? What if she resented me for moving on with my life? What if she was catatonic and didn't respond at all? Worst of all, I had a nagging fear that the diaries would set her off instead of fill a need in her.

Mostly, though, I just wanted to embrace my old friend and talk to her — just two women on the porch enjoying the spring, taking comfort in each other's company. Would she let me?

The hospital was a stately old colonial in good condition. My heart pounded as I walked up the porch steps and into the front hallway. It smelled of lemons, and paintings of the mountains and surrounding hills hung on the walls. It was a pretty place.

I saw a sign hanging outside the door on my left that read OFFICE, and when I walked in, a nurse with blond hair and small brown eyes gave me a warm smile.

"Welcome to Highland," she said. "Are you a visitor?"

"Yes, ma'am," I said, and placed the heavy bag on the ground. "I'm here to see Zelda Fitzgerald."

The woman's eyes lit and her smile stretched across her face. "Anna?"

That she knew who I was calmed me, and I nodded.

"Here, honey," she said. "Sign in and I'll

443

take you right to her. She's painting in the garden."

Painting in the garden. Of course she was.

As I signed my name with trembling fingers, the nurse placed her hand over mine. "She's going to be overjoyed to see you."

"Me, too," I said. *You have no idea.*

She led me down the quaint hallway, through a recreational room, and out to the back veranda that overlooked a garden full of creeping ivy, mature budding trees, and pockets of spring bulbs newly pushed up through the soil.

"Follow the path," she said. "You'll find her just around the corner."

I walked down the stairs and onto the crushed gravel, and felt as if I'd stepped into another world. The trees folded softly over me, and I was reminded of the paths at my parents' home in Maryland. The ripple of a nearby fountain gave a pleasant texture to the air, and I knew all would be well in spite of my trepidation.

When I rounded the bend in the path, I saw her. She stood at the end of the lawn, next to a stone wall with her easel, facing the mountains. Her back was to me, and I stopped and watched her for a moment without her knowing I was there. I wanted to take a picture of her here, at peace in a garden, creating, but as soon as I'd lifted the camera, I placed it back in the bag. I didn't want to use her.

She turned her head to the side.

" 'Had I on earth but wishes three, the first should be my Anna,' " she said.

She put down her brushes and I my bag and we ran to meet each other in the garden.

Now that I had her, I didn't want to let her go.

We stood at the easel, arms wrapped around each other, joined at our sides. She looked at me and I at her, and her bold smile lit up her face.

"Look at us," she said, and ran her hand down the line between our bodies. "A line of symmetry. Two halves of a whole. Two peas in a pod. A pair of queens. Though your card, I must observe, has aged better than mine, which has been played too often."

I laughed. How I'd missed her.

"You flatter me, Zelda," I said. "I've never seen anything lovelier than you at your easel, painting the mountains. It is the first time, I think, that I've ever seen a complete portrait of you, the woman, Zelda."

"I'll argue with you until I run out of air

about my physical state. I'm plump as a Heffalump. I will agree with you, however, about my emotional state. I've never felt better."

"But your letter," I said. "It was frantic. I feared the worst."

"I'm sorry," she said. "I am at my worst in the night, and it's when I think of you most and need you, and fired off that plaintive missive. But in the day, I can cope. They've started sedating me at night, and it's one pill I don't protest."

"Nights are hard for anyone who has lived long enough," I said.

"A truer observation was never made," she said. "When I go home, they'll send me with sleeping pills. I'll be fine in the days. Mother needs me, anyway. She's been sending me the same kind of letters I sent you."

"When will you return to Montgomery?"

"I could've gone last week," she said. "I just wanted to make sure, though. I check in and check out of here when I need it, but I find I need it less and less. I think I've realized that the worst for me has passed."

I was somewhat shocked to learn that she could check herself in and out, and had been for years. Why had it taken so long for her to write to me? She must have seen my confusion, and took my hands in hers.

"I'm still not right, Anna, and I don't think I ever will be. I'm just righter some days than others. I'm sorry it took me so long to reach out to you, but I was convinced I'd poison your life when it was going so well. I do that, you know."

My heart sank and I shook my head. "You could never poison me, Zelda. Is that really why you didn't write?" My God, all the wasted time, and she had thought she was protecting me.

"At first it was like I said in the letter: I was too raw. But over the years, reading your letters, I could feel how well your life garden had blossomed, and I didn't want to come stomping my weeds through it. You deserve better."

I shook my head again and squeezed her hands tighter. "Please promise me that from now on you'll never keep yourself from me again. Promise."

"I promise," she said.

We let the moment pass, and then Zelda's face lit with a smile.

"Scottie just had her second baby," she said. "She's coming down next month to visit, with the children, and I can't wait. Grandbabies are life's great gift. If only Scott could have known them. I tell him about them, of course, but it's not the same as holding them."

I felt a shiver and tried to dismiss her mention of communicating with Scott. She said it with such nonchalance — like it was an everyday occurrence — that I worried for her. Hearing voices was never a good thing.

"Oh, here's Nurse Anna now," she said, snapping me out of my thoughts. "Your face just turned six shades of gray. Yes, Scott talks to me. No, it is not a voice in my head. And no, you don't need to worry about me."

I couldn't help but smile. "Am I so easy to read?"

"An open book."

We sat on a nearby bench overlooking the mountains and talked for an hour, as if not a day had passed. Zelda told me that she lived modestly off of the annuity Scott's executor and friend had set up for her. Her demeanor was peaceful, and her Southern drawl had reasserted itself in her root surroundings. Her language hadn't lost any of its vivid color, and she still twisted her hands all over each other while she talked. I could have stayed there all day, but I began to sense the presence of the diaries in the nearby bag. They were so close, I could almost feel them quivering to be placed into her hands, reunited with their author, but something else held me back. Was it my fear that our calm meeting would be disturbed? I decided that I had to show her soon, but I thought it might be best done alone, in her room.

"Zelda, I have something for you, but we should go somewhere private before I share it with you," I said. "Could we go to your room?"

"If you'd prefer the sterile, barred room at the tower top, certainly, but it's so much more pleasant out here."

"I would actually prefer the room."

She looked at me and saw my earnestness. It struck me how, in spite of the wear in her face and in her body, her eyes were totally unchanged. She could have been nineteen, staring at me from those large, active eyes. She blinked slowly, as if she understood that what I had for her might stir a strong reaction, and nodded.

"Do I need to prepare myself mentally?"

"Yes," I said. "But I think it will do you a great good."

She looked at me for a moment more, then turned, picked up her watercolor off the easel, and started back for the house, with me following.

I watched Zelda's pink dancing slippers as I

trailed her up several flights of stairs, and I had to catch my breath at the top. She looked back at me without a touch of fatigue.

"I'm used to it," she said. "We hike five miles a day up and down mountain slopes."

I nodded, and followed her down a corridor that, as she'd promised, took on the sterility of the psychiatric environment. None of the charm from the lobby was on this floor, and I could feel drafts as we walked down the hall. We passed a woman shrieking in a room that appeared to be locked, and an orderly knocked into me on his way to the room.

What was Zelda really doing here? Wasn't she disturbed by those more troubled than herself, or was she simply putting on a good face for me? No, when Zelda was agitated it was impossible for her to wear any countenance but agitation. That I knew for sure.

When we arrived in her room, she propped her watercolor of the mountain against the wall, motioned me in, and shut the door behind us. Though the room was small and white, the view faced the mountains, and there were items around it that made it distinctly Zelda's: great vases stuffed full of flowers, canvases propped on all available surfaces, a pale pink tutu resting upright in the corner like a ghostly ballerina. While I took it all in, Zelda sat on the bed, closed her eyes, and breathed in and out three times. Then she opened them.

"Okay, I'm ready."

My hands trembled as I placed the bag on the floor and reached inside.

I heard her gasp.

She knew what the books were before they were in her hands, and she began to cry. I worried for a moment, but when I looked at her, she did not seem frantic, only very, very moved. Her hands trembled as I placed the books in them. She ran her fingers over the worn brown leather covers.

"Anna, how did you . . . Where did you . . ."

"Westport, in a cellar crawl space. I'm sorry, but they are terribly decomposed. I had hoped you'd be able to actually read them."

She met my eyes.

"You crawled in the dirt for me? Where else did you go and leave your life for me? You went other places, didn't you?"

"Delaware, Princeton, New York."

She touched the diaries again, one by one, then stood to embrace me.

"I don't deserve this," she said. "I made my life and I wrecked it. I don't deserve redemption."

"You do," I whispered. "I have something else for you."

I turned and pulled the scrapbook I'd made out of the bag and we walked over to the bed, where we spent the next hour or more poring through photos, sighing, laughing, and crying. I told her about the haunt at Ellerslie, and how I had imagined Scott appearing to me beside the sign to Princeton, leading me to safety.

"It was him," she said. "I'm sure of it."

I waved her off.

"You believe what you want," she continued, "but he tells me when trains will be late, when Scottie will write, and when I'll have visitors. He told me you'd come this week."

I couldn't help but roll my eyes, and redirected her to the album and the picture of the Princeton boys at the bar.

"They wanted you to know that they love you," I said. "They are going to read *Save Me the Waltz.*"

She clapped her hands in delight. "I always stirred up the Princeton boys. It's because they know a good Southern girl when they see her."

After reading my scrapbook, she carefully began to work her way through her old diaries. When she was able to see the words, she read aloud from newspaper clippings and ran her fingers over faded dance cards, photos of old beaux, and letters from Scott. Some of the pages were in decent shape, but most were rotten. While turning pages in her debutante diary, she stopped when she got to a dried corsage of pressed nasturtiums, and her face grew serious. I know she was thinking of the day that Scott called her a faded lapel flower, and maybe she felt it was true, but she did not speak of it. Instead, she turned the page, and a picture of the country club in Montgomery was before us.

"Do you know what they played for us last night during our painting class?" she asked. "*La Gioconda* and the 'Dance of the Hours,' and it was as if all time and space dropped like stage curtains and rose on the scene of me and Scott at that country club all those years ago. And just when the magic of that moment seeped through me, the setting changed again, and my imaginings jumped to you and me in the Maryland Theatre, the night you took me to the show. Except this time I did not leave in hysterics, but allowed the beauty of the music and of what you were trying to do for me to heal the scars, to seep into the injury in my soul like sweet balm, leaving it fresh, clean, and mended. When that painting session and the music concluded, I tell you that is precisely what I was left with — cleanliness, calm, healing. So thank you, Anna. All these years later, your tender medicine worked and I feel such peace."

I was too moved to respond, but I knew she understood my thoughts.

"And I don't think I'll burn these, after all," she said.

"I was hoping you wouldn't," I said.

She closed the books and took my hands in hers. "I'm ready to leave Highland and never come back. This is what I needed. Case closed. You may sign my file."

I smiled at her and pretended to stamp her forehead, and we embraced again.

A soft knock on the door interrupted us. It was the nurse who had welcomed me.

"I'm so sorry to say that visiting hours are over. Zelda will need some time to rest before supper."

I glanced at the clock on the wall and couldn't believe I had been there for three hours. The scream of the woman down the hall traveled into the room, and my heart began to hurt. I didn't want to leave Zelda here. I wanted to take her with me. Urgently so.

"May we have just five more minutes?" said Zelda. "Please, Jane."

The nurse looked down the hall with nervous eyes and then back at us. "I'll leave you for five more minutes. I'll just say I had to take care of our friend down the hallway. Five minutes."

With that, she was gone.

"Zelda, can you check out now?" I asked. "You've checked yourself in. You can stay with me at the inn down the street tonight. We'll have breakfast tomorrow and I'll drive you home to Montgomery. Will told me to take as long as I needed."

She looked away from me and all around the room, and it appeared that she was actually thinking about taking me up on my offer. Then she sighed.

"If we only had more time today, I'd say yes, but I have so much packing to do, and so many good-byes. I can't just leave. I'm never coming back after this," she said. "I'm sure of it."

The woman screamed again and the sound went right through my stomach.

"I'm not ready to be done with you," I said. "Please come with me."

"I want to," said Zelda. "I'll leave with you tomorrow. That will give me time to say my good-byes at supper and pack tonight

455

before they lock the doors and send me off to Luminal land in my sleep. You come first thing tomorrow morning and we'll go."

She broke into a huge smile and stood, pulling me up with her.

"Oh, Anna, I can't wait for you to go to Montgomery. If you can stay a night I'll take you to all of the sights in town, and we'll have lemonade with Mother, and visit the old places Scott courted me."

"I can't wait," I said.

I knew it made sense this way, but I hated to leave her. Nurse Jane was back in five minutes, however, just as she had promised. I collected my bag, empty now except for my camera. We all walked together down the long flights of stairs and out to the front porch. I asked Jane to take a picture of us, but to my dismay I had run out of film paper.

"Next time," said Zelda. "When I've had my hair set."

We laughed, and Jane left us on the porch to say our good-byes, but I could not speak, and my eyes filled with tears.

"It's just one night," said Zelda as her eyes also filled. "Tomorrow we set off."

I nodded.

She leaned in and kissed me gently, and we embraced once more before I started the walk back to the inn. Just before I rounded the turn I looked back. She waved at me and blew me a kiss. Then she bowed like a prima ballerina.

THIRTY-THREE

In the dream, I was back in the garden at Highland, overlooking the forests and mountains, enveloped in warm sunlight. A tiny purple butterfly worked its way over the wildflowers just on the other side of the fence, and a brown hawk glided in a wide, lazy arc over the treetops. Down in the valley, there was a man who looked like a monk. He held up his hand to me and I saw that he had a bloody hole in his palm. The heavy floral fragrance seemed to come from him in a way I could almost see, and as I inhaled, I felt a great peace fill me.

Over the bubbling of the fountain in the garden, I heard the strains of Sorin's song "Anii." I turned to try to locate the source of the music, and was surprised to see Scott standing under a wisteria-covered tree, neatly dressed and pressed. He did not see me, because he was gazing anxiously at the house behind us, which instead of Highland

Hospital looked a little like the house at Westport and the Montgomery Country Club all at once.

I followed his gaze to the house, and after a moment the door opened and Zelda stepped through rather abruptly, looking surprised. When she saw him she smiled, and the years slipped away and she was in the bloom of her youth. She stepped down off the back of the veranda and began walking toward him and he toward her, until they were running, and locked in an embrace. He pulled back and put his hands on the sides of her face, kissed her, and hugged her again. I could hear her say, "Oh, my love, my Goofo, my sweetheart."

The long wail of a siren suddenly grew closer, breaking the stillness, but the Fitzgeralds did not seem to hear. The garden fell away and I bolted up in bed at the inn. It took me a moment to orient myself to this time and place, and register that the siren was passing by on the street outside.

I lay back on the pillow and rolled over, thinking how sweet the dream had been, and began to drift off when a second siren pierced the silence, again screaming past the inn and down the street.

I was thoroughly awake now, and as I stared up at the ceiling in the dark I became unsettled. The sound of a third siren began to approach, and I heard voices on the front porch below my room. Being a nurse, I wondered whether I could be of some assistance in whatever emergency was taking place, so I climbed out of bed, put on my robe and shoes, and left my room.

Amelia and an older man stood on the porch in their nightclothes, watching as a fire truck rushed past the inn and turned down the street. She gave me a worried look as the smell of smoke hit me.

"Fire," she said. "Bad one, by the smell of it."

"My goodness, I wonder where it is?"

"Looks like it's just up the street there," said the man.

A cold, hollow feeling began in my stomach. My thoughts began to race. My dream, the diaries, the salamander.

My God, she couldn't have.

I shot off the porch like a bullet and began running down the route I'd traveled to and from earlier that day. Amelia called after me, but I ignored her and ran faster.

It didn't take me long to reach Zillicoa Street and Highland Hospital, blazing like a pocket of hell. I was unable to move for a moment while I watched the flames digesting the old wooden building with sickening speed. Fire trucks and ambulances surrounded Highland, and people ran to and from the front of the hospital. The heat from the fire singed my face and made it hard to breathe.

I ran to a group of patients crying and screaming by a tree. A doctor tried to calm them, and looked like he'd been badly burned. I scanned their faces but did not see Zelda. *My God!* Zelda said she was sedated and locked in her room at night. She couldn't have started the fire, but how could she get out?

A terrible howl sounded from inside the building, an anguished sound such as I'd heard in the war all those years ago, and I screamed, "Zelda!"

Without thinking I raced toward the entrance and climbed the stairs, plunging into the inferno. A fireman passed me carrying a woman in pajamas who clutched him around the neck. "No, you have to get out of here," he yelled.

"My friend, I have to get my friend!" I cried.

I didn't stop to negotiate with him, but started up the stairs.

Nurse Jane passed me, dragging two patients behind her.

"Jane, do you have her?"

She shook her head, sobbing, and continued down the stairs.

Black swells stung my eyes and made a vise around my throat. I looked up to the upper floors but couldn't see anything except flames and smoke. Another scream pierced the night from above, followed by a terrible cracking sound.

I tore off my robe and covered my face, trying to form a pocket where I could breathe, when a fireman suddenly lunged at me from behind. He began to pull me down the stairs, and when I tried to resist, he lifted me and carried me screaming out of the house.

He ran with me out to the lawn, and just as he dropped me under a tree, a large section of the roof collapsed, sending a firestorm of sparks into the air. A burst of heat washed over us, and as the terrible screams from inside stopped, I lost consciousness.

"Anna. Anna."

I could hear Will's voice through the fog and I opened my eyes. Everything was blurry, so I blinked until I had a clear picture of my love standing over me with fear in his red-rimmed eyes.

"Anna!"

I felt his hands on my sides, the oxygen

mask pressing into my face, and a terrible burning pressure in my chest. My head ached.

"Anna, thank God, you're awake. Are you okay?"

I nodded and he pressed into me, beginning to cry. I started to cough, deep rasping coughs, and pulled off the mask until the fit subsided. I'd never felt such pain in my head before, and I squeezed my eyes shut to block out the light coming in from the hospital window.

"Close the curtain," I said in a hoarse whisper.

He jumped up to close it, and came back to me, taking my hand in his.

"I'm so sorry," I said, feeling the tears well up in my own eyes. It actually felt good for them to spill out, because it relieved some of the pressure in my head.

"No," he said. "Don't apologize."

I knew he understood. He'd been in war before, and knew what you did for your friends. I also knew the truth, but I needed to ask him and for him to speak the words. "Did she . . ."

He nodded and ran his hand over my head.

"Did they find her?" I said.

He inhaled and sighed deeply. "Do you

want to talk about this now?"

"No," I said. "But I have to."

He nodded again. "They identified her from a charred dancing slipper that was with her body."

Nausea rose in me and I closed my eyes, determined to fight it. When the feeling subsided, I opened my eyes again.

"Did they determine how the fire started?" I asked.

I held my breath, waiting for his answer. I knew that Zelda would have been sedated, but I feared that she could have hidden the pill and not taken it, and burned her diaries the way she'd burned her confessions. Though I really couldn't believe that, based on her state of mind when I'd been with her.

"They don't know yet," he said.

My tears began to fall again. He reached up and brushed them away.

"When you called me after you met with her," he said, "you told me how peaceful she'd been, and how moved she was to have the diaries, and her excitement over going to Montgomery with you. She didn't start that fire, Anna."

I reached for him and he leaned down to hug me. I felt warm and safe, and so relieved to be with him. I buried my face in his neck and kissed him.

"I want to go home," I said. "I need our home. I need to see the children. And Peter and Dad."

He pulled back and rested his chin on his hand on the bed. He reached for my hair again and smoothed it. Then he reached for my hand and kissed it.

"I think she's finally at peace," he said.

I took in his words, and remembered my dream of Scott and Zelda in the garden, and I prayed that he was right.

He was right.

As it turns out, the fire began in the kitchen. Zelda had been locked in her room that night. There was no way she could have started the fire; nor could she have escaped it.

We laid Zelda to rest in Rockville, Maryland, with Scott, on March 17, 1948, on a warm, peaceful St. Patrick's Day.

Scottie was there, poised and beautiful. She hugged me and thanked me for coming and for being her mother's friend. I told her that I'd been with Zelda the day she'd died, and that she'd spoken so fondly of Scottie. I did not tell her about the diaries, for some reason. It seemed to me something that would burden Scottie rather than lift her.

Mrs. Turnbull, the owner of La Paix, placed two delicate wreaths of pansies at the grave. They were Zelda's favorite flowers from the estate, and the wreaths stood side by side over the Fitzgeralds' grave, over a picture of Scott and Zelda together in their younger years, before the trouble began.

When everyone left, I remained at the grave, praying for Zelda and for Scott, listening to the toll of the church bells. While I stood there, I felt a warm breeze pass over me, carrying with it a light, sweet fragrance like magnolia. I looked up at the photograph of the writer and his muse and remembered the day on the way to New York when the two of them had fallen asleep together on the train, their heads resting against each other, their arms entwined.

I still think of them this way every day, and I rest knowing that they are finally at peace — the mythic salamander and her one true love.

ACKNOWLEDGMENTS

I knew I wanted to write about Zelda while I researched my novel *Hemingway's Girl,* because Ernest Hemingway's hatred of her intrigued me. I know Hemingway didn't mean to do it, but I fell in love with Zelda, and for that I want to thank him.

I want to thank God for timing, serendipity, and inspiration, and for giving me the most supportive family on earth.

To my mother-in-law, Patricia Robuck, whose work as a nurse who stayed long past her shift inspired that aspect of Anna's character. To my parents, Robert and Charlene Shephard, whose complete love and support inspired the characters of Anna's parents. To Richard Robuck, father-in-law, war veteran, and babysitter extraordinaire. To my uncle, Richard Shephard, for information about working with copper to make wind chimes. To the priests I've known who have been some of the best friends and spiritual guides in my life. To my early readers not mentioned above: Jami Carr, Alexis McKay, and Heather Pacheco. To Dave Tieff, songwriter and enthusiastic cheerleader of other artists. To all of you, I extend my heartfelt thanks.

To my writing partners, Jennifer Lyn King and Kelly McMullen — two women on two sides of the world and as far from me in location as they could possibly be — who have championed, critiqued, listened, counseled, and supported me so much. There are not enough languages to properly express my gratitude to you.

I am so grateful for my agent, Kevan Lyon. She has been such an enthusiastic supporter of my work and a friend. Also my editor, Ellen Edwards, who so precisely knows how to draw the depth out of my work and inspire me to complete the story the way it wants to be revealed. I also want to thank everyone at NAL/Penguin who has given me so much time, attention, and support, including Kara Welsh, Craig Burke, Fiona Brown, Sarah Janet, and so many more. Thank you.

To the Oregon Retreat Women: Kristina McMorris, Sarah McCoy, Therese Walsh, Jael McHenry, Julie Kibler, Margaret Dilloway, Marilyn Brant, and Sarah Reed Callender: You all are like the sorority sisters I never had — XO.

To Book Pregnant. You know who you are and why you are so incredibly important to me.

For assistance with the historical aspects of this novel, I extend my deep thanks to Mare Thomas of the Maryland Historical Society, Doug Skeen of the Enoch Pratt Library, and Gabriel Swift at Princeton University. Thank you to Taft Utermohl, docent at the Johns Hopkins Evergreen Museum, who so kindly escorted me through *Choreography in Color,* an exhibit of Zelda Fitzgerald's paintings, arranged by Laura Maria Somenzi. I'd also like to thank Gwendolyn Owens, who so generously trusted me with the documentary *Marked for Glory* that her father made about the Fitzgeralds, and for her kind assistance answering questions about Zelda.

Finally, over the ten years I've been seriously committed to the novel form, my husband, Scott Robuck, has been my partner in every sense. He has listened enthusiastically to endless talk of dead writers, read very rough drafts of my work, and taken wonderful care of our three sons while I traveled to book clubs, writing conferences, or simply coffee with writing partners. He is the very definition of what a husband should be, and writing about such dysfunctional spouses was easy because I simply had to write about the opposite of what I've experienced over the life of our marriage. I love you, Scott.

BIBLIOGRAPHY

The first and best source comes from the words of the subjects themselves. I found the most inspiration from Zelda's novel *Save Me the Waltz* and her short stories and essays, and Scott's novels and stories. Letters, medical files, photos, and the occasional rare and beautiful video footage were also instrumental in presenting the Fitzgeralds as completely as I could.

Some of the books I consulted during this project are listed below, and are excellent resources for both the curious reader and the scholar.

Bruccoli, Matthew J., Scottie Fitzgerald Smith, and Joan P. Kerr. *The Romantic Egoists: A Pictorial Autobiography from the Scrapbooks and Albums of F. Scott and Zelda Fitzgerald.* New York: Scribner, 1974.

Cline, Sally. *Zelda Fitzgerald: Her Voice in*

Paradise. New York: Arcade Publishing, 2003.

Fitzgerald, F. Scott. *A Life in Letters,* edited by Matthew J. Bruccoli. New York: Simon & Schuster, 1995.

Fitzgerald, Zelda. *The Collected Writings,* edited by Matthew J. Broccoli. New York: Scribner, 1991.

Lanahan, Eleanor. *Scottie: The Daughter of . . . The Life of Frances Scott Fitzgerald Lanahan Smith.* New York: HarperCollins, 1995.

————. *Zelda: An Illustrated Life.* New York: Harry N. Abrams, 1996.

Meyers, Jeffrey. *Scott Fitzgerald: A Biography.* New York: HarperCollins, 1994.

Milford, Nancy. *Zelda: A Biography.* New York: HarperPerennial, re-issue edition, 2011. Originally published by Harper & Row in 1970.

■ ■ ■ ■

READERS GUIDE
CALL ME ZELDA

ERIKA ROBUCK

■ ■ ■ ■

A CONVERSATION WITH ERIKA ROBUCK

Q. Your last novel was about Ernest Heming-way. This one is about Zelda Fitzgerald. Have you made a deliberate choice to write about literary figures?

A. It may sound strange, but I feel as if they have chosen me. I was working on a sequel to my self-published novel about slavery when I visited Hemingway's house in Key West. I've felt haunted by Hemingway ever since. While I researched him, I became fascinated by his relationship with the Fitzgeralds. That's when Zelda wouldn't leave me alone.

The subject of my current work in progress, Edna St. Vincent Millay, entered my consciousness as I read about two Princeton classmates of F. Scott Fitz-gerald's, Edmund "Bunny" Wilson and John Peale Bishop, who were both in love with Millay. I had long enjoyed Millay's poetry, but after reading about her personal life, I found it every bit as interesting as her work. That's when I knew she would be my next subject.

Q. *What about Zelda at this particular time in her life especially interested you, and what kind of research did you do in preparation for writing the novel?*

A. I live in Maryland, and have spent a lot of time around the old Baltimore Fitzgerald haunts. I had made several trips to Johns Hopkins Hospital, but had never known about the Phipps Psychiatric Clinic until I learned about Zelda's time there. Also, my grandmother, now deceased, was a psychiatric nurse, so I knew a bit about mental health care. Because of my proximity to these places from this phase of the Fitzgeralds' lives, my family background, and the fact that little has been written about their lives "after the party," I knew I wanted to highlight this time.

In addition to reading numerous biographies by critics and family members, I visited Princeton University to research the Fitzgerald archive there. I've also been to the Phipps Building where it still stands, have attended an exhibit of Zelda's art at Johns Hopkins Evergreen Museum, and have paid my respects at the Fitzgeralds' graves in Rockville, Maryland.

Q. Did Zelda really write diaries, and did her husband really "steal" material from them and include it in his novels? Do we know what became of the diaries?

A. Yes, Zelda really did write diaries that Scott took, allowed friends to read, used in his fiction, and ultimately hid or destroyed after theater critic George Jean Nathan read them in the Westport basement and suggested they publish them. I was unable to find any mention of the diaries after the Westport days, but did find a possible allusion to them from the Fitzgeralds' time at La Paix. It is possible that the diaries were saved from the fire there, and stayed in a storage locker while Scott moved to North Carolina, but I have not been able to trace anything definitive.

I sent a letter to the current owner of the house at Compo Road in Westport to ask about the inside configuration of the rooms and basement, and if they had ever found any Fitzgerald artifacts. They wrote me back very kindly (for it must have been a strange letter to receive) but said they did not find anything.

Q. What did you learn about Zelda, and the Fitzgeralds in general, that most surprised you, details that perhaps didn't make it into the novel?

A. What most surprised me was their continued devotion to each other in spite of all of their miseries, affairs, and tragedies. It was truly as if they were connected at the soul.

Something else that surprised me was Zelda's dedication to dance and how far her talent almost took her. She did not take up ballet until her later twenties, and was offered a position in a prominent ballet company in Italy, which she ultimately declined. She made extraordinary progress in ballet for having begun at such an "advanced" age for dancing.

Another interesting detail was that Zelda became an accomplished painter. She had exhibitions in Baltimore, New York, and Montgomery, Alabama, and not just because she was the wife of a famous author. She showed true artistic genius and originality in her work.

Q. Why did you decide to make Anna Howard, a fictional character, the narrator? Did you think it was important for Anna to experience a tragedy in her past, so that she could be more sympathetic toward Zelda during her emotional breakdown?

A. Anna came to me, in part, after I read a short story by F. Scott Fitzgerald called "One Interne" about a resident in love with an anesthetist at Johns Hopkins: "A dark-haired girl with great, luminous eyes" who shared an apartment with a female musician from Peabody, and who had a brass sculpture by the artist Brancusi in her apartment. Later, in my research, I read about Zelda's ill-fated trip to her New York art showing at Cary Ross's gallery, that she had traveled with a nurse, and that Zelda had to be sedated on the train back to Craig House in Beacon, New York. These ingredients blended together, and Nurse Anna emerged.

It was very important to me that Anna have her own tragic past. I wanted Anna to connect to Zelda and be needed by Zelda to draw herself out of her past pain, and to give more than would have been required in caring for Zelda. Without a tragic past, Anna could not have empathized with her friend and patient, or wanted to help her so badly. In helping Zelda, of course, Anna is helping to heal herself.

Q. *In both* Hemingway's Girl *and* Call Me Zelda, *you explore the harm that writers can do when they use the people in their lives to create their work. But isn't it inevitable that writers draw material from their own lives, and especially from their relationships? As a writer yourself, how do you deal with this paradox?*

A. The irony is not lost on me that I use these writers as I condemn them for using others in their fiction, but what I do is different. First, I don't use my living family or friends as characters. While I may use details, personality traits, or events in creating my characters, none of them is a perfect representation of a living acquaintance. Also, my mission is one of redemption, especially of these tortured, dead writers. I feel connected to them and wish for their ultimate peace. My writing is a prayer for them.

Q. Call Me Zelda *strikes me as, above all, a novel about female friendship. Anna takes great risks in trying to help Zelda, and at one point Zelda saves Anna's life. In your opinion, is it necessary to take risks in a relationship in order to make it truly meaningful? Are we sometimes guilty of avoiding a deeper involvement by telling ourselves we have no business telling a friend how to live her life?*

A. Yes, I think taking risks and allowing

oneself to be vulnerable to another makes for a deeper relationship. In opening one's heart to another, sharing one's passions and fears, one is exposed. It is mutual exposure and acceptance that knit us to one another.

Such a level of intimacy is difficult, though. It allows others to have power over us, power to judge or to hurt. On the other side, however, it can form connections that endure across time and space, and give us the security of knowing that someone, somewhere understands us and would risk anything for us — even laying down her life for us. This form of friendship is rare and beautiful, and I hope I was able to illustrate it through Anna and Zelda's relationship.

Q. Music plays an important role in the novel. In fact, I found myself wanting to listen to the pieces that are mentioned as I read. Did you always intend for music to play a role? And can you include a playlist, for those of us who would like to seek out the pieces?

A. Yes, I always wanted music to play a role. Music is essential to my creative process. I listen to classical piano music while I write to get in the "zone." What I hear in the music often inspires scenes: from the very light, to the frenzied, to the frightening, romantic, or dramatic. Music also calms me, and as I was researching the past of Walter Reed, I read about the music therapy program for shell-shocked soldiers. I thought it would add an important layer to the book to show a creative art as a healing practice, in contrast to what the creative process often did to Zelda.

Some of the musical pieces mentioned in the book are Mendelssohn's *Songs Without Words,* Mahler's *Kindertotenlieder,* and Ponchielli's "Dance of the Hours" from the opera *La Gioconda.* "Embraceable You" by Gershwin is playing on the phonograph the night Anna and Will have their first kiss. I listened to that song on repeat while I wrote the scene. It still gives me chills.

Q. What would you most like readers to take away from reading Call Me Zelda?

A. Some of the themes that I hope resonate with readers are the depths of true friendship, the danger of using others, and the power of confession and atonement. I also wanted to explore the concept of how beautiful we can become if we first go through trials and allow ourselves to be transformed and purified. If readers want to go deeper into these themes, and the theology that informs most of Peter's character in the novel, they might seek out the writings of Caryll Houselander, which are profound.

Q. As we write this, your previous novel, Hemingway's Girl, *is about to go on sale. What has the experience of writing and publishing that book been like for you so far, and what are you most looking forward to as it becomes available to readers?*

A. The response to *Hemingway's Girl* has been a phenomenal experience. From my publishing team, to blogger support, reader feedback, and social media enthusiasm, I'm being showered with positivity. It took about ten years for me to find an agent and publisher, and there were times when I wanted to give up. Ultimately, I kept at it because writing is my passion, and I knew I'd do it whether or not I had a publisher. Getting to travel now to so many wonderful conferences and bookstores, seeing enthusiastic reader reviews, and hearing about news outlets that will cover the book is overwhelming and gratifying beyond words.

What I'm most looking forward to is meeting with all of the book clubs and readers who were behind me when I was a self-published author, and not only showing them where I am now, but also thanking them for their incredible support. I really couldn't have done it without them and without the encouragement of my family and friends.

Q. *What is your next novel about?*

A. My next novel takes me into the strange, compelling, bohemian world of the first woman to win the Pulitzer Prize for poetry, Edna St. Vincent Millay. Based on themes from *The Scarlet Letter,* the novel will immerse readers in a judgmental New England town full of secrets and scandal. A seamstress, a sculptor, and the poet are just some of the characters in this historical suspense novel that weaves a tapestry of truth and fiction.

QUESTIONS FOR DISCUSSION

1. What did you most enjoy about *Call Me Zelda*? Did you make an emotional connection with the characters?

2. The novel depicts the marriage of F. Scott and Zelda Fitzgerald as one of soul mates who destroy each other even as they can't quite live without each other. Why do we find such relationships so fascinating? Can you think of others like it? Are they more common in literature than in life?

3. Zelda does not narrate the story, but the title bears her name and she is obviously central. Discuss the triumph and tragedy of her life. What do you feel for her? Do you understand her? What aspects of her character most fascinate you, and what relevance does her life story have for us today?

4. Does Anna blur the boundaries between

her professional care for Zelda and her personal feelings for her? Are there times when Anna's affection for Zelda causes her to make poor choices regarding Zelda's care, and in her own personal life? How would you have handled the situation?

5. When the novel opens, Anna is stuck in life, having spent years mourning her lost husband and child. What is preventing her from moving forward? What ultimately allows her to embrace life more fully, and what role does Zelda play in that change?

6. Does the novel suggest that there is an honest link between the drive for artistic expression and out-of-control behavior that sometimes masks the artist's inner torment, and can even lead to mental illness? Does the novel suggest that artists are justified in "acting out," or is that just an excuse for their bad behavior? Consider Zelda's attempts at self-expression, and Scott's struggle to finish his novel. Consider Sorin's musical composition and his explanation to Anna of his creative process.

7. What is Peter's role in the novel? Why did the author include a Catholic priest, and give him such a close relationship with the narrator, Anna? What is Sorin's role? Is it

important that he turns up late in the novel, after being absent for many pages?

8. Discuss how the various mothers in the novel express love for their children. Is it different from the way the fathers express love?

9. Why do you think the author includes the ghost at the abandoned home where the Fitzgeralds once lived? Is Anna's sensing a ghost all that different from the inner voices that Zelda hears?

10. When Anna decides to try to find Zelda's diaries for her, Peter quotes a verse from the Bible: "There is no greater love than to lay down one's life for one's friends." Discuss how both Anna and Zelda, and other characters, take risks and make sacrifices for one another. In your own life, how have your friendships been shaped by the sacrifices you've made?

11. Toward the end of the book Anna takes a journey by car in 1948 that is quite different from what a similar journey would be like today. Drawing from your own experience and understanding of the day, talk about what travel and communication were like back in the 1920s through the 1950s,

especially before the interstate highway system was built after World War II and before long-distance phone calls became routine.

12. Compare the psychiatric care that Zelda receives in the 1930s to what she would likely receive today. In what ways might her care be improved and in what ways might it be worse? Would she have as many choices now as she did then?

13. Have you read Zelda's novel *Save Me the Waltz* or Scott's novel *Tender Is the Night*? Does reading this novel make you want to take on the challenge of reading and comparing them?

14. Finally, what do you think you will take away from having read *Call Me Zelda*? What aspects will resonate and linger for you?

ABOUT THE AUTHOR

Erika Robuck is a contributor to the popular fiction blog Writer Unboxed, and she maintains her own blog, Muse. She is a member of the Hemingway Society and the Historical Novel Society, and she lives in the Chesapeake Bay area with her husband and three sons.